WIFEY

The explosive national bestseller—more than three million copies sold!

"One for the grown-ups!"
—*Los Angeles Times*

"You will enjoy reading this book. . . . Hide it where the children won't see it!"
—*The Cincinnati Enquirer*

"Adulterous fun!"
—*The Philadelphia Inquirer*

SMART WOMEN

A *New York Times* bestseller for more than four months!

"Blume's sensitivity to a child's viewpoint elevates this book . . . the children are splendid in their richness."
—*The New York Times Book Review*

"Filled with good insights and great, quotable one-liners. . . . Blume's style is so open, so honest, so direct. . . . Her artistic integrity is to be admired."
—*The Washington Post*

Books by Judy Blume

Forever . . .
Letters to Judy
Smart Women
Wifey

Published by POCKET BOOKS

Judy Blume

WIFEY
SMART WOMEN

POCKET BOOKS
New York   London   Toronto   Sydney   Singapore

This book is a work of fiction. Names, characters, places and incidents are products of the author's imagination or are used fictitiously. Any resemblance to actual events or locales or persons, living or dead, is entirely coincidental.

An *Original* Publication of POCKET BOOKS

 POCKET BOOKS, a division of Simon & Schuster, Inc.
1230 Avenue of the Americas, New York, NY 10020

Wifey copyright © 1978 by Judy Blume
"Taking a Chance on Love," by John LaTouche, Ted Fetter, and Vernon Duke, copyright 1940 by Miller Music Corporation; copyright renewed © 1968 by Miller Music Corporation. All rights reserved. Used by permission.

Smart Women copyright © 1983 by Judy Blume
The author gratefully acknowledges permission from Holt, Rinehart and Winston, Publishers, the Estate of Robert Frost, and Jonathan Cape Ltd. to quote from "Stopping by Woods on a Snowy Evening" from *The Poetry of Robert Frost,* edited by Edward Connery Lathem. Copyright 1923, © 1969 by Holt, Rinehart and Winston. Copyright 1951 by Robert Frost.

Published by arrangement with Penguin Putnam, Inc.

ISBN: 0-7434-3757-8

First Pocket Books trade paperback printing October 2001

10 9 8 7 6 5 4 3 2 1

POCKET and colophon are registered trademarks of
Simon & Schuster, Inc.

For information regarding special discounts for bulk purchases,
please contact Simon & Schuster Special Sales at 1-800-456-6798
or business@simonandschuster.com

Cover photo by PhotoDisc

Printed in the U.S.A.

These titles were previously published individually in hardcover by
Penguin Putnam, Inc., and in mass market paperback by Pocket Books.

Contents

WIFEY

To Claire and Phyllis, *for believing*
To Randy and Larry, *for enduring*

In terms of affluence America in the 60's reached a stage that other societies can only dream of.

from Good Times *by Peter Joseph*

1

SANDY SAT UP in bed and looked at the clock. Quarter to eight. Damn! Last night she'd told Norman she might sleep all day just to catch up. No kids for once, no demands, no responsibilities. But the noise. What was it, a truck, a bus? It sounded so close. And then the empty sound after the engine cut off. She'd never get back to sleep now. She slipped into her robe, the one the children had given her for Mother's Day. "Daddy picked it out," Jen had said. "Do you like it?" "Oh yes, it's perfect," Sandy had answered, hating it. Imagine Norman choosing the same robe for her as she had sent to his mother and her own.

She traipsed across the room to the window, rubbing her eyes to keep them open, spitting her hair out of her face. She looked down into the wooded backyard. He was in front of the crab apple tree, hands on hips, as if waiting for her, dressed in a white bed sheet and a stars and stripes helmet, standing next to a motorcycle. What was this? A kid, playing Halloween? A neighborhood ghost? No . . . look . . . he threw off the bed sheet and stood before her, naked, his penis long and stiff. Sandy dropped to her knees, barely peeking out the window, afraid, but fascinated, not just by the act itself, but by the style. So fast, so hard! Didn't it hurt, handling it that way? She'd always been so careful with Norman's, scared that she might damage it. Who was he? What was he doing in her yard? *Nineteen, twenty, twenty-one,* Sandy counted. He came on twenty-seven, leaving his stuff on her lawn, then jumped on his bike, kicked down with one foot, and started up the engine. But wait. It stalled. Would she have to call Triple A and if so how was she going to explain the problem? *Hello, this is Mrs. Pressman . . . there's a . . . you see . . . well . . . anyway . . . and he's having trouble with his motorcycle . . .* No. No need to worry. The engine caught and he took off, zooming down the street, wearing only the stars and stripes helmet.

She called Norman first, at the plant, and he asked, "Did it make ridges in the lawn?"

"What?"

"The motorcycle, did it make ridges in the lawn?"

"I don't know."

"Well, find out."

"Now?"

"Yes, I'll hold."

She put the phone down and ran outside.

"Yes, there are ridges," she told Norman. "Two of them."

"Okay. First thing, call Rufano, tell him to take care of it."

"Right. Rufano," she repeated, jotting it down. "Should he reseed or what?"

"I can't say. I'm not there, am I? Let him decide, he's the doctor."

"But it doesn't pay to put money into the lawn when we're moving, does it?"

"We haven't sold the house yet. It would be different if we'd already sold."

"Norm . . ."

"What?"

"I'm a little shaky."

"I'll call the police as soon as we hang up."

"I'm not dressed."

"So get dressed."

"Are you coming home?"

"I can't, Sandy. I'm in the middle of a new solution."

"Oh."

"See you tonight."

"Right."

Sandy showered and dressed and waited for the police.

"Okay, Mrs. Pressman, let's have it again." She'd expected, at the very least, Columbo. Instead she got Hubanski, tall and thin, with a missing tooth and an itchy leg. He sat on the sofa and scratched the area above his black anklet sock. Plainfield, New Jersey's, finest.

"My husband told you the whole story, didn't he?"

"Uh huh."

He whipped his notebook out of his pocket and made squiggles with his ballpoint pen. "Doesn't seem to be working today."

"Try blowing in it," Sandy suggested. "Sometimes that helps."

Hubanski blew into the end of his ballpoint and tried again. "Nope, nothing."

"Just a minute." Sandy went into the kitchen and came back with a pen. "Try this one."

"Thanks," he said, printing his name.

Sandy sat down on the love seat opposite him, tucking her legs under her.

"Okay, now I want to hear it from you, Mrs. Pressman. You say it was about quarter past eight?"

"No, quarter to."

"You're sure of that?"

"Yes, positive, because as soon as I woke up I looked at the clock."

"And the noise that woke you sounded like a motorcycle?"

"Well, I didn't know it was a motorcycle then. I just knew it was a noise, which is why I went over to the window in the first place."

"Now, we have to be very sure about this, Mrs. Pressman."

"I looked out the window and there he was," Sandy said. "It's very simple."

"He didn't ring the bell or anything, first?"

"Why would he have done that?"

"I'm only trying to set the record straight, Mrs. Pressman, because, you know, this isn't our everyday, ordinary kind of complaint. So just take your time and tell me again."

"He was wearing a sheet and he was looking up at me."

"Now, this here's the important part, Mrs. Pressman, and I want to be sure I've got it one hundred per cent right. You're telling me that this guy rides up on a motorcycle."

"Yes."

"And he's got a bed sheet over him."

"That's right."

"Like your ordinary everyday kind of bed sheet?"

"Yes, plain white, hospital variety."

"Okay, I get the picture. So let's take it from there, Mrs. Pressman. Now, you look down from your bedroom window and he looks up. Is that right so far?"

"Very good, you're doing fine."

"Look, Mrs. Pressman, you might not believe it, but this is no picnic for me either."

"Sorry."

"Okay, so he takes off the sheet."

"Right."

"And he's stark naked."

"Yes, except for his helmet . . . stars and stripes . . ."

"Yeah, I already got that. So, go on."

"Well, then he masturbated. And that's about it."

"You say *about*. Is there something else?"

"No, he got on his motorcycle and rode off. That's it."

"Naked?"

"Yes, I told you that."

"So where's the bed sheet, Mrs. Pressman?" He held up his hand, a hint of a smile showing on his face for the first time.

"I don't know."

"You didn't pick it up when you went out to inspect the lawn?"

"No."

"And you didn't see him pick it up either?"

"No, but he might have. Because I was pretty upset at the time, as you can imagine. I might have missed that."

"What I don't get, Mrs. Pressman, is how come you watched the whole thing. I mean, you could have called us right off. We might have been able to get over here in time."

"I was scared, I guess. I just don't know."

"How about a make on the motorcycle?"

"It was chrome."

"Come on, Mrs. Pressman. You can do better than that. Was it this year's model, a 1970? Or would you say it was five to ten years old?"

"I don't know. They all look the same to me."

He clicked the pen closed, stood up, and handed it to Sandy.

"Keep it," she said, "I'm sure you'll need it."

"Thanks. Say listen, what about the dog? Your husband said you have a dog."

"We do, a miniature schnauzer, Banushka. But he slept through it."

"You're sure he was white?"

"Who?"

"The guy—the exhibitionist."

"Oh, yes."

"Because a lot of these mixed races can look almost white."

"No, he was white. Like you."

He sighed. "Well, you haven't given me much to go on, Mrs. Pressman."

"I'm sorry."

"Look, if you remember anything else, no matter how small, give me a call, okay? And in the meantime I'll do my best."

"That's all anyone can ask for, sergeant . . ." Sandy paused. What the hell was his name?

"Hubanski. U-ban-ski. The H is silent."

"I'll remember that. Good-bye . . . and thank you."

As Hubanski was walking down the front steps Sandy called, "Oh, sergeant?"

He turned. "Yeah."

"I just remembered . . . he was left-handed."

"Hubanski didn't believe me," she told Norman that night, over chicken piquant. She was really pissed about that.

"It is an incredible story, Sandy."

"Don't you think I know that?"

"How come we're having chicken tonight? It's Monday, we always have chicken on Wednesdays."

"I didn't stop to think. I just defrosted the first thing I saw when I opened the freezer. Besides, with the kids away, what's the difference?"

"The difference is that I count on chicken on Wednesdays, the way I count on pot roast on Thursdays and some sort of chopped meat on Tuesdays. I had chicken salad for lunch."

"Oh, I'm sorry."

"Did you get this recipe from your sister?"

"No, from *Elegant but Easy.*"

"Not bad. You should have browned it first, though."

"It's a pain to brown chicken. That's why I made this one, you don't need to brown it first."

"It would look more appetizing if you did, next time."

"So close your eyes!"

"I'm just making a suggestion, San. No need to get so touchy about it."

"Who's touchy?"

Norman took off his glasses and wiped them with his dinner napkin. "I think what you need is new interests, especially now, with the kids away for the whole summer."

Was he doubting her story too? "I have plenty to do. There's the new house and besides that, I'm going to read. I'm going to do the classics. I told you that."

"But you need to get out of the house more, to mingle," Norman said.

"I don't need to be around people all the time."

"You lack self-confidence."

"What's that supposed to mean?"

"I'm trying to tell you, trying to help you, if only you'll let me."

"Do you want more rice?"

"Yes, thank you. I think The Club is the answer, San."

"Oh, please, Norm, don't start that again."

"I thought we agreed that as soon as the kids left you'd give it another try."

"Look, I told you when you joined that it wasn't my thing . . .

that I didn't want any part of it. So don't expect . . . don't ask me to . . ." She got up to clear away the dishes.

"Look at your sister," Norman said.

"You look at her."

"Four years older than you."

"Three and a half, but who's counting?"

"She loves The Club, practically lives there."

"She was always the family athlete."

"Tan and firm, in terrific shape."

"I failed gym in eighth grade, did you know that?" She put a plate of cookies on the table and set two cups of cold water, with tea bags, in the new microwave oven.

"You're not in the eighth grade any more, Sandy." He took a bite of one of the cookies. "Pepperidge Farm?"

"No, Keeblers." The microwave pinged and Sandy carried the teacups to the table. "Myra got straight A's in gym, all the way through school. She won letters. She was a goddamned cheer-leader!"

"You ought to learn to do more with the microwave than just heat water."

"I don't like gadgets."

"Because you lack self-confidence."

"What does self-confidence have to do with the microwave?"

"What do gadgets have to do with it?"

"I tried The Club, Norm. I took two golf lessons and two tennis lessons and I was awful. I just don't have the aptitude, the coordi-nation."

"Don't give me that shit, Sandy. You could be as good as most of the girls if you'd make the effort." He crunched another cookie. "Why don't you have your hair done . . . buy yourself something new to wear . . . you used to look terrific yourself."

"Jesus, you sound like my mother now."

"So she's noticed too?"

"I've been sick, Norm!"

"That was months ago. That's no excuse for now."

Sandy went to the sink and turned the water on full blast.

"I guess I'll walk Banushka," Norman said.

"You do that!"

"Oh, San, for God's sake." He tried to put his arms around her but she brushed him away. "You're so damned *touchy* these days," he said. "I can't even talk to you any more."

Any more? Sandy thought. But she didn't say it.

As soon as she heard the back door close she picked up a plate and flung it across the kitchen. It smashed into tiny pieces. She felt better.

2

OKAY. SO SHE didn't look her best. But that wasn't her fault, was it? She'd had a rough couple of months and was just beginning to feel healthy again. After an illness like hers it could take a year to get back to normal. And it hadn't been a year yet. It had started last Halloween, at the supermarket. She'd felt sick at the checkout counter and had to be helped to the Ladies Room by the cashier. She thought she was going to pass out, but once she got her head down, she was okay. The manager had carried her groceries to the car, even offered to drive her home, but she assured him she was fine, that it was just the combination of the overheated store and her heavy jacket. Too warm for October.

In the car, on the way home, she'd been overcome by a wave of nausea and sharp pains in her head. She'd pulled over, feeling very much the way she had when coming down with mono, years ago. In a few minutes that passed too and she was able to drive the rest of the way home. Jen had greeted her at the door. "Oh, Mom, you look so cute with those Halloween decorations on your face."

"What decorations?"

"Those little hearts."

Sandy had run to the mirror. Good God, she did have little heart-shaped marks around her eyes and on her cheeks.

William R. Ackerman, M.D., P.C., Diplomate in Internal Medicine, with a sub-specialty in livers, had seen her late that afternoon. By then, the heart-shaped marks had disappeared.

"Scarlet fever," he'd said, relating her condition to Bucky's recent strep infection. He'd taken a throat culture, then prescribed penicillin; one capsule, three times a day.

Within the week she'd improved enough to resume her family responsibilities, although she certainly wasn't feeling great. Ten days later it returned, but much worse. A fever of 105, aches and pains in her joints, a strange rash suddenly covering her body; hivelike on her arms, measlelike on her stomach, blotches on her swollen face. She wanted only to sleep.

She was vaguely aware of routine household activity. Aware, but not caring. Aware of the children. "Is Mom going to die?" asked in the same casual tone as *Is Mom going shopping?* Aware of Norman's anger. She never could understand his anger when she or the children were sick, when life didn't go as planned, as if it were all her fault. Aware of her mother, called in by Norman to take charge, because in eleven and a half years of marriage he had never missed a day of work or a golf or tennis game. "Oh, my God, my God," Mona had cried. "My little girl, my darling Sandy."

This time Dr. Ackerman had stood at the foot of Sandy's bed, not because he made house calls, but because it was Sunday and he lived across the street and it was more convenient for him to see her at home than to drive across town to his office. He stood there, looking down at her, ticking off possibilities on his fingers. ". . . or it could be indicative of thoracic cancer, leprosy, leukemia, lupus, or a severe allergic reaction."

Sandy closed her eyes. She didn't want to hear any more. *Please God, don't let it be leprosy,* she prayed.

"I think we'll go with the allergic reaction theory and start her on steroids right away," Dr. Ackerman said.

"But what exactly is it?" Norman had pressed.

"Erythema multiformi. Debilitating but not fatal."

So, she wasn't going to die this time.

"There must be something she can do to prevent these illnesses," Norman said. "Take vitamins or something. I haven't got the time for all of this."

And later, after the doctor had left, she opened her eyes to find Norman's Nikon pointing at her. "What are you doing?"

"Just a couple of shots," Norman told her.

"But, Norm . . ."

"Just in case."

"In case, what?"

"Medical malpractice, you never know."

Norman read the *AMA Journal* religiously, unusual for a man in the dry-cleaning business. Was he a frustrated physician? Or did his morbid interest stem from Sandy's physical problems? Dr. Ackerman once told her she was the healthiest *sick* person he had ever treated. Healthy, because basically there was nothing wrong. She had been tested and re-tested. Everything was in good shape, although Dr. Ackerman once suspected her stomach of being in her chest cavity because he heard gurglings while listening to her heart. Not an illness, he'd told her, reassuringly, but a condition *we* should know about, for *our* records. He'd sent her to a radiologist who served her a tall glass of lime-flavored barium. But the X-rays only proved that her stomach was exactly where it should have been.

Camille, Aunt Lottie had called her as a girl. But Mona said, "It's not her fault, she has no resistance!"

She had her first important illness at ten. Pilitis, pus in the kidney. It had burned when she peed. How comfortable, how warm and safe, to crawl into bed and have her mother take care of her. Mona was a somewhat nervous but gentle nurse, catering to Sandy's every need, every wish. The first few days she'd been too sick to do anything but just lie there, dozing off and on. Mona fed her the yucky chocolate-flavored medicine the doctor had prescribed and when the lab technician came to the house for a blood sample Sandy had vomited it all over him. Mona was terribly embarrassed. "Why didn't you ask for the bucket?"

"I didn't know," Sandy had said. "I'm sorry."

She had lain in bed for two weeks that time, listening to soap operas on her radio, doing movie star cutout books, reading Nancy Drew mysteries, and practicing upside-down tunnels with her tongue, learned during speech class, before Mona had rushed into school, demanding that Sandy be removed because "There is nothing wrong with my daughter's speech!" "It's her *ing* endings,"

Miss Tobias had explained. "Her *ing* endings are as good as your *ing* endings, maybe better," Mona had argued. And won.

In junior high it had been a three-year battle with atopic dermatitis. Everybody else had plain old acne but Sandy suffered through eczemalike patches all over her body and had to sleep with white cotton gloves so that if she scratched during the night she wouldn't tear her flesh open. In high school she'd been tested for diabetes because of her fainting spells but the tests were negative. And then, as a college freshman, mono. A year later she married Norman, and marriage brought with it a never-ending parade of physical problems. Recurring sore throats, assorted viruses, stomach pains, a ganglian cyst in her right wrist, plantar warts on the bottoms of her feet, combined with two children who had inherited her low resistance, carrying home every available bug, and then, once she'd nursed them back to health, passing each disease on to her. But this, this erythema multiformi, was the most frightening, yet most exotic illness yet.

Sandy responded to the cortisone treatment, without side effects. "Lucky girl," Dr. Ackerman had said, and within two weeks all the symptoms had disappeared, leaving her ten pounds lighter, tired out, and looking like hell.

They'd gone to Jamaica over the Christmas holidays. Myra and Gordon had insisted. "Look at you," Myra had said, "a bird could blow you over. What you need is sunshine, sunshine and rest and besides, if there's any trouble Gordy can look after you."

"Gordon's a gynecologist," Sandy had said. "This isn't a gynecological problem."

"You think just because he's a gynecologist all he knows about are pussies? I'll have him talk to Bill Ackerman. We'll let *him* decide what's best for you."

And Dr. Ackerman had given his blessing.

They had flown down to Montego Bay together. Myra, Gordon, and their twin daughters; Sandy, Norman, Bucky, and Jen. "If this plane should go down, God forbid," Mona had said, seeing them off, "then I'm taking pills . . . maybe gas . . . my whole life's on board!"

"You should be coming with us," Myra said.

"I don't fly, period!" Mona answered. And then she repeated her story about taking pills or gas to the ticket agent, who smiled and said, "No problem." With what . . . the pills . . . the plane . . . Sandy wondered, taking every word literally. Flying was no joking matter.

She was a nervous flier but she played it cool for the kids. *See how brave Mommy is.* Once on board she prayed every half-hour and tuned in to strange noises, odors, flickering lights, calls for the flight attendants, suspicious-looking characters likely to carry bombs in their luggage, or whatever. And during takeoffs and landings she grabbed Norman's hand and squeezed as hard as she could. He once got an infection because her fingernail pierced his skin.

Her oldest and dearest friend, Lisbeth, who was into psychology, explained it as Sandy's need to control her own destiny. "If you were the pilot," she said, "you wouldn't be afraid. What you really ought to do is take flying lessons."

"Oh, sure," Sandy said, "I don't have enough trouble driving the car. I still don't back into parking spaces."

"And your terror of thunderstorms is the same thing," Lisbeth had said one summer day when the sky turned black and rumbly. "You have no control over nature."

"So who does?" Sandy had asked.

"Nobody, but most people accept that."

"Your explanation is very sensible, but accepting it doesn't help me."

"You've got to fight to overcome your fears, believe me, I know."

And Sandy wanted to overcome her fears, was willing to fight, but not on this particular flight. She was too worn out to try anything new.

They'd landed safely, five minutes early, and were welcomed at the airport by a steel band and complimentary daiquiris. Myra had shipped three hundred dollars' worth of meat with her baggage, packed and frozen in dry ice by her butcher in South Orange. She'd arranged to find the meat broker in front of the Air Jamaica counter but so far he hadn't shown. Without him her meat would be confiscated. Sandy drank two more daiquiries while Myra ran through the airport in a frenzy, searching for him.

Bucky and Jen, hot and bored, were chasing each other. The twins, sullen, as usual, complained about the lack of air-conditioning, and fanned themselves with magazines.

After an hour it was clear that the meat broker was not going to show and they lined up to go through customs. "Bastards!" Myra hissed. "It's so unfair. They make it hard on us when we're the ones bringing in the money . . ."

"Relax, lady," the customs official said, "you got tree days to claim it before it's confiscated . . ."

"And I'm supposed to trust you to keep it frozen for three days?"

"Sure lady . . . you come back wit de meat broker . . . you take de meat home wit you . . ."

"You expect me to give up a full day of vacation to come back here, unnecessarily?"

"Yes, lady. Dat's de rule."

"Oh, you people!" Myra shook her frosted head at him. "No wonder it's like . . . you think . . ." She pointed at him. "Someday you'll see."

"Yes, lady."

Myra walked off in a huff, gold bracelets bangling, chains swinging around her neck, and were those really perspiration stains under the arms of her beige silk shirt? Sandy had never seen Myra sweat.

The car was there, waiting for them, but even in the Buick Rancho wagon it was tight. Jen fished a piece of wool out of her goody bag and worked a cat's cradle on her fingers, while Bucky polished off the rest of the cookies, melted by now. Connie and Kate sacked out. Sandy had trouble keeping her eyes open too. It took an hour and a half to get to Runaway Bay. At least none of the kids got carsick any more.

Myra and Gordon had bought the house eighteen months ago, after falling in love with the area. It came complete with furnishings, four servants, a Rhodesian Ridgeback, and a name. Sandy had seen endless pictures of it but even they didn't prepare her for the real La Carousella. Round, as its name implied, with a swimming pool in the middle, the roof opened to the sky above it, four bedroom suites around the pool, and a large, glass-walled living room overlooking the golf course, a separate building to house the servants, and a brand new Har-tru tennis court with adjacent thatched-roof bar.

"Hollywooooooood . . ." Myra sang, dancing around the pool.

"Mother, please!" her daughters cried.

"Can't I even enjoy my own house?" Myra asked. "So what do you think, San?"

"I can't . . . that is . . . I'm speechless!"

"Can we go swimming, Aunt Myra?" Bucky asked.

"Yes, go and change. Everybody go and change. Last one in's a rotten egg!"

Sandy, exhausted from the trip, said, "I think I'll take a little rest first." She didn't wake up until the next morning.

3

BY NEXT HALLOWEEN she was sure she'd be fully recovered. Maybe she'd even encourage the kids to throw a costume party, a good way to help them make new friends once they moved, Sandy thought, sweeping up the broken plate. She finished the kitchen and was sitting in the den, watching the Monday-night movie and wondering how Bucky and Jen were doing at camp when Norman returned with Banushka. "Three sticks and two wees," he said. "Would you mark his chart, San? I've got to make an important phone call."

Sandy waited until the first commercial, then went back to the kitchen and marked Banushka's chart. Banushka's chart had been Norman's idea. He'd recorded every pee and crap the dog had taken since they'd brought him home from the kennel, four years ago. When the children were born Norman had insisted that Sandy keep charts for them too. Careful records of their temperatures and bowel movements, with the appropriate descriptions, exactly as his mother, Enid, had kept for him when he was a boy. Sandy threw away the children's charts three years ago, when Bucky was eight and had checked off seven bowel movements in one day. She'd given him a huge dose of Kaopectate before finding out that it was Bucky's idea of a joke. Norman had never forgiven her. He and Enid still discussed bowel movements and their bathroom cupboards were filled with disposable Fleet enema bottles, just in case.

They got ready for bed without speaking. Sandy brushing her teeth with Crest, making blue spit in her sink, Norman using Colgate, as he had all his life. He got into his bed, wearing striped permanent-press boxer shorts, Sandy got into hers, dressed in peach nylon baby dolls, her hair pinned up with barrettes because lately she'd been perspiring in her sleep, strands of hair sticking to the sides of her face, causing an acnelike rash. An adolescent at thirty-two. Norman turned his back to her, she turned hers to him.

Sandy shivered and rolled herself into a ball, pulling the covers up around her head. Norman kept the house like a goddamned refrigerator, the air-conditioning always turned up too high. But he was never cold. He had body heat. That's what he called it, not that it did Sandy any good. He didn't like sleeping close so they had twin beds, attached to one headboard, a royal pain to make in the mornings, but why should she complain? Florenzia made the beds four mornings a week.

One bed for Norman, with cool, crisp sheets, preferably changed twice a week, not that he didn't want fresh ones daily, but even he knew that was an unreasonable, never mind impractical, request. And one bed for Sandy, where once a week, on Saturday nights, if she didn't have her period, they *did it*. A Jewish nymphomaniac. They fucked in her bed, then Norman went to the bathroom to wash his hands and penis, making Sandy feel dirty and ashamed. He'd climb into his own bed then, into his clean, cool sheets, and he'd fall asleep in seconds, never any tossing, turning, sighing. Never any need to hold hands, cuddle, or laugh quietly with her. Three to five minutes from start to finish. She knew. She'd watched the digital bedside clock often enough. Three to five minutes. Then he'd say, "Very nice, did you get your dessert?"

"Yes, thank you, dessert was fine."

"Well, then, good night."

" 'Night, Norm."

She'd learned to come in minutes, seconds if she had to, and she almost always made it twice. No problem there. She almost always got her main course and her dessert. But usually it was a

TV dinner and an Oreo when she craved scampi and mousse au chocolat.

And there was no agonizing itchy pussy for Norman either, to keep him up half the night. It was driving her wild. Scratching, scratching, all night long, reminiscent of her junior high condition but concentrated only in her vaginal area. Digging her nails into the soft delicate flesh of her lower lips, tearing them open and in the morning, when she sat down to pee, the unbearable sting of her urine hitting the open wound. She'd tried creams and lotions and powders and cornstarch and antihistamines and cotton underpants, but so far nothing worked.

"We've ruled out the possibility of a fungus," Gordon told her, "and there's no sign of infection. We're still considering an allergic reaction, to Norm's semen, but at the same time we also have to consider the possibility that it's strictly functional . . ."

"Functional?"

"Yes, psychosomatic, relating to your sex life. So how is your sex life, Sandy?"

My sex life? Oh, you mean my *sex* life. Yes. Well. Let's see. Ummm, if you want to judge it strictly on the basis of orgasms it's fine. Terrific. That is, I masturbate like crazy, Gordon. You wouldn't believe how I masturbate. God, I'm always at it. Driving here, for instance, this morning . . . driving, get that, in traffic, no less . . . no, not the Cadillac, Norm took that to work. The Buick . . . driving the Buick, I hear this song on the radio . . . from my youth, Gordy . . . like when I was seventeen or something . . . *Blue velvet, bluer than velvet was the night* . . . it reminds me of Shep . . . and I get this feeling in my cunt . . . this really hot feeling . . . and just a little rubbing with one hand . . . just a little tickle, tickle on the outside of my clothes . . . just one-two-three and that's enough . . . I'm coming and I don't even want to come yet because it feels so good . . . I want it to last. And guess what, Gordy? I never itch after I come that way. I itch only after Norman. So, you see, it must have something to do with him. Maybe I *am* allergic to his semen . . . maybe I'm allergic to his cock . . . maybe I'm allergic to him! Wouldn't that be something?

Oh, you'd rather hear about my sex life *with* Norman? Yes. Of Course. I understand, Gordy. Bearing on the case. Certainly. Well. Every Saturday night, rain or shine, unless I have my period. Variety? You mean like in the books? Well, no . . . Norm isn't one for variety. Changes make him uncomfortable. And I'm not one for making suggestions, Gordy. You think I should? I don't know . . . I'd have to think about that . . . maybe . . .

Oral sex? Oh, Gordy . . . now you're getting so personal. Must we? I mean, really. Well, of course I see that it's part of my sex life. Yes, certainly we've tried . . . but the one time Norm put his face between my legs . . . well, poor Norm . . . he gagged and coughed and spent half an hour in the bathroom gargling with Listerine afterward and I felt terribly guilty. He was like a cat with a hair ball. All that suffering just to please me. And then there's the problem of smell . . . odor, you know . . . Norman hates the smell of fuck. He always complains the morning after, opens all the windows in the bedroom and sprays Lysol. That's why I douche with vinegar . . . cunt vinaigrette . . . to make it more appetizing . . . you know, like browned chicken.

"So how is it, Sandy?"

"What?"

"Your sex life."

"What does that have to do with my problem?"

"It could have a lot to do with it."

"I don't think I can discuss it with you, Gordon."

"Would you like me to send you to someone else?"

"No, I don't think I could discuss the subject at all."

4

SHE USED TO look like Jackie Kennedy. Everybody said so. In 1960 she won the Jackie Kennedy look-alike contest sponsored by the Plainfield *Courier-News*. Norman's mother had sent in her photo. She hadn't even known she was a contestant until they'd called her to say she'd won and they were running her picture on the front page, two columns wide. A celebrity. A star.

Of course she'd voted for Jack. It was her first presidential election and there was no way she was going to support Norman's candidate, even though Norm was treasurer of the Plainfield Young Republicans' Club at the time. But Norman didn't know, didn't guess what she was up to. He thought his politics were her politics; his candidate, her candidate. Oh, the thrill of pulling the lever for Kennedy, defying Norman, even secretly!

"You should be out there ringing doorbells with me," he'd told her, during the campaign.

"If you tell them I'm pregnant, they'll understand."

"All right, as long as you do your share like a wife should." So Norman brought home lists of registered voters and every night during election week Sandy sat at the phone making calls. The Young Republicans' Blitz.

She'd done her share to support her husband. She'd earned the right to celebrate secretly over Jack's election. For the first time Sandy had been touched by politics, by a current event. There had been no depression or world war to affect her life and Mona and Ivan were determined to spare their children the insecurities, the anxieties they had known. She had once asked her mother, after spending two weeks in the country with Aunt Lottie, "How is the war in Korea?" And Mona had answered, "The same, and don't worry your pretty little head about it. It has nothing to do with you."

Until now. Sandy and Jackie. They'd been pregnant together. John-John was born first, in November, and Bucky followed, in December. Sandy didn't watch the delivery in the overhead mirror although Dr. Snyder wanted her to. It was bad enough that he'd placed the baby on her belly fresh out of the oven, all bloody and ugly. She was high on Demerol. "Take him away," she'd cried, "he's a mess."

Dr. Snyder had laughed. "You don't mean that, Sandy. This is the happiest moment of your life."

She'd dozed off. Later, a nurse had carried Bucky to her, clean and wrapped in a soft blanket, all cuddly and warm. And the nurse had undressed him so that Sandy could examine his tiny fingers and toes, his navel, his miniature penis, and acknowledge the fact that she and Norm had produced a perfect baby.

They'd named him Bertram, after her grandfather, but agreed to call him Bucky until he was old enough to handle such a serious name.

"Bucky?" Enid had snickered. "What kind of name is that for a Jewish boy?"

"It's as good as Brett," Sandy had answered, tossing out the name of Enid's other grandson.

"From Miss Piss I expect a name like Brett," Enid had said. "From you I expected something better."

Miss Piss was married to Norman's brother, Fred, a California Casualty agent in Sherman Oaks. Other people called her Arlene. They saw each other only on rare occasions and Sandy always marveled over Arlene's never-ending change of hair color.

Six months later, when Norman's father, Sam, dropped dead while firing a cashier for pocketing cash, Enid had cried to Sandy, "If only you were having the baby now, he could have a proper name. Who knows how long I'll have to wait for Miss Piss to give me another grandchild. Or for that matter, you."

Jen had come along two and a half years later, just months after Jackie had lost her infant, Patrick, to hyaline membrane disease. Sandy had named her Jennifer Patrice. Jennifer because she loved the name; Patrice for Jackie's baby.

"Don't you think we should name her Sarah, after my father?" Norm had asked.

"Sarah can be her Hebrew name," Sandy said, and Norman hadn't argued. After all, she'd done all the work. And they'd both found out, through Bucky, that Norman's idea of *father* meant paying the bills, period.

Enid and Mona had arrived together, for afternoon visiting hours, each bearing a gift for the latest grandchild. A musical giraffe from Mona, a pink and white orlon bunting from Enid. Sandy had a small private room, filled with cards and flowers, the most elaborate a bouquet from Norman. To make up for the fact that he hadn't been around to drive her to the hospital? Sandy wasn't sure. By the time he'd been located on the sixteenth hole she'd already delivered the baby.

She wore the pink satin bed jacket Myra had sent when she'd had Bucky, and she'd pinned her hair up in a French twist, sprayed herself with Chanel, and put on makeup, denying the fact that under the blanket she sat on a rubber doughnut to ease the pain of her stitches and that she was slightly fuzzy from the Darvon Dr. Snyder had prescribed to numb her tender, swollen breasts.

At night the nurse provided ice packs to hold under her arms. "It's always you little girls who fill up that way . . . such a shame to let it all go to waste."

"I don't believe in nursing," Sandy told her. "I was nursed for eight months and I've always been sick."

"You should have told that to your doctor. There are shots, you know."

"I did tell him."

And Dr. Snyder sympathized with Sandy's discomfort. "I thought you'd change your mind this time," he'd said.

"I'll never change my mind about breast-feeding."

"Well, next time we'll give you a shot right after delivery so you won't have to suffer this way."

Next time? Who said anything about next time? She'd been expected to produce two children, preferably one of each sex. She'd fulfilled her obligation.

The first time Norman had been so impressed with the sudden growth of her breasts he'd brought his Nikon to the hospital, snapping pictures of Sandy in her bed jacket, unbuttoned enough to show some cleavage. This time he was less enthusiastic, realizing that the change was only temporary and would leave her as small-breasted as before, unlike her sister, Myra, who had inherited Aunt Lottie's mammoth breasts, and who had, two years ago, undergone a breast reduction operation because "you can't imagine what it's like to carry around a pair of tits like these!"

"Too bad she can't give some to you," Norman had said at the time, adding, "ha ha . . ."

"Yes, too bad," Sandy had answered. "Ha ha ha . . ."

"So, when is my little Sarah going home?" Enid asked, reading the cards lined up on Sandy's dresser.

"Her name is Jennifer," Sandy said, "Jennifer Patrice. Didn't Norman tell you?"

"He said *Sarah.*"

"Well, yes, in Hebrew it's Sarah, but we're going to call her Jen."

"I don't believe it!"

"It's true," Sandy said. "I've already signed the birth certificate. Jennifer Patrice."

"Mona, tell me I'm dreaming," Enid said, with one hand to her head, the other to her chest.

"The baby is hers to name," Mona said. "You had your chance with Norman and Fred."

"Oh, God, oh, God." Enid swayed, then sat down. "I feel weak, like I might faint."

Mona poured a cup of water for Enid. "Try to relax," she said, "don't get yourself all worked up for nothing . . ."

"Nothing? You think my son didn't want to name his own baby after his father, may he rest in peace. No, it's her . . ." Enid said, with a nod toward the bed. "She thinks she's too good for a simple, beautiful, biblical name like Sarah." She sipped some water.

"It's not that . . ." Sandy began.

"Miss High and Mighty!"

So she'd been christened too.

"Miss High and Mighty is too good to care about her poor old mother-in-law and did I or didn't I once send her picture to the *Courier-News,* making her a celebrity?"

"Please . . ." Sandy said.

"And how much time do I have left? A little happiness is all I ask."

"Stop it . . ." Sandy said, "please, stop it!"

The nurse poked her head in the doorway. "Ladies, could we try to remember we're in a hospital?"

Enid turned to face Mona. "I'll tell you this, my enemies treat me better than my daughter-in-laws. You don't know how lucky you are to have girls instead of boys. With boys you wind up with tsouris . . ."

"At least be happy the baby has the Hebrew name you want," Mona told her.

"To me she'll always be Sarah, no matter what Miss High and Mighty calls her."

"Her name is Jennifer, dammit!" Sandy shouted. "And I've got the birth certificate to prove it!" She could no longer hold back her tears.

"Ladies, ladies." The nurse returned, shaking her head at them. "I'll have to ask you to leave now. Look at our patient."

Sandy was crying hard. "Take care, darling," Mona said, kissing her cheek. "I'd better go too. She shouldn't drive like this."

The nurse gave Sandy a sedative and she slept through feeding time and missed evening visiting hours.

Sandy was filled with guilt. It wasn't just that she liked the name Jennifer, and certainly she didn't dislike the name Sarah. It was that she couldn't, wouldn't name her child after Samuel D. Pressman. Sam Pressman had never addressed Sandy by name. He'd called her *girl* or *you,* not entirely without affection, but without concern. Samuel David Pressman, owner of Pressman's

Dry Cleaning Establishment, a chain of four stores in Plainfield, Roselle, and New Brunswick, catering to the *Black is Beautiful in Cleaned and Pressed Clothes* business. And in each store a dober-man slept in the front window, a reminder that burglars should take their business elsewhere.

Two months after the funeral Enid decided to give up her organizations, her luncheons, her shopping expeditions to Loehman's and her afternoon Mah-Jongg games for the sake of the business. "I can't expect my boy to do it all by himself, can I?" And she established herself as manager of the Plainfield store, leaving Norman free to expand and improve the business. And he had. He'd opened three new stores that year and four more since then. He was always up to his elbows in a new solution.

Sandy was under the dryer at Coiffures Elegante in downtown Plainfield that gray November afternoon in 1963, her head cov-ered with giant blue rollers, which, after an hour of intense dis-comfort would turn into the popular bouffant hairstyle of her look-alike. She was flipping the pages of the latest issue of *Vogue* with the stub of her fingers, careful not to mess up the freshly applied Frosted Sherbet on her nails, when the news came over the radio. Sandy didn't know what was happening since she couldn't hear anything but suddenly there was a lot of activity in the shop. She raised the hood of her dryer. "What's wrong?"

"The president's been shot!"

"Is it serious?"

"Looks like it."

"Oh God."

And the other women pulled their dryers back down over their wet heads. But not Sandy. She'd jumped up, knocking over the manicurist's table, tiny bottles of polish crashing to the floor. She ran through the shop to the back room, where her coat hung, and as she tore out the door the last words she heard were spoken by her neighbor, Doris Richter. "Alex . . . could you tease it a little higher on the left because it always drops by the next day . . ."

She drove home quickly, rushed into the house, found Bucky snuggled next to Mazie on the sofa in the den, the baby asleep in her lap, the TV on. "Oh, Mrs. Pressman," Mazie cried, "the president's dead. He's been shot in the head. Lord help us our president's dead."

Bucky made a gun with his finger. "Bang bang, the president's dead!" He studied Sandy for a minute. "You look funny like that, Mommy . . . like a moonman."

Sandy took him in her arms, cried into his warm, puppy-smelling head, then went to her room, took the rollers out of her hair, laid out her black dress and shoes, dug out the black veil she'd worn to Samuel's funeral, and prepared for mourning.

"What the hell," Norman said, when he got home and found Sandy dressed in black.

"I'm sitting shiveh for the president."

"Are you crazy?"

"No."

"You didn't sit shiveh when my father died."

"That has nothing to do with this."

"And the Kennedys are Catholic!"

"So what?"

"I think you're really going off your rocker this time. I think you're really going bananas."

Sandy shrugged. "I don't expect you to understand . . . you didn't even vote for him."

"And neither did you."

"That's how much you know." She gathered several sheets from the linen closet and draped one over the mirror in their bedroom.

"Jesus Christ, now you're going Orthodox?"

"This is the way we did it when Grandpa died," Sandy said, "I remember."

"I can't believe this. You're not Jackie, you know, just because you won that fucking contest."

How could Sandy explain? In a way she was Jackie, with blood and brains all over her suit. "I know exactly who I am and exactly what I'm doing."

"We're due at the Levinworths' in two hours. You better do something about your hair. It looks like hell."

"You'll have to call to say we can't make it."

"Not *we,* Sandy. I'm going anyway."

"Don't you have any feelings? Don't you know the whole country's in mourning?"

"So we'll mourn at Lew's house. It's not going to make any difference. It's not going to bring him back."

"No!" Sandy headed for the dining room, to cover the mirror above the sideboard.

"Pardon me, Mrs. Pressman," Mazie said. She'd changed out of her uniform into a green wool suit and she carried a small suitcase. "I'm going to take a few days off to go down to Washington . . . to the funeral . . . you know . . ."

"That is absolutely out of the question, Mazie," Norman said. "You can see what condition Mrs. Pressman is in."

"Same as me," Mazie said, "sad and sick." She put down her suitcase and helped Sandy drape the sheet over the mirror. "I don't know just when I'll be back, Mrs. Pressman . . . maybe three or four days . . . after the weekend. I just don't know."

"Maybe you didn't hear me, Mazie," Norm said, raising his voice, "but there's no way you can have time off now. Who's going to take care of the children?"

"Take care of them yourself, Mr. Pressman."

"If you go, you can kiss this job good-bye!"

"Norman!" Sandy came alive. "What are you saying? Mazie loved the president! If she wants to go to his funeral . . ."

"It's just an excuse, Sandy, can't you see that? Every goddamned fucking excuse."

"I won't tolerate no language like that," Mazie said. "I'm sorry, Mrs. Pressman, but I can't work for no Communist!"

She picked up Jen, who was in her infant seat, and carried her down the hall to her room. Bucky followed, wailing, "Mazie . . . Mazie . . ." Sandy followed too. Mazie put the baby into her crib and kissed both children. "Good-bye, sugars, you be good for your mommy, hear?" Then she grabbed her suitcase and marched out the front door. "Goodbye, Mrs. Pressman. I'm really sorry."

"Oh, Mazie," Sandy cried, "I don't know what we're going to do without you." She closed the door, trying to keep out the chill night air, and said to Norman, "I can't believe you did that. I'll never forgive you. Mazie was wonderful." She brushed past him and went to the bedroom. Suddenly she felt very tired. She had to lie down. To contemplate. How did Jackie feel at this moment? A widow, with two young children. And Caroline used to parade around in her pumps, interrupting his meetings . . .

The phone rang. Norman picked it up. "Yes, Lew, how are you? . . . Well, certainly, we were just about to call you . . . No night to celebrate, that's for sure . . . Yes, that's right, Sandy feels especially close to Jackie, always has. I can hear Hannah crying . . . yes, same here, they're very emotional . . . You too, another time. Uh huh . . . Bye . . ." He hung up. "That was Lew."

"Hypocrite!"

"That's the thanks I get for covering for your emotional immaturity?"

"Mommy, I'm hungry," Bucky called.

"Just a minute," Norman called back. "Mommy's coming." He whispered, "Your children are starving. Will you quit this idiot act and take care of them?"

But Sandy wouldn't budge, wouldn't speak, and Norman, unable to cope with the situation, frantic at the idea of feeding the kids supper by himself, and convinced that Sandy was really going off the deep end, phoned Gordon, as if Gordon could look into Sandy's head the way he could look into her cunt. Gordon advised two aspirin and a good night's sleep.

And then, while millions of TV viewers, including Sandy and Norman, watched Jack Ruby shoot Lee Harvey Oswald, the call came from the highway patrol. Sandy's father, Ivan Schaedel, had had a flat tire on the Pulaski Skyway. Mona had sat on the hood of the car, shooing away cars with her scarf, as Ivan attempted to change the tire. But he never finished. He was smashed by a Juniper Moving Van and killed instantly.

And then the shiveh began in earnest.

5

LAST DECEMBER WHILE Sandy was recuperating in Jamaica, Norman was making a name for himself as athlete of the century. He'd jump out of bed at six, jog around the grounds of La Carousella for half an hour, perform Royal Canadian Air Force exercises for twenty minutes, swim a dozen laps, play eighteen holes of golf, rush out to the new court for doubles, followed by singles, followed by mixed doubles, and before dinner, while the others were napping, he was back in the pool, holding his breath under water.

"Daddy can count to one hundred," Jen told Sandy. "How high can you count under water?"

"If I hold my nose I think I can make it to five."

"That's not very good."

"It's good enough. I don't expect to ever have to hold my breath under water."

"But suppose you do?"

"I'll drown, I guess."

"But Daddy says . . ."

"Never mind what Daddy says this time. Go and get ready for lunch."

"Can I eat in the kitchen with Lydia?"

"I guess so, if she doesn't mind."

"She likes me and I like her. She's the best cook. Why don't you ever make fried bananas?"

"I never thought about frying them but I used to feed you mashed bananas when you were a baby."

"Mashed bananas, yuck! Will you fry them when we get home?"

"Maybe, now go and find Bucky and tell him to wash up for lunch."

On the twenty-seventh Myra threw a party for her friends, three couples from The Club who were also vacationing at Runaway Bay, two of them in rented houses, and the third staying at the hotel on the beach. All were thinking seriously about buying a piece of property of their own so that they could continue to vacation together. Besides, it was tax deductible, they reminded each other, daily.

Before the party, while Myra scurried around filling candy dishes, rearranging furniture, and checking the bar, Sandy asked, "Don't you find it boring to be down here with the same people you see all the time at home?"

"Not at all," Myra answered. "We love it."

"But don't you want to meet new people down here?"

Myra dumped a jar of Planters dry-roasted nuts into a silver bowl. "It would be awful." She tilted her head back and dropped a handful of nuts into her mouth.

"I think it would be nice."

"Awful to have to find games, I mean." Myra chewed and swallowed the nuts, then brushed off her hands. "Take golf . . . they could say they're class A players when they're really B's, and if I had to play with beginners, well, frankly, I'd rather not play at all. And then there's tennis," Myra said. "Playing with people who aren't in your class is *horrendous*. There are people who'll tell you they're high intermediates when by your standards they might be low intermediates or, worse yet, high beginners."

"What are you?"

"I'm low advanced, but I can handle any average advanced player and upward. Norman, for instance, is headed for high advanced, but he and I can still have a good game. How do you think the candy looks? Do you like it piled high or spread out in rows?"

"Piled high."

"Me too. Remember how Mona used to spread out the after-dinner mints?"

"Yes."

"Where'd you get that dress?"

"It's not a dress, it's a skirt and top." Sandy fingered the material, an Indian cotton print in bright colors, with elephants marching around it. She enjoyed the comfortable wraparound style. "Do you like it?"

"It's cute."

Sandy felt that Myra was waiting to be admired. "I like yours too."

"I couldn't have worn this in the old days," Myra said, "but now I can go braless if I feel like it." Her dress was a long, clingy, black jersey with a high neck in front, plunging to the waist in back. Her frosted hair hung to her shoulders and framed her face, like a lion's mane. And under the black jersey Sandy could see the outline of Myra's perfect 34-B breasts, of her perfect, rose-colored nipples, each one the circumference of a quarter, where Sandy's were only the size of dimes.

"I wish to hell Gordy could play tennis like Norman," Myra said. "If he could, we'd win all the married couples tournaments at The Club. As it is I'm embarrassed having a shelf full of trophies when Gordy's never won anything."

"Does he mind?"

"He says he doesn't."

"Well, then, don't worry."

"I'll bet Norman's great in bed."

"Myra!"

"Does that embarrass you?"

"Not exactly."

"They say you can tell a lot about how a man performs in bed by watching him play tennis." Myra was at the bar now, arranging brandy glasses on a tray.

"I've always heard you can tell by the way a man dances," Sandy said, "and Norman can't dance at all."

"Are you saying he's no good then?" She looked over at Sandy, raising her eyebrows.

Sandy looked away. "I'm not saying anything, one way or the other."

"You're not having trouble, are you?"

"No, who said anything about trouble?"

Myra sighed. "I remember when Daddy told you that Norman was *phlegmatic* and you left the room in tears. I was shocked myself. Who would have guessed Daddy even knew such a word . . ."

"That was years ago."

"But Mona said he was a good catch," Myra added, "and she turned out to be right, as usual."

"Yes."

"You used to tell me everything, San . . . you used to come to my room with questions, remember? I wish we could be that close now."

"I don't have any more questions."

Myra busied herself with the cocktail napkins, counting out equal piles and distributing them around the room. "Tell me something," she said in a low voice, looking around to make sure no one was in sight or hearing distance. "Do you suck?"

"Myra, please!"

"Oh, come on. You can tell me. Everybody's doing it these days."

"Including you?"

Myra shrugged. "Of course. So how about you and Norm?"

Sandy hesitated. "Certainly."

"Do you swallow?"

"Do you?"

"I asked you first," Myra said, "and anyway, it's pure protein, it can't hurt you."

"I know."

"Mother!" Kate called in her fishwife's voice. "I think your friends are here. I heard a car drive up."

Myra ran her hands over her hair and her tongue across her teeth. "I don't have lipstick on my teeth, do I?" she asked Sandy, making a horse face.

"No, you're fine."

"Why don't you run in and put some on. You could use the color . . ."

"I think I'm getting a herpes . . . I'm using Blistex . . ."

"Hello . . . hello . . . hello . . ."

Barbara and Gish. Lucille and Ben. Phyllis and Mickey. Myra's friends. It was hard for Sandy to keep them straight. She'd watched them on the court each day but dressed in their Head color-coordinated outfits they all looked the same. They'd tried to get her to join them, tried to make friends. "I'd love to play," she'd explained. "But I've been sick and I have to take it easy for a while."

Now here they were, out of their daily uniforms, into their evening ones. The women wore clingy jersey dresses, like Myra's, and the men were all in plaid slacks and Lacoste shirts. During the week, Sandy had given the women code names, to help her remember who was who. Brown, Luscious, and Funky instead of Barbara, Lucille, and Phyllis. Sandy thought she might like Funky, with a bandana tied around her head, loaded down with Indian jewelry, best, until they got into a discussion about Plainfield.

"Plainfield, my God!" Funky said. "I thought Plainfield was all black."

"Not quite."

"You mean not yet! If I were you, I'd get out while the going's good and move up to the Hills. We built our final house in Watchung last year. We can see the lights from our living room, just like stars. It's fantastic . . . you'd love it . . . is your Plainfield house your first house?"

"Yes, we bought it from Norman's mother after his father died."

"Oh. Because I was going to say if it was your final house then I could understand your reluctance to leave it, but with your first house . . ."

"It's very nice," Sandy said, feeling defensive about Enid's house for the first time. "It's in Sleepy Hollow."

"But the schools . . ."

"The children go to private school."

"In Watchung you could send them to public school. We have

only two black families in the town and both of them are professional."

"It's really not a racial thing," Brown said, joining them.
Brown's nails were filed to squares instead of points and polished
in frosty brown, to match her frosty brown eye shadow, her frosty
brown hair, her frosty brown suntan, her frosty brown dress. "It's
more of a socioeconomic thing, don't you think?"

"Yes and no," Funky said. "Yes, in the sense that the professional
ones tend to think more like us and want what's best for their children. No, in the sense that they're still different no matter how
hard you try to pretend they're not. I mean, put one in this room,
right now, and suddenly we'd all clam up." She took a cheese puff
from the tray offered by Elena, the black maid. "Thank you."

Sandy was trying to sort out the men. Ben was the urologist
with the vasectomy button on his collar. Had he performed his
own vasectomy? No, how could he see over that belly? It might be
nice if Norman had a vasectomy. Sandy hated her diaphragm. It
was so messy. And the Pill made her sick. She'd have to approach
the subject carefully, though, because Norm was very sensitive
about his genitals.

Mickey had a lot of hair and some kind of engineering company. Then there was Gish. He practiced law in Newark, special-
ized in personal injury work and was, according to Myra, cleaning
up. He and Brown were neighbors of Myra's in Short Hills. Sandy
didn't like the way he looked her up and down every time she
crossed the room. It made her uncomfortable.

So much for the men.

"Your husband," Luscious said, settling next to Sandy on the
sofa, "is such a tiger! That serve . . . what a smash! I told him, don't
let up on me just because I'm a girl, and he didn't . . . aced me
every time . . . you must be really proud of him . . ." Luscious, tiny,
blonde, and perfect, looked like an aging Barbie Doll.

"Yes," Sandy answered.

"And his backhand is nothing to sneeze at," Brown said, sitting
on Sandy's other side. "Wicked, absolutely wicked!"

"He really enjoys his games," Sandy told them.

"It's not just a question of *enjoy*," Funky added, leaning over the back of the sofa so that Sandy could feel her breath on her neck. "It's talent. Pure, unadulterated talent."

Pure, unadulterated bullshit, Sandy thought, wishing she were brave enough to say it out loud.

"I should be so lucky!" Brown said, laughing down her vodka and orange juice.

"Normie . . . tiger . . ." Luscious called across the room to where the men had gathered. "Will you play with me tomorrow . . . singles . . . for just a little while?"

"Sure thing," Norman called back. "Let's say, from three-thirty to three forty-five."

And later, after dessert, while they were sitting around sipping brandy, Ben said to Norman, "You should join The Club."

"I've been telling him that all week," Myra said.

"And I've been thinking about it," Norman said.

That was certainly news to Sandy.

"It makes a lot of sense," Norman said.

Gish, who was seated next to Sandy on the small sofa, turned to her and said, "What do you think?"

"What . . . oh, me?" Sandy asked, surprised to find herself in the conversation. "Well, I'm not an athlete so it's hard for me to say if we should invest that much in The Club."

"But Sandy," Myra said, "it's more than a club . . . it's a way of life . . . it's not just golf and tennis . . . you'd make wonderful friends . . . look at us . . ." She smiled and extended her arms.

"And your children will meet the right kinds of young people too," Funky said.

"Playing those public courses is a waste of time," Ben told Norman. "How long do you have to wait to tee off on weekends?"

"I get up at six so I usually don't have to wait."

"Wouldn't you rather sleep till nine?" Funky asked.

"I'm not a late sleeper," Norman said.

"So, you'd have time for a quickie," Ben said.

"We just love our Sunday-morning quickies," Luscious told them all.

Gish put his arm around Sandy's shoulder and whispered, "I'd like to make it with you, quick or slow, your choice."

"And Sandy," Brown said, "once you take lessons you'll love it like everybody else. We're not all born athletes like your husband."

"I'll bet you don't need any lessons in the sack," Gish whispered.

"And on Thanksgiving and Mother's Day and all the other holidays you'll always have a nice place to go," Funky said.

"And The Club does a terrific job on affairs," Brown said.

Affairs? Sandy thought.

Myra stood up. "I think I have a Club booklet somewhere." She went into her bedroom and returned with it. *Green Hollow Country Club. Rules and Regulations.* "Read this, San, it'll give you a better idea."

"Thanks." Sandy stood up too. "It's been very nice," she said, "I hope you'll excuse me . . . I'm really tired . . ." She looked across the room, at Norman.

"Sandy's recuperating, you know," Myra said. "She's been quite sick. Take care, San. Get a good night's sleep."

"I'll be in soon," Norman told her.

"Yes, see you all tomorrow."

Sandy got into bed with the green booklet. *Had Gish been serious? No, it was just a joke.* She opened the booklet. There were General Rules, Golf Course Rules, Tee Off Procedures, Club House Rules, Guest Rules, Tennis Regulations, Pool Regulations, Rules Pertaining to Children on the Premises, Rules Pertaining to Restaurant Minimums, and Rules Pertaining to Sons of Members Who Wished to Caddy.

Suppose Gish had been serious? He was attractive.

No, it was out of the question. He'd just been kidding around. Flirting, but not seriously.

There were Lessons For All, including but not limited to Private Tennis Instruction (by the hour or half-hour), Golf (by the hour or half-hour), Playing Lessons (nine holes or eighteen), Having the Pro Play in Your Foursome . . .

Sandy dozed off, the bedroom light still on.

6

Two days later Sandy, Myra, and the twins were having their lunch on the patio. "It's just wonderful to be able to share your vacation with your family," Myra said, squeezing Sandy's hand in a sudden burst of enthusiasm. "You're looking so much better, San. How do you feel?"

"Stronger . . . healthier . . . I always feel good with a tan."

Myra inhaled deeply and stretched. "I can't think of any place on earth I'd rather be."

"Well, I can!" Kate said. "And I'd also like to know why we can't ever have anything besides blended salad for lunch?"

"Because blended salad is good for you," Myra said. It was her latest kick in fad foods. She bought romaine lettuce by the crate. Sandy found it hard to take herself, but instead of complaining she just waited until the others left for their afternoon activities, then made herself a peanut butter sandwich.

"Green mush!" Kate moved it around on her plate.

"Seaweed!" Connie added. "And Bucky and Jen are in the kitchen eating hamburgers and fried bananas, is that fair?"

"Bucky and Jen are little children," Myra told them, "but you are young women and need to watch your weight."

"Bullshit!" Kate said, pushing back her chair.

"I thought I told you to watch your language," Myra said, clenching her teeth.

"Oh, come off it, Mother. Aunt Sandy knows we're human. Let's go, Con." She and Connie got up and stalked off.

Myra tried to laugh it off. "Just wait until Bucky and Jen reach adolescence." She sipped her mint iced tea. "It isn't easy." She flicked her hair back. "Did I tell you I made appointments for them with Dr. Saphire?"

Dr. Saphire had performed Myra's breast reduction surgery.

"No, aren't they too young?"

"Nose jobs . . . not the other . . . not yet . . ."

"Oh, I didn't know he did those."

"Yes, he's the best in the business."

"When are they going in?"

"Early July."

She nodded. She was always surprised that Myra had produced such unattractive children. It must be hard on them, having a gorgeous perfectly groomed mother, like Myra, Sandy thought. But no matter how hard she tried to like them, to find some redeeming feature, she couldn't. It was so unpleasant being around them. Bucky and Jen felt it too. Just that morning Jen had said, "I hate Connie and Kate, don't you?"

Bucky answered, "I hate Kate. Connie's just dumb."

"I don't want to hear you talking about your cousins that way," Sandy had said.

"Why not? It's true," Bucky told her.

"Yeah," Jen said, "they never laugh or have any fun and they're so ugly."

"But they sure do have huge tits," Bucky said.

"Will mine grow like that, Mommy?" Jen asked.

"I doubt it," Sandy told her. "You're small-boned, like me. The twins are built more like Aunt Lottie."

"I hope mine grow bigger than yours," Jen said. "Yours are so little."

"Big breasts aren't everything," Sandy said.

"Yeah, I'm an ass man myself," Bucky said. "Like Dad."

"Like Dad?" Sandy asked.

"Yeah, he told me the other day when we saw Aunt Myra's ass."

"Bucky!"

"Well, we did and it wasn't our fault either. She was standing there talking on the phone and it was sticking out for everybody to see."

"You should have looked the other way," Sandy said.

"Dad didn't."

Norman, an ass man? He'd never told her that, but she should have guessed, given his fascination with the product of that part of the body.

Bucky and Jen were not happy that afternoon, when Connie and Kate piled into the car with them. They poked each other and whispered but Sandy was determined to make it a pleasant outing.

"Now remember, Mom," Bucky said, "you drive on the *left* here."

"I know, I know."

It was a short ride down the hill to the small, private, home-owners' beach which was adjacent to the long beach belonging to the Runaway Bay Hotel. Often, Sandy and her children were the only ones there. The other homeowners and tenants had their own swimming pools, like Myra, and spent most of their time playing golf or tennis anyway. Norman hated the beach. "All that sand," he'd say. "It gets up my ass and between my toes . . . who needs it?" But Sandy loved the beach. The warm sand, the endless blue-green sea, the salty air. "Isn't the water beautiful down here?" she asked the twins.

"It's all right," Connie said.

More than their looks, it was Connie and Kate's apathy, their lifelessness, that bothered Sandy. The twins took off their beach shirts, revealing bikinis. Their loose flesh hung around their middles and poured out from their bikini bottoms. They weren't fair-skinned like Sandy and Myra. They were more like Gordon's family. Gordon had olive skin and tanned deeply, changing his looks. Otherwise, during the winter months, Gordon appeared to have faintly green skin. He was balding and combed his remaining hair carefully across his head. His eyes were deep-set and his cheeks becoming jowly, but he still had a hard, compact body, although at just under five five, Myra dwarfed him.

How lucky Sandy was to have Bucky and Jen. Lovely little Jen, small and delicate with wispy hair and an almost constant smile. And Bucky, growing up to look like Norman, with a square body and almost no neck, set on broad shoulders. But Bucky would be warmer than Norman, warmer and kinder and unafraid of his feelings.

Jen ran off to hunt for shells and Sandy settled down for her afternoon nap. Just as she was dozing off, Kate screamed. Sandy jumped up and ran to her. "What is it?"

"My belly . . . my belly . . ."

Appendicitis? Would she be able to find Myra or Gordon? Oh, Jesus, she should have left them home. They were nothing but trouble.

"He burned it! It's killing me."

"Burned it . . . who . . . what?"

"Bucky! With his fucking magnifying glass."

"What? He did what?" Sandy looked over at him. He was sitting under a palm tree, holding his magnifying glass, a sheepish look on his face.

"I didn't know it would happen so fast," Bucky said. "It takes a long time for leaves to burn."

"I'm not a leaf, you fucking imbecile!"

"Okay, okay," Sandy said, "let's calm down now. Bucky, apologize to Kate and give me your magnifying glass."

"Do I have to?"

"Yes, and now."

He handed her his magnifying glass. "Can I have it back tomorrow?"

"No."

"Day after?"

"I doubt it."

"When?"

"We'll see."

"You always say that!"

"Apologize to Kate, please."

"Oh, Mom."

"We're waiting, Bucky."

"Okay, I'm sorry."

"I don't think he really means it, Aunt Sandy."

"I do so," Bucky said.

"I'm sure he does," Sandy told Kate.

"What happened?" Jen asked, racing back, her Baggie filled with shells.

"Bucky burned Kate with his magnifying glass," Connie said. "Look at that red mark on her belly."

Jen examined Kate's belly and held back a laugh.

"It hurt like hell," Kate told her. "I thought a snake bit me, or something."

"They don't have snakes on the beach," Bucky said.

"The hell they don't."

"Do they, Mom?"

"I really don't know." Sandy rummaged through her beach bag. "Look, why don't the four of you go over to the hotel and have a drink. Here's five dollars. You can bring me the change."

"Five won't buy us all drinks," Kate said, "not down here."

"Oh, I suppose you're right," Sandy said, fishing out another five. "Take ten then and bring back the change."

"They're having crab races this afternoon," Jen said. "I love crab races. Please, please, can we go?"

"Oh, all right . . . I suppose it can't hurt."

"Thank you, thank you." Jen jumped up and down and planted a kiss on Sandy's cheek. "You're the best mother that ever was."

Sandy laughed. "Go on, have a good time."

She watched as they ran down the beach, Bucky and Jen out front, Kate and Connie behind them. Then she made a pillow out of two beach towels, settled back on her blanket, and closed her eyes, her face lifted to the sun. Ah, the hot sunshine. It felt so good. She began to drift off . . . the sun hot on her face, her belly, her legs. Hot between her legs. Yes, good and hot . . . so nice . . . so long since she'd had that feeling . . . since before she'd been sick. Norman hadn't . . . that is, they hadn't fucked since before. He wanted to, she knew, but she told him she was still too weak. Nice to know it was still working, that the cortisone hadn't affected her that way. She opened her legs a bit more, letting the

hot sun warm her there, warming her all over . . . on her
nipples . . . erect now . . . she ran her hand across her belly . . .
fuck me . . . fuck me, sunshine . . . so delicious, as it crept up her
legs, to her thighs, to her cunt . . . kiss me there . . . lick me . . .
oh, please . . . oh, hurry . . . She pictured the beachboy, the one at
the hotel who set up lounge chairs and handed out towels. A
beautiful boy, with white blond hair and deeply tanned skin. A
beautiful body too. She could see every muscle in his back.
Strong arms. And a line of pale fur extending from his navel to
the top of his bathing trunks . . . and beyond? Yes, probably
beyond. She could see the outline of his cock, of his balls,
through his tight little Speedo suit. Everytime she passed him, as
she walked along the beach with the children, everytime she
looked, although she promised herself she wouldn't any more . . .
she saw his bulge. How nice it would be to feel him against her. If
he walked by right now, she would say, *Lie on me,* and he would,
rubbing against her. Rubbing, rubbing, but not putting it inside
her. It would be exciting enough that way, just rubbing on the outside of her suit, the way Shep used to do because she'd told him, *I
can't Shep . . . I promised my mother . . . I can't do it . . . not all the
way . . . but we can do this . . . and this . . . yes, Shep, yes . . . I can feel
you through my clothes . . . can you feel me? Yes, I can come this way.
I'm coming, Shep . . . oh, God . . . I'm coming . . . now now now . . .*

"I think I love you."

Sandy opened her eyes and sat up. A middle-aged man in
madras bathing trunks was sitting opposite her, drawing in the
sand with a stick. "I'm sorry, did you say something?" Sandy
asked, rearranging her bathing suit, hoping she hadn't been
squirming, that the man had no idea what she'd been thinking.

"I said I think I love you."

Sandy jumped up, gathered her things in a hurry, and took off,
running down the beach.

He called after her. "Don't go, I said I love you and I mean it.
Come back. Come swim with me."

Jesus, a pervert on the private beach! She ran until her side
ached, until she reached the safety of the crowded hotel grounds.
God, he could have killed her. He could have bashed in her head

with a coconut. Never again. From now on she was going to make her headquarters on the hotel beach.

She used the Ladies Room near the hotel pool, got herself together, then went up to the crab races and found Bucky and Jen.

"Hi, Mom, what are you doing here?" Bucky asked. He didn't wait for her answer. He was too engrossed in the crab race. "Go little guy . . . go . . . look at that . . . go number three . . . go . . ."

"I lost," Jen said. "I bet on number six and then he turned around and walked the wrong way."

"Maybe that will teach you a lesson about gambling," Sandy said. "Where's Connie and Kate?"

"Oh, they went off with the ganja man," Bucky said.

"The ganja man?"

"The dealer."

"What dealer?"

"You know, Mom, quit acting dumb."

"Bucky, I do not know what you're talking about."

"Ganja . . . it's like grass . . . like dope . . . pot . . ."

"Marijuana?"

"Yeah, down here they call it ganja."

"And they went off with him?"

"Yeah, but they'll be back, don't worry."

"They're just down the beach," Jen said pointing, "but Kate said if I told anybody she'd kill me. She said she'd hold me under water until I turn blue. That's why I have to learn to hold my breath till one hundred, like Daddy."

"Nobody's going to hurt you," Sandy said. "Now, listen . . . you two stay right here and watch the rest of the crab races . . . don't move . . . I'll be back with Kate and Connie and then we're going home."

Just what she needed. Where the hell were they and what was she supposed to do about them? And if they'd used her money, she'd kill them. The bitches!

She found them in a clump of trees, laughing their heads off. "Hi, Aunt Sandy," Kate said. "What are you doing way down here?"

"I was just going to ask you the same question. I thought you were going to stay with Bucky and Jen."

"Bucky and Jen aren't babies. They can take care of themselves."

"Have you been smoking pot?"

They laughed again.

"Do your parents know you smoke?"

"I don't know," Kate said. "We've never discussed it."

"Are you going to tell them?" Connie asked.

"Of course she's not," Kate said. "What purpose would that serve?"

"Look," Sandy said, "I'm not feeling well and I want to get home."

"Gee, that's too bad, Aunt Sandy," Kate said. "Would you like a joint? That might help."

"No, let's just get out of here."

That night Norman asked, "Feeling stronger, San?"

"Yes." She was already in bed, reading.

"You're getting a nice tan. Are you ready for a little something?"

"I think so."

"Got your diaphragm in?"

"No, I forgot."

"Where is it?"

"In the bathroom cabinet."

"I'll get it for you."

"Okay."

He came back and handed her the case, then looked the other way while she reached under the covers and inserted it. "Ready," she said when it was in place. Norman turned out the light and climbed into bed beside her.

Rules and Regulations for a Norman Pressman Fuck.

The room must be dark so they do not have to look at each other. There will be one kiss, with tongue, to get things going. His fingers will pass lightly over her breasts, travel down her belly to her cunt, and stop. He will attempt to find her clitoris. If he succeeds, he will take it between his thumb and forefinger and rub. Too hard. He will roll over on top of her. He will raise himself on his elbows, and then . . .

Norman kissed her. He tasted like Colgate toothpaste. She hated

Colgate. Question: Did she also hate Norman? Answer: Yes, sometimes.

Norman's cold tongue was darting in and out of her mouth. One kiss. That was enough for him. Sandy didn't mind. Her lip hurt. Besides, his kisses no longer pleased her, no longer offered any excitement.

"Ready, San?"

"Yes." Sandy raised her hips to catch him. In and Out. In and Out. She closed her eyes, and imagined herself with the beachboy. She would be on top, bouncing wildly. Almost thirty-two years old and never been on top. How unfair! Uh oh . . . Norman was beginning his descent. Three more strokes and it would be over. *Hurry, Sandy . . . hurry, or you'll be left out.* She moved with Norman but it was too late. No main course tonight.

"Sorry," he said, "it's been a long time. I couldn't wait. Wake me in twenty minutes and we'll try again."

"It doesn't matter," Sandy said. *Liar. Liar. Of course it mattered.*

Norman used the bathroom. She heard him gargling. Was he afraid that her kisses still bore germs? He returned to his own bed, across the room. In seconds he was asleep, snoring softly. Sandy masturbated, continuing her fantasy with the beachboy. The climax she reached alone was stronger and more satisfying than any she had had with Norman. When she could breathe easily again she said, "Norman, do you love me?"

She knew he was asleep. She didn't really expect him to answer. And he didn't.

7

1970. NOT ONLY a New Year but a New Decade. When they returned from Jamaica Sandy was full of resolutions. She would learn to be a gourmet cook. She would get a slinky dress. She would become an outstanding mother of the year. She would clean out all the closets and organize them. She would make sure the baseboards were as clean as Norman claimed Enid's were. She would read *Time* magazine from cover to cover and make interesting, occasionally startling, comments. She would devour three books a week from the library and only one of them would be fiction. She would be sexy. Yes, she would be very sexy. Always. Looking her best. Never in need of a shampoo. Shaving her legs before it was necessary. Dental floss between her teeth morning and night. Regular douches with vinegar, maybe wine vinegar for variety, and not just the morning after. She would please Norman in every way. If she made him happier, if she concentrated on his every wish, then she would be rewarded. She would become a happier person. A better person.

"Make his interests your interests. Make his friends your friends. When he's in the mood, you're in the mood. Dress to please him. Cook to please him. What else matters? A happy husband is the answer to a happy life," Mona Schaedel said to her daughters, Myra Suzanne and Sondra Elaine, December, 1954, upon the former's engagement to Gordon Michael Lefferts, third-year medical student, excellent catch, who the night before had presented Myra Suzanne with a perfect, blue-white, three-carat Marquise cut diamond engagement ring, purchased from his uncle Jerome, who, thank God, was in the business and got him a terrific price, because someday when Gordon was a specialist and Uncle Jerome was old, Gordon would take care of him and there would be no charge. Uncle Jerome never thought to ask about Gordon's future plans. Maybe if he had he wouldn't have been so generous. On the other hand there was Aunt Fanny and her hysterectomy to consider.

Myra let Sandy try on her ring and from that moment on Sandy's goal in life was to become engaged.

They'd been back from Jamaica for two weeks when Sandy bought a pictorial sexual encyclopedia. "I have an idea," she said to Norman. "Let's do it every night for a week."

"Are you serious?"

"Yes, and a different position everytime."

"Starting when?"

"Tonight?"

"You've got yourself a deal!"

But when she tried to explore his body he tensed. "No, not there," he said, when her hands touched the soft patches of hair under his arms. "I don't like to be touched there."

"Oh, sorry." She kissed his neck, then made her way down to his chest.

"No," he said, squirming, as her fingers rested on his nipples. He took her hands in his. "What do you think I am, a fag?"

"I'm just exploring," Sandy said, "like the book says."

"To hell with the book!"

She had planned to work her way down to his feet, where she would bite and kiss his toes, and then, hopefully, he would follow her lead and do to her all the lovely things she had done to him. He would lick her nipples, round and round, and kiss her inner thighs until she was wet, until she had to have him; and only then would he enter her, long and stiff and they would move together for hours, maybe all night.

But she could see now that there was no point in going on. It wasn't going to work. She might as well get on with the different position. She climbed on top of him.

"What are you doing?"

"Let's try it this way."

"No, not with you on top."

"It's a very common position, Norm . . ."

"For dykes, for women's libbers who want to take over."

"No, it has nothing to do with that. It's supposed to feel good this way . . ."

"I'm the man in this family. I get on top."

"That's silly, Norm, it has nothing to do with being the man."

But he was on top of her now, pushing into her. "You're my wife, not some whore."

"I could pretend to be a whore, just for fun."

He pushed harder. "You're my wife . . . there, there . . ." he said, coming into her.

Every night for a week, proving that he was the man.

Every night for a week, and Sandy was sore.

So much for her New Year's resolutions.

Norman joined The Club in early February and was promptly asked to serve as chairman of the Grievance Committee. "That's some honor for a new member!" Myra told Sandy. "You should be very proud."

"Oh, I am. Anything that makes Norm happy."

And he was *very* happy. His enthusiasm for The Club carried over to the children. "Can I learn to play golf?" Bucky asked.

"Of course, there's a practice range and a putting green and you can take lessons this spring."

"What about me, Daddy?" Jen asked. "Can I take lessons too?"

"Certainly, Princess."

"What about Mommy?" Jen and Bucky looked at her.

Sandy shook her head but Norman said, "Mommy's going to learn to play golf and tennis too."

"Come on, Norm . . . don't tell them that . . . you know it's not my thing."

But for her birthday Norman gave her a set of matched clubs in a lemon yellow bag, brown and white golf shoes, reminiscent of her beloved junior high saddles, and a dozen pairs of peds with different color trim.

And for Mother's Day he presented her with a Davis Classic racquet, Tretorn tennis shoes, two Head outfits, a tennis sweater, and three cans of fuchsia balls.

All right. She would try. She'd make an effort. After all, eighth grade was twenty years ago. Her coordination might have improved. She'd had babies since then and masturbation took coordination, didn't it? Especially while driving.

8

THE MAN ON the motorcycle returned on Monday morning, but this time he was dressed in jeans and a T-shirt although he wore the same helmet and rode the same bike. As soon as Sandy looked out the window he unzipped his jeans and dropped them to his ankles. No underwear. Interesting. He worked quickly, making it on the nineteenth stroke. After, he waved to her. She didn't wave back. At least he didn't ride up on the lawn this time.

Sandy didn't call Norman. She didn't call the police either. What was the point? They hadn't believed her before. Besides, he wasn't hurting anyone. But who was he? And why had he singled her out? Or did he go to a different house every day? Yes, last time he had come on a Monday too. Maybe Monday was *her* day. *Some day he'll come along, the man I love . . . and he'll be big and strong, the man I love . . . maybe Monday . . .* Oh, the possibilities were endless.

She had to hurry if she was going to make the nine-thirty-two train. She had a date to meet Lisbeth in New York for lunch and wanted to do some shopping first. She needed something for the Fourth of July formal at The Club, something black and slinky like Myra and her friends had worn in Jamaica. Maybe she'd get her hair cut too, if there was time.

The phone was ringing when she stepped out of the shower. She wrapped herself in a towel and answered.

"Mrs. Pressman?"

"Yes."

"This is Hubanski."

"Who?"

"Sergeant Hubanski, Plainfield PD."

"Oh . . . yes . . . of course . . ."

"We found a sheet."

"You did?"

"Yes, plain white, exactly the kind you described."

"Where?"

"The corner of Sunset and Morning Glory."

"That's not far from here."

"We know."

"When?"

"When, what?"

"When did you find it?"

"Oh. Yesterday afternoon. I was off. My boys picked it up, so I didn't know about it until this morning. We're checking out the laundry marks now. When we've got something we'll give you a call."

"Yes, please."

"Just wanted you to know we're hot on his trail."

"Yes. Well, thank you for calling, sergeant."

So, they'd found a sheet. Was it his? Was that why he was dressed differently today, because he'd lost his sheet? Unlikely. He must have more than one sheet. This one that Sergeant Hubanski had come up with probably belonged to some neighborhood child who had been playing tent and left it outside.

"Good morning, Mrs. Pressman," Florenzia called from downstairs, slamming the front door. "That's just me."

"Good morning, Florenzia," Sandy called back.

"You got some mail . . . You like to see?"

"Yes, please." Sandy met her halfway down the stairs. Florenzia handed it to her. "Thank you."

"It be very hot today."

"You can turn the air-conditioning back on now. I turned it off for my shower."

"I be doing downstairs today in case somebody come looking to buy house?"

"Yes, that's a good idea."

"Mr. Pressman, he tell me to keep house looking good and he be giving me a raise."

"Oh?"

"That's so. He tell me two weeks ago."

"I didn't know, Florenzia, but we're certainly very pleased with the way you keep the house." How like Norman to offer a raise when they were about to move.

Sandy took the mail to her bedroom and closed the door.

Nothing from Bucky yet but there was a card from Jen. The first.

DEAR MOMMY,
Camp sucks! I am starving to death. There is no steak. There is no roast beef. Only one cookie a day. You should see me. I am all bones. Please, please, get me out of here. And hurry!
                                         Your daughter,
                                         JENNIFER P.

That proved it! Jen was too young for camp. She shouldn't have listened to Norman. Just because Enid sent *him* off to camp when he was five didn't mean Jen was ready. Poor little Jen. Sandy had a mental picture of her behind barbed wire, crying. Painfully thin. A concentration camp for overprivileged youngsters.

Oh, God.

But wait. She had visited Camp Wah-Wee-Nah-Kee last summer. Had seen how lovely it was. Across the lake from Bucky's camp. Iris Miller, the director, had shown them around. Pretty little bunks lined up at the crest of the hill. Manicured lawns. Flower beds. Modern bathrooms. Tennis courts. A dining room with a view of the mountains. And certainly no barbed wire. Jen would be all right. She had to be.

Sandy picked up the phone and dialed.

"This is Camp Wah-Wee-Nah-Kee in the heart of the Berkshires." A cheery voice sang out.

Sandy asked for Iris Miller, then waited while she was paged.

"Yes, this is Iris Miller."

"This is Sandy Pressman, Mrs. Miller . . . from New Jersey . . . Jennifer's mother . . ."

"Yes, Mrs. Pressman. I saw Jennifer at breakfast. She's doing beautifully."

"But, Mrs. Miller, I just received a very disturbing postcard from Jen saying that she's starving."

"Really, Mrs. Pressman," Iris said, laughing, "I promise you, she's not starving."

"Something about no steak and no roast beef."

"She's been here less than a week . . . she's a first-year camper . . . there's always a period of adjustment . . . and as it happens we had steak on our first night. But we refer to it as beef here. We certainly give our campers the very best, believe me."

"Well, I hope so, but you can understand how upset I was when I got Jen's card."

"Of course. But don't worry. She'd have written a letter if she was really unhappy. The postcard is a sign that everything's fine."

"I'd like to talk to Jen."

"You know that's against the rules, Mrs. Pressman. No phone calls before visiting day. Write her cheerful letters. Believe me, she's well cared for here."

"I guess it's just that . . ."

"See you on visiting day and don't hesitate to call whenever you're concerned."

"Yes . . . well . . ." Sandy began, but Iris had already hung up.

She'd have to write to Jen tonight, explaining about the beef, suggesting that if she was hungry to demand peanut butter and to promise that on visiting day she would bring her all sorts of goodies. Pepperidge Farm cookies, fruits, potato chips, candy. No, that was wrong. Jen had to learn to get along without her. That was what camp was all about, wasn't it? That's what Norman said. Sandy didn't know. She'd never gone herself. Mona didn't trust camps. "You want polio, that's a good way to get it," Mona had argued when Myra begged to go to sleep-away camp. "But it's hot and I want to go swimming," Myra whined. "You're hot, go sit in the bathtub," Mona answered.

*   *   *

Sandy barely made the nine-thirty-two and found a seat in no-smoking. She'd been looking forward to this visit with Lisbeth. They hadn't seen each other in months, not since January, when Sandy had returned from Jamaica. And on that day Sandy was sporting a full-blown herpes virus on her lower lip.

"You still get those things?" Lisbeth had asked.

"From the sun."

"So why don't you wear something to protect your lips, like zinc oxide?"

"Zinc's so ugly, all that white goo."

"No offense, San, but it's not as ugly as a fever sore."

"I know, and from now on I'm going to cover my lips before I go out in the sun. I've made up my mind, it's crazy to suffer this way."

"Didn't you have one when you and Norman were married?"

"Yes, a very small one."

"And when your father died?"

"Yes, at his funeral. I had the tail end of one at my Sweet Sixteen Party too."

"Do you think they come from emotional upheavals?"

"No, from the sun."

"But your father died in November, didn't he? The same time as JFK?"

"You know something, you're right. I never thought about that."

"You see, there's more to it than the sun."

"Maybe . . ."

Lisbeth Moseley. Born Zelda Rabinowitz. Changed her first name on her fifteenth birthday, refusing to speak to anyone who didn't address her as Lisbeth from that day on. It was she who encouraged Sandy to change the spelling of her name from Sandra to Sondra, not that it mattered. Everyone continued to call her Sandy. Lisbeth. Editor in chief of the Hillside High *News.* Girl Most Likely To . . . with straightened black hair and an inexpensive but successful nose job. The only one of the old crowd to go to Barnard. Lisbeth, who married a goy, when Sandy wasn't even brave enough to date one. A genuine goy who also happened to be her professor. An elective poetry course for those students exempt from freshman English. Blond and tall and slim, he smoked a pipe and wore tweed jackets with elbows patched in leather. The stereotypical professor. Vincent X. Moseley, from Connecticut. With background. Never mind that he also had a chunky, snub-nosed wife and two little boys in a crowded apartment on West 116th Street.

He *did it* with Lisbeth anyway.

"Really, all the way?" Sandy asked.

"Yes, and it was wonderful . . . wonderful . . . much better than we ever thought when we used to play our silly games."

"It didn't hurt?"

"No."

"Did he use a rubber?"

"No."

"But Lisbeth, suppose you get pregnant?"

"I'm going to marry him, anyway."

"But he's already married."

"She doesn't understand him. He's a poet. He's very sensitive. All she understands are diapers and bottles. He's asking for a divorce."

Their child, Miranda, was two years older than Bucky. Lisbeth's mother looked after her until Lisbeth got her degree, and then, when she had a job, a job with a real future, as a textbook editor at Harper's, Miranda went to live with her parents in New York. "She's brilliant, beautiful, and sophisticated, just as you'd expect," Lisbeth said, matter-of-factly, to anyone who asked about Miranda.

They lived in a co-op on Riverside Drive now, and had a cabin off the coast of Maine with no indoor plumbing. Lisbeth had shown pictures of the three of them, frolicking in the outdoor tub, naked.

Lisbeth, whose mother kept kosher when the rest of the crowd ate bread over Passover, whose mother never tired of singing "How Much Is That Doggie in the Window?" to her daughter's embarrassment.

Lisbeth, Sandy's best friend. Sandy's first lover.

*　　*　　*

They were twelve, going on thirteen. It was New Year's Eve. The bedroom door was closed but not locked. There were no locks on the doors in Sandy's house. A child might get locked in that way. And God forbid, in case of fire . . .

Mona and Ivan were in the basement recreation room entertaining their friends. Myra was out on a date. Sandy and Lisbeth were in Sandy's bed, under the quilt. Sandy was on top, being the boy. She moved around and around, squiggling, rubbing against Lisbeth until she got that good feeling. Then it was Lisbeth's turn to do the same. Sometimes they played *Rape* and other times it was *Just Plain Love*. They touched each other's breasts, but never *down there*.

The door opened. It was Mona. "Happy New Year!" she sang, slightly tipsy, a glass of champagne in one hand. "What are you doing in the same bed?"

"Keeping warm," Zelda/Lisbeth answered.

"You're cold?"

"Yes," Sandy said.

"I'll turn up the heat, but first, come downstairs and say Happy New Year to our friends."

"Do we have to?"

"Yes, everybody wants to see you."

"Like this?"

"Put on your robes and slippers."

Mona didn't know that under the quilt the girls were naked.

"We'll be right down," Sandy said. "Could you close the door so nobody can see us in our pajamas?"

"There's nobody here but me," Mona said.

"Please, Mom, Zelda doesn't want you to see her in just pajamas."

"Since when?"

"Since I've gotten modest, Mrs. Schaedel. It just happened a few weeks ago."

"I see," Mona said. "All right, but hurry down because then you have to go to sleep even if it is New Year's Eve."

"Whew . . ." Zelda/Lisbeth said, when Mona was gone.

They got into their pajamas and robes and went downstairs, where they were hugged and kissed by Mona and Ivan's friends. Friends from the Sunday Night Club, where the women played Mah-Jongg and the men played poker, friends from the Tuesday night group, where the women played canasta and the men played poker, and friends from the Friday Night Dance class, where Mr. Zaporro came to the house and taught them the cha-cha-cha.

Sandy had to call the friends *Uncle* or *Aunt,* and let them pinch her cheeks. When she and Zelda/Lisbeth went downstairs, Aunt Totsie spilled champagne on Sandy's robe and Uncle Jerry was too busy to kiss her because he had his hand up Aunt Ruthie's dress. Aunt Ruthie wore black stockings and the girls could see clear up to her garters, even caught a glimpse of her black girdle. That was really funny because Aunt Ruthie was married to Uncle Ned and Uncle Jerry was married to Aunt Edie.

"Do you think they're going to do it?" Zelda/Lisbeth whispered to Sandy.

"No, they're just good friends."

"She has her hand on his fly."

"I know, but they're just good friends, believe me. Sometimes good friends act that way."

"I never knew that."

"Yes. When it's New Year's Eve anything goes."

"Oh."

Lisbeth had such dreams! Getting married and having babies was enough for the rest of the crowd but not for Lisbeth. She dreamed of being president of Lord and Taylor's. After all, she read the New York *Times* and longed for a zebra-covered sofa and a Manhattan apartment when the rest of them were concerned with Saturday night dates and being felt up.

And later this same Lisbeth marched on Washington and no longer dreamed of zebra-covered sofas because her consciousness had been raised to such a degree that she insisted that her mother get rid of her cherished Persian lamb coat and hat. Mrs. Rabinowitz,

who had a friend, who had a cousin, who knew a man who manu-
factured Borgana coats and the summer before they went off to
college had schlepped both girls into New York, to the wholesale
house, where each bought a Borgana coat for freshman year.
Lisbeth had whispered to Sandy, "It feels so good against my skin
I'd like to turn it inside out and wear it naked." And later, after
she'd met Vincent, called Sandy to say, "You know that coat . . . the
Borgana one . . . well, Vincent and I made love on it . . . in his
office . . . on the floor . . . you ought to try using yours for that,
San . . . it's terrific!"

"Sandy! It's been so long . . ." Lisbeth sang, hugging her, outside
the Plaza. "Are you all right?"

"Yes, I'm fine, why?"

"I don't know. You looked tired."

"I've had a busy morning."

"Well, let's get a table. I've got so much to tell you."

Lisbeth was in French pants and a shirt unbuttoned halfway to
her navel. Sandy felt very suburban in her linen suit.

"We're leaving for Maine on the first, taking the whole month
off. Vincent is thinking about doing a book."

Vincent was always thinking about doing a book.

"I'm just going to relax, unwind, be free."

"Sounds wonderful. How's Miranda . . . is she going with you?"

"Of course. She has friends there. You should see her, San . . . I
should have brought pictures . . . she's got tiny breasts and just had
her first period. I taught her to use Tampax right off. Remember
how we had to put up with those disgusting pads?"

Sandy nodded.

"Let's order. Then I want to hear all about you."

Sandy scanned the menu. "Did you ever have the chicken salad
here?"

"Yes, you have to toss it yourself."

"You mean it's dry?"

"Yes, chunks of chicken."

"Good . . . that's what I like."

"And there's shredded lettuce on the side and mayonnaise or
Russian dressing, I forget which."

The waiter came to take their order.

"Is the chicken salad all white meat?" Sandy asked him.

"If you request it," he answered.

"Yes, please, with mayonnaise on the side and shredded lettuce."

"We're not serving it shredded any more. It's leaf style now."

"Oh . . . well, that's all right."

"So . . . what's happening in suburbia these days?" Lisbeth asked.

"Oh, the usual. Plus we joined The Country Club this year."

"You didn't!"

"Norman's playing a lot of golf and tennis. It made sense."

"But what about you?"

"Oh, I'm taking lessons. Norm's head of the Grievance Committee."

"Terrific!"

Sandy laughed. "He loves it."

"I'll bet."

"His first complaint had to do with a woman who ran from the golf locker room to the parking lot in her bathing suit."

Lisbeth shook her head. "How's the new house coming?"

"We hope it'll be finished by Labor Day."

"Did you sell the Plainfield house yet?"

"No, we've had a few offers but Norm says they're not enough."

"Are you going to sell it to blacks?"

"Norm says, no, even though three out of four lookers are black."

"That's illegal, you know."

"I know, I know, I've tried to tell that to Norm, but Enid would never forgive him. You know how she feels about them."

The waiter brought their lunch. "Mayonnaise on the side," he said, plunking Sandy's plate down in front of her.

They ate quietly for a moment. Then Sandy asked, "How's your mother?"

"Not too well. She's been undergoing all sorts of tests. Lost the feeling in her left arm."

"I'm so sorry. Is she in the hospital?"

"She was. She's out now. How's yours?"

"She's okay."

"And how are things with you and Norman?" Lisbeth asked, looking up from her shrimp salad.

"What do you mean?"

"In general . . . I just finished a course called Marriage in a Changing Society and I'm interested."

"We're the same as always." Sandy tossed some more of the chicken in mayonnaise. "Did I mention that Jen hates camp, that she wants to come home? And that I have this fungus or something that I can't get rid of. It's driving me crazy."

"No, you didn't mention that."

"And that sometimes I . . ."

"What?"

"Oh, I don't know."

"Are you sure you're all right?"

"I don't know that either." Sandy choked up and took a long swallow of iced tea.

Lisbeth reached across the table and patted Sandy's hand. She spoke softly. "Tell me," she said. "You'll feel better."

Sandy shook her head. "It's nothing. I'm just tired. I tire easily."

Lisbeth put down her fork and leaned close. "I'm going to tell you something, San, because I think it might help. A few months ago Vincent and I were having our problems . . . boredom with the relationship, snapping at each other . . . the usual . . . but now we've got it back together . . . better than ever . . . and it's all due to a fantastic new arrangement . . . Thursday nights off . . ."

"I don't get it."

"Thursday nights off from each other, from the marriage."

Sandy still wasn't sure what Lisbeth was trying to tell her.

"Every Thursday night I go out with another man and he goes out with another woman and then we come home and tell each other everything."

"Sleep with, you mean?"

"Yes, of course. Isn't it incredible that something so easy should bring us back together?"

"Who do you go with?"

"Right now it's this art director. He's young, his wife and kids are out at the beach for the summer, so we go to his place and just fuck, fuck, fuck."

"And Vincent?"

"He's got some graduate student doing her thesis on eighteenth-century poets."

"And do *they* know about your arrangement, the graduate student and the art director?"

"Of course. Everything *must* be out in the open . . . that's the only rule . . . no secrets . . . you see, San, it's secrets that cause problems . . . this class I took last semester in Contemporary Relationships was fabulous . . . showed us how secrets cause strains. This openness has been such a boon to our marriage . . ."

"Well, I don't know what to say."

"Don't say anything. I'm only telling you because I think it could do a lot for you and Norman."

"Norman is very conservative."

"I know, you'd have to approach the subject carefully, but I'm still convinced it could work for you."

"Maybe. I'm not sure."

"Oh, I almost forgot . . . I've got something for you." She opened her purse and pulled out a paperback book. "You haven't read it yet, have you?"

"No," Sandy said as Lisbeth handed it to her. The title was *Diary of a Mad Housewife.*

"I think you'll really enjoy it. It's funny and true. It has a lot to say."

Did Lisbeth think she was a mad housewife too? Was that why she'd given her the book? "Thanks, I'll start it on the train going home."

But on the train going home, she saw Shep. God, she hadn't seen him in what . . . almost eight years. Since she was pregnant with Jen and they'd bumped into each other at the Towers Steak House on Route 22. She'd been sitting at the bar, with Norman and another couple, and he'd walked in with a group of friends. She'd introduced him to Norman and then he'd introduced her to his wife, Rhoda. "One of my old friends," he'd called Sandy. She'd tried hard to stay calm, cool, but she'd farted when she first saw him, silently, thank God, and after he'd been shown to his table she'd squeezed her whiskey sour glass so hard it had broken in her hand, cutting her palm. The bartender had had to give her a wet towel to sop up the blood.

Shep.

"He'll never amount to anything," Mona had warned. "*Handsome* doesn't put food on the table. You can't eat love." Some people might disagree with you on that one, mother.

He'd fooled Mona all right. Fooled all of them. He'd made it big, in shopping centers. *Handsome* puts food on the table after all. And were they eating love, he and Rhoda? Probably.

They'd met at Myra's wedding. He was the date of one of Myra's bridesmaids, Margie Kott. Mona had advised Myra to choose her plainest friends as bridesmaids so that she'd really stand out. And she did. She looked as if she'd stepped right out of *Bride's* magazine. Sandy was maid of honor, in pink organza. Everything was pink and white at Myra's wedding, including the cageful of doves that were released as the happy couple said *I do*. Before they completed their circle around the room, one of them let out his stuff on Shep's head. Sandy saw it happen and couldn't help laughing.

"Jesus!" he'd said as she handed him a pink napkin with *Myra and Gordon* printed across it. "Thanks, kid. Did I get it all?"

He bent over and Sandy inspected his hair. It was thick and dark. "Yes."

"Does it stink?"

She sniffed his head. "No, you're okay."

He smiled at her. "You know something, kid? So are you."

Oh, that smile. Slightly crooked. Dazzling. Making Sandy's tummy turn over. "I'm not a kid. I'm a senior in high school. I'm seventeen. I have a driver's license."

"No, really?"

"Yes, how old are you?"

"Twenty-three."

"Myra's twenty."

"Myra?"

"My sister, the bride."

"Oh, that's your sister? Great-looking girl, Myra."

"Everybody says so."

"But I prefer you." Again, the smile.

"Who are you, anyway?" Sandy asked. "I mean, what's your name?"

"Shep. Shep Resnick, think you can remember that?"

"I'll try. I'm Sandy Schaedel."

After dinner he came over to her table and said, "Let's dance, Sandy Schaedel."

He held her close and they danced to "Blue Velvet." "You shouldn't wear a padded bra, kid."

"You can tell?" Sandy looked up at him, feeling her face turn red.

"I can always tell. And you sure as hell don't need that girdle," he told her, patting her ass.

"Shep, please!" she giggled nervously. "Everybody wears . . ."

"Never mind everybody. Next time we dance I want to feel *you* next to me, not padding and rubber." He pulled her closer and hummed into her ear.

He called the following Wednesday. Was she free on Saturday night? Was she!

He picked her up at eight and they rode around town in his 1950 Nash. "I've got no money, kid, sorry, but I blew it all renting that monkey suit for your sister's wedding."

"That's okay."

"I guess most of your dates take you to the movies."

"Yes, that's what we usually do."

"And then for a hamburger."

"Most times."

"And then what?"

"Oh, well, that all depends."

"On what?"

"You know, how much I like him."

"And if you like him what?"

"Well, then maybe we'll go back to my house and sit in the rec room and listen to records and . . . you know."

"I'm a lot older than you, Sandy. I'm not sure what kids do nowadays."

"Make out."

"What exactly does make out mean?"

"Shep, are you teasing me?"

He reached for her hand. "Would I tease a nice kid like you?"

So they'd gone back to her house after she was sure her parents were asleep and he made coffee because she didn't know how and she served them each a slice of Mona's homemade chocolate layer cake and sat with him at the kitchen table drinking a glass of milk and he told her she looked like a commercial for the dairy industry. She was almost sure that was a compliment. And then they'd gone downstairs to the rec room and she'd played her favorite making-out records, starting with "Blue Velvet," followed by "The Morningside of the Mountain" and "She Was Five and He Was Ten."

They danced. "Much better," he said, patting her ass, "much, much better." And then he kissed her. She'd kissed a lot of boys but never anyone like Shep. Never anyone with *experience*. His mouth was hot. He licked the corners of her lips then pushed his tongue into her mouth, running it over her teeth, then above them. He moved his lips across her cheek, to her ear, and he breathed into it licking the outside, then the inside, nibbling on her lobe. Sandy knew suddenly that she was in great danger and she pushed him away.

"What's wrong?" Shep asked.

"It feels too good when you kiss me like that."

He laughed and hugged her.

"I'm scared of you," she said.

"You don't have to be. I won't hurt you, I promise. And I won't do anything you don't want me to do either, not ever, understand?"

She took a big breath and nodded. "Okay."

He had a job in New York that summer, in the garment industry, and she was at the Jersey shore, working as a mother's helper. He drove down to see her one weekend. He had money this time. He took her to the movies and then for a hamburger and then for a ride in the Nash, parking it along the beach, showing her how the front seat folded down to make a bed. And he kissed her again and again, his body stretched out next to hers, his hands reaching under her sweater. Sandy tensed. She had to be ready to spring up if the situation demanded it. How could she allow herself to relax and enjoy it when her entire future was in jeopardy?

He unhooked her bra, his fingers on her bare breasts. Okay. She had decided it was all right to go this far, but no farther. He never stopped kissing her. Touching her. And then his hand was on her belly, his fingers creeping lower and lower . . .

She sat up. "No, Shep, you promised!"

"But, Sandy, what am I doing wrong?"

"I don't know. I just have this feeling."

"You like me to touch you?"

"Yes, you know I do."

He took her hand and pressed it to his pants. "How far do you go with your other boyfriends, Sandy?"

"I've gone this far but it wasn't the same. Besides, I don't have any other boyfriends right now . . ."

"I'm glad to hear that. You understand that I go out with other girls . . . with other women . . . because I have to . . . but you're my favorite, kid. I really mean it, I like you the best."

"Thank you."

"The others, well, they're just for sex because I'm a pretty hot guy, Sandy, and I really need it."

"Yes, I understand."

He started to laugh. "Hey, do you believe everything I tell you?"

"Yes."

He put his arms around her. "Sandy, Sandy, I want to be your first lover. Will you remember that? Some day when you're ready I want it to be me."

"Not until I'm twenty-five or married, whichever comes first."

"Twenty-five?"

"Yes. My mother thinks I should wait until I'm thirty if I'm still single but I've decided that twenty-five makes more sense."

He laughed again, then reached inside her sweater but this time he rubbed her back. "How many cashmeres do you have?"

"Twenty-seven, why?"

"Just wondering."

"That's a pretty funny question."

"But you had the answer, didn't you?"

"Everybody counts their cashmeres."

"You see. Is your father rich, Sandy?"

"Not rich, but we're well off. He's got a tire business."

"I'm poor, but I'm going to make it someday."

"I hope you do, Shep, if you want to so badly."

"And I'm going to be able to buy my kids twenty-seven cashmeres at once."

"I didn't get them all at once. I collect them."

"I know, I'm just telling you how it's going to be for me."

He seemed so different when he talked that way. More like a little boy. Certainly he wasn't a threat when he was sharing his dreams with her. Sandy found this side of Shep very appealing. She could handle the little boy in him. It was the man that terrified her.

Sandy went off to Boston U. that fall and didn't see Shep until Thanksgiving. He was sharing an apartment with three other guys in the Hotel Albert on University Place, working for Pilgrim Knitwear, as a salesman, and taking courses in business administration at NYU, nights.

Sandy wore her beige wool dress, three-inch heels, seamless stockings, gold bangle bracelets, green eye shadow, and her Borgana coat. The picture of sophistication. She thought.

He took her out for a drink, then up to his place.

"Sandy, Sandy," he said, looking her over. "What's happened to my little girl?"

"I've grown up, Shep."

"Not too much, I hope."

"Enough." She smiled knowingly, trying to keep her voice husky, her legs from trembling. She'd rehearsed this moment for two months.

"Seeing a lot of guys?"

"I go out."

"That's not what I'm talking about."

"Well, what are you talking about?"

"You know damn well!"

"I told you once, twenty-five or marriage, whichever comes first."

He took her in his arms. "I thought you said you've grown up."

"I was just pretending."

"I'm glad."

It felt so good to have him hold her again. She wanted it to stay this way forever. He unzipped her dress and she tensed. "It's all right," he whispered, easing it over her shoulders and down, until she stepped out of it. "It's all right." He held her close. She was in her lacy beige nylon slip, her beige garter belt, her beige lace bra and matching panties. She'd bought it all in September, at Filene's, with some of her living allowance, and every day she took the set out of her dresser drawer, fondling it, thinking about how it would be when she wore it with Shep. And every day she came, picturing them together.

But she'd never tried it on. No, that would have spoiled it. She hadn't even worn it to the Tufts Homecoming Ball and her date, Norman Pressman, was a senior, vice-president of the graduating class, a BMOC. She'd let him kiss her goodnight, twice, but that was it.

"I bought it just for you," Sandy told Shep. "Do you like it?"

His answer was a sliding kiss, from her mouth to her neck to her shoulder. He picked her up and carried her to his bed. Scarlett O'Hara and Rhett Butler. He lay next to her, kissing, kissing, until she thought she would die. He lifted her slip and took it off, over her head. He unhooked her beige lace bra and tossed it to the floor. He looked down at her and kissed her bare breasts. One, then the other, making her nipples stand up, sucking on them. "Oh, Shep ... God ... please ... no ... I can't ... I ..."

And he rested his hand on the soft flesh on the inside of her thighs, between the tops of her stockings and her beige lace panties, and then, he let his hand rest on the panties themselves.

"So wet," he whispered, "your pussy is so wet." His hand was suddenly inside her panties, his fingers touching her, *There*. The first person she'd ever let get inside. "No, Shep, I ..."

"Shush . . ." He kissed her again and kept playing with her, one finger moving around inside her, the other squeezing her lips.

"I love you, I love you," she called as she came.

"I know," he answered. "I've always known."

She kissed him.

"Was that nice?" he asked.

"You know it was. I never came that way before. I never let anyone touch me *there*."

"So how did you come?"

"Oh, by myself, mostly . . . rubbing . . ."

"Like this?" And he rolled over on top of her. When had he taken off his slacks? He was just in his jockey shorts now and she could feel him against her, feel how long and hard he was. They moved together and she could imagine what it would be like to have him inside her. Yes, she could imagine it. She could want it. "No . . . stop, Shep . . ." She pushed him away.

"Sandy . . . Sandy . . . it hurts . . . please . . ." He reached inside his shorts and pulled out his penis.

She looked away.

"Don't be afraid, Sandy, come on."

"I can't, Shep."

He took it in his hand, his fingers wrapped around it, pulling, rubbing. "See, that's all you have to do."

He took her hand and put it around him. "There . . . there . . . see how easy that is?" He kept his hand over hers and together they made him come, into his handkerchief.

At Christmas he was begging her to kiss it and wanting to eat her. But she couldn't, couldn't do that. It was unhealthy, abnormal. Shep was pushing her too far.

Mona warned her. "I won't forbid you to see him, Sandy, but I want you to know how unhappy Daddy and I are about this. He's not the right kind of boy for you. He has no background. His mother scrubs floors. Did you know that?"

"No."

"A Jewish scrubwoman. They're not our kind of people, Sandy. And God forbid, he could make you pregnant."

"Mother! I'm not doing anything like that."

"I hear he's already made twenty girls pregnant."

"Who told you that?"

"Margie Kott's mother. Margie had to stop seeing him because she couldn't trust him."

"I don't believe that."

"You better believe it before it's too late . . . did you know a girl can get pregnant without doing . . . *you know what . . .*"

"No!"

"It's true. So don't go losing your head over him. He could ruin the rest of your life . . . remember that . . . look at Myra . . . look how happy she is . . . you find yourself a nice boy, like Gordon . . . somebody with a future . . . with a profession or a good business and you go after him . . . and give him enough to keep him interested but don't give him everything . . . because once he's got everything from you he'll never marry you . . . believe me, I know what I'm talking about. I gave Myra the same advice . . . and look what she got. What about that nice boy who took you to the Ball?"

"Norman?"

"Why don't you see him over vacation?"

"I might."

"He calls every day . . . a nice boy from Plainfield . . . the same background . . . that's what counts, Sandy. Remember, you can't eat love . . ."

"Please stop saying that."

So Sandy went out with Norman Pressman. He took her to the Chaim Chateau for dinner and dancing, and although he couldn't dance at all, it turned out to be a very nice evening. No pressure. Two good-night kisses. And the next day he asked her to dinner at his house and his mother served a roast and his father carved it at the table. Three days later Norman drove her back to school in his new Oldsmobile.

Still, she dreamed of Shep. She dreamed of kissing him *there* and over midwinter vacation had a sudden urge to take him in her mouth. What was she going to do about these disgusting thoughts? Decent people, normal people, didn't do those things . . . didn't even think about them. Shep was perverted. But she let him do that to her. Just once. And oh, it was so good. Like nothing she had ever experienced. She came over and over, as he licked and kissed and buried his face in her. Until she cried, "Stop . . . please stop . . . I can't take any more . . ."

And then he kissed her face and she tasted herself on him. And she liked it.

If her mother knew, she would grow faint and say: Sandy, a nice girl like you! I can't believe it. How could you? That's against our religion. All those years of Sunday school . . . didn't you learn anything?

And her sister would add: Sandy, I'm shocked! Gordy and I are married and we *never* do anything so disgusting. Didn't you take Health in school? Don't you remember what Miss O'Shea taught us? That if you engage in abnormal sexual practices you'll give birth to abnormal babies. Don't you want healthy babies, Sandy?

But it feels good, Sandy would argue.

So do a lot of things, Mona would tell her. But we don't do them.

Like what? Sandy would ask.

And then Mona and Myra would look at each other and shake their heads.

Sandy knew she had to be strong. Strong enough to stop seeing Shep before he ruined her life.

Fortunately, he was drafted before Easter and after six weeks at Fort Dix was scheduled to go overseas, to Germany.

Mona relaxed.

Shep called to say good-bye. "Will you wait for me, Sandy?"

"Are you asking me to?"

"I can't, Sandy. I'm going to be gone a long time, but someday I'll be all yours. I promise."

"I don't know, Shep. I've got to think about it."

She thought about it while she went out with Norman Pressman. To dinners at expensive restaurants. To fraternity parties. To dances and movies and plays.

By the end of the summer they were pinned.

By November engaged.

She understood Norman. Felt comfortable with him. Safe. With

Norman she was in control of the situation. She didn't have to be afraid. He knew the rules.

DEAR SHEP,
I haven't heard from you in ages, but I just thought I should tell you that I am engaged to marry Norman Pressman. He went to Tufts but graduated last June and is now in his family's dry-cleaning business in Plainfield. We plan to be married in August. I will probably transfer to Douglass next fall.

Please Shep . . . call and tell me not to do it and I'll listen. Come home and kiss me, Shep . . . hold me . . . and I'll call it all off. My knees don't shake with Norman, Shep. My stomach doesn't roll over . . . but you can't eat love, can you? I mean, really? I know what kind of life I'll have with Norman. I don't know about you, Shep. With Norman there won't be any surprises and that's good, isn't it? My mother says so . . . my mother says surprises can only mean trouble . . .
Norman fits in, Shep. You don't. You'd never be satisfied with just me . . . would you? And I couldn't stand it, Shep, if we got married and then you went with other women . . . I'd die . . . I have an engagement ring. A two-carat, emerald-cut, blue-white diamond. And we're going to Puerto Rico on our honeymoon. And we're renting a new garden apartment in Plainfield. Five and a half rooms. And I'm choosing my china and crystal and silver and linens . . . oh, I'm so busy choosing everything . . . and my picture is being done by Bradford Bachrach next week, Shep . . . and please, if you care . . . if you want me the way I want you . . . please, hurry and send a telegram before my picture is in the paper and everybody knows I'm going to marry Norman Pressman . . . before it's too late, Shep . . .

She moved into the seat behind Shep on the train, willing him to turn around. But he didn't. He had longer hair now, brushing his shirt collar. She thought about touching the back of his neck. Remembered how he'd shivered when she'd kissed him there. Funny, she'd never kissed the back of Norman's neck. Ten minutes later they pulled into Newark. Sandy had to change trains. She walked out past him. He was reading his paper and never looked up. She was clutching the book Lisbeth had given to her.

Sandy and Norman went out to dinner that night. Not to The Club, The Club was closed on Mondays. To the new Chinese restaurant in Scotch Plains. Everyone was raving about it. And the owner, Lee Ann Fong, had recently joined The Club herself. Sandy told Norm about Lisbeth and Vincent and their arrangement. Their Thursday nights off.

"I could never tolerate anything like that," Norman said. "Marriage is a contract."

"But Lisbeth says it's helping their marriage."

"Lisbeth is full of shit . . . always has been." Norman stirred his Scotch with his index finger as he spoke.

"Did you know McCarthy did that?"

"Did what?"

"Stirred his drinks with his finger."

"You think I'm like Joe McCarthy? Is that what you're saying?"

"No, Norm, one thing has nothing to do with the other. It's just a peculiar habit."

"You shovel corn niblets with your fingers."

"It's hard to get corn niblets onto the fork."

"It's uncouth to shovel with a finger. That habit of yours has bothered me for years."

She pushed her salad around on her plate. "I told Lisbeth you wouldn't go for the idea."

"Go for? You're not suggesting . . . Jesus . . ."

"No, of course not!"

"I wish you'd stay away from her. She's nothing but trouble. I wish you'd concentrate on making new friends, at The Club."

"I got a dress for Fourth of July."

"Good, I thought you were going to have your hair cut, too."

"I was, but I didn't have time."

"Make an appointment before the holiday weekend."

"I will, I will. It's just that I'm so busy. I've got so many lessons . . ."

"Make an afternoon appointment. I cut out a picture for you."

"A picture of what?"

"The way you should have your hair cut. Remind me to give it to you when we get home."

But when they got home Norman was ready for a little something. And when she came, when she got her dessert, she called out.

"What'd you say?" Norman asked.

"Nothing."

"I thought you said *schlep*."

"No, why would I say that?"

"I don't know, that's what I'm asking."

"No, I didn't say anything."

But she must have. She must have called *Shep*. She'd been thinking about him as she came.

9

WHAT NORMAN LIKED best about The Club was that it wasn't one hundred percent Jewish. Besides Lee Ann Fong, there were nine Japanese members, all from Manhattan, three Italian families, all in the disposal business, two ordinary Christians, and a black assistant pro named Roger. Norman felt it was good for the children to meet all kinds of people. Not that they'd actually met any of the Japanese members because they kept pretty much to themselves but they had, at least, seen them eating dinner in the Grill Room along with everybody else.

Sandy took golf lessons from Roger. Three mornings a week, at nine-thirty, she reported to the driving range dressed for battle. Three mornings a week Roger steadied her head with one hand as she swung at the ball. Roger smelled of Sen-Sen and old English Leather after-shave. He was determined to get her off the practice range and onto the front nine by mid-July.

"Eye on the ball, Mrs. Pressman," Roger said. "Watch your club strike the ball . . . left arm straight . . . no, no, look at that elbow . . . is that a straight arm? Get comfortable . . . move those feet around . . . look at that club waggling . . . we can't have that . . . now, take it back again, nice and slow . . . no need to hurry . . . nice and easy . . . don't try to kill the ball, Mrs. Pressman . . . are you comfortable . . . you don't look comfortable . . ."

I'm not, dammit! Sandy wanted to scream. *How can I be com-*

fortable with you holding my head? But she said, "I'm comfortable . . ." and she swung at the ball. And missed.

"You've got to *watch* the ball, Mrs. Pressman . . . I can't put it any plainer than that . . . if you don't *watch* the ball, you're never going to hit it."

"I'm trying," Sandy said, "but I'm not especially coordinated."

Roger sighed.

Sometimes Roger would stand behind her and put his arms around her and actually hold the club with her and some of those times Sandy felt what it would be like to really hit the ball well. And some of those times Sandy could imagine what it would feel like to have Roger put his hands on her breasts, as he stood behind her with his cock hard, pressing against her ass.

After each lesson Sandy was expected to stay at the practice range, hitting two buckets of balls. Then she was permitted a break.

Two afternoons a week she was scheduled for tennis lessons with Evan. Evan was not as determined as Roger. Evan favored his more promising students. He stood across the net from Sandy, tossing balls to her and delivering instructions in a bored monotone.

"Racquet back . . . step to the side . . . bend your knees . . . watch the ball . . . control, Mrs. Pressman . . . we're after control . . . where's that follow-through . . . don't try to kill it . . . easy, swing easy!"

And after Evan had used up his bucket of balls, it was Sandy's job to retrieve them. Then they'd begin again, with Sandy panting and Evan cool and smug.

"Can I ask you a serious question, Mrs. Pressman?" Evan said after Sandy's fourth lesson.

"Yes."

"Do you like this game?"

"Not really."

"Then why?"

"Because my husband wants me to learn for our retirement."

Evan shook his head and smashed a few balls across the net.

"Very nice," Sandy said, walking off the court.

She began to pray for rain.

The phone rang as Sandy was dressing for her Wednesday golf lesson. She was trying to match a pair of peds but all she could find was one with pink trim and one with yellow.

"Hello . . ."

"This is Hubanski."

"Oh, yes, sergeant."

"Can you be down to headquarters in half an hour?"

"Well, I've got a nine-thirty appointment."

"This is very important. Can you cancel, because we've traced the laundry markings on the sheet and we've picked up the guy it belongs to."

"Who is he?"

"Can't go into that now, but we're holding him. What we want to do is put him in a lineup and see if you can identify him."

"A lineup?"

"Yeah."

"Like on TV?"

"Yeah, like that."

"Okay, I'll be there."

Sandy called The Club and canceled her lesson, assuring them that it was an emergency and that she would return tomorrow morning, as usual.

She drove downtown, to police headquarters.

Would she be able to identify the man on the motorcycle? Did she even want to?

"Now, look, Mrs. Pressman," Hubanski said, directing her to a small auditorium, "all you got to do is look them over. They can't see you, so don't worry."

"Are they all criminals?"

"We can't discuss that now. The important thing's for you to identify the guy. You got that, Mrs. P?"

"Yes." So now she was Mrs. P. How cozy.

"Here we go," Hubanski called. "Okay, Jess, send them out."

Sandy slouched down in her seat in the darkened room.

Number One wore a business suit. He had graying hair and was far too pudgy to be her man. Number Two wore jeans and a T-shirt. She mustn't be fooled by dress, though. He had a lot of red hair. Attractive. Young. The right build. But red hair? No, then he'd have red pubic hair too, wouldn't he? And freckles? Her man had dark pubic hair and no freckles, at least none as far as she knew.

She leaned over to Hubanski and whispered, "You know, I didn't see his face."

"Try to identify him by body."

"If I could just see them naked."

"Mrs. Pressman!"

Number Three was young, pimply, and skinny. Too skinny. Number Four wore slacks and a sport shirt. Nice build. Could be . . . could be . . . clean-cut face . . . brown hair . . . she had no trouble imagining him naked . . . nice . . . very nice. Number Five was big, with a craggy face, about fifty, looked like a caddy at The Club. God, he *was* a caddy at The Club.

"I know that man," Sandy whispered to Hubanski. "Number Five. He caddies at The Club."

"Is he the one?"

"No, he's too old."

"You're sure?"

"Yes, positive."

"Well, do you see anyone else?"

"I can't be sure, but Number Four might be the one."

"Number Four is my assistant, Mrs. Pressman. And I can assure you that on the day of the incident in question my assistant was right here, working with me."

"I'm sorry. How was I to know? The only other possibility is Number Two but his coloring is wrong. I don't think the man we're after has red hair." She wanted to say, *if only I could see them in the act I'm sure I'd recognize him . . . my man has a certain style . . .*

But then Hubanski would say, *let's not get carried away, Mrs. P. There's no way I can give you a lineup of guys jacking off.*

I don't see why, she would argue.

Hubanski stood up. "Well, this is very disappointing, Mrs. P. Very depressing, you know? I was hoping the guy with the sheet."

"Which one owned the sheet, anyway?"

"I can't go into that now. Let's just say you didn't mention him at all."

"Are they all left-handed?"

"No . . . but I'm not convinced the man we're looking for is either. He could have used his left hand to throw us off the track . . ."

"Do they all ride motorcycles?"

"I can't divulge that information either."

"Well, I'm sorry, sergeant, but you certainly don't want me to lie."

"Certainly not, except that now we're back to nowhere."

When she got home the phone was ringing. Florenzia never answered the telephone and made no calls herself. She'd made it clear from her first day on the job that she would have nothing to do with that machine.

Sandy threw down her purse and car keys and ran to the kitchen wall phone. "Hello," she answered, breathlessly.

"Mrs. Pressman?"

"Yes."

"May I fuck you today?"

"Excuse me?"

"I said, may I fuck you today?"

Sandy hung up. *Jesus!*

It rang again.

She picked it up. "Yes?"

"Or would you rather have me suck you?"

She slammed down the receiver. If it rang again, she wouldn't answer. Maybe Florenzia had the right idea after all.

"You got mail," Florenzia said. She was wiping out the cabinet under the kitchen sink. "I put on your bed."

"What? Oh, thanks."

"The phone be ringing all morning. I no answer."

"Yes, okay." Sandy went upstairs to look over the mail.

DEAR MOMMY
Grandma is writing me letters addressed to *Sarah*. Will you tell her to quit calling me that. Everybody in my bunk is calling me Sarah now, all because of Grandma. I still hate camp and want to come home. My counsellor got fired for doing it in the woods. That's what the seniors told us. They are big kids who know everything. We have a new counsellor now. Her name is Fish. Isn't that a dumb name? She's dumb too. She bounces a quarter on my bed every day to make sure the covers are tight enough. I miss Banushka. Send me some of her fur. Also, I hate Bucky. He was mean on brother-sister day, just because I cried.

Love,
JENNIFER P.

This letter was dictated by Jennifer P. to Deborah Z. of Bunk 16.

And a postcard from Bucky.

DEAR MOM AND DAD,
Jen is a jerk. She cried at brother-sister day. I'm not going to any more of them. I had twenty-six splinters on the bottom of my foot. The nurse counted them when she took them out. That's the most any kid at camp has ever had at one time. She put them in an envelope so you can see them on visiting day. I have thirty-one mosquito bites. You might get to see them too. Camp is great. I'm fine. See you soon.

Your son,
BUCKY PRESSMAN

The phone again. If it was *him* she'd tell him to fuck off. To get it up with someone else. She was too busy for crazies.

"Yes?" she said, picking it up on the fourth ring, sounding annoyed.

"Sandy?"

"Yes."

"This is Vincent."

"Who?"

"Vincent, Vincent Moseley."

"Oh, Vincent . . . hi . . . sorry . . . I didn't recognize your voice."

"How are you, Sandy?"

"Oh, just fine, how about you?" Why would he be calling her unless he had bad news. "And the family, how's the family?"

"They're fine, as well."

"Oh, good, for a minute there I was worried."

"No, everything's okay. Lisbeth told me she had a nice visit with you the other day."

"Yes, we don't see each other often enough."

"Look, Sandy, I was wondering if you could meet me for dinner next Thursday?"

"The four of us, you mean?"

"No, Lisbeth's busy on Thursday nights. Just the two of us . . . informally . . . a chance to talk . . ."

"Thursday, you said?"

"Right."

"That's Thursday, the seventh?"

"Let me check. Yes, Thursday, the seventh. Let's say Gino and Augusta's at six-thirty . . . that's on West Sixty-fourth, near the park. Is that okay, Sandy?"

"I'm writing that down. Sixty-fourth, near the park?"

"Right, you'll be there, then?"

"Well, I guess so."

"Good . . . see you then . . . really looking forward . . ."

"Yes. Bye, Vincent."

Vincent X. Moseley? On Thursday night? What was this all about? Unless . . . oh, it *couldn't* be that! Not Vincent. Then why? Strange. Vincent calling out of the blue that way. She'd just have to wait and see.

10

THEY'D PUT THE house on the market in March, right after Myra and Gordon had returned from their midwinter vacation in Jamaica. The four of them had met in New York for dinner at Le Périgord Park. "We were robbed," Myra said, over paté. "We didn't want to tell you on the phone, we knew you'd worry."

"Robbed, my God!" Sandy said.

"Robbed," Myra repeated. "They held a machete to my throat. I was this close to death." And she held her thumb and index finger together so that Sandy and Norman could see exactly how close to death she had been. "I'm telling you, this close," she said again.

"A machete, Jesus!" Norman said.

"Those fucking schvartzas . . . look at these marks." Myra pulled her Lanvin scarf away from her neck. "That's where he had his hand . . . one hand on my throat . . . the other holding the machete over me . . . they broke in through the shutters, right into our bedroom . . . in the middle of the night . . ."

"What did you do?" Sandy asked.

"What could we do?" Gordon answered. "I gave them everything. My money, Myra's jewelry, everything. They would have killed her if I hadn't."

"You did the right thing," Sandy said. "You had no choice."

"The girls slept through it all," Gordon said.

"And Mona is never to know," Myra told them. Sandy and Norman nodded in agreement.

"We put La Carousella up for sale the next day . . . we told the agent to sell it fast . . . just to get rid of it . . . never mind if we have to take a loss . . . I never want to see the place again . . ." Myra went back to her paté. "Besides we were getting tired of Jamaica." She swallowed, sipped some wine, and continued. "We want to learn to ski next winter . . . maybe get a place in Aspen or Vail . . . more invigorating than the heat of the islands . . . better atmosphere for the twins . . . and have you seen the latest ski clothes? They're fantastic!"

Later, when Sandy and Myra went to the Ladies Room Myra said, "Gordy is ashamed of himself, can you tell?"

"No, why?"

"Because he begged and pleaded with them. He even cried."

"But that's only natural. They were threatening your life."

"And his. They said they'd kill us both, first me, then him."

"Oh, Myra, I'm so sorry," Sandy said, hugging her sister. "It must have been awful."

"And after they were gone he vomited . . . got diarrhea . . . had a nosebleed . . ."

"It was a terrible experience for him," Sandy said.

"I'm the one who almost died."

"I know, but . . ."

"And I didn't vomit, for chrissakes!"

"How did you react?"

"I don't remember. Gordy says I was angry at him for giving them my jewelry, but I honestly don't remember."

"You were probably in shock."

"Probably. I just can't wait to start skiing."

They went back to their table and ordered Courvoisiers. "I'll tell you this," Gordon said, mainly to Norm, "the natives are restless everywhere. It's only a matter of time before it really hits here. Remember the riots in Newark in '67? Plainfield is next. You better get out before it's too late."

When they got home, after Norman had paid the baby-sitter and seen her out to her car, he said, "There's something I think you should know, San."

"What's that?"

"I've got a gun."

"You've got a gun?"

"Shush, you'll wake the kids."

"Since when . . . where . . . "

"I got it during the riots in Newark. I never wanted you to know, but now, well, Gordon is right. It's only a matter of time so I'm going to show you how to use it just in case."

"No, Norm, I don't like guns. They terrify me. I don't want to know."

He grabbed her hand and led her into his study. "Look," he said, "I keep the gun locked in this cabinet." He tapped one of the wall units. "And the key to the cabinet is here, in the bookcase, behind *Bartlett's Quotations.* Now, the ammunition is locked in a steel box in the bottom cabinet." He tapped again. "And the key for *it* is in the third drawer of my desk, under the business envelopes, so you don't have to worry about the kids getting into it."

"But Norm, if somebody breaks into the house, by the time you unlock the cabinets and the ammunition box and load the gun we'll all be dead anyway, won't we?"

"You don't understand, Sandy, but then, I didn't really expect you to."

"First, we'll try selling the house ourselves," Norman said. "No point in paying a commission if we don't have to."

So, on Monday morning, Sandy placed ads in the *Courier News,* the Newark *News* and the New York *Times,* and made appointments with three realtors to look at houses in Watchung. In May she found the right house. With a view. At night you could look down and see the traffic on Route 22. You could see the lights of the houses in Plainfield, twinkling. A fireplace in the family room. Three bathrooms. Lots of stone. Lots of glass. Lots of class. And all for just ninety-nine thousand five hundred dollars. Not only that, but the builder, Joe Fiori, who was putting the house up for speculation, would let them choose their own bathroom fixtures, their kitchen cabinets, their wall colors.

Now all they had to do was sell the Plainfield house. In any other suburb it would be worth eight-five thousand dollars, at least. Here, they'd be lucky to get forty thousand dollars for it. Plus, they had to contend with Enid, had to promise they wouldn't sell to blacks, not even to a black doctor or lawyer. A foolish promise, since there were very few white buyers in Plainfield. But Enid refused to have *ductlas* living in the house she and Samuel D. had built.

Ductlas. Enid claimed she had invented the word because *they* had figured out what *schvartza* meant. This way she could say, *Do you have a decent ductla? How does she iron? My ductla eats me out of house and home. I have to hide everything.* And they would never guess what she was talking about.

All of the Pressman stores were staffed with blacks. A smart business move, initiated by Norman, when he took over. And the best way to keep them from stealing you blind was to hire a black manager for each store, give him a share of the profits, and let him contend with the rest of the employees. That way Norman never had to play the bad guy. And he would never drop dead while firing a cashier for stealing the way his father had. Sometimes, Sandy wished Norman would drop dead. Because then she'd be free. Oh, she knew that was a terrible thought, a wicked thought and she certainly didn't wish him a long, horrible, cancerous death. Maybe an accident with the car or a blood clot to the brain, something clean and quick. *Free, free, free.* She'd never been free, could only imagine what it might be like. She'd never been on her own. She'd gone from Mona and Ivan straight to Norman. Little girl to little wife.

Sandy and Norman took Enid to The Club for dinner. Enid was dressed to a tee, as she liked to put it. And tonight she wore her thick, ash-blonde wig, turquoise eye shadow to match her Trevira knit dress, and the most curious pair of spectator pumps. Enid never got rid of old shoes, believing that if you held onto them long enough they'd come back into style. "Today's are all made of plastic," she'd once told Sandy, slipping off her shoe and holding it out. "Smell this, genuine leather top and bottom, 1947."

As soon as they were seated and studying the menu, Roger

came over to their table. "I missed you today," he told Sandy.

"Oh, sorry, something came up, but I'll be back tomorrow."

"I like your haircut."

Sandy's hand went to her head. "Thanks."

Giulio had invented a cut just for her, at least that's what he told her. It looked neat and would require very little care. Norman didn't like it, she could tell, even though he said it was cute, that she looked like an elf. "And anyway," he'd told her earlier, "it'll grow out by September and then you can have it restyled."

"But I like it this way," Sandy said.

"Don't get me wrong, for the summer it's okay," Norman had answered.

"Well," Roger said to all of them, "enjoy your dinner." And then, just to Sandy, "See you tomorrow."

"They allow *ductlas* in here?" Enid asked, as soon as Roger was out of earshot.

"He's the assistant golf pro," Norman explained. "Sandy is taking lessons from him."

"They couldn't find a white one?"

"Roger is very good," Norman said.

"Well, if you don't mind, why should I mind?" But suddenly Enid wasn't that hungry. "A salad is all I feel up to, that and some soup." And she sighed.

"Jen wrote asking me to tell you she's very unhappy about the way you've been addressing her letters to camp," Sandy told Enid. "Her name isn't Sarah, you know. You're embarrassing her in front of her bunkmates. Do you think that's fair?"

"A name like Sarah, a beautiful, biblical name like Sarah should embarrass a child?"

"No, that's not the point. It's not the name that embarrasses her, it's the idea. Everyone at camp knows her as Jennifer. That is, after all, her name."

"Not her *real* name," Enid protested.

"Oh, yes, her *real* name."

"Look, Mom," Norman said, "it would be better if you wrote to *Jennifer*. She's at that age now."

Enid sighed again and picked something out of her salad. "Look at this. You'd think such a high-class club could wash their salad more carefully."

And that wasn't the only thing wrong with dinner. Enid's soup was served lukewarm. "There's nothing less appetizing than cool soup," Enid said, calling the waiter. "Please take this back. Soup should be served steaming hot." She turned to Norman. "You'd think a place like this would know."

And the coffee was weak.

And the cream for it might or might not have been sour, but from the looks of it Enid wasn't taking any chances and ordered tea instead. But the tea wasn't brewed, it was served with a bag on the side.

"Did you shop around before you joined this place?" Enid asked. "I'm sure there are plenty of other country clubs."

"My sister belongs here," Sandy said. "It's supposed to be the best."

"Maybe tonight's an off night," Enid said.

"Yes, maybe."

"She's getting difficult," Norman said later.

Getting? Sandy thought. But she said, "Yes."

"She's driving everybody in the store up the wall."

"What are you going to do?"

"I don't know, but I've got to get her out of there."

"What about Florida?"

"I only wish."

"Your Aunt Pearl is there."

"You know they don't get along."

"That was years ago. It might be different now that they're both widows."

"And this business about not selling the house to blacks. We haven't had a decent offer yet. If we're going to be in the new house in time for school we've got to sell now."

"Maybe you could talk to her about it, explain how we need the money from this one in order to close on the new one."

"She won't listen. Nobody can make her listen, you know that. But I have another idea."

"What?"

"We can sell to a realtor, then the realtor can sell to a black family. A lot of people who don't want to sell directly to blacks are doing that."

"Oh, Norm, I don't know. I'd rather we sell it ourselves or just list it with a realtor."

"I'd rather sell it myself too because I doubt that we can get forty to forty-five selling it to a realtor, but if we haven't sold it ourselves by August first, I think that's what we should do."

"That doesn't give us much time."

"If worst comes to worst you can drive the kids up to Watchung for the first month or two of school."

"But that would eat up my whole day."

"You don't have anything better to do."

"Until you said that I thought we were having a real conversation. We were actually exchanging ideas, but you had to go and ruin it with that stupid statement!"

"What statement, what are you talking about?"

"That business about me not having anything better to do!"

"There you go again. No wonder we can't ever have a conversation—you're too goddamned touchy!"

And later, when they were in bed, ass to ass, Sandy asked quietly, "Norman, do you love me?"

"You know what I think of that question."

"Do you?"

"I'm here, aren't I?"

11

THE UNWRITTEN LAW. She had broken the unwritten law with that question. He'd told her once, when he'd asked her to marry him. "I love you, Sandy. I love you and I want to marry you. I don't think it's necessary to tell you that again."

And he hadn't.

And Sandy was ashamed for wanting him to, for wanting him to confirm and reconfirm his feelings for her. But that was her problem. And she would have to deal with it herself.

They'd been married at The Short Hills Caterers, a newer wedding palace than Clinton Manor, where Myra had married Gordon. And instead of the two hundred and fifty guests of Myra's wedding, Sandy and Norman had had only ninety. "We don't owe so many obligations this time," Mona told her. It was a more intimate wedding, more elegant, Sandy thought, without doves, without a ceremonial parade, without the bride feeding the groom. A no-nonsense wedding, with Norman breaking the glass on his first try and with a band who played the horah, just once, which disappointed both families. "That's the way the happy couple wants it," Mona explained, shrugging.

Sandy had worn Myra's wedding dress, taken in, and Myra and Lisbeth were co-matrons of honor in vivid blue, the tiny twins were flower girls, in pale blue organdy, toddling down the aisle, stealing the show.

Cousin Tish caught Sandy's bouquet and one month later ran

off to Europe with Norman's Uncle Bennett, whom she'd been seated next to at the wedding dinner. He left his wife and three children, he quit his job with IBM, to live with the love of his life, who was twenty years younger and who still slept with a retainer in her mouth, although her braces had been off for years. And to think that he'd met her in New Jersey, of all places. That they'd fucked in the bride's changing room at The Short Hills Caterers, between the prime ribs au jus and the baked Alaska. Rumor had it that they were still together, running a small inn somewhere in the south of France, that they were deliriously happy, and that her teeth hadn't shifted.

Sandy and Norman spent their wedding night at the International Hotel at Kennedy Airport, found a bottle of Taylor's Brut on ice awaiting them in their room with a card reading *Thank you, thank you, thank you! We wish you a long happy life together.* Signed, *Uncle Bennett and Cousin Tish,* which neither of them understood at the time.

Norm had opened it and they'd toasted each other, then Sandy poured the rest of the bottle into her bathwater, having read somewhere that champagne baths were sexy. She emerged from the bathroom powdered and perfumed and dressed in her Odette Barsa bridal peignoir set, to find Norman already under the covers, on his back, one hand draped across his eyes.

"I drank too much," he said.

"Oh, I'm sorry, are you feeling sick?"

"Just the beginning of a headache."

"Can I get you anything?"

"No, I'll be all right. Just turn out the lights, okay?"

"Okay." Wasn't he going to open his eyes? Wasn't he going to admire his bride in her Odette Barsa peignoir set? Obviously not. Oh well, there was always tomorrow night. She untied her peignoir, laid it carefully over the chair, and climbed into bed beside him.

How strange to be in bed together. She'd never been in bed with a man. On a bed, yes, with Shep, but never *in* it, never under the covers.

He turned to her. "Hello, wifey, how's my little wifey?"

Sandy felt the champagne, the baked Alaska, the au jus, working their way up to her throat, thought she might be sick in her wedding bed, on her new husband. Oh, God, her husband! What a terrifying thought. Why had she done this stupid thing? Why, oh why, had she gotten married . . . and to Norman Pressman, of all people!

Norman rolled over on top of her, pushing her night gown up above her belly.

"Look," Sandy said, "we don't have to . . . if you don't feel like it . . . there's always tomorrow . . . I mean, we're going to be married for a long . . ."

"No, I'm okay and I want to, unless you . . ."

"No, it's not that."

In the rec room, in Sandy's parents' house, she and Norm had shared the couch, week after week, listening to music, kissing for hours, feeling each other, dryhumping until they both came, with Norman having to change his underwear. Even then he came quickly. Rub-a-dub-dub and it was all over. He'd always carried an extra pair of boxer shorts in a Safeway bag.

Sandy needed that kissing and hugging, that petting, but maybe Norman didn't know, didn't understand, because now he was pushing his penis against her, trying to get inside. "Norm, I'm not ready yet . . . please . . ."

"Relax, San, I know you're scared. It's okay."

"No, it's just that . . ."

"It'll be over soon. Just close your eyes and try to think of something else. I put Vaseline on the rubber so it'll go in easier."

"No, Norm, wait. Please."

But he wasn't listening. He was pushing, pushing inside her. She was dry, dammit.

Sandy closed her eyes and prayed that it would be over quickly. *Some wedding night! Shep . . . oh, Shep . . . I want it to be with you . . .* "Norm, it can be good if you wait for me. Norm . . ."

Push. Shove. In. Out.

"Norm . . . ow . . . please . . ."

"Shush . . . can't wait . . . sorry, San . . ." In and In and In and then it was over. Norm shuddered once, kissed her cheek, said

"Now you're really my little wifey," then rolled over and fell asleep.

Sandy was sore and bleeding. She bled so heavily they'd had to call Gordon the next morning.

"Relax," Gordon told her. "It'll stop in a day or two. Wear a Tampax and enjoy yourself! See me as soon as you get back. I'll cauterize you and fit you with a diaphragm."

She'd left a trail of blood all over Puerto Rico, but by week's end she was beginning to enjoy the feeling of Norm's penis inside her. She was still sore but she liked the way it felt moving in and out. And she was coming, coming the way she had in the rec room, coming once or even twice every time. She wanted it more and more. She wanted it morning, noon, and night. And Norman was impressed with her responsiveness. He'd had other girls, he told her, but none like her. None who could come so fast, so hard. None who wanted it so often. It looked like it was going to work after all.

So where did things go wrong, Norm? So what happened? It seemed all right then. Comfortable. Safe. We had our babies. We made a life together. But now I'm sick. You can't see it this time. There isn't any rash, no fever, but I'm sick inside. I sleepwalk through life. And I'm so fucking scared! Because every time I think about life without you I shake. I wish somebody would tell me what to do. Make the hurt go away. I wish a big bird would fly up to me, take me in its mouth and carry me off, dropping me far away . . . anywhere . . . but far from you. I want my life back! Before it's too late. Or is it already too late? Is this it, then? Is this what my life is all about? Driving the kids to and from school and decorating our final house? Oh, mother, dammit! Why did you bring me up to think *this* was what I wanted? And now that I know it's not, what am I supposed to do about it?

12

SLINKY JERSEY WAS out. Flowing chiffon was in. Sandy had guessed wrong again. Norman would be disappointed.

This was Sandy's first Club Formal. They'd missed the Memorial Day Dance because Bucky had been sick. Norman looked handsome in his new tuxedo with his blue ruffled shirt. She'd told him so before they'd left for the Club. And he had admired her too, saying, "That's a very unusual color for a summer dress."

"Yes. The saleswoman called it *wine*. I think you can wear it all year round, don't you?"

"Yes, I suppose so."

Sandy had a secret. Like the man on the motorcycle, she wore no underwear tonight. She hadn't planned it that way, but she found that her panties showed through her slinky dress, spoiling the line, and it was too warm to wear panty hose. So she wore just a Tampax under her new dress, insurance against leakage. The jersey felt good against her naked bottom and her secret made her feel sexy. But she wasn't going to tell Norman. Let him discover it on his own.

Norm brought Sandy a whiskey sour. "Drink it slowly," he said, "so you don't get dizzy."

Sandy nodded.

Sherm Hyatt, who was Norman's partner in the holiday tournament, walked toward them with his guests. "I'd like you to meet Rhoda and Shep Resnick," he said. "Rho . . . Shep . . . say hello to two of our new Club members, Norm and Sandy Pressman."

Sandy squeezed her whiskey sour glass.

He spoke first. "Sandy Schaedel!"

"Yes."

"What a surprise!"

"Yes." She would not break her glass this time. She would not sweat or stutter or fart. She would remain calm, cool, and sophisticated.

"Well, it's certainly been a long time."

"Eight years."

"Eight years . . . imagine . . . Rhoda," he said, turning to his wife, "this is Sandy Schaedel, a friend from the old days."

"Oh, yes," Rhoda said, extending her hand, "we met once at some restaurant."

"The Towers," Sandy reminded her.

"That's right . . . of course . . ."

Shep kept smiling at Sandy while Norman and Sherm heatedly discussed the latest Club Incident. Ed Braidlow had peed on the floor of the steam room and three other Club members had lodged a complaint against him.

"Norm is chairman of the Grievance Committee," Sandy explained.

"Must be interesting," Shep said.

"This is his first important grievance."

"I see."

"Do you live around here?" Rhoda asked.

"In Plainfield but we're moving to Watchung soon. We're building a house there."

"We're in Princeton."

"Oh. It's supposed to be nice there."

"It is, especially for the children."

"How many do you have?" Sandy asked.

"Four but we're expecting our fifth any day."

"Oh, really? You can't tell."

Shep and Rhoda laughed together, making Sandy feel foolish.

"Rhoda's not pregnant," Shep told her. "We've adopted our last two kids and our latest is coming from Vietnam."

"She's three and a half," Rhoda added, "and adorable. I can show you her picture." She opened her purse and pulled out a mini photo album. "There she is, isn't she a darling?"

"Oh, yes, lovely."

"And these are our others." She flipped the pages so that Sandy could admire all five children. "We've got two boys of our own and two girls from Korea."

"I think that's terrific," Sandy said. "Really, just so nice."

"Rho," Lexa Hyatt called, "over here . . ."

"Excuse me," Rhoda said, "I think Lexa wants me to meet some of her friends."

Which left Sandy alone with Shep.

"So," he said.

"So," she answered.

"You're looking good, Sandy."

"Thank you." Pause. "Rhoda seems very nice."

"She is."

"And all those kids."

"She collects kids the way some women collect recipes."

"But you must enjoy them too."

"I've always enjoyed kids." Pause. "Norman seems nice, too."

"Oh, yes, he is. And we have two children, a boy, ten and a girl almost eight. They're away at camp." Pause. "My sister's here. You remember Myra, don't you?"

"How could I forget? I met you at her wedding."

Sandy's mouth was dried out. She licked her lips, then tried sipping her whiskey sour but found her hand was shaking. "I saw you on the train last Monday."

"Why didn't you say something?"

"I had to get off in Newark, to change trains. There wasn't much time."

"Where are you sitting for dinner?"

"Over there," Sandy pointed, "at the table in the corner with my sister and her friends. How about you?"

"Back there, that long table. Save me a dance, will you?"

"No problem. Norman doesn't dance."

The band leader announced dinner and the parade to the tables began.

Gish sat next to Sandy, whispering, "You look sensational in that . . . shows off your little body just right . . . love your little tits . . . you know the old saying . . . anything you can't fit in your mouth . . ."

"Cut it out, will you?" Sandy whispered back.

She tried to concentrate on the meal, drank more than she should have, waited until she saw Rhoda Resnick dancing cheek to cheek with Sherm Hyatt, and knew that he would come for her soon.

"Pardon me, ma'am," he said, standing behind her, "but could I have this dance, for old time's sake?"

She pretended to be surprised. "Oh, Shep, how nice." And she excused herself from the table.

Shep took her hand and led her to the dance floor.

"So," he said, looking down at her.

"So."

"Here we are again."

"Yes."

"I feel like I'm back at your sister's wedding."

"And I've just wiped the bird crap off your head."

He laughed. "I haven't been crapped on by a blue dove since then."

"Pink, wasn't it?"

"Was it?"

"I think so. Everything was pink and white."

They were quiet for a while. The electricity was still there. Her knees were weak, she felt very warm, her hands were sweating. He held her tight. "Are you happy, Sandy? Do you have what you want?"

She didn't answer. Couldn't.

"Sandy?"

"I don't know. What about you?"

"I'm reasonably happy."

"And successful, I hear."

"Yes, but bored. I made it too fast, too soon. I miss the struggle."

"What about all those kids?"

"That's Rhoda's department."

The music ended but Shep didn't let go of her hand.

"Do you play around, Sandy?"

She shook her head.

"Norman was the first and only?"

"Yes."

"And you're proud of that, aren't you?"

"Not especially."

The music began again. He pressed her to him, then changed his mind. "Let's go for a walk."

"I can't, they'll notice."

"No they won't. Look at Norman with that little blonde."

"That's Luscious. She admires his tennis game."

"I thought you said he doesn't dance."

"He doesn't. She's dancing, he's just standing there."

"Yeah, I guess you're right. And look at Sherm. He thinks if he dances with Rhoda all night he'll get the contract on my next shopping center."

"Will he?"

"Probably. Come on." He led her through the lobby to the double doors.

Outside it was hot and dry. Sandy smelled roses and wisteria. She had trouble breathing. What now?

Shep held her hand and they walked quickly across the eighteenth fairway and down the road to the pool. Then, off to the side of the pool, behind the cabanas.

He turned to her, took her in his arms, and kissed her. He still had that delicious way of kissing, licking the corners of her mouth, running his tongue along her teeth, sucking on her lower lip. His breath was hot on her face, in her ear, on her neck. How different from Norman's cold, toothpaste kisses. Shep tasted of wine, of salad dressing, of sex. Shep was hard. Oh yes, she could feel it against her. Very hard. He laughed.

"Feel that," he said, placing her hand on his trousers. "Just like the old days."

"Shep, Norman would never forgive me. I have to get back."

He put his hands on her ass and squeezed. "You're not wearing anything under this are you?"

"No." She felt faint, unable to swallow, to get a deep breath, scared she might pass out from the excitement of it, grateful for the Tampax, holding in her juices, keeping her dry so he wouldn't know, wouldn't guess how hot she was for him, how close to coming just from his kiss, just from his hands on her ass.

"I have to go now," she told him. "Norman . . ."

"Norman will never know." He was easing her dress up, his fingers on her naked bottom now.

"You don't understand . . ."

"Relax." He was kissing her again, one hand tightening around her breast.

"I can't, Shep, I can't take the chance."

He let go and stepped away from her.

"Life is one big chance, Sandy. If you're not willing to take it, you can't play the game."

"Then I guess I'm not ready for the game," she said slowly, hating herself.

"Call me if you change your mind," he said and walked away, leaving her alone in the dark. He never was one to force the issue, damn it!

Sandy went back to the Clubhouse, to the Ladies Room, where she splashed cold water on her face. "I know how you feel," a strange woman said to her. "I've had a wee bit too much myself."

"Oh, there you are," Norman said when she got back to their table.

"I got hot. I needed some fresh air."

"Don't have anything more to drink."

"No, I won't."

Steph Weintraub rushed up to her. "Sandy, you haven't signed my petition yet. We want all the new members to sign."

"What petition is that?"

"A refusal to accept the archaic laws of this Club which state that women cannot tee off on Wednesdays, weekends, or holidays until one P.M. I mean, we're members too, aren't we? So why should we just go along with this shit? I play as good a game as most of our *male* members. Why should I have to wait until one P.M.?"

"You shouldn't," Sandy said, and reached for Steph's pen.

"Bullshit!" Gish said. "The difference, my dear, Stephanie Ball Breaker, is that *we* work our tails off all week, supporting you charming creatures, while *you* get to play every goddamned day of the week. So is it too much to ask that on Wednesdays, weekends, and holidays we get to tee off first? Talk about fair, talk about selfishness, Jesus H. Chreeist!"

"Maybe Gish is right," Sandy said. "I hadn't thought about . . ."

"Think for yourself, Sandy!" Steph argued.

"I never learned how." Sandy handed the pen back to Steph, without signing her petition.

13

MYRA AND GORDON threw a swim party the next night. They'd just had the pool landscaped and lit. Mona assured Sandy that Myra's pool was the talk of Short Hills, just as her house had been a few years earlier, with its staircase straight out of Tara and its eight and a half bathrooms.

Sandy and Norm arrived early for a private tour of what used to be the backyard. "Fantastic!" Norman said over and over as Myra and Gordy pointed out the newly planted sights. "Absolutely fantastic! I only hope some day we can do the same thing in Watchung."

"You've got to give him full rein," Myra said of their landscaper, who called himself the Greek. No relation to Jackie's Greek. "He's a kook, but very talented. If you try to tell him what to do he'll quit. I told him I wanted something that blooms so the next morning I look out my window and here's this bush with the most gorgeous purple flower you ever saw. So I rush outside to get a closer look and the Greek, who's watching the whole thing, gets hysterical, laughing. Because it's plastic! His idea of a joke!"

"And you've got to be willing to pay," Gordon added, "through the nose."

Tiny lanternlike lights hung from the trees, glowing softly. The shrubbery was lush, with narrow footpaths running to the house, to the side yard, to the pool itself. Railroad ties, gravel, wood chips, wild flowers, they'd created a wooded paradise out of a bare acre lot. Sandy heard the soft sound of water splashing. She turned. Of course. A miniature waterfall tucked between the rocks. She should have known. And while it was not quite Jamaica, it was certainly as close as one could hope to get in suburban New Jersey. And not only that; it was safe here. Safe, because of an intricate burglar alarm system, hooked up to a private surveillance company who monitored it twenty-four hours a day. No one was going to get close enough to hold a machete to Myra's throat here. If someone or something weighing over twenty-five pounds fell into the pool, or wandered onto the grounds once the alarm was set for the night, it would go off, first silently, warning the family, then with a blast. "We can sleep without worrying now," Myra told them. "We can leave the girls and know it's okay."

Myra shimmered in a caftan of flimsy organza, her matching bikini showing through. Gordon had on tennis shoes and socks, bathing trunks, and a Lacoste shirt. His hair was arranged carefully to cover his bald spot. Sandy and Norman changed into their swimsuits as the other guests arrived, twenty couples, many of them Gordy's colleagues. Doctors and their wives. Norman loved it, loved to surprise them with his knowledge of diseases and treatments by tossing out statements from last month's issue of the *AMA Journal*.

Soon the party was in full swing with Justine and her forces in charge. Justine was the ultimate caterer, the finest, the classiest, the most *gourmet*. Sandy knew the menu by heart. So did all the other guests. There would be no palatable surprises. But no one would go hungry. Crab fingers, marinated mushrooms, miniature pizzas, cheese and spinach quiche, tiny shells filled with chicken a la king, giant shrimp to hold by the tail, and later, at midnight, Justine herself would emerge from the kitchen, offering whole fillets of beef, sliced before your very eyes and placed on squares of hot garlic bread, eliminating the hostess's need for renting china or silverware. And later still the buffet table would be laden with delectable French pastries and freshly brewed coffee. *Oh, delicious . . . delicious!* they would cry, even though they used Justine for all of their parties too. Myra threw three of them a year. The seasons would change, Myra's hostess gowns would change, but Justine's menu would remain the same. And next week and the week after that they would attend other parties at other homes, catered by Justine, and at midnight, would rave about the scrumptious sliced beef on garlic bread and how dependable Justine was, how you could count on her food being perfect, every time.

The women gathered in the shallow end of the pool, comfortable in the eighty-eight-degree water, drinks in hand. The men were treading water or hanging onto the sides in the deep end, less concerned about wetting their hair. Into this steamy wonderland Norman jumped with his waterproof stopwatch, impressing them all with his ability to hold his breath under water.

Steph Weintraub was still trying to convince The Club members to sign her petition. She squatted at the pool's edge, begging for signatures, while trying to keep her paper dry, the ink from smudging. From their end of the pool the men threatened to drown her and teased Warren, "If you were a *real* man, you'd keep her in line."

"Fuck you," Steph yelled at them.

The response was more laughter.

At ten, a five-piece band arrived, complete with electric guitar and bongo drums, something for everyone. Sandy drank carefully although her glass seemed to fill up automatically each time she looked away. She was sure that before long someone would pass out and fall into the pool and was relieved that the house was full of doctors, just in case. Following the steak sandwiches someone declared that the *girls* should go topless. Myra was the first to discard her top, flinging it into the pool with a great whoop, then dancing a bouncing frug with Gordon's friend, Dave Immerman. The best-breasted followed Myra's lead, while the padded and the drooping wisely kept covered.

Gish sneaked up behind Sandy and untied her top. "Take it off . . . take it off . . . take it all off . . ." he chanted.

Sandy held her suit to her and ran for the house, away from the circus. As she passed the pool she saw that Norman was still performing his breath-holding act, as a group of bare-breasted women circled around him, oohing and aahing and shrieking for him to come up.

Sandy went to Gordon's study, a quiet, dark room at one end of the house, and she lay down on the floor, closed her eyes, and thought about Shep. Regrets, regrets . . . her life seemed to be made up of nothing but a series of regrets. Why hadn't she let herself go last night? It would have made more sense than this . . . this insane party. Fear of pregnancy had kept her a virgin, now it was fear of being caught, of having to face the consequences, that kept her faithful . . . shit . . .

"Sandy."

She sat up. "Oh, Gordy."

"It's okay, don't get up."

"I needed to get away from . . ."

He nodded. "Me too."

"It's a lovely party, really."

Gordon sat down on the floor, next to her, and rubbed her back. His hands were warm, firm. He massaged her neck, relaxing her. "You know something, Sandy, I hate this fucking house, this stupid party."

"You're drunk, Gordon."

"Goddamned right I am. Stinko, but not so drunk I don't know my life is shit, that I've had it up to here."

"Come on, Gordy, you don't mean that."

"I do. I do. I want out."

"Don't talk that way. It's the booze, that's all."

"*That's all, she says.* What am I doing here, answer me that."

"You love Myra and the twins. That's what it's all about."

"Love? I don't know the meaning of that word. I used to think I did, but no more."

"Gordy, you're talking in cliches. You better go to bed."

"Good idea," he said, pulling her down with him, kissing her on the mouth.

"What the hell?" Sandy said, pushing him off her.

"I've always wanted you, Sandy . . . always loved your little ass . . . your cunt . . . everytime I examine you I want it . . . want to kiss it . . . to fill it . . ."

"Gordon! Are you crazy?"

"Yes, but I know what I want. Please, Sandy, please let me." He was tugging at her bikini top, pushing down her pants.

"Look, I can't. I haven't got my diaphragm in."

He jumped up. "I'll get you one. What size?"

She started to laugh. "Gordon, this is insane."

"What size?"

"Eighty . . . but I can't . . . really . . ."

He opened a cabinet and pulled out a box. "Eighty, eighty, here's one." He ran to the door and locked it, ran back to her, and said, "I can make my cock dance inside you. Just wait, you're going to love it."

He kneeled in front of her and pulled down her bikini pants. "I'll put this in for you, what kind of jelly do you like?"

"I don't use jelly."

"You use foam?"

"No, nothing."

"You don't use anything with your diaphragm?"

"No."

"You have to use something. You could get pregnant without it."

"So far I haven't. Look, Gordy, we can't . . . somebody . . ."

"It's all right."

She had never been attracted to Gordon, but now he kneeled in front of her, his penis, fat and inviting, sticking straight out from his black bush. As he inserted her diaphragm he whispered, "So beautiful . . . sweetest pussy . . ." And then he put his face between her legs and sniffed her cunt, actually put his nose into it and kissed it. She found herself not just aroused, but actually wanting him very much.

He rolled her over and entered her from behind, one hand squeezing her right breast, the other holding her pussy. It felt good. Very good.

"Your fucking sister won't let me do it this way. Says it's for animals, but we are animals, aren't we, Sandy."

He pulled out and flipped her over abruptly. "And now for my cock dance," he said. "Lie still, don't move."

She lay quietly, obediently, as his cock slid into her and then she felt it moving, seemingly on its own, *dancing,* my god, he really could make it dance. Could others do that too? Or did Gordon, her short, balding brother-in-law have some special talent?

"Myra . . . Myra . . . so cold . . . hates to be dirty . . . have to come into a rubber so I don't mess her up . . ."

This can't be happening, Sandy thought. But she couldn't lie still any longer, was too excited now, had to move with him, and then she was coming, coming and moaning and wrapping her legs around him as he shot into her, calling, "Yes, my pussy, my love."

Sandy laughed. She shouldn't have, she knew, but it all seemed terribly funny. She expected Gordon to laugh with her. To say it hadn't really happened. Instead he sobbed.

"I should be shot, I should be hung or castrated or both. I'll never forgive myself. Never. I'll blow my brains out . . . throw myself out the window . . . drive the Citröen off a cliff . . . I've ruined you, Sandy, and I've humiliated my wonderful wife . . . my beautiful Myra . . . I love her so much . . . you just don't know . . ."

"Of course you do, Gordy. Take it easy. It's okay, no one will ever know, I promise."

"My children, what would they think . . . fucking my sister-in-law . . . oh, Jesus . . . they hate me anyway . . . hate us both, me and Myra . . . I loved them once . . . when they were babies . . . soft and small . . . now they're strangers, Sandy . . . hostile, moody strangers . . ."

"They're going through a stage, Gordy. It won't last forever."

He was crying hard, had trouble catching his breath. "I want them back the way they were. I want my babies back. Most of the time I want to die, Sandy. I want to be dead, done with it. It's too hard to keep going."

Sandy stroked his hair and cradled him in her arms, the way she would Bucky or Jen.

"I want to be a little boy again."

"Of course you do. You can be my little boy." She held him, kissing his forehead.

"Thank you, Sandy, that's the nicest thing anyone's said to me in a long time."

And Sandy cried with him.

14

SANDY AND GORDON sat in his Citröen in the parking lot of Sip n' Sup on the highway. Gordon had ordered two hamburgers with french fries and Cokes and now, as they unwrapped their lunches and prepared to eat them, Sandy said, "Oh, God, I've got to go again," and she leaped out of the car and raced inside to the Ladies Room. She'd had stomach pains and diarrhea since 4 A.M., following her episode with Gordon. She knew it was nerves. Nerves and tension and anxiety. The fear of being caught. Having to face the consequences. She could see it all too clearly.

Her mother would say: I raised her to be a wonderful wife and this is what I get. She does it with Gordon, my beautiful Myra's husband.

But mother, Sandy would cry, it was Gordon's idea.

You can't blame the man! All men want to do those things. It's up to the woman to say no. Didn't I teach you to carry a magazine on every date so that if you had to sit on a boy's lap you could spread the magazine out first? I'll bet you didn't have a magazine with Gordon, did you?

No, mother. I never even thought about a magazine.

There, you see? What did I tell you? God will punish you, Sandy. He'll never let you forget how you've sinned. Thou shalt not covet they sister's husband. That's one of the Ten Amendments.

Commandments.

That's what I meant.

Except it's not.

If it's not, it should be.

Besides, I don't covet him. I fucked him but I do not covet him!

And Enid: Whore. Harlot. Just like a ductla! I knew from the start she wasn't good enough for my Norman. He only should have listened to me then. Miss High and Mighty. With her brother-in-law yet!

And the twins: Really? We had no idea Daddy could still get it up!

And Bucky and Jen: You did it with Uncle Gordon? Eeuuuww ... *gross!*

And Myra: I'm suing Gordy for divorce. I'm taking the house, the cash, the investments, the cars, forty-five thousand dollars a year in alimony, and The Club membership. As for you, Sandy, I'll never forgive you! I understand why you did it. Oh, yes, I understand very well. Jealousy. You've always been jealous of me because I was the favorite child. But frankly, I think you're a fool for having done it with Gordon. All he's interested in is sticking it up somebody's asshole, and him a gynecologist!

No, Myra, you've got it all wrong. It feels good from behind, you should try it. And besides, he can do a fantastic cock dance.

Cock dance? Don't make me laugh! He hasn't even learned to do the Twist!

Norman: Norman would throw her out. Throw her out and forbid her to see her children. Marriage is a contract. You broke the contract. You're out. Without a penny from me. I don't want to see you again. Just pack up and leave. I can't imagine why you'd go and do it with Gordon, of all people. Jesus, he can't even play net!

Sandy returned to Gordon's car, looking pale and worn out. "How long will it take before the Lomotil starts working?" she asked.

"You should feel better in a few hours," Gordon said.

Sandy nodded.

"What I wanted to talk to you about, Sandy . . ."

"Don't tell me," Sandy said, interrupting. "Myra knows!"

"No, nobody knows, at least not as far as *I* know. What I want to say and I couldn't over the phone, is that I'm willing to marry you."

"Marry me?"

"Yes. I've thought it all over and decided that's what we should do. We'll fly down to Juarez, or wherever you go for a quickie divorce these days, and marry before we come home. That way we can get things settled up over the summer. We might have to move away. Nevada's a possibility or New Mexico. I'll have to look into the logistics, have to arrange to sell my practice here." He sipped his Coke. "And who knows, maybe Norman and Myra will get together too. They have a lot in common."

"Gordy, in spite of my diarrhea, I know that Sunday night just happened and the best thing we can do is to forget it."

"Really? You really mean that?"

"Yes. I don't want to marry you."

She could see his relief. "I'll never be able to tell you how sorry I am it happened, San, I could apologize for the next ten years and you'd still never know."

"I do know, Gordy . . . really . . . it's okay . . . it was my fault as much as yours . . . I could have stopped you . . . I wasn't that drunk . . . as long as nobody ever finds out . . . that's all I care about . . ."

"You're a wonderful woman, Sandy."

"Did you really think I'd marry you?"

"I wasn't sure. But I felt I owed it to you to ask."

"That was very nice, unnecessary, but nice." She leaned over and kissed his cheek.

He hugged her. "It was good, wasn't it?"

"Yes."

"We could go across the street and take a room for a few hours."

She laughed. "No."

"I guess you're right."

"Oh, I almost forgot," she said, opening her purse and pulling out a small packet wrapped in Kleenex. "I brought you the diaphragm."

"Keep it."

"I can't."

"Oh, go on, I have plenty. Think of it as a memento of our time together."

"Okay, if you're sure." She put it back in her purse and opened the car door. "Bye, Gordy."

"Bye, San, take care and let me know if you don't feel better soon."

"I feel better already." She walked across the parking lot to her own car and drove home.

Sandy couldn't remember the combination number for her locker at The Club. Rather than admit this and have the handyman break into it, she carried her things back and forth in a canvas tote. She still tried her locker each time, hoping that one of these days she would hit on the right combination. 30-45-15 45-13-30 15-35-42 Nothing.

"What's the matter?" Steph asked, catching Sandy in the act.

"Oh, nothing, why?"

"It looked like you were having trouble with your locker."

"Me? No, I was just rearranging some of my things."

"Could you zip me up?" Steph asked.

"Sure and if you're still interested I've decided I'd like to sign your petition."

"Terrific!" Steph opened her locker, which was across from Sandy's, and handed her the petition and a pen. "This means we have just seventeen holdouts and every one of them is scared shit of her husband. Glad I had you figured wrong, Sandy. Are you going to play in the ABCD tournament?"

"No, I'm not ready for tournaments yet. I'm having my first playing lesson today."

"Well, I'll talk to Roger about it. He'll tell me if you're ready or not, and if you are, I'll try to get you in my foursome. I'm glad you joined The Club. We can use some new faces around here. Not to mention some new ideas."

"Thanks," Sandy said, surprised and flattered.

It was Ringer Day. Every Tuesday was Ringer Day. A large posterboard chart hung on the wall behind the row of dressing tables. Each member's name was neatly printed down one side. On Tuesdays, after they had played their rounds they posted their best score for any one hole. Their *Ringer*. Members without official handicaps, like Sandy, were automatically assigned a 36, the highest. She imagined the chart on Labor Day, all the little squares neatly filled in with fives and fours and threes. Except next to her name. Next to her name would still be a blank row. Oh, shit! Who cared?

Sandy had to hurry. Roger would be waiting. They were going off the back nine. Sandy had never been out on the course, except in a cart with the children when they had first joined The Club.

"Hey!" Roger called, clapping his hands. "Here she is ready for her big debut!"

"Roger, please don't make it worse. I'm very nervous as it is."

"Relax, Sandy. This is supposed to be fun. Steve is going to caddy for us. Steve, this is Mrs. Pressman."

Steve nodded and said her name softly.

She had seen him before, waiting around. He wasn't an A caddy, that much she knew, probably not a B either, but he had a nice smile and seemed shy. Good. She didn't need any wise-ass caddy following her around. Most likely he was the son of a member, home from college for the summer. He picked up her bag and walked behind them.

"Now, listen, Sandy," Roger said, "you're going to stand up to the ball. Forget about everything else and hit it. The practice range is for thinking about what to do. When you're out here you stop thinking and just let it happen."

"Suppose it doesn't?"

"That's not the attitude we want to start with, is it?"

"I'm just being realistic."

"Never mind. Confidence is what we want to stress today to prove to yourself that you can do it. Get that?"

"Yes. Sure."

Two hours later Sandy was back at the locker room. She'd lost eight balls, had come close to getting smacked in the head when her tee shot on fifteen hit a tree and rebounded, had spent twenty minutes trying to get a shot over the water on seventeen, and had promised Roger she would come out every day to hit two buckets of balls, take a lesson twice a week, and play nine holes as often as she could.

"After next week you should start playing regularly," he said. "And sign up for the ABCD tournament."

"I can't play in a tournament."

"Sure you can. Plenty of women out there can't hit the ball as well as you."

"I'll see."

Roger held out his hand. "Next year you're going to say, remember when . . ."

Sandy scraped her shoes on the mat outside the Ladies Locker Room, then went inside and collapsed on the floor in front of her locker. One thing she knew for sure. She hated the game of golf. So why had she made an appointment with Steve to caddy for her at Friday morning at eight? Because she was expected to. Because she always did what she was told. Because she was such a good little girl. Such a good little wifey.

15

NORMAN CAME HOME at five, an hour early. He took two aspirin and lay down on the sofa in the den.

"What's wrong?" Sandy asked.

"A terrible day."

"What happened?"

"Jake died."

"Jake who?"

"This is no time to be funny."

"I'm not being funny. I don't know who you're talking about."

"Jake, the doberman in the New Brunswick store."

"Oh, the dog."

"Is that all you can say?"

"I didn't know him personally."

"He was poisoned."

"Poisoned!"

"Had convulsions in front of the customers. Died before we could get him to the vet."

"Were you there when it happened?"

"Yes, what a mess."

"Who could have done it?"

"That's what we're trying to find out."

"Are you going to get another dog?"

"I've already called the kennel."

Sandy nodded. Then, to cheer him, she said, "I had my playing lesson today. I hit my tee shot over the green on eleven."

"This is no time to talk about your playing lesson."

"I thought you'd want to know."

"For God's sake, I just told you one of our dogs was poisoned, Sandy!"

"You didn't carry on this way when Kennedy was killed. Or when my father died!"

"Just what the hell is that supposed to mean?"

"Nothing, forget it."

She went into the kitchen, cut up the salad, and set the table. Then, feeling guilty, she poured a glass of lemonade and carried it to Norman. He sat up and sipped it.

"We got two letters from Jen and a card from Bucky," Sandy told him. "Bucky just signed his name but Jen sounds like she's adjusting and having fun."

"I told you she would."

Sandy nodded. "I made stuffed peppers for dinner."

"I don't think I can eat tonight."

"But stuffed peppers are your favorite."

"Save them for tomorrow."

"I won't be home tomorrow. I'm going into New York, remember?"

"No."

"Yes, I told you. The twins are being operated on tomorrow morning. I'm taking my mother in and then spending the night with Myra at the St. Moritz."

"I guess I forgot."

"Can I bring you some soup or maybe tea and toast?"

"Soup would be good."

"Okay. And Norm, I really am sorry about Jake."

"And I'm sorry I snapped at you. I'm glad the playing lesson went well."

Sandy sat down next to him. "Hold me."

He put his arms around her. She rested her face against his. "We can make it better, can't we?"

"What?"

"Us."

"What do you mean?"

"I mean if we try, really try, we can still make it work."

"I don't get you."

"Us . . . you and me . . . the marriage . . ."

"Don't start in tonight, Sandy. I'm tired and my head aches."

Sandy picked up Mona at eleven the next morning and drove into New York, leaving the car on the Port Authority parking roof. It was hot, but breezy, and Mona protected her hairdo with a pink, gauzy scarf for the short walk to the building.

"I was up all night," she told Sandy. "I'm so worried about the girls."

"They'll be fine. It's easy surgery. They don't even have to put them out. They get a local."

"In their noses?"

"I don't know how they do it."

"It must be very painful."

"I don't think so. If it was, you wouldn't hear about so many girls having it done."

"It's a shame they got the Lefferts' nose instead of ours. We all have such good noses."

"I'm sure they'll look great when it's over."

"Did you know it costs eighteen hundred dollars a nose but because they're twins and because of professional courtesy they're getting a break—two thousand dollars for both."

They entered the building and waited for the elevator to carry them down to the main floor.

"We'll take a cab?" Mona asked.

"Yes. The hospital's uptown."

"I get confused in the city."

"So do I."

Mona held Sandy's arm as they walked through the lobby of the Port Authority building. "Sandy," she began, then looked around as if to make sure no one was listening, "I have something to discuss with you."

"What is it?"

"Not here, outside."

They went through the double glass doors and caught a cab. After Sandy had given the driver the address of the hospital she turned to her mother. "Go on." Was it possible that Mona had somehow found out about her and Gordon? What a thought!

"I met a man," Mona whispered.

"That's wonderful!" Sandy told her, relieved.

"I knew him years ago before either one of us was married and now I ran into him again at Ruth Berkow's house. He's still married. But he wants to see me. I don't know what to do."

"Do you like him?"

"If he wasn't married I could be persuaded. He brought me a bottle of perfume over the weekend—Joy. And he sent me a dozen roses for the Fourth of July—yellow."

"He must have fallen for you in a big way."

"But he's married."

"Maybe they don't get along."

"They don't, but they have a truce, he says. No love, no *you-know-what* but they still live together."

"And he wants to *you-know-what* with you?"

"Sandy, God forbid! I have my reputation to consider."

"So what does he want?"

"Companionship, he says."

"So what's wrong with that?"

"He's *married*. A *married* man, Sandy. How would it look? Divorce your wife, I told him, and I'll think about it. *She'd kill herself*, he says."

"So what are you going to do?"

"I'm going out to dinner with him Saturday night. Then I'll decide."

"That makes sense."

"But I'm nervous. If his wife finds out, I could be named coordinator, God forbid."

"Correspondent."

"That's what I said."

"And you can't be named just for having dinner with him."

"It's all so easy for your generation!"

"It's not easy at all. But you're an attractive woman, mother, a widow, you should be going out with men. I've told you so since Daddy died."

"If you remember, I tried once."

"That was a bad experience. I agree."

"You're telling me? You don't know the half of it. That one went to Charlie Chaplin's doctor in Switzerland. *My hormones are like a boy's,* he tells me. First we go for a ride in his new Cadillac, to south Jersey, to the cemetery where his late wife is buried, and after, he takes me to dinner at Howard Johnson's."

"I never knew that."

"You think I wanted anyone to know he took me to Howard Johnson's for dinner? And that's not the end of it either. When we get back to my place he asks if he could please come up for some coffee. *Of course, coffee and a piece of Sara Lee cake, maybe?* I say. *Sounds beautiful,* he says. *And Mona, so are you.* I should have known then, but no, I had to go and believe him. Miss Innocence. So he looks around my apartment, admires every-thing, and asks if he could please lie down on my bed. He's not feeling well all of a sudden. Right away I start worrying that he's going to have a heart attack in my bedroom and how will that look to the world? But he's not having a heart attack. Not him! He grabs me and pulls me down on top of him. Can you imag-ine! He wants to *you-know-what* with me on the first date! I tell him if he doesn't let go in a hurry I'm going to scream. *Good,* he says. *I like my women to scream.* A meshugunah! I tell him I'll kill him and I mean it. I'm already thinking about my sewing scissors. Then he laughs and lets me go. *I thought you were a sport,* he says, *but let's just forget it. I have plenty of women, more than I can handle, so who needs you?* And then he gets up and walks out. Such an experience! Is it any wonder I haven't gone out since?"

The cab pulled up in front of the hospital and Sandy paid the driver.

"You should have told me before," Sandy said as she and Mona walked into the lobby.

"You think I like to bother you and Myra with my personal problems?" Mona looked around. "This is a hospital? It seems more like an office building to me."

"It does, doesn't it." They walked toward the elevator. "Does Myra know about your new friend?"

"Morris . . . Morris Minster. No, she's got too much on her mind right now, the noses and everything."

The elevator door opened and they stepped inside. "What floor did Myra say?"

"Four, I think."

Sandy pressed the button.

"Sandy, I hope you're careful with Norman."

"Careful, how?"

"Careful so you don't get into trouble."

"We're not planning on any more children if that's what you're worried about."

"Not that."

"Then what?"

"Divorce," Mona whispered.

"Divorce?"

"Yes. My friend Nettie's daughter, who lives in Connecticut, in a very swanky neighborhood, is getting a divorce. It's making Nettie sick. Her blood pressure's up to God knows what. You should take good care, Sandy. Make Norman happy. Nettie's son-in-law, a lawyer, ran off with another woman from the same street!"

"That's too bad for Nettie's daughter but it has nothing to do with me and Norman."

"I'm just saying there's so much going on these days, everything is different from when your father and I were your age. You should just watch out. I told Myra the same thing."

"Don't worry about us, Mother, we're just fine."

"Thank God."

They got out on the fourth floor and Mona went up to the receptionist. "We're looking for a Mrs. Lefferts," she said, "Mrs. Myra Lefferts. Her twins were operated on this morning."

"Oh, yes, of course, Room four-sixteen. Mrs. Lefferts said her family would be here around noon."

They started down the hall but coming toward them were two girls with huge brown rubber noses held on by white, blood-stained tape running across their cheeks and up to their foreheads.

Mona swayed and reached for the handrail. "Oh."

"Shush," Sandy told her.

"I feel sick."

"They've just had nose jobs, that's all."

"They look like the walking dead."

"Come on, Mother. Connie and Kate will have the same kinds of bandages. You better get used to it."

"It's good I saw *them* first. Otherwise I might have fainted, see-ing my grandchildren that way."

The door to Room 416 was partially opened. Connie and Kate, in identical zombie masks, were asleep. Myra sat by the window, reading the latest issue of *Vogue*. She looked up, held her finger to her lips, then joined Sandy and Mona outside, in the hall.

"How are they?" Sandy asked.

"Fine, back in their room by nine-thirty. He did one right after the other. They were awake but groggy. Now they'll doze on and off all day."

"Thank God it's over," Mona said. "Could you see anything? Could you tell how they look?"

"No, it'll take three weeks before we can tell how they're going to look but Dr. Saphire stopped by a few minutes ago to say it went very well. No problems."

"Now, if they'll just lose some weight," Mona said.

"They will, Mother," Myra answered, annoyed. "They needed the incentive. Give them a few months and you won't recognize them. I've already made appointments at Sassoon for the day the bandages come off."

"You want to go to lunch?" Sandy asked.

"Yes. I could use a little break. The nurse will look in on them while I'm gone." Myra went back into the room and wiped off the blood trickling down from Connie's exposed nostril. She smoothed back Kate's hair, planted a gentle kiss on each girl's cheek, and tiptoed out of the room.

*   *   *

Sandy put Mona on the four o'clock bus back to Hillside, then went to Myra's room at the St. Moritz to shower and change for her dinner with Vincent. When she'd made the date with him she hadn't realized how well it would work out, had forgotten that she was to keep Myra company for a day or so while the girls were hospitalized.

She still wasn't sure exactly what Vincent had in mind. A good visit, she hoped. Maybe he wanted to talk with her about Lisbeth, about their arrangement, or maybe he wanted to ask her to help out with Mrs. Rabinowitz when he and Lisbeth went to Maine in August, or maybe he wanted to . . . No! She wouldn't think about that. They were meeting for dinner, that was all, like old friends. Nothing wrong with having dinner with an old friend, was there?

Come off it, Sandy!

Look, I'm not going to jump to conclusions.

She walked up to the restaurant. She was ten minutes early and decided to wait outside. She wore her green dress and carried her white blazer over her arm. She was always cold in air-conditioned restaurants. Thin blood, Norman told her. She watched the people walk by. Quite a selection. A dwarf, two shirtless men arm in arm, a group of little girls in Danskins, a stunning woman who looked like . . . my God, Sandy thought, taking off after her. Was it? Yes, she was almost sure. *Jackie!* The woman walked to the corner and turned left. Sandy followed. The woman had slightly bowed legs. The right hair. Sandy crossed the street and walked quickly to the corner. Jackie reached her corner and waited for the light to change. Sandy crossed at the same time, coming face to face with her. It *was* Jackie! She wore big sunglasses but there was no doubt. Sandy knew. Jackie knew she knew. They smiled at each other. Sandy wanted to hug her, to tell her how sorry she was about her troubles, but not to worry, that things would be better. In a second they had passed each other. Jackie walked down Central Park South, not hurrying, but with long confident strides.

Sandy rushed back to the restaurant. Vincent was waiting. They kissed hello. "You won't believe this," Sandy told him, breathlessly, "but I just saw Jackie Kennedy."

"Of course I believe it," Vincent said.

"Well, I almost didn't!"

"You've always had a lot of interest in her, haven't you?"

"Yes."

"Well, shall we go inside?"

"Fine."

"Have you ever seen her in person?" Sandy asked.

"Several times."

They were shown to a table in the corner. They each had two drinks, fettuccine, a green salad, a half bottle of Bolla Soave, and cappuccino. They talked about their children, the pros and cons of fad dieting, the war in Vietnam, where it all would end, how his students weren't as bright or eager as they used to be, and marriage and its future in America. Sandy found it exciting to engage in a real conversation, found she had ideas she hadn't been aware of herself.

When the check was presented, Sandy asked, "How's Mrs. Rabinowitz?"

"Not well at all. She's going in for more tests. They suspect a brain tumor . . ."

"I'm sorry."

"Yes, difficult . . ." Vincent signed the BankAmericard receipt and checked his watch. "Well, it's just seven-forty-five. How about a movie?"

She tried to hide her surprise. She hadn't considered the possibility of anything as ordinary as a movie. "I don't know."

"Oh, come on, it's still early and you're spending the night with your sister, you said."

"Yes."

"Well then there's no hurry, is there?"

"I guess not."

"Good. I know just the film. It's playing up near Columbia. We can make the eight-twenty show."

It would probably be some artsy foreign film with titles, and after it Vincent would ask her all kinds of deep questions about its real meaning and Sandy would either have to admit, *I don't know* or make something up, the way she used to when Lisbeth dragged her to films full of relevance way back when. Yet Sandy wasn't anxious to get back to the hotel, didn't want to meet up with Gordon.

"X-rated?" Sandy asked, when she saw the marquee.

"Yes, but very high class," Vincent assured her. "I've already seen it but I'd like very much to share it with you."

"I've never seen a porno film."

"This isn't porno, Sandy, it's artistic. There's quite a difference."

"If you say so." Sandy giggled, more from nervousness than anything else. So, it wasn't to be ordinary after all.

Vincent bought the tickets and they went inside.

The picture began. A girl was walking down the street. She entered a building, climbed up several flights of stairs, let herself into an apartment, went directly to the bedroom, undressed, and was raped by two young men who had been hiding in her closet. Or maybe she wasn't raped. Because she enjoyed it very much. Possibly the two young men were just playing games with her. But there was no time to try to figure out the plot because she was already with a third man. This time she sat on him, her hands caressing her own breasts, as she moved up and down. Was this simulated or real sex? Oh, wait a minute . . . it was real . . . his penis was inside her . . . yes, from this camera angle you could see it gliding in and out. And now she was sucking him . . . and here were the two young men again, one of them fucking her, the other one . . . very complicated . . . Sandy lost track of which body belonged to which player. After fifteen minutes more of various sexual acts Vincent leaned close and whispered, "Does watching make you wet?"

Sandy didn't answer. She'd been dripping right from the start, shifting in her seat, trying to make the heat go away, trying to forget that Vincent was sitting next to her and most likely had plans.

"Does it?" he asked again.

"Yes," she said, thinking over her options. She could walk out, take a cab back to the St. Moritz and never see Vincent again. That was what she *should* do. But she hated to make hard feelings. Vincent's hand was on her bare thigh now. Any second now he would feel how wet she really was.

"Vincent, this is crazy."

"You're right," he said, "let's go." He grabbed her hand, practically pulled her out of the theater, across the street, down another street, past a row of stores.

"Where are we going?" she asked.

"To my office, it's right around the corner."

Oh, so that was it. "But Vincent . . ."

"Look, Lisbeth told you about our Thursday nights, didn't she?"

"Yes, but . . ."

"I was sure you understood when you accepted my invitation."

"No, I thought . . ."

"But it's *Thursday*. I made that clear when I called, didn't I? I said, *Thursday,* the seventh."

"Yes, but you see . . ."

"Never mind. Here we are." They stood in front of a small, ivy-covered building on campus, across the square from the library. Vincent fumbled in his pocket for his keys, found them, unlocked the front door, escorted Sandy up a flight of wooden stairs, unlocked the door to his office, stepped inside, turned on a table lamp, took her in his arms, and kissed her with more tongue than she found comfortable. He squeezed her breasts and whispered, "My little panda, my little bear, my mountain goat, my baby burro." Was she hearing right? Was he kidding? He pushed her down to the floor, easing her dress up and her panties down.

"Vincent, no." She tried to get him off. "I can't. I haven't got my diaphragm, for one thing."

"Not to worry," he said, licking her exposed right breast. "I've had a vasectomy. Didn't Lisbeth tell you?"

"No."

"It's all right, my little sparrow, my coyote, my wolverine, my lion cub." He had her dress pushed up around her neck now, and her panties around her ankles. He was working on her shoes, trying to unbuckle the straps, instead of just slipping them off.

"Does Lisbeth know you're with me tonight?"

"It was her idea."

"Really?"

"Well, in a way. She asked me if I could think of anyone who might be right for you . . . said you were ready to explore . . . *someone who isn't terribly intellectual,* she said . . . *someone sexy but not overpowering, someone Sandy can trust* . . . So I thought of myself. Of course I'm quite intellectual but not a snob about it like some of my colleagues. And I'm sexy, don't you think so, but not over-powering." He kissed her ankles as he removed her panties. "My little alligator, my sand shark, my turtle . . . and you can trust me . . . so why look further . . ." He had given up on her shoes and was kissing her knees.

"Oh, no . . ." Sandy said, suddenly. "I just remembered . . . I left my jacket in the movie . . . what'll I do?"

"Fuck me and then we'll go back and try to find it," Vincent answered, kneeling over her, his erection long and slim, like the rest of him. He had blond pubic hair and was circumcised. She'd often wondered about that. Vincent grabbed hold of his cock, letting the tip brush against her cunt, teasing, then pulling it away.

Sandy arched her back and raised her hips off the floor, like the girl in the movie had.

"My little kangaroo is hungry . . . hungry to fuck . . ." He slid into her and she tightened her cunt around him, but as she did she felt him disappear.

"Oh, dammit. Dammit to hell!" he cried.

"What's wrong?" Sandy asked. "Did I do something?"

"No, I lost it."

"But why?"

"Because I lose it every goddamned fucking Thursday night." He rolled off her and lay on his back.

"I'm sorry, Vincent."

"It's not your fault. It's psychological, guilt or anxiety or some-thing."

"Is it this way with Lisbeth too?"

"Hell no, with Lisbeth it's great."

"Then why bother with Thursday nights?"

"Because she wants to."

"Does she know about you?"

"No, I make up stories for her. Actually, she's better at screwing around than I am. And that's what really hurts!"

"We could keep trying," Sandy suggested, feeling sorry for him now and needing to prove to herself that she could keep him aroused.

"No, I've tried and tried."

"Maybe you need someone with a lot of experience."

"I've tried professionals too."

"What will you do now?"

"Go home and make it with Lisbeth. It's always very good on Thursday nights."

Sandy leaned on one elbow. "Vincent, did it ever occur to you that maybe Lisbeth's inventing stories too? That maybe neither one of you is really doing anything?"

"She reeks of sex when she gets back. You can smell her a mile away. I love it."

"Oh." Sandy stood up and began to get dressed.

"Look, if you're still hot I could suck you," Vincent said. "I wouldn't mind. I'm quite good at it."

"No thanks. I've got to get back to the hotel. Myra will be wondering what happened to me. And Vincent, I'd appreciate it if you didn't mention any of this to Lisbeth."

"I've no intention of mentioning it to her."

"But I thought you don't believe in secrets . . ."

"*She* doesn't believe in secrets."

"Oh, I see."

They went downstairs and walked out to the street. Vincent hailed a cab and told the driver to take Sandy to the St. Moritz. "Thanks for dinner," Sandy called.

"We'll have to do it again some day," Vincent answered.

Fat chance, she thought.

When she got back to the hotel she realized they'd never gone back to the theater to look for her jacket.

Myra was in bed, reading *Cosmopolitan.* "I was getting worried," she said.

"We went to a movie. How are the girls?"

"They fell asleep around nine and Gordy and I went out for a cup of coffee. Norm called an hour ago. He'd forgotten you were having dinner with Lisbeth."

Forgotten, no. She hadn't mentioned it to him in the first place. "Well, it's too late to call him now. Did he say what he wanted?"

"No."

"I'll call him in the morning," Sandy said yawning. "I'm very tired. I think I'll get ready for bed." When she had finished in the bathroom she climbed into the other bed, still rubbing in her hand lotion. "Okay if I turn out the light?" she asked.

"Sure," Myra said, closing her magazine. "I'm tired too."

"Night. I'm glad the surgery went well."

"Yes, me too."

Sandy was dozing off when Myra whimpered, "Oh, San . . ."

"What . . . what is it?"

Myra's voice caught and she began to cry. "Oh, Sandy, I don't know what to do . . ."

Sandy sat up and switched on the light. "What's the matter?"

"It's Gordy."

"What about him?"

"I think he's having an affair." She cried hard, her shoulders shaking, her face buried in her hands. Sandy could remember having seen Myra cry just once before. Myra must have been about fifteen and Mona had taken her to the beauty parlor for a haircut. Myra came home wailing that she had been ruined for life and that she would never forgive Mona or that fruitcake, Mr. Robert. Sandy got out of her bed and sat down next to Myra, handing her the box of Kleenex from the night table. "I can't believe it," she said, "not Gordy!"

"I know. I can't believe it either, but look what I found." Myra blew her nose, then reached under the covers and pulled out a plain white envelope. She handed it to Sandy. "Read this."

Sandy's fingers shook as she opened it and took out a greeting card. The front of it showed two tiny animal creatures and a huge foot. Inside it read:

It's bigger than both of us! And then, in Gordon's almost illegible doctor's script:

I miss you.

It was wonderful.

Let's do it again some day soon.

Just bring your memento and name the time and place.

G. . . . .

Jesus! He must have written it to her, unless he gave out mementos regularly. But, luckily, he'd never addressed it. "It could be some sort of joke," Sandy said, trying to sound convincing.

"Come on, San."

"Okay, I admit it's incriminating, but still, Myra, it doesn't necessarily mean he's having an affair. It could have been a one-night stand."

"He wants to see her again. He says so."

"Yes, but he never mailed it. He obviously thought it all over and decided it was a mistake."

"I don't know what to do. If I ask him about it he might bring up . . ."

"What?"

"Oh, San, I'm so ashamed. Years ago, when the twins were babies and Gordy was at the hospital night after night . . ."

"Go on."

"I had an affair."

"Myra!"

"I know, I know. It makes me sick just to think about it."

"Who was he?"

"Frank Monzellini . . . our neighbor in the apartments . . ."

"I remember him. He and his wife used to have terrible fights and we used to listen."

"Yes. We only did it three times, not that he didn't want to keep it up but I couldn't. I was so scared and I didn't really like him, but he was very sexy."

"Does Gordon know?"

"I don't think so, but maybe I'm wrong and this is his way of punishing me. After all, he left the card in a very conspicuous place as if he wanted me to find it."

"Where?"

"With the household bills."

"It could have been a mistake."

"I guess."

"You didn't say anything to him tonight, did you?"

"No. Suppose I do confront him and he says he wants a divorce. What do I do then?"

"I'm sure he doesn't want a divorce," Sandy said, reassuringly. "He loves you, anyone can see that. If I were you I'd just forget the whole thing."

"That's easy for you to say, but suppose you found out Norman was playing around."

"Well, I'd be shocked."

"And?"

Sandy nibbled on her finger. "I'm not sure."

"There. You see?"

"Do you love Gordy?"

"Of course I love him. I've never considered not loving him. I never even think about it. I love him just like I love the twins and the house and The Club and my friends and you and Mona."

Sandy had trouble falling asleep after their conversation, couldn't help picturing Myra, at twenty-three, with Frank Monzellini, who wore an undershirt, Marlon Brando style, showing off his hairy armpits. Frank was a plumber. Sandy remembered him carrying in Myra's groceries, playing with the twins on the floor, and one day, to her surprise, when she'd dropped by unexpectedly, finding him there without his shirt, under or regular, and Myra in her robe, flushing. "The toilet's stopped up," Myra had said. "Frank is fixing it for me." Myra and Frank had exchanged looks, then Frank left. Sandy hadn't guessed, hadn't even suspected what was going on. How naive she'd been then.

Thinking about Myra and Frank brought back Sandy's unfinished sexual feelings. The movie. Vincent's office. Gordon, writing her that stupid note. That fool, she thought, touching herself softly, finishing what Vincent had started. *Fool, fool, fool.* Yet she was a fool too. A fool for going with Vincent, for playing with Gordon, for her why not attitude.

16

THE NEXT DAY, when she got home, Sandy phoned Gordon. "Myra found your greeting card."

"My what?"

"You know, *It's bigger than both of us!*"

"No!"

"Yes. And she thinks you're having an affair."

"I forgot all about that card. Did she mention any names?"

"No."

"That's good."

"Gordon, this is very serious. Why did you do it?"

"I don't know. I was looking for get-well cards for the girls and I came across that one and it appealed to me. It reminded me of us."

"You better think up a good explanation."

"I'll say it was for Mrs. O'Neil."

"Who's she?"

"Our bookkeeper. Myra's crazy about her. She's about sixty . . ."

"You expect Myra to believe that?"

"I don't know."

"Maybe we'll get lucky, maybe she won't ask." Sandy paused. "Gordy, that card *was* to me, wasn't it?"

"Well, of course it was."

"I just wanted to make sure."

"Doesn't anybody trust anybody any more?"

"It keeps getting harder."

That night, in bed, Norman looked up from the July issue of the *AMA Journal* and said, "I didn't know you were going out with Lisbeth when you were in New York."

"Her mother's very ill," Sandy said. "They think it's a brain tumor."

"That's too bad."

"Yes."

"I picked up the new dog today. The employees voted on a name for him. It's Lester."

"That's a nice name."

"I would have preferred something with a little more class, but it's important for the employees to feel involved."

Sandy closed her book and said, "Norm . . ."

"What?"

"Have you ever seen a porno film?"

"What has that got to do with Lester?"

"Nothing, I'm changing the subject. Have you?"

"Not since my college days. Why?"

"I thought it might be fun to see one together sometime."

"That sounds like Lisbeth. You know, San, she's nothing but trouble. I've warned you again and again . . . begged you to make new friends at The Club."

"This has nothing to do with making friends at The Club."

"I'll bet her fag of a husband needs porno flicks to turn him on, but I don't." He switched off the bedside lamp, pulled down her blanket, and climbed in next to her. "I'm always ready," he said, dropping his boxer shorts to the floor. "I'm ready right now."

"Yes, I know."

Three minutes from start to finish. Sandy thought about Frank Monzellini. Frank and Myra. No time for a main course tonight. Tonight she got just a snack.

After, when Norman had finished washing and gargling and

was tucked safely into his own bed, Sandy asked, "Norm, are you happy?"

"You ask too many questions lately."

"I need to know. Are you?"

"Yes, I'm happy."

"All the time?"

"Who's happy all the time?"

"I don't know. That's what I'm trying to find out."

"I'm happy enough. And so would you be if you had half a brain. Now go to sleep."

Half a brain. If she had half a brain she'd appreciate him. That's what he meant. But how could she when he treated her like a trained animal? Like Banushka. No, he treated Banushka better. With more care, more respect. Well, she had news for him. She had more than half a brain. It just hadn't been working lately. Hadn't been tuned up for a long time. She'd just been letting it sit there. Going bad. Rotting away. Atrophy. Atrophy of the brain. There now, that was a grown-up word, an intellectual word. *Someone not too intellectual,* Lisbeth had told Vincent. Imagine her saying that!

I'm going to read the classics this summer. But summer was getting away. Next weekend was visiting day at camp. That meant it was half over. Half over and half a brain. Half over and what had she accomplished? Painful golf and tennis lessons. And what did she have to look forward to? More of the same. And come September? The new house. The final house. Shit. Fuck.

She thought about calling Shep, about telling him that she was ready, at last. She went to the phone, lifted the receiver off the hook but couldn't go through with it.

Why not, Sandy? Why couldn't you dial?

I'm scared.

Of what?

Suppose he says *no*?

He won't.

He might. Besides, the man on the motorcycle hasn't shown up all week.

So . . . maybe he's on vacation . . .

Maybe . . . or maybe he doesn't find me very exciting any more . . . and if he doesn't . . . will Shep?

What does one have to do with the other?

Look, I had my chance at the dance and I blew it.

And now she was due at The Club. Due at eight to struggle through nine holes, with Steve dragging his ass behind her, yawning all the way.

"Know what you need, Mrs. Pressman?" Steve said, as she tried to chip over the water and onto the seventh green, missing by inches. "You need a good ball retriever, that's what."

"I'll tell my husband," Sandy answered.

She lost six balls—not that it mattered since Norman gave her his discards—and finished with a score of 72 for nine, not counting her tee shot on eight, when, after five tries, she finally picked up her ball and carried it up the hill, where she took her three wood and really blasted it, surprising herself. "Great shot!" Steve called.

She was finished and scraping her shoes on the mat at nine-forty-five. She showered and changed, the only member in the locker room. It was nice that way, quiet and peaceful. She tried six new combination numbers on her lock, without luck. Oh well. She'd go grocery shopping now, then home to sit on the porch and read. Yes, she'd stop by the library and get something she could sink her teeth into. Something that would make her think.

She got into her car, but instead of going directly to the A&P, as planned, drove straight to the Parkway, headed South, and thirty minutes later turned off at the Mattawan Exit, where she followed signs to Ye Olde New England Village, Shep's shopping center.

Sandy was impressed by its size, by the interesting layout and the attractive shops. She browsed through them, hoping to bump into Shep. She bought a bracelet to bring to Jen at camp, some rubber band glider planes for Bucky, canasta cards for Mona, a set of lemonade glasses in a chrome carrier for the new house, a dozen terry cloth dish towels, a knit shirt with a pocket for Norman, and everywhere, she watched for Shep, turning around quickly, expecting to find him there, smiling at her. And then they would stroll off together, for lunch in a quaint country inn, followed by a walk in the woods, and there, on a rug of pine needles with the sunlight filtering through the trees, they would make love and it would be beautiful, meaningful, perfect.

"Do you, by any chance, know Mr. Resnick, the owner of this shopping center?" Sandy asked the clerk in the bookstore, where she had just bought the number-one best-seller of the summer. Fourteen weeks on the New York *Times* list.

"Certainly," the clerk said. She was an older woman with a sweet face and Sandy could see how lovely she must have been.

"Is he here today?"

"I really couldn't say. He stops by maybe once or twice a week to see how we're doing. Very nice man, very friendly and interested."

"Yes, he's an old friend of mine. I thought I might say hello."

"No telling where to find him. He's got other shopping centers and an office in New York."

"Well, thank you."

"Enjoy the book."

"Yes, I'm sure I will."

Sandy stopped for lunch at one of the two restaurants within Ye Olde New England Village. The waitresses wore long cotton skirts. "Ready to order?"

"Yes," Sandy said. "I'll have half a brain with cottage cheese on the side."

"I'm sorry, did you say . . ."

Sandy looked up and slowly repeated her order. "Half a cantaloupe, cottage cheese on the side."

The waitress laughed. "For a minute I thought you said half a *brain*. Boy, my ears must really be clogged." She tapped the side of her head with one hand.

Had she really said half a *brain*, she wondered, on the drive home? Was her subconscious beginning to take over? Could that happen? No, of course not. She had complete control. She knew exactly what she was doing and saying. Didn't she?

She wasn't home five minutes when the phone rang.

"Mrs. Pressman?"

"Yes."

"This is the plumber over at the new house."

"Yes?"

"We've got a little problem here."

"What is it?"

"You ordered American Standard fixtures in Desert Sand."

"That's right."

"And we just got word from the company that Desert Sand has been discontinued. They're putting out two new colors though, one's called Beechnut and the other's Suntan. I've got the samples here. If you'd come up we could put the order in right away."

"It's almost four."

"I can wait."

"Well, it'll take me half an hour . . . I might run into traffic."

"The sooner the better but like I said, I'll wait."

"Okay."

Sandy went outside, got into the car, and drove toward the new house. . . .

He was waiting for her, as promised, standing next to his truck, guzzling Budweiser from the can. *Hello, Mrs. Pressman.* He wiped his mouth with the back of his hand. *I'm Frank Monzellini, the plumbing contractor.*

Frank Monzellini?

That's right. I work with Joe Fiori, the general contractor. I've met your husband but I don't think I've met you.

Are you the Frank Monzellini who used to live in Tudor Village Apartments?

Yeah, how'd you know that?

This is so funny, Sandy said. *You used to live next door to my sister, Myra Lefferts. Of course, it was a long time ago. The twins are going on fifteen.*

Sure, I remember now. Myra Lefferts, how about that?

Frank was about forty-five, graying, with a beer belly, but still attractive, although the undershirt had been replaced by a blue work shirt.

So you were Myra's little sister . . .

Yes I'm Sandy.

All grown up now, huh?

She smiled and fiddled with the belt on her skirt.

Small world, isn't it?

Yes, Sandy said, *and about those samples . . .*

Oh, sure, right here, in my truck. He reached in, took out the samples, and handed them to Sandy. *We were pretty good friends, me and Myra.*

She mentioned that just the other day.

She did?

Yes. Do you think I could look at these tiles in the bathroom, the light might be different.

Yeah, sure. He followed her inside and up the stairs. They went to the master bath first. *Now, this here's the Beechnut and this here's the Suntan,* he told her, spreading them out on the floor, his thigh brushing against hers.

I always liked the hair under your arms and all over your chest, Sandy said.

Well, I still got it. He took off his shirt. *You see.*

Very nice, Sandy said, running her hands across his chest. *Here, let me do that,* she told him, unbuckling his belt. She unzipped his work pants, reached inside, and pulled out his cock. It was soft, but as she held it, it grew hard. *Oh, you're big!*

Yeah, ten inches, stiff.

I guess I knew you would be. Myra said you were sexy although I've read that size doesn't mean a thing. It's what you do with it that counts.

Yeah, well, I'll tell you what I'm going to do with it, he said. *I'm going to bury it in you. I'm going to move it in and out real slow until you scream.*

My mother had a friend who liked his women to scream.

Never mind your mother.

Don't hurt me, Frank. Please. You're so big I'm afraid.

Don't be scared. I never hurt a woman.

Is this how you did it to Myra? Sandy asked, her legs around his back, in a semi-sitting position, the unfinished floor rough and uncomfortable beneath her.

Yeah . . . yeah . . .

Does it feel better with me?

Yeah . . . yeah . . . real good . . .

Fuck me, Frank . . . harder . . .

Yeah . . . yeah . . . scream now . . . scream . . .

He was waiting for her on the front steps. "Mrs. Pressman?"

"Yes."

"I'm Carl Halloran, the plumber."

"Thank you for waiting."

"I have the samples upstairs, in the bathroom. I figured you'd want to see them up there, the light might be different."

"Yes, of course."

He followed her up the stairs, down the hall, and to the master bath. Sandy looked at the samples, thought for a minute, and said, "I think the Suntan is more what I had in mind."

"I figured you'd pick that one but I couldn't be sure."

"Yes, you can order it for both upstairs baths."

"Very good. I'll call first thing in the morning."

"Thank you."

17

ON SUNDAY AFTERNOON Sandy and Norman played in the mixed doubles tournament at The Club. It seemed foolish to Sandy to participate in a tournament when she'd played only two games of tennis in her life, plus, of course, her series of twenty-five lessons, which weren't over yet, but Norm had it all figured out. "You just keep out of the way," he said that morning. "I'll return everything. You've got to serve and receive serves, but other than that, every shot is mine. Just move fast, away from the ball, and we can take anybody, got that?"

Sandy nodded.

"Can you get your serve in yet?"

"I think so."

"I hope so."

Before their match began Norm said, "Why don't you wipe that white goo off your mouth?"

"I can't," she explained. "I need it—it's zinc—without it, in this sun, I'll have a herpes tomorrow."

"Couldn't you use lipstick instead, just for our match?"

"We're not on TV, you know!"

"But there's a crowd. You want to look good, don't you?"

"I thought all that matters is how I play."

"No, that's not all. It's our image as a couple too."

"Well, I'm sorry, Norm, but I can't go out there without zinc."

"Oh, all right." He grabbed both his racquets, adjusted his sweatbands and eyeglasses and they walked onto the court.

Sandy was already sweating, one of her peds crept down inside her shoes, and she had the remains of a blister on her right thumb, which hurt, even though it was covered by two Band-Aids.

They played against Millicent and Harvey Sommers. Millicent couldn't return Sandy's serves. "They're just too slow," she cried, "too soft. Are they even legal?"

"Damn right!" Norman called.

And Harvey said, "Just keep your eye on the ball, dear."

Bounce . . . thwack . . . bounce . . . thwack . . .

"Look at that!" Millicent cried again. "He's taking all her shots. Is that fair? Is it even legal?"

"She's serving and receiving our serves," Harvey said. "That's all she has to do, dear. Just keep your eye on the ball and try to concentrate."

"I think it's very unfair! We might as well be playing singles against *him!*" Millicent threw her racquet to the ground.

Norman ran up to the net. "As chairman of the Grievance Committee it is my duty to inform you that throwing your racquet on the court is a punishable offense. Look at that mark you've made."

"Try to control yourself, dear," Harvey said. "It's only a game."

"It's not *only* a game," Millicent informed him through clenched teeth. "It's a goddamned tournament!"

Sandy and Norman won their match 6-3, 6-2. Norman was ecstatic. "What'd I tell you?" he laughed, hugging Sandy. "You're great. I always knew you could do it."

"But Norm, I didn't do anything. You did it all."

"Never mind, never mind. As a team we're great. The best. Unbeatable!"

Until their next match, when they were knocked out of the competition by Luscious and Ben, who smashed every ball directly at Sandy.

"Jesus," Norman muttered, storming off the court. "Six-two,

six-one. I told you to move out of the way, didn't I? But you didn't. You just stood there like a lump of clay."

"I was moving . . ."

"In the wrong direction. You moved toward the ball every god-damned time."

"How was I to know where they were going to hit it?"

"Anticipation! Hasn't your teacher taught you anything?"

"Which teacher?"

"Your *tennis* teacher . . . what's wrong with you . . . don't you listen?"

"I tried my best," Sandy told him, feeling the beginning of tears and hating herself for letting him get to her this way. "Do you think I enjoy this . . . this humiliation? Do you think this is any fun for me?"

"Oh, Christ! Stop crying. Everyone can see."

He took her by the arm and tried to lead her away from the crowd but she shook him off shouting, "Let me go."

They didn't speak to each other until Monday night, when she told him she'd been busy and hadn't prepared any supper. They went to Lee Ann Fong's. Lee Ann sat down at their table and said, "Tomorrow's the ABCD tournament. It's my first. Boy, I can't wait!"

Sandy called for the weather report at seven-thirty the next morning. "Hot and humid . . . chance of thundershowers . . . temperature ranging from the mid-eighties to the upper nineties, inland . . ." She hung up and thought about staying in bed. But Norman would never forgive her. No, she had to go, had to play in the tournament. She dressed and drove to The Club. The sky was already gray and threatening.

Sandy checked the board in the locker room and found that the rest of her foursome consisted of Millicent Sommers, Brown, and Lee Ann Fong.

Great, she thought.

"It's going to be a hot one," Myra said as Sandy tied her shoelaces.

She nodded. "What did you decide to do about Gordy?"

"I haven't decided anything yet. I'm still thinking about it."

"Don't do anything foolish."

"I don't intend to."

Outside, Lee Ann Fong was waiting in a golf cart, calling, "Sandy, Sandy, you ride with me."

Millicent and Brown were in another golf cart, ready to go. If a foursome took two carts, they were also required to take along a caddy, to carry their putters and spot their balls. The lowest-ranking caddies were awarded this job.

"Oh, not him!" Millicent cried, as the caddymaster beckoned to Steve. "He's so slow. Can't we have someone else?"

"He's not that slow," Sandy said. "I take him every day."

"Oh, what do you know?" Millicent muttered.

Sandy didn't answer. She could feel the storm brewing and hoped that it wouldn't hit until they'd finished the front nine.

"Let's go . . . let's go . . ." Millicent called, as Sandy missed several shots in a row, winding up in the heavy rough. "You could use some lessons!"

"I'm just having an off day," Sandy told her. "I'm sure you've had your share of those." She wanted to smash her with a golf club.

They stopped for hard-boiled eggs and Welch's grape juice at the Halfway House, wet paper towels and draped them around their necks, and in ten minutes were on their way again. Sandy dreaded the back nine. The holes were long and tedious. She was already tired and hot. The sky was still gray and the humidity oppressive.

Just as Millicent hit her tee shot on twelve it began to thunder. They were as far as they could get from the safety of the clubhouse. An open shelter stood nearby but that didn't ease Sandy's fear. "Listen," she said, "wasn't that thunder?"

"Probably," Brown answered.

Try to stay calm, Sandy told herself. "Don't you think we should go back?"

"No," Millicent said.

But at her first sight of lightning Sandy, trying to keep her voice from breaking, said, "Look, it's going to storm. I really think we should head back now."

"One-two-three-four-five-six," Brown counted. The thunder followed. "It's at least six miles away." She teed off and landed in the sand trap to the right of the fairway. "Oh, shit!"

At the second lightning, when the thunder came after the count of three, Sandy told them, "I'm going. This could be dangerous. Anyone else joining me?"

"This is a tournament," Millicent reminded her. "You can't walk out on a tournament."

And Lee Ann said, "I'm playing too good to quit now. This might be my best round."

Brown said nothing.

So Sandy jumped into a golf cart and took off.

"Come back here, you bitch!" Millicent yelled. "You've got our clubs!"

Oh, god, the clubs! Rule Number One: *If caught on a golf course in a thunderstorm get rid of the clubs.* Sandy stopped the cart, dumped the clubs off, then remembered Rule Number Two: *Get rid of your spiked shoes.* She kicked hers off and left them with the clubs, jumped back into the cart, and floored it.

"You're going to live to regret this!" Millicent screamed across two fairways.

Sandy didn't turn around. *Hurry, hurry . . . lightning to the left . . . don't think about the storm . . . just concentrate on getting back.*

She left the cart outside the locker room door and rushed inside, shaking. But she was safe now. It was going to be all right.

The storm hit ten minutes later and the golfers followed, in groups of four, rushing into the locker room, drenched, some laughing, others, kvetching. Sandy hid in a toilet stall. She didn't want to see any of them.

Click . . . click . . . click . . . the sound of spiked shoes on the tiled bathroom floor. Millicent: "Just wait till I get my hands on that little bitch. Where is she?"

Myra: "Who?"

Millicent: "Your sister."

Myra: "I don't know. What'd she do to get you so riled up?"

Millicent: "Took off in *my* cart with *my* clubs before it even started to rain!"

Myra: "Sandy's afraid of lightning . . . always has been . . ."

Millicent: "That's no excuse!"

Steph: "Calm down, Mill, the tournament's been called anyway."

Millicent: "You can ignore this if you want to, but we'll see what the Grievance Committee has to say about it!"

Myra: Laughing. "Sandy's husband is chairman of the Grievance Committee."

Millicent: "I know!"

What shit, Sandy thought. What was she doing here? What was she trying to prove anyway? And to whom? *You need to control your own destiny,* Lisbeth had said. *Yes,* Sandy answered to herself. *Yes, I want to control my own destiny.* All her life she had let others decide what was going to happen to her. Maybe now it was time to please herself. Call her own shots. She laughed out loud, remembering the two times she had made her own decisions; to vote for Kennedy and to name her baby Jennifer. Two times in thirty-two years that her decision was not based on someone else's feelings, someone else's choice.

As soon as the sky was light again Sandy left the empty locker room, ran across the parking lot to her car, and drove home.

She took a hot bath and wrote to the children.

At three the doorbell rang.

Florenzia answered and called, "Mrs. Pressman, you got some company."

"Who is it?" Sandy asked.

"Some boy. He be riding a motorcycle."

Was he back? Was he really here, in person, ringing her doorbell? Should she call Hubanski? No, not yet. After all, she wasn't alone. Florenzia was here. He wouldn't do anything in front of Florenzia, would he? She ran downstairs and peeked out the window next to the front door. It wasn't him. It was Steve. Relief, and then, disappointment.

She opened the door. "Hi, Steve. I didn't know you had a motorcycle."

"For two years."

"What kind is it?"

"Honda . . . XL 175 . . . do you ride, Mrs. Pressman?"

"No." She laughed at the idea. "Just curious. Well, come on in." She turned to Florenzia, who was standing right behind her. "It's all right, Florenzia."

Florenzia disappeared down the hall and Steve followed Sandy into the house. "This is nice," he said.

"Thanks. It's for sale. We're moving soon, to Watchung."

"It's nice up there too." He held out a brown grocery bag. "I brought your golf shoes."

"Oh, thanks, that was very thoughtful." She took the bag and set it on the floor, under the foyer table, thinking about Norman, and how he'd carried his damp underwear out to the car, after their dates.

"And I took your clubs to the storage room and cleaned them off."

"Thanks again."

"And I just wanted to tell you that I appreciate what you said this morning when Mrs. Sommers was complaining about getting me."

"I told the truth, that's all."

"Well, thanks. It was real nice of you." He wiped his forehead with the back of his hand. "Sure is hot. Storm didn't help much."

"No."

"Could I by any chance trouble you for a drink, Mrs. Pressman?"

"Sure. Lemonade?"

"Sounds great." He followed her into the kitchen and placed his helmet on the table.

"Have you seen *The Graduate?*"

"Yes, I have."

"I've seen it three times. I really dig that Mrs. Robinson."

Sandy carried the pitcher of lemonade and two glasses to the table.

"She's older but very . . . very, uh . . ." He made circles with his hand.

"I've always liked Anne Bancroft."

She filled both glasses. He gulped his down without stopping for a breath.

"I'll tell you something, Mrs. Pressman, you're the nicest woman at The Club."

"Thanks, Steve."

"Some of the others are okay but mostly, when you get right down to it, they're a bunch of bitches, you know?"

"Yes, I know." *Okay, Mrs. Robinson, get him out of here now.*

"Mind if I have another glass of lemonade?"

"No, please, help yourself." She fingered his helmet. It was bright yellow with a tomato stenciled on one side and his name on the other.

"I designed it myself. You like it?"

"Yes, very much. I have a friend who wears a stars and stripes helmet."

"Oh, yeah, they were very big last year. The moon landing and all that, real American . . ."

"Do a lot of people still wear them?"

"Oh, yeah, a real lot. So what kind of bike does your friend ride?"

"I'm not sure. I really don't know one from the other."

"There's a couple of real good buys around now. I'm thinking of selling mine and getting a Yamaha instead."

"Oh." *Come on, Sandy, say goodbye before it's too late.* "Well, thanks for coming by, Steve . . . and for bringing my shoes . . ." She offered her hand.

He looked at it for a minute, then stood up, realizing he was expected to shake it. His fingers closed around hers. His hand was warm. "Bye, Mrs. Pressman." He looked into her eyes.

She lowered hers, walked him to the front door, closed it after him, and sighed.

18

"I STILL DON'T understand how you could have made such a mistake," Norman said. "Do you have any idea how embarrassing this is for me?" They were driving on the Massachusetts Turnpike, on their way to visiting weekend at camp.

"I've already told you, it was lightning and I was scared. I just wanted to get back to the clubhouse and I jumped into the closest cart. I never stopped to think it was Millicent's, not mine." Sandy was working on the needlepoint pillow she'd started, but somehow never finished, last summer. She cut off a snip of wool and threaded the needle again.

"Just because I'm chairman of the Grievance Committee doesn't mean I can get you off . . . it has to go before the whole committee. I wish to hell you *had* stopped to think this time."

"I don't expect you to get me off. I've told you how I feel about the whole thing and I'm sorry I've caused you so much trouble." She turned her canvas upside down and started another row.

Norman stretched his arms out against the wheel, took a deep breath, let it out, and said, "Okay, I've given it a lot of thought and I've decided maybe it's better all around if you don't play any more golf or tennis."

"I'm glad you finally see it my way."

"That doesn't mean I'm not disappointed."

"I know and I'm sorry about that too, but it's making me miserable and if you care about me at all . . ."

"If I care? Who paid for all those lessons?"

"Paying isn't caring, Norm."

"You know your trouble? Your trouble is you don't know how good you have it."

"Here we go."

"Never had to work a day in your life . . . everything handed to you on a silver platter . . . you've got no *real* trouble so you've got to go looking for it . . . inventing it . . ."

"That's not the way it is at all. I might even like to go to work." She accidentally stuck her thumb with the needle, watched the blood ooze out, then sucked on it.

"Oh, sure, doing what?"

"I don't know yet." She examined her thumb, wrapped a Kleenex around it, then went back to stitching the canvas.

"Your first duty is to make a home for me and the kids. After that, you want a little part-time job, it's fine with me."

"Norman, sometimes I get the feeling that you don't know me at all."

"And sometimes I get the same feeling about you."

"But I *want* to know you . . . I want to know your needs . . ."

"My needs are very simple. I come home from work tired. All I ask is time for a drink before dinner, a chance to read the paper in peace and quiet, some good food, and a pleasant, relaxing evening."

"Those are your needs?" She looked over at him. "Your emotional needs?"

"I told you they were very simple."

"Norman, listen to me . . . please . . . I'm scared . . . I really am . . . I don't like what's happening . . . I don't like myself . . ."

"It hasn't been easy to like you this summer."

"Okay. I admit it. Let's see a marriage counsellor as soon as we get back."

"There's nothing wrong with me. You're the one with the problem. You want to see a marriage counsellor, fine. I'll foot the bill, but don't expect me to waste my time that way."

"It only works if both partners go."

"It's not our marriage that's wrong, Sandy. It's you."

"How can you say that . . . if I'm unhappy . . ."

"Aha . . . there . . . *you're* unhappy . . . you just said it . . . but I'm not . . . I don't want to change anything . . . you're unhappy because you haven't got a life without the kids. I tried to help you develop new interests, healthy interests, but you blew it."

"Dammit, Norm, I tried."

"Not hard enough."

"I think part of the trouble is that I don't feel your love," she said.

"What do you mean, you don't *feel* it?"

"It's hard to explain. I just can't *feel* any love."

"What am I supposed to do, run around kissing you twenty-four hours a day?"

"No. But there's a lot inside me," Sandy said. "A lot you don't know about."

"Have you been reading that book again?"

"What book?"

"The one Lisbeth gave you."

"This has nothing to do with Lisbeth or books. It's me and it's you. It's us!"

"I'm a busy man, Sandy. I work my ass off for you and the kids . . . to give you everything. I don't need this aggravation. I don't have the time for it. Do *you* understand *that?* So when we get back you get yourself together. You get yourself together before the kids come home from camp." He turned off at the exit to Pittsfield. "Give me a peach, would you."

She handed him one from the bag. "It's not enough to work your ass off."

"Not enough?"

"Norm, be careful, you almost sideswiped that car."

"You want to drive?"

"No, just be careful, that's all."

"I'd like you to trade places with me for just one week . . . to let you see what my life is like . . . Christ, you have no idea . . . dealing with *ductlas* day in and day out . . ."

"You mean blacks."

"I mean *ductlas!*"

"Norm . . ."

"You've got it so fucking good, what more do you want from me?"

"Love. Understanding. Tenderness."

He pushed the button to lower his window and spat out the peach pit.

Sandy began to cry, quietly at first, then harder, louder, until she couldn't control the sobbing. Her tears fell on her needlepoint canvas. There was an ache in her throat, her head, her guts.

"Stop it," Norman told her. "That's enough. You wanted conversation, you got it. You wanted communication, you got it. But you can't take it, can you? No, because you're still a little girl. You have to have everything your way. Emotionally immature."

"I am not a little girl!"

"Ha ha ha . . . look at the baby cry . . . ha ha . . ."

"Shut up, you bastard!"

"Don't shout, little girl. I'm sitting right next to you. I can hear you just fine."

"Norman, stop the car. I think I'm going to vomit."

He pulled over quickly, the brakes screeching. "Get out . . . don't do it in here . . ."

Sandy opened the car door and threw herself to the ground, feeling faint and nauseated.

Norman remained in the driver's seat, his head turned away from her. She could see him through the open car door. Control. Control. She had to get control of herself, of the situation. Perspiration on her forehead but the nausea was passing. She was not going to be sick this time. Being sick didn't solve anything. Yes, it was passing. She felt stronger now. In a few minutes she climbed back into the car.

"Did you?" Norman asked.

"Yes," she lied.

"I can smell it."

"Really?"

"I'll pull in at the next gas station so you can wash. You know that smell is enough to make me sick." He pulled in at a Gulf station and Sandy got out to use the Ladies Room. She splashed her face with cold water, combed her hair, applied fresh lipstick, and pulled her T-shirt down inside her denim skirt. There, that was better. She fished around in her purse for a breath mint and dropped it into her mouth, then sprayed a little cologne on her neck, wrists, behind her knees.

All right. All right. It was true that Norman worked hard and provided well for her and the children. So, was she wrong to want more out of life? She wasn't sure any more. A good wife wouldn't complain. If he beat her, she could complain. If he drank, she could complain. If he ran around, she could complain. But Sandy had no *real* reason to complain. Not an acceptable reason anyway. *Nobody loves a kvetch,* Mona had said. *Remember that, Sandy . . . especially not a man who's worked hard all day.*

I'm sorry, Mother.

I'm sorry, Norman.

I'm sorry, everybody.

What happy, smiling faces they put on for the children. What a wonderful family they appeared to be for the counsellors, the camp directors, the other parents. What wonderful families they all were for each other, ignoring the rules that had been so carefully spelled out in the visiting day brochure. *Please do not bring any food into camp. All food will be confiscated. Please do not bring bunk gifts. We suggest a book or a game instead. Please do not tip our staff. Our counsellors are professionals who are paid a professional salary.*

But that didn't stop Sandy and the other mommies from arriving with carloads of fresh fruit, cookies, pretzels, sugarless bubble gum, and bunk gifts. And it didn't stop Norman and the other daddies from tipping the counsellors, to make sure that *their* children received special attention.

Norman's Nikon captured visiting day at Camp Wah-Wee-Nah-Kee. Jen, diving into the lake. Imagine that! Little Jen who used to be afraid to put her face in the water. Jen, playing third base in a lower camp softball game, at dramatics, in a rowboat. Jen, running off with her bunkmates, laughing.

At rest hour Sandy trimmed Jen's toenails and handed out bunk gifts. "Oh, Mom," Jen said, her face full of disappointment, "I told you to buy something different. You're the third mother to give out jacks."

"I'm sorry, honey, I thought jacks *were* different."

That afternoon Bucky and the other brothers from across the lake were brought over to visit. And Norman caught him showing off his mosquito bites, with a mouthful of watermelon and teasing Jen's bunkmates with a fake snake.

When it was time to say good-bye the children walked them down to the field where they had parked. All the Cadillacs and Continentals and Mercedes were neatly lined up. Sandy had never seen so many low-numbered license plates in one lot. She put on her sunglasses so the children wouldn't see her tears. They're on their way to becoming independent, she thought. Soon they won't need me at all. Maybe that was why Mona had never let her girls go away to camp.

"I'm ready for a little something," Norman said that night when they got into their beds at the motel.

"Oh, Norm . . . I'm so tired . . . and tomorrow will be just as hectic at Bucky's camp."

"It'll make you feel better. It always does."

"And I didn't bring my diaphragm. I didn't think we'd need it."

"But it's Saturday night."

"I know."

"And I'm in the mood."

"You certainly don't want to take a chance, do you?"

"No."

"Then . . ."

"I'll pull out in time . . ."

"Coitus interruptus, at our age?"

"Just this once." He pulled down her covers and lay beside her, taking her hand and cupping it around his balls. "Ready, San?"

She'd never refused him. Not once in almost twelve years. *When he's in the mood, you're in the mood.* Oh, Mother, go away. Please, please, go away!

"You're sure this is safe?" she asked, as he entered her.

"Yes."

"Because I really don't want to get pregnant."

"You won't, although another baby might be just what you need. Another baby would keep you busy, San."

"No, that's not a good enough reason to have a baby."

He came on her belly and feeling him against her like that, feeling his wetness, excited her. "Rub it into me," she said.

"Here's some Kleenex."

"No . . . I want you to rub it into me . . . all over . . ."

"Come on, San . . . don't talk like that . . . you better go wash up or you'll be all sticky in the morning."

He got out of bed and went to the bathroom. She heard the water running, then Norman, gargling. Some things never change, she thought. She masturbated, remembering the way Shep had once rubbed his cum all over her.

Norman returned to his bed, pulled the covers around his head, and said, "I know you've been tense lately, San, but I think you'll be a lot happier once we move into the new house. It's going to change your whole outlook."

"It's not the house, Norm. It's us."

"You're going to have to stop talking like that. Everything's fine between us. It's just like always except you haven't had enough to do this summer. It's just a little depression at having the kids away. As soon as they're back you'll be fine."

"It's not that easy."

"It is! We have a good life together and don't you go messing it up."

19

On Monday morning Hubanski called. "How're you doing, Mrs. Pressman?"

"Just fine. Anything new with our case?"

"I'm sorry to tell you, Mrs. Pressman, we aren't making much headway . . ."

"Well, he hasn't been around here lately."

"Lately, did you say *lately?*"

"What I meant was, I haven't seen him since . . . since the first time."

"Oh, it sounded as if . . ."

"No . . . I meant that he hasn't come back here at all."

"I see." She heard him smack his tongue against his teeth. "We'll just have to keep trying, then."

"Yes."

Sandy wondered about the man on the motorcycle, even worried about him. The last time he'd paid her a visit he'd waved to her when he'd finished his act, and she'd waved back. Maybe that was what had scared him off, her aggressiveness.

Aggressiveness. Yes. Okay. It was time. On Tuesday morning she called Shep's New York office.

"He's at the Berkeley Heights site today. He can be reached at area code 201-KL-5-5579."

"Thank you." Sandy hung up, then dialed the New Jersey number.

"Yeah, hello." It was a man, but not Shep.

"I'd like to speak to Shep Resnick, please."

"Yeah, hang on." She heard him call, "Hey, Shep, for you . . ."

And then *his* voice. "This is Shep Resnick."

Control. Control. Keep your voice steady. He can't see you . . . has no way of knowing you're shaking. Or you could just hang up. Hang up now and forget about it. No . . . no! "Shep . . . it's Sandy . . ." There. Not bad. But he didn't respond right away so she added, "Sandy Pressman . . . Sandy Schaedel . . ."

"Sandy! What a surprise."

"You said to call."

"And I meant it, but I didn't expect it."

Her turn. "I'd like to see you, Shep." An uncomfortable pause. Why didn't he say something? Answer me, dammit. "Shep, are you there?"

"I'm thinking," he said. "How about lunch. Let's say Linda's Fireside at twelve-thirty, that's by the old bridge going up to Berkeley Heights. You know where that is?"

"I've passed it, I think. I'm sure I can find it."

"Good. I'm glad you called, Sandy. See you soon."

Oh, God, she'd done it. She'd actually done it. Committed herself. Would have to face the consequences this time. But wait, she could still change her mind. Just lunch. It didn't have to be more than that.

She showered and shampooed and nicked both her legs shaving. Worse than an adolescent. She inspected herself in the full-length mirror, naked, and was shocked to find hairs on the back of her thighs. She'd never thought of shaving there before. She trimmed and polished her toenails, buffed her fingernails, douched with vinegar, and inserted her diaphragm, just in case. Oh, hell, who was she kidding? Of course they were going to make love. But she didn't have to. She would only do it if she really wanted to. She was through giving in to Norman because he was in the mood, through saying *why not* to Gordon or Vincent or whoever. From now on it was to be her choice. And her choice was Shep. Had always been Shep.

What to wear? She looked over everything in her closet and settled for a simple shirt and skirt. Casual, as if she were going to the A & P. But underneath she wore her best beige lace-trimmed bikini panties. Just like the old days. And no bra. Should she put rouge on her nipples? She'd read that some women did that. But suppose it rubbed off against him? No, better to just leave well enough alone.

She drove up ahead of time, in case she got lost. He was already there, waiting for her in his white Porsche. "Hi Shep . . ." How girlish she sounded. *Remember, Sondra Elaine, you're not seventeen any more. You're supposed to be a woman now.*

"Hi, Sandy, I phoned for a table," he said, getting out of his car and taking her arm.

"I've never been here but I've heard it's good."

"Linda makes a great veal piccata."

"I usually eat peanut butter for lunch."

"I'm not surprised." He laughed.

They went into the restaurant and were shown to their table. "So . . ." he said, after they were seated.

"So . . . did your little girl arrive from Vietnam yet?"

"No, the latest word is the end of September. There's a lot of red tape involved."

She pretended to read the menu. The waitress approached their table. "Have you folks decided?"

"Sandy?"

"I think I'll have the chef's salad." She looked over at Shep. "I'm not very hungry," she explained.

"Make it two," he said, "and a bottle of Pouilly Fouissé."

The waitress left and Sandy said, "I thought you were going to have the veal."

"Changed my mind. I'm not that hungry either."

They looked directly at each other for the first time. Sandy cleared her throat twice, felt her face grow hot, her stomach climbing into her chest cavity. Maybe Dr. Ackerman had been right, after all. "Shep . . ."

"Yes, Sandy . . ."

"I'm scared."

"About what?"

"You know . . . this . . . everything . . ."

He took her hand and held it between both of his. "It'll be all right."

She nodded.

After lunch they went out to his car. Sandy, feeling fuzzy from the wine, got in beside him and flipped her sunglasses up on her head. "Too bad you gave up your Nash." She touched the soft leather upholstery. "This one's not bad but the seat doesn't go back, does it?"

"I don't have much use for a car seat that turns into a bed these days. In fact, I haven't since the summer of . . ."

"Fifty-five, wasn't it?"

"You have a good memory."

"I haven't forgotten one minute of it." She faced him. "Kiss me."

He put his arms around her. "I will . . . I will . . . but first I want to just hold you close."

She placed her cheek against his, her hand on the back of his neck. Her fingers played with his soft, curling hair. She touched his face tenderly, then kissed him on his lips. A soft, gentle kiss, without the urgency, the passion of that night at The Club.

He kissed her back, harder now, stronger, his tongue in her mouth. She sucked on it, trying to keep a part of him inside her. "Can we go someplace?" she whispered.

"Not today. I want you to think it over first. I want you to be very sure of what you're doing."

"I'm sure. I'm sure right now and I want you so much."

"I want you too and if you feel the same way tomorrow, we'll go someplace, I promise."

Driving home, she considered the possibilities. He was too busy this afternoon. He had meetings that he couldn't possibly cancel at the last minute. He had another woman lined up for today.

He had to discuss it with Rhoda.

He wasn't attracted to her any more.

He'd become impotent since July Fourth.

Endless possibilities.

Or, the truth. He really wanted her to think it over, to be sure she knew what she was getting into.

Yes, she liked the truth best.

She found Myra waiting for her in the den when she got home. "Hi . . . Florenzia said you'd be back soon."

"Is everything all right?" Sandy asked. Myra wasn't in the habit of dropping in this way.

"Yes, sure, everyone at The Club is asking for you."

Sandy sank into the sofa, her legs tucked under her. "I've given up on golf and tennis . . . with Norman's permission."

"But San, that's so silly. Millicent's a bitch. Everyone knows that. Her complaint won't be taken seriously."

"It's not just that."

"Steph wanted you to play with her one day this week and a lot of the other girls were rearranging their schedules to include you in some games . . ."

"That's nice of them, but I'm not going back."

"That's crazy, San. I'd hoped . . ."

Sandy shook her head. "It's just not my thing."

Myra sighed. "I suppose you haven't heard the news."

"What news?"

"Barbara and Gish . . . they're splitting up . . . and I'm just sick about it . . . I was with her last night . . . it's awful . . . her kids will be back in a few weeks . . . they don't know yet."

"What happened?"

"Oh, who knows? She says Gish wanted out . . . ever since his brother died he's been different . . . afraid he's missing out . . . freedom . . . that whole number . . ."

"I knew he was a flirt, but . . ."

"Everyone knew that, including Barb, but she accepted it and look where it got her. He's keeping The Club membership . . . she can't afford to join another one. I don't know what she's going to do, how she's going to manage." Myra reached into her purse for a Kleenex and blew her nose.

"He'll have to support her and the kids, won't he?"

"Oh, sure, up to a point."

"I'm sorry to hear it but I can't say I'm surprised."

"Who can be surprised any more? It's happening all around us." They were quiet for a moment. "I have to admit, I've considered divorce myself . . . especially since I found out about Gordy's affair. I can't go to bed with him. I keep imagining him with *her,* whoever she is. I've decided not to go to the AMA convention, even though I adore San Francisco. I'm going to tennis camp instead. I need to get away by myself to think things over . . ."

"I know Gordy loves you, My. Don't turn his one mistake into a reason for divorce."

Tears came to Myra's eyes. "I really don't want a divorce. What would my life be like without Gordy? What am I without him? With him I'm a somebody, I'm a doctor's wife. Oh, I get lonely, but I fill my days with activities, keep as busy as possible." She blew her nose again, harder this time. "If I divorced him, I'd have to give up the house and move to an apartment in Fort Lee, with all the other divorcees, eat at Howard Johnson's instead of Périgord Park, get a job in a department store. My friends would invite me to dinner parties, trying to fix me up with some recently divorced man. It's all too terrible to even think about. Poor Barb, that's the kind of life she has to look forward to now. I think I'd kill myself first, I honestly do. The only way to a decent divorce is through another man, but where am I going to find another man who can give me all that Gordy can?"

"I've thought about divorce too," Sandy said, quietly, the first time she'd ever said it out loud.

"Sandy!"

"I can't help it. I'm not happy with Norman." There, she'd admitted it. It was on the record now. It was official.

"Sandy, I'm shocked, truly shocked."

"Don't be. Norman and I are very different. I'm emotional and he's . . ."

"Phlegmatic."

"Yes."

"Daddy was right."

"Yes. He was right about a lot of things."

"Do you ever wonder what kind of marriage he and Mona had?"

"Sometimes."

"I've been thinking a lot about them lately. I'm beginning to see things the way they really were."

"Daddy wanted a dog, did you know that?"

"No."

"He took me to a kennel once . . . it was our special secret . . . he picked out a puppy for me . . . for us . . . but we never got him . . ."

"He *let* her bring us up . . . he didn't have to withdraw . . ."

"He didn't like making waves."

"She would have appreciated him more if he had."

"Maybe."

"Well, no point in dwelling on the past, is there?"

"I guess not."

"Could I have a glass of juice?" Myra asked.

"Oh, sure." They went into the kitchen and Sandy poured two tall glasses of grapefruit juice.

"Thanks," Myra said, taking a long swallow. "I've signed up for a course in art appreciation this fall . . . art is going to be very big next year . . . everyone is getting into it . . . why don't you come with me . . . it's going to be fun . . . Wednesdays in new York . . . lunch . . . a tour of the galleries . . . I may even start collecting . . . and you'll need some things for the new house . . . they say art is a wise investment . . ."

"I don't know . . ."

"Keep busy, Sandy . . . when you're busy you don't have time to brood . . ."

"Life should be more than keeping busy."

"Maybe it should be, but for most of us, it's not." Myra stood up. "You know, San, you don't have a bad life with Norman . . ."

Sandy's eyes filled up and she chewed on her lower lip.

"I've got to run," Myra said, hugging Sandy. "I feel closer to you than I ever have. I hope we can keep it this way. Take care. Talk to you tomorrow . . ."

20

SHEP CALLED AT nine the next morning. "So what's the verdict, kid?"

"Guilty," she told him. "So where should I meet you?"

"You're sure?"

"I'm sure."

"Okay, twelve-thirty at the Monterey Motor Inn on Route 1, South. Park your car in the bowling alley lot next door and I'll park mine across the street in the shopping center."

"You certainly think of everything."

"I have to . . . and Sandy . . ."

"Yes?"

"I'm glad you didn't change your mind."

A few minutes later Norman called. "Four Corners made an offer."

"Who?"

"Four Corners . . . the realtors . . . they're offering thirty-seven thousand, five . . ."

"What do you think?"

"I'd like to get them up to forty."

"Did you explain about Enid?"

"I can't, how would that look?"

"I see what you mean."

"We have to do what's right for us at this point. I'll call you back when it's firm."

"I'm leaving before noon. I've got an appointment."

"What time will you be back?"

"I don't know, late this afternoon, I guess."

"Maybe we can reach an agreement before you leave."

The phone rang almost as soon as she hung up. What now? Shep, canceling?

"Mrs. Pressman."

"Yes?"

"May I fuck you today?"

"Oh, not you again!" She hung up and waited, knowing that he would call right back. He always did, at least once a week. Her friendly caller. She should have mentioned *him* to Hubanski. Maybe next time she would. Maybe there was some connection between him and the man on the motorcycle. "Go to hell!" she shouted into the phone when it rang again, before he had a chance to say anything. She slammed the receiver down. At least she'd be rid of *him* when they moved to Watchung.

She went into the bathroom, repeating yesterday's rituals, except for polishing her toenails. They still looked fine. She looked for her diaphragm but couldn't find it. It wasn't in its blue plastic case or any of the bathroom drawers. Damn! Then she remembered and laughed with relief. She'd forgotten to remove it yesterday afternoon. She washed it out and inserted it again.

Norman called back at ten-thirty. "Thirty-eight thousand seven hundred and fifty is as high as they'll go."

"What'd you say?"

"I told them I'd have to think it over."

"Enid won't like it."

"Enid won't know."

"I'll bet she finds out."

"Look, I think we should take it, San. It's the only decent offer we've had."

"Okay, whatever you decide is fine with me."

"I'll call him and get right back to you."

She sat on her bed and waited. When the phone rang she picked it up immediately. "Yes, hello?"

"It's a deal," Norman said. "We sign the papers tonight at six-thirty, our house. And after, we'll go out to celebrate."

"With Four Corners?"

"No. Just us."

There was a knock at Sandy's bedroom door. "Mrs. Pressman . . . that's me, Florenzia . . ."

"Yes, Florenzia?" Sandy opened her door.

"So many telephones today . . . everything is all right?"

"Yes, fine."

"I no like when so many telephones."

"I know and there shouldn't be any more for a while."

"Good, because my ears be ringing. It be making me very *nervous*. I no can clean with so many telephones."

"Yes, well, I'm sorry. It should be quiet now." Florenzia was right. Sandy spent too much of her life on the phone, dealing with trivia.

She drove to the motel and parked in the bowling alley lot, as instructed. Shep was waiting for her, sitting on the steps, a wicker basket at his feet.

"I brought a picnic lunch," he said.

"You really do think of everything."

"I try."

They walked over to the motel. "We're in Room twenty-eight," Shep told her. "Mr. and Mrs. Shepherd."

They smiled at each other, Shep took the key out of his pocket, unlocked the door, and they stepped inside. "Hmm . . . let's see . . ." he said, setting the wicker basket on the bureau top. He moved a table and two chairs out of the way, making room on the floor for their picnic. He spread out the checkered tablecloth and unpacked the basket. Cold chicken, potato salad, and a chilled bottle of champagne.

"Beautiful!" Sandy said.

"You're not bad yourself, kid." He pulled a small tape recorder out of the basket. "For you." He handed it to her. "Turn it on."

She turned the switch. Nat Cole was singing "Blue Velvet."

"Shep, you remember everything . . ."

He reached for the champagne. Taylor's Brut. *Uncle Bennett and Cousin Tish. Sandy and Norman's wedding night. A champagne bath. Oh, shit . . . don't think . . . don't . . . you'll spoil it . . .*

It popped when he uncorked it and dribbled down the front of him, wetting his shirt and pants. They both laughed. He poured them each a glassful and raised his in a toast. "To us!"

She clinked glasses with him. "To us!"

He offered her a chicken leg.

"I'm not sure I can swallow," she said. "I'm too . . ."

"I know. That's why we're having lunch, first, to relax you."

"I'd feel better if you kissed me," she said.

"All right, but just one."

"Just one. I promise."

He leaned across the picnic cloth and kissed her lightly. "No more now. First you have to eat."

She nodded, kicked off her sandals, and attacked her lunch.

When they'd finished, Shep wrapped everything up in the cloth and stuffed it back in the basket. "Now," he said. "Now I'm going to love you." He pushed her gently to the floor and kissed her. The tape recorder was playing *Here I go again . . . I hear the trumpets blow again . . . all aglow again . . . taking a chance on love . . .*

She held him to her, inhaling him, tasting him, her hands in his hair, her mouth open to his. He unbuttoned her shirt, slowly, watching her, then kissed her breasts, sucked on her nipples, slipped off his own shirt so that he could rub his chest against her nakedness. "Please, Shep . . . please . . ." she begged.

"Not yet . . . not yet . . ." he said, lifting her onto the bed. He unzipped her skirt and slid it off, then got out of his denim pants and jockey shorts. She looked down at him. How ready he was. How stiff and beautiful. She told him so.

He laughed and said, "I've put on some weight."

"I don't mind." She reached for his penis and held it in her hand, tracing his swollen tip with two fingers. A silky mushroom. She squeezed him and felt a drop of his liquid, exciting herself even more.

Now he moaned softly, pulled down her panties, kissed her belly, her inner thighs, licked his way back up to her breasts, to her face. He kissed her lips and she buried her tongue in his mouth.

"I love you," she told him. "I've always loved you!"

"You didn't come," he said, after.

"I know . . . I couldn't . . . I was too excited."

"Too excited to come?"

"Yes."

He laughed. "That's a new one."

"I'll come next time," she told him.

"I hope so," he said. "I'd hate to think I've lost my touch."

Next time was in half an hour and she came three times, which pleased him. "Soup, main course, and dessert," she said without thinking. Then she blushed. How could she play Norman's game with Shep?

"Tomorrow, Sandy?" Shep asked as they soaped each other in the shower.

"Yes."

"How about a five-course meal?"

"Maybe, but I'm not always that hungry."

"Don't eat any breakfast."

"I always have breakfast. Rice Krispies and toast."

"Always?"

"Well, sometimes I have cornflakes."

"I'm glad you haven't changed, kid."

"I'm glad you haven't either."

21

THAT NIGHT SHE and Norman signed the papers, selling their house, Enid's house, to Four Corners Realty Company, who, in turn, would almost certainly sell it to blacks.

"We hope to move by the second week in September," Norman explained to Mr. Podell, the representative from Four Corners, "and we'd appreciate it if you didn't show the house until we've gone."

"We understand your feelings on this matter," Mr. Podell said, scratching his head.

"It's not us," Norman added, hastily. "It's my mother. She and my father built this house, spent a lot of years in it . . ."

"Of course, of course." Mr. Podell examined the fingernails on the hand that had scratched his head. What did he expect to find there? "Don't worry, Mr. Pressman, we're known for our discretion at Four Corners. We'll bring our clients in after dark, on nights when you and the family are out."

Norman nodded.

"Is that legal?" Sandy asked.

Mr. Podell flushed.

"Damn right it's legal!" Norman told her.

"We'll keep an exclusive on it until you move so that we can control the prospective buyers. Then, if we still haven't sold it, we'll put it on multiple listing, but by that time you'll be comfortably settled in Watchung and I seriously doubt that we'll have to go to that. I have in mind a very successful attorney. I think this might be just what he's been looking for."

Norman and Mr. Podell shook hands, then Sandy showed Mr. Podell to the front door. "You made a wise decision," he said.

"Yes." She went back into the den, where Norman was carefully studying the ten-thousand-dollar check of deposit. The balance was due at the closing, in a few weeks.

"We're on our way to Watchung!" Norman sang, hugging her. Banushka barked, jealous of the attention Norman was showing Sandy. Norman scooped him into his arms. "You're going to like it up there, little fellow, just you wait."

"I hope he doesn't have an adjustment problem," Sandy said. "Dogs sometimes do, don't they?"

"Not our little guy. He'll be fine. How many sticks did he make today?"

"Two sticks and four wees," Sandy lied.

"That's good, I didn't see it on his chart."

"Oh, maybe I forgot to mark it."

"I wish you'd try to remember that, San. It's important for me to know how he's doing." He put Banushka down. "Well, we better get going. Lucille and Ben will be waiting."

"Lucille and Ben! I thought we were going out by ourselves."

"Ben called this afternoon, to check on our weekend game, and asked if we'd like to join him and Lucille for dinner at The Club. I accepted."

"I don't want to go there, Norm."

"You'll have to get over that, Sandy, the sooner the better. It's still *our* Club and I intend to make the most of it."

"To Watchung!" Lucille and Ben toasted. "To a happy and healthy new life there!"

"Hear . . . hear . . ." Norman raised his glass to theirs. "I'll drink to that . . ."

To us! Sandy thought. *To a new life.*

"Sandy," Ben said, "you can't be serious about quitting golf . . ."

"I'm serious."

"It doesn't take much to upset Sandy," Norman said. "She's very . . ."

"I'm emotionally immature," Sandy told them, before he'd finished. "In fact, I've only got half a brain. Right, Norm?"

Lucille and Ben looked at each other. "To each his own," Ben said, drinking.

"Isn't it terrible about Barbara and Gish?" Luscious asked.

"It's the women's lib thing," Norman said. "None of them know how good they have it . . ."

"Oh, no . . . you've got it all wrong," Sandy said, "Gish walked out . . ." But the others weren't really listening.

When they got home and into bed Norman snuggled up to her and said, "I feel like a little something."

"Well, I don't."

"What do you mean, you don't?"

"I'm tired."

"You don't have to do anything but lay there and open your legs. I'll do all the work."

"No, Norm."

"What do you mean, *no?*"

"I mean, *no!* I mean I don't *want* to."

"This is supposed to be a celebration."

"We celebrated over dinner. I drank too much. I'm feeling very gassy."

"A little something will make the gas go away."

"A little something will probably make me fart."

"Forget it," he said, rolling over.

She got a letter from Jen the next morning.

DEAR MOMMY,
Since visiting day I had a fight with Beth. She used to be my best friend. Now I hate her. She is getting everyone in my bunk to hate me. I think I should come home right away.
　　　　　　　　　　　Your poor little unhappy daughter,
　　　　　　　　　　　JENNIFER P.

Sandy shook her head. No point in calling camp this time. No point in writing about it either. By the time her letter arrived at camp bunk politics would have changed, possibly more than once. And camp would be over in less than two weeks. Jen and Bucky would be home. They'd be a family again. She'd have to start sorting out junk, deciding what to take to the new house and what to get rid of. They'd have to arrange for the movers and start packing. She'd have to shop. They'd need new linens, new kitchen dishes. Maybe she should work with a decorator. Myra did. Oh, shit, she wouldn't think about any of that now. Wouldn't think about real life. She was going to spend the afternoon with Shep. And that was all that mattered.

"Hello, kid . . . how's it going?"

They met at the Holiday Inn on Route 22, where it meets the Parkway.

"Look what I have." She showed him the sexual encyclopedia she'd bought last January, when she was still full of new New Year's resolutions.

Shep laughed. "We don't need that."

"Maybe you don't but I do. I don't have any experience."

"You don't need experience to know what feels good."

She thought about that, then dropped the book to the floor and kissed him. "You're right . . . you're always right . . . and I love you, Shep . . ."

"I love you too."

"Do you know I've never been on top?"

"You've never?"

"Never."

"You've got a lot to make up for . . ."

She wasn't sure whether she liked the sex best or the closeness following. She felt so safe sleeping in his arms, their bodies curved around each other.

"Come away with me for the weekend, Sandy."

"How can I?"

"You'll think of a way if you really want to."

"I want to . . . I want to . . . it's just that . . ."

"No excuses this time."

"What about you? What will you tell Rhoda?" There. The first time she'd said *her* name to him. She didn't want to think about Rhoda, didn't want to acknowledge her existence. She hated Rhoda, hated her for having Shep all these years, for sleeping next to him and waking up with him and having babies with him and sharing life with him. She wished Rhoda were dead. Rhoda and Norman, killed in an accident together. How easy that would make it for them. How wicked she felt for her thoughts. Rhoda was a decent person, raising four, soon to be five, kids. Who was *she* to wish her dead?

"Rho and the kids are going to the beach this weekend. We have a place down on Long Beach Island."

"Don't you go with them?"

"Usually, but there are times when I have to go looking at land."

"What'll I tell Norman?"

"That's up to you."

"Where will we go?"

"I'll think of someplace. Let's get an early start. Say, nine at Newark Airport."

She nodded and wrapped her arms around him. "There's so much time to make up for. So many years."

"I know. You were such a scared little girl then. Always thinking your mother was looking over your shoulder."

"She was."

"And now?"

"Now I don't care any more."

"I'm going to make love to you all weekend until you can't take any more."

"I can take a lot."

"We'll see who gives up first."

"I love you, Shep. I don't know how to tell you how much I love you."

"I can feel it."

On the way home she remembered that she'd left the sexual encyclopedia on the floor of the motel. Oh, so what? It didn't have her name in it. Maybe the maid would appreciate it. With Shep there was no need for how-to's. She laughed out loud, feeling giddy. Giddy with sex and adventure and love.

She could imagine what they'd say when they found out she was going to divorce Norman and marry Shep. Norman wouldn't believe her at first, wouldn't take her seriously. *What are you talking about . . . a divorce . . .*

Just that, she would tell him, I'm in love with another man and we're going to be married. It's very easy to understand if you try.

You're crazy.

No.

Emotionally immature.

Not that either.

I'll get custody of the children. You'll never see them again. You're an unfit mother and I can prove it.

You can't scare me with that crap, Norman.

All right . . . go ahead . . . get a divorce! You'll come crawling back to me in a year . . . you've never known how good you have it with me . . . now you'll find out the hard way . . . and you won't get a penny . . . I can promise you that . . . not one fucking penny from me.

I don't want a penny from you. I don't want anything from you.

Enid would phone Norman: What did I tell you? Right from the start I said she's going to bring you trouble, didn't I? So now you've got it. I warned you, Normie, but that's water over the dam . . . so now you might as well say good riddance to the whore . . . you can do better . . . I know plenty of women who would give their eyeteeth for you. She'll live to regret it, don't worry . . . she'll get her comeuppance . . . I only hope I'm still around to see it.

The children would say: What? You and Daddy are getting a divorce? That means next year at camp we can have two visiting days . . . all the kids with divorced parents get two visiting days . . . one for their mother and one for their father. Where will we live? Will we live with you or Daddy? Who wants to live with Daddy? He can't cook.

Mona: Oh my God . . . a divorce . . . how can you do this to me?

What am I going to tell people? What about the new house? What about the children? Who's going to support you? I can't afford to touch my principal, you know that. What? You're going to marry Shep Resnick? Why didn't you say so in the first place? I hear he's done very well for himself . . . in shopping centers, no less . . . I don't like the idea of divorce . . . but I'm grateful that you've found another man to take care of you. A woman shouldn't be without a man to take care of her . . . believe me, I know.

Myra would give her blessings. I told you, San, the only way to do it is to go straight to another man. And you certainly didn't waste any time. I'm proud of you. Not only that but he's rich. You've got it made. I should only be so lucky.

Yes, she could almost look forward to telling them. Telling the whole world. Special to the New York *Times*: Mrs. Mona Schaedel announces the marriage of her daughter, Sondra Elaine Schaedel Pressman, to Shepherd James Resnick. Mr. Resnick is in shopping centers and Mrs. Resnick is in love. Their six children attended them. The bride wore pale beige lace bikini panties . . .

"Norm, I'm thinking about going away for the weekend."

"What?"

"I'm thinking about going away for the weekend to visit Lisbeth in Maine. She called and invited me up today."

"You know what I think of Lisbeth."

"That doesn't matter. I'm not asking you to go with me. I know you've got games all weekend."

"I don't like the idea of it, Sandy."

"Well, I do. And I've already told her I'll be there. I'm flying to Boston in the morning and taking the bus from there. I'll be back on Monday."

"Monday? What's wrong with Sunday."

"It's a long trip, Norm, it doesn't pay to travel on Friday and come back on Sunday. I'd get too tired. You know how tired I get when I travel."

"If you're so tired, you should stay home and sit at the pool at The Club."

"I didn't say I'm tired. I said I *get* tired when I travel too much all at once. I need to get away, Norm, to think."

"The less thinking you do the better off you'll be."

"That's a new one."

"Most wives wouldn't desert their husbands over a weekend."

I will not answer that statement. I will not get into a fight over this. "Myra and Gordon are taking separate trips this week. He's going to the AMA convention in San Francisco and she's going to Amherst, to tennis camp."

"What's that got to do with us?"

"Nothing, I'm just making conversation."

"What'll I eat?"

"Come on, Norm, you're a big boy. You can eat at The Club."

"Suppose there's an emergency?"

"Then you'll take care of it."

"Leave your phone number."

"Lisbeth doesn't have a phone in Maine, but I'll call from a booth and let you know I arrived safely, okay."

"No, it's not okay, but it looks like I have no choice."

That's right. This time the choice is mine.

"You need money?"

"No, I have enough."

"What about the airline ticket?"

"I'll write a check."

"Here . . ." he said, reaching into his pocket, "take some . . ." He counted out five twenties. "You never know . . ."

She turned the money over in her hand and felt a lump come up in her throat. "Thanks, Norm . . ."

"Just be careful."

"I will."

"Who knows . . . maybe the change will do you good."

She nodded.

"But don't plan on taking off whenever you feel like it . . . because there's only so much I can tolerate . . ."

She nodded again.

When she went downstairs the next morning she found a list taped to the refrigerator.

Sandy: Before the end of next week

1. Arrange for movers
2. Arrange for painters
3. Arrange for fixtures with electrician
4. Arrange to get Banushka to the vet for shots
5. Arrange for the kids to transfer to the schools in Watchung
6. Arrange for live-in Ductla for new house

Arrangements and more arrangements. Sandy didn't know whether to laugh or to rip the list in shreds.

The phone rang just as she was about to leave the house. "Sandy, it's Myra. I've changed my mind. I'm going to San Francisco after all."

"I'm glad. I've thought you should go all along."

"Our plane leaves at noon."

"Have a wonderful time."

"I hope so. See you next week."

"Right, bye."

Sandy drove to the airport, wishing she were going away for good, never coming back to Norman or the house. But what about the children? Oh, she'd send for them. Maybe.

Sandy! What are you saying? You'd give up your children?

I don't know.

You should be punished for even thinking that!

I'm sorry! I don't know what got into me. You're right. I should be punished.

Of course she wanted the children. They needed her, didn't they?

Are you sure? At camp they . . .

Yes, but that was only for eight weeks. They knew they were coming home afterward.

They might do just as well without you.

No! I am not giving up my children. I know what he'd do to them. Make them just like him. No! The children are mine. And that's final. Shep and I will marry and I'll get custody. He can't prove I'm an unfit mother. I'm not! Well, I'm not, am I?

Would a fit mother be running off with another man for the weekend, leaving a trail of lies behind her?

One thing has nothing to do with the other. Look at Myra. She was fucking Frank Monzellini when the twins were babies.

So maybe that's what messed them up.

No, it's just a phase they're going through. It's adolescence. Ask Myra. She says they're coming out of it now. They've already lost twenty pounds at their fat camp in Southampton. So, you see, she is a fit mother and so am I!

Sandy pulled into the airport. *Long-term parking, short-term parking,* where was *weekend parking?* Why did they have to make it so confusing? Finally, she parked successfully, grabbed her bag, and locked the car. She'd better write down the section and number or she'd be looking for the car all day when she got back. *If* she got back. Suppose they flew somewhere and the plane crashed? Would Norman and Rhoda put two and two together? So what if they did? She and Shep would be dead anyway. But the children. What would Norman tell them? That Mommy ran away with another man? No, he'd never admit to that. That wouldn't do his image any good. Besides, it wasn't going to happen. Flying was safer than driving. Everyone said so. The statistics proved it. And if the plane was going to crash, it had to be on the way back so they could at least have their weekend together. Making love until she couldn't take any more. That's what he promised. Her knees felt weak just thinking about it.

Upstairs, in the terminal, she had pains in her stomach. Just nerves, she told herself. Relax, relax, don't give in to them and they'll go away.

She searched for Shep at the Eastern counter. He had said Eastern, hadn't he? So where was he? Suppose she saw someone she knew? *Hi, there . . . going away for the weekend? Me too . . . my old girlfriend . . . Maine . . . plane to Boston . . . how about you?*

Where are you, Shep?

He must be on his way. He should be here any minute, unless . . . unless . . . No! That was too terrible to think about.

Shep, lying on the street, blood pouring out of his head. Shot . . . like Kennedy? No, an automobile accident. The slick highway. Last night's rain. Ambulance attendants bending over him, shaking their heads.

"Hello, kid."

She turned around. "Shep!"

"Who were you expecting?"

"I'm just so glad to see you. I thought . . ."

"Sorry I'm late, traffic."

"It's okay now."

"Here's what I thought we should do. Take the shuttle up to Boston, rent a car and drive out to the Cape. I've found us a little cabin on the ocean."

"Sounds wonderful. And you won't believe this but I told Norman I was flying up to Boston, then taking the bus to Maine to visit my old friend, Lisbeth."

"Now you can show him your ticket and prove it."

"Yes. It's all working out for us, isn't it?"

"Did you think it wouldn't?"

"I wasn't sure."

"Have faith, Sandy."

"I'll try."

"Let's go. There's a nine-forty-five shuttle."

As they lined up to get on board Sandy noticed Mickey. Oh, shit! Was Funky here too?

She whispered to Shep. "I know that man and I think he's seen me."

"Just play it cool."

"Hey, Sandy, I thought it was you," Mickey said, approaching her. "What are you doing here?"

"I'm on my way to Maine to visit my friend for the weekend. How about you?"

"Business in Boston. Just for the day."

"Oh."

"I heard about that episode at The Club. Phyllis tells me you've stopped playing because of it."

"No, it's not that."

"Because, hell, some guy once lodged a complaint against me. I just paid my fine and forgot about it. That's what you should do."

"It's not just the complaint . . ."

"Say, why don't we sit together on the plane?"

"Do you smoke?" She knew he did.

"Yeah."

"Sorry, but I'm in *no smoking*."

"Oh, well, have a nice weekend. If you feel like hanging around in Boston for a couple of hours, I'd be happy to take you to lunch."

"That's very nice of you, Mickey, but once we land I've got to run. My bus to Maine . . ."

"Oh, yeah, I forgot about that."

"Oh, and if you happen to see Norman over the weekend tell him we were on the same plane."

"I'll do that . . ."

"Whew," Sandy said, when he'd finally left.

"You handled that very well. I'm impressed."

"I don't like lying."

"I know."

They boarded the plane and Sandy held Shep's hand tightly as they took off.

"Don't tell me you're a white-knuckle flyer," Shep said.

"Sort of."

"I should have guessed."

The flight attendant was tall, blonde, green-eyed, and overattentive, especially to Shep. At first Sandy found it funny, but by the fourth time she paraded up the aisle, pausing at their row, Sandy began to feel uncomfortable, and then slightly nauseous at the way Shep eyed her back, at the way their hands touched as she handed him his raincoat when they landed.

"Good-looking girl," Sandy said as they deplaned.

"Who?" Shep asked.

"The flight attendant."

"Really, I hadn't noticed. I only have eyes for you," he said, patting her ass.

*   *   *

The cabin smelled of mildew but it didn't matter. They threw down their things, changed into bathing suits, and raced down to the ocean's edge. The water was freezing. They only wet up to their ankles, then sunbathed, took a bath in the oldfashioned tub in the cabin, and made love. Endless hours of lovemaking, as promised, with Shep climbing on top of her each time he neared his climax, pumping her full, making her come one last time when she was sure there was nothing left in her. They slept in each other's arms, Shep more soundly than Sandy. She awakened every few minutes, kissed his face, his neck, his arms, and dozed off again.

She didn't remember to call Norman until Saturday morning at seven. "Where were you last night?" she asked. "I tried and tried . . ." She was ready with all sorts of excuses if he said he'd been home all evening, waiting for her call. *Out of order. Operator's error. Tiny village. Crossed lines.*

Norman yawned into the phone. "I was at The Club playing in the Twi-niter, then Lucille and Ben convinced me to stay for the dinner-dance." He yawned again. "I didn't get home till after one."

"No wonder I couldn't get you."

"You didn't want me to sit home all alone, did you?"

"Of course not. I'm glad you had a good time. I just wanted you to know I'm here and everything's okay."

Shep rolled over and began to kiss her breasts.

"Mickey told me he saw you on the plane."

"Yes, wasn't that a coincidence?"

"He was surprised."

"So was I."

"Well, have a good weekend."

"You too, Norm."

"See you on Monday. You'll be back before dinner, won't you?"

Shep's hand was between her legs.

"Yes, I think so."

"I hope so!"

She hung up and Shep kissed her. "I've never kissed anyone without brushing my teeth first," she told him.

"Then it's time you did," he said, sweeping the inside of her mouth with his tongue. And then Shep was on top of her but suddenly he cried out and jumped off the bed. "Jesus . . ." He paced up and down.

"What is it?" Had she done something? Hurt him in some way?

"My leg, it's my leg."

Polio? A blood clot?

"A cramp . . . God, it hurts . . ."

"Can I do something?"

"No . . ."

She waited quietly.

"It's letting up now." He came back to bed and lay down. He was covered with perspiration. She got up, went to the bathroom, and returned with a wet washcloth. She mopped off his face, pulled the covers up, held him in her arms, and watched him sleep.

When he awoke again it was nine-thirty and he reached for the phone to call Rhoda at the beach.

"Hi, honey . . . how are things . . . good . . . and the kids . . . good . . . send them my love . . . miss you too . . . take care . . . see you Monday . . . yes . . . kisses to all of you too . . ."

Sandy turned her back to him, hurt by the concern, the love, in his voice.

"Sorry, kid," he said, after he'd hung up.

"It's just that . . ."

"I know. Let's try to forget about it, okay?"

They went to breakfast at Josie's House, a beautiful, old Cape Cod, turned into a restaurant, where the tables were set with white lace paper doilies and baskets of fresh flowers. The waitresses were suntanned girls, their shiny hair tied back, their long, sleek legs exposed beneath miniskirts. Sandy wondered how Shep could want her, love her, when there were so many more beautiful girls in the world, every one of them ready to jump into bed with him. She could feel it. The way the redhead looked at him as she poured his coffee. The way the one with the brown eyes smiled at his smile. Sandy couldn't help feeling jealous, jealous of their beauty, their youth, their freedom. Yes, most of all, their freedom.

"Let's have the works," Shep said, "cereal, bacon, eggs, muffins. I'm famished. We forgot to have dinner last night."

"I know. We were too busy."

He smiled and took her hand, kissing her fingers.

"I love you, Shep. I want to live with you forever."

"I know."

"I want to wake up next to you every day."

"And I want to wake up with you in my arms, looking at your funny, sleepy face."

So what are we going to do about it? she felt like asking. But she couldn't. Not yet.

22

THE PHONE WAS ringing as Sandy unlocked the front door on Monday afternoon. "Yes, hello?"

"Sandy? It's Vincent."

"Vincent, what a surprise."

"We've been trying to get you since yesterday."

"I was away for the weekend. I just got back."

"Lisbeth's mother died. The funeral's tomorrow at ten. At Apter's."

"Oh, Vincent, I'm so sorry."

"It's a blessing, actually. She'd been going steadily downhill and at the end she didn't even recognize Lisbeth."

"I'll be there tomorrow," Sandy said, her voice cracking. "Send Lisbeth my love and my sympathy."

"Yes, I'll do that."

"And Vincent . . ."

"Yes?"

"You didn't by any chance reach Norman, did you?"

"No, there was no answer at all. Why?"

"No reason. See you tomorrow."

"Right."

Trying to get us on the phone all day yesterday, Sandy thought. Suppose Norman had answered. Then what? Then she would have had to face the consequences. Luck was with her and Shep. Somebody up there liked them. Wasn't that what Mona used to say? Yes, when she fell off her bicycle and came home with only scraped knees, Mona said, *Well, it could have been worse. Somebody up there likes you, Sandy.* And Sandy used to wonder what the somebody looked like. Was it God, himself? Was it one of his angels? Was it Moses, or Esther? What a mess it would have been if Norman had been home to take the call. Not that Sandy wasn't prepared to leave him. She was. But first she wanted to put everything in order. She had to discuss it with Shep. The sooner the better. Before something like this came up again. Before Norman could gather evidence to use against her in a custody battle. Wednesday. She would tell him on Wednesday afternoon when they met at the Country Squire Inn in Basking Ridge. She couldn't go on sleeping with Norman, playing wifey, when all she could think of was Shep and the way she loved him.

"Her mother died while you were visiting?" Norman asked that night.

"Yes."

"And they flew back but you stayed?"

"Yes, I stayed to get things in order up there."

"You stayed all alone in some godforsaken cabin in the woods?"

"Yes."

"Did you ever stop to think of what might have happened to you with no phone, no running water. Jesus!"

"Nothing happened. I'm home and I'm fine. The funeral's tomorrow morning."

"I hope you don't expect me to go."

"I don't."

"Because I'm really bogged down at the plant. August vacations and . . ."

"I said I don't expect you to go."

Lisbeth conducted the service for her mother. She read poetry, then told the small gathering of friends and relatives how her mother had always encouraged her, how she'd brought her up to believe that she could become anything she wanted. That it was her life, her only life, and the decisions were hers to make. "I'll always be grateful to the wonderful woman who was my mother. And I'll remember the happy times we had together. I know she'd want you to remember those times too."

Miranda, every bit as poised and lovely as Lisbeth had said, spoke next. "My grandma took care of me when I was a baby. She loved me even when I was bad. She let me sit on the kitchen counter while she baked. She gave me dough to play with and laughed when it got stuck in my hair. And as I got older, I still loved to go to stay with her. She was old-fashioned in lots of ways, but not in loving. She really knew how to love. And I'm going to miss her a lot." Miranda put a pink rose on the closed coffin. "Good-bye, Grandma. I miss you already."

Sandy's tears were confused. They were not only for Lisbeth and Miranda and Mrs. Rabinowitz, but for herself. For her life, her only life, and the decisions she had never made.

After, Sandy kissed Lisbeth's cheek. "I'm so sorry."

"I know."

"It was a beautiful service."

Lisbeth nodded. "Come to the house after the cemetery. I want to talk to you."

"Okay."

Mrs. Rabinowitz's neighbors had set up a feast. Such a delectable spread of goodies that Sandy could have sworn she was at a catered affair, maybe even at The Club. Cheeses, breads, vegetables, salads, white fish, herring, homebaked cookies and cakes. She could never understand why people felt so hungry after funerals but she knew it was true. She remembered it from her own father's funeral and from Samuel D. Pressman's. She remembered it from when she was small and wasn't permitted to go to family funerals. They always came home from the cemetery starving and Sandy wondered what they did there to get themselves that hungry. Now she knew. A celebration of life, through death.

Sandy and Lisbeth went upstairs, after lunch, to Lisbeth's old bedroom, which was exactly as she had left it sixteen years ago to go off to Barnard. They sat on the bed together the way they had when they were teens; Lisbeth propped up against the pillows, Sandy, hugging her knees to her chest.

"Vincent said you were away for the weekend."

"I was."

"Without Norman, I gather?"

"Yes."

"Well, tell me all about it."

"I went to Cape Cod, with a man, but Norman thinks I was with you, in Maine. That I was there when the call came through about your mother. I've turned into an incredible liar. I hate myself for it."

"Don't worry, I'll cover for you any time. So who is he?"

Sandy hesitated.

"Come on, San . . . this is me, Zelda, remember?"

"Zelda?"

"I've been thinking about changing it back. Did you know my mother named me for F. Scott Fitzgerald's wife?"

"No."

"I just found out myself. Supposedly I was named for my great-grandmother, but when my mother realized she was dying she told me the truth. So who is he and do you love him or is it just a fling?"

"I love him. It's not a fling."

"How long have you been seeing him?"

"Just a week, but it seems like months . . . years . . ."

Lisbeth shook her head. "It's serious, isn't it?"

"Very."

"You know something, Vincent and I have given up our Thursday nights off. We've decided it's just too risky. And to tell you the truth, it was getting boring. I love Vincent. I don't *need* anyone else and he feels the same way. It's as if we've discovered each other all over again. Ever since my mother got sick, he's been just wonderful. I've fallen in love with him, Sandy, like a schoolgirl."

"I'm glad for you." *Thank you, Vincent . . . thank you for not telling her about us . . .*

"I've often wondered why you've stayed with Norman this long."

"It takes guts to get out."

"Sandy, did you hear what I said at the funeral? You can't wait around for your next life. This *is* your life. It's very short, very precious. Don't waste it."

Sandy cried. Lisbeth put her arms around her and said, "It'll be all right."

On her way home Sandy stopped to pick up some cold cuts for supper. She and Norman ate early, then he took Banushka for a walk while she cleaned up the kitchen. The doorbell rang before she had finished. She wiped her hands on her pants and went to the front door. It was a man she had never seen before. "Yes?"

"Mrs. Pressman?"

Sandy nodded.

"I'm Mr. Martinez. Is Mr. Pressman in?"

"He'll be back any minute. He's walking the dog."

"I'll wait in my car, then."

"Is it about the house?"

"The house? No, it's a private matter."

"I see." She double-locked the door, and watched from the front window. What kind of private matter? Someone from the Anti-Defamation League? Someone who found out they'd sold to a realtor instead of a black? Now they'd really be in for it. She'd warned Norman. He should have listened. Could he be sent to jail for not selling directly to a black family? How many years? Five . . . ten? Could she divorce him if he was in prison? She saw Norman approaching with Banushka. Mr. Martinez got out of his car. Norman seemed angry. Martinez held up a portfolio and shook it at him. Both men walked up to the house. Sandy ran to the front door and unlocked it. "Hi," she said to Norman.

"Sandy, this is Mr. Martinez. Martinez, my wife, Sandy."

"Yes, we've already met," Sandy said.

Martinez followed Norman into the house. "I'll be right with you," Norman told him. He ushered Sandy into the kitchen.

"What's going on?" she asked.

"Myra came to me weeks ago, suspecting Gordon of having an affair. She asked me to help her. I hired Martinez. He's a private detective."

"Oh, no."

"When you told me Gordon was going to San Francisco and Myra was going to tennis camp, I put Martinez onto it."

"Oh, no."

"He's got the goods on him now. Photos and everything."

"But, Norm . . ."

"Let's go have a look."

"Caught him red-handed," Martinez said. "In the act. Wait till you see these." He tapped his portfolio.

"Go ahead," Norman told him.

"In front of the little woman?"

"It's her sister we're trying to help."

"If you say so." He untied the portfolio and spread out the evidence on the dining room table. Six 8x10 black and white glossies of Gordon and Myra. Two of them showing the happy couple fucking in the missionary position, two showing them sucking, one, making it from the rear.

"Jesus Christ!" Norman said, holding up a picture.

"I tried to tell you," Sandy said.

"Pretty good, huh?" Martinez asked. "Really professional."

"This is my sister-in-law, you idiot!" Norman said, holding the picture under Martinez's nose.

"What?"

"His wife! This is his wife!"

"This woman is his wife?" Martinez asked.

"Yes. I showed you pictures of her, didn't I?"

"Yes, but I thought . . ."

"Never mind what you thought. You're off the job. Fired! Give me the negatives and get the hell out of here."

"But my expenses . . ."

"I'll pay your goddamned expenses but not one penny more. Now, give me the negatives."

Martinez reached into his portfolio and dropped the negatives on the table. Then he hightailed it out of the house.

"Stupid goddamned fool!" Norman muttered.

"I can't believe you hired a detective."

"Your sister came to me crying. What was I supposed to do?"

"I don't know. You could have discussed it with me."

"With you? If she had wanted you to know, she would have gone to you in the first place."

"She did. She told me all about it."

"She told you?"

"Yes, I advised her to think it over carefully. Not to do anything foolish . . ."

"Wait till I tell Hubanski about this guy."

"Hubanski! What's he got to do with it?"

"I called him, asking him to recommend someone. I'm not in the habit of hiring private detectives, you know."

"And Hubanski recommended Martinez?"

"Yes, they used to work together. Did you know your sister was going to San Francisco?"

"Yes, she called me right before I left on Friday morning. I didn't think it was that important. I didn't know you were having Gordon tailed."

Norman picked up one of the pictures. "Myra looks great, doesn't she? And who would have thought Gordon had it in him? You just never know . . ."

I know, Sandy thought.

Norman made a fire and burned the pictures and negatives.

Later, he wanted a little something. Sandy knew he would. He was excited by the pictures of Gordon and Myra. So was she. But she couldn't do it with Norman. Couldn't be unfaithful to Shep. So she said, "I'm very tired . . . the funeral . . . and now, this . . ."

"Come on, Sandy."

"No, not tonight, Norm."

"What is this shit? You've been away all weekend and now it's *no, not tonight, Norm.*" His imitation of her came out sounding like Enid.

"I just don't want to."

"It's your marital duty."

"Oh, shut up. What do you know about marital duty?"

"There's only so much I can take, Sandy. You're pushing me to my limits."

"Go to sleep."

"Bitch!"

She met Shep the next afternoon. "I've missed you," she said. "So much has happened in only two days."

"And I've missed you."

They made love, then talked. Sandy told him about Mrs. Rabinowitz, how Lisbeth and Vincent had been trying to reach her all weekend, how Norman would have found out something was wrong if he had been home to answer. She told him about Myra and Gordon and the detective, and then about refusing Norman last night, and his anger.

"I couldn't make it with Rhoda either. Told her I thought I was coming down with a bug."

"Shep, we've got to do something. I can't go on like this." *So tell me that you're leaving Rhoda tomorrow . . . that you're going to marry me . . .*

"I know, I've been giving it a lot of thought. I just didn't think it would come up this soon. I thought we'd have six months, maybe a year, before this happened."

"I love you, Shep. I'm ready to leave Norman now."

"I know you are."

Then say it . . . say it . . . "We'll be happy together."

He held her in his arms, brushing the hair away from her face.

"I want to spend the rest of my life with you," she told him, kissing his neck, then his face. *Please tell me you feel the same.*

"I wish it were possible, kid."

She looked up at him. "It is. It has to be."

"I can't leave Rhoda and the kids. Not now."

She shook her head and felt her throat tighten. "But you love me."

"Yes."

"Then?"

"I love her too."

Sandy panicked and wriggled away from him.

"Try to understand," he said.

"Understand?"

"Rho and I have shared a lot. Come a long way together."

"Now you tell me!"

"Sandy, this has been the best week of my life. I mean it."

"Stop it. Just stop it, will you."

"I don't want to let you go." He reached for her but she wouldn't let him touch her. She couldn't think. Couldn't get beyond the tears, beyond the hurt and humiliation. She had been so sure.

"We could arrange something," Shep said. "Get a little place . . . see each other twice a week . . ."

"I hate arrangements!" she cried. "I can't live that way."

"It's a lot to ask, I know," he said, "and I don't want to push you, but a lot of people do live that way, Sandy, and it works."

"Don't tell me what works. I'm not a lot of people."

Shep sighed. "I warned you, didn't I? I warned you to think it over carefully."

"And I did. I did."

"No, you never thought about the ending."

"I didn't know there had to be one." She knew how ugly she looked when she cried. How her face contorted. But she couldn't stop. "I thought we were going to get married and live together happily ever after. What a little girl I am. What a silly, stupid little girl . . . with little girl dreams!"

"Sandy, Sandy." He stood behind her and put his arms around her. "I'm so sorry."

"Don't be," she told him, trying to control herself. "It's my fault. I should have known. What did I expect in just a week?" *Just a week . . . but it seems like months . . . years . . . my whole life . . .*

"If you don't love Norman, leave him. I'll help all I can—money, a job, a place to live."

"No! I'm not going to live a lie."

"At least let me be your friend. I can help make the transition period easier for you."

Her friend. Yes, she wanted him as her friend, but she wanted him as her lover, as her husband too. "I had it all figured out. Don't you see, I had everything figured out."

"Leave him. You'll be better off. Find yourself, kid."
"I don't know where to look."

She'd never felt such despair, such hopelessness. Nothing mattered now. Life was over because life had become Shep. Crying didn't help any more. The empty feeling inside her remained. The love of her life and her passport to freedom, all gone, down the drain together. What now, Sandy? What now? She thought about getting sick. A high fever. A raging virulent infection. Oxygen tanks. Intensive care. The critical list. Shep would rush to her bedside, blaming himself. *No!* That wouldn't solve anything. No more illnesses. No more fantasies. Divorce Norman anyway? And then what?

Myra would say: Sandy, are you crazy? You want to live on Kentucky Fried Chicken and pizza? Work in Bloomingdale's and get varicose veins? Come home exhausted to nasty children who blame you for messing up their lives? Think! The only way to a decent divorce is through another man. So get busy and find one if you're so unhappy. Never mind Shep. It's not practical for you to go on loving him.

Mona would catch her breath: Sandy! A divorce? I can't believe it. Don't do this to me. Don't do it to the children. Don't do it to yourself. You have a good life with Norman. So what if you don't love him the way a schoolgirl loves her boyfriend? Love changes as you grow older. Accept him for what he is. You're lucky. A lot of women would give their . . .

Yes, Mother, I know, their eyeteeth for a man like Norman.

Exactly.

She would tell the children: Daddy and I are getting a divorce. We're not going to have much money from now on.

Then we'll live with Daddy. He's got plenty.

But you belong with me. Don't you want to live with me?

Not in some crummy apartment, Bucky would answer. We want to live in the new house.

Why doesn't Daddy get an apartment? Jen would ask. And we'll live in the new house with you.

Because I can't afford it. And besides, I wouldn't be happy there without Daddy.

Then why are you getting a divorce? they'd say together.

Bitch, Norman would cry. Goddamned bitch!

And so, what was left? What were her choices now?

I keep the gun locked in this cabinet and the key to the cabinet is in the bookcase, behind *Bartlett's Quotations.*

Sandy went downstairs, to the den, unlocked the cabinet and looked at the gun. *A way out. The end.* She touched it. How cold it was. She lifted it and pressed it against the side of her head, feeling dizzy. She pictured her brains splattered all over Norman's desk, all over the Mark Cross desk set she'd given him on their tenth anniversary. Better do it someplace else. The bathroom? Yes, it would be easier to clean up the mess in there. Mr. Clean, Windex, Ajax—that should do the job. Would she hear the explosion as she pulled the trigger? Had Jack heard it? She remembered the blood and gore on Jackie's pink suit and looked down at her robe, her Mother's Day robe. The children might take that personally. Maybe she should change first. No, the undertaker would get rid of the robe. Or did he send his customers' clothes out to be cleaned and pressed so that he could return them to the bereaved family? She didn't know. She'd have to ask Norman about that. But if she pulled the trigger now she wouldn't be able to ask him. She would die without knowing whether or not he got business from the local morticians. Oh, so what! Besides, you don't always die, she reminded herself. If you miss, you could wind up a vegetable. She'd read about a man who'd missed. He'd blown off half his face but they'd managed to save him so that he could lie in a nursing home, a blob, a nothing, the rest of his life. Would their insurance cover the cost of a nursing home or would Norman leave her to rot in some public institution? No. How would that look to the family, their friends? No, she'd have a private room somewhere, plenty of fresh flowers, and every Sunday after tennis Norman would drag the kids to see her. *That ugly thing isn't Mommy,* Jen would cry, pointing. *Yes, it is, you dummy!* Bucky would tell her. *It's Mommy with her brains blown out.*

You know, Luscious would announce at the Labor Day Dance, *she had only half a brain to start with. She told me herself the last time we had dinner together.*

Sandy laughed out loud at that one. Oh, what the hell . . . she didn't know how to load it anyway and with her luck she'd probably blow off a foot. As she put the gun back she noticed an envelope inside the cabinet. Funny, she hadn't seen it before. The warranty? The instruction manual? She opened it. How strange. A canceled check, dated November 19, 1969, made out to Brenda Partington Yvelenski for five thousand dollars. What was this all about? Who was Brenda Partington Yvelenski? November 19, 1969—the week Sandy had been so sick. The week Dr. Ackerman had stood at the foot of her bed, listing possibilities. Thoracic cancer . . . leprosy . . . leukemia . . . lupus . . .

Who was this Brenda Partington Yvelenski to whom Norman was writing a substantial check while she lay upstairs, desperately ill? Unless . . . unless she was a faith healer and Norman had been so frightened at the idea of her impending death he had actually contacted a mystic, called Brenda Partington Yvelenski, who agreed to pray for her swift return to health for the meager sum of five thousand dollars. But Norman didn't believe in the spiritual. He didn't even believe in Bar Mitzvahs. Still, as a last resort? No, that's crazy! Then what else? Then why hide the check?

Blackmail. No, for what? A homosexual, Norman? Come on, not Norman! Okay, so the wife is always the last to know but . . .

A hooker. A specialist in black leather boots, chains, whips because he's too ashamed to tell her what really turns him on. A year's supply at once, three times a week. No. Not likely.

A landlord. He's rented a small apartment from Brenda Partington Yvelenski. A place to rendezvous with . . . Who? Luscious . . . Brown . . . Funky . . . all three at once? Myra, to get even with her for fucking Gordon? The twins . . . for kicks? Her mother? No. Absolutely not! He didn't have the time for anything like that. Okay, so they can always make time, but Norm wouldn't give up his golf or tennis or holding his breath under water just to get laid, would he?

A shrink? Yes, could be. He's finally realized he's got problems and has decided to deal with them. Dr. Brenda Partington Yvelenski, Shrink. Except that Norman didn't believe in shrinks. Besides, he would have made out the check to *Dr.* Yvelenski, in that case . . . tax deductions and so forth.

She put the check back in the envelope, the envelope back in the cabinet, relocked it and put the key in its place, behind *Bartlett's Quotations,* then went to Norman's desk. She took out the check register and thumbed through it. November . . . November . . . yes, here it was. Number 402, Nov. 19, Brenda Partington Yvelenski: Investment.

She's a broker? Then why hide the check? What sort of invest-ment? Black Angus cattle, like Gordon and his friends? An adult gift shop on the highway, sex aids and porno books? Worse yet, the cleaning stores are a front? Norman's mixed up with the mob . . . bookies, pimps . . . Jesus, you think you know someone and then . . .

She'd ask him tonight. She'd say, *Norman, who is Brenda Partington Yvelenski?*

And he'd say, *Why do you ask?*

And she'd say, *Because you gave her five thousand dollars.*

And he'd say, *How do you know that?*

And she'd say, *Because this afternoon, as I was about to kill myself, I found the canceled check in the gun cabinet.*

And he'd say, *You have one hell of a nerve reading my canceled checks!*

She gave Norman a little something that night. He patted her shoulder and said, "Glad you're feeling better, San."

"Do you ever say what you mean?" she asked.

"Does anybody?" he answered.

WHEN IT DIDN'T matter any more it began to rain. It rained for two days, a heavy, steady downpour, sure to flood the second hole and close the golf course, which, a few weeks earlier, would have delighted Sandy. On the first day she stayed in bed and slept, glad that Florenzia was taking the week off to drive to South Carolina with her family. She dreamt that the man on the motorcycle was really a woman called Brenda Partington Yvelenski and that Norman had hired her to drive Sandy insane.

On the second day Sandy realized that sleeping wasn't the answer either. So she got up, dressed in old jeans and a torn shirt, tied a bandana around her head, and decided to keep busy. She would tackle the attic first.

As a child Sandy was terrified of the attic in her house, imagining all sorts of creatures up there, just waiting to do her in.

She still wasn't completely comfortable in the attic, although this one was well lit. Even so, the man on the motorcycle could be hiding up there, could have walked right in while she was out with Banushka, and as she reached the top of the stairs he would be waiting . . .

For what?

Rape . . . murder . . .

No, he's gentle . . . shy . . .

You call tossing his thing around that way gentle? He's probably violent. He'll probably strangle you first, then stab you, then . . .

Oh, grow up, Sandy!

She carried the radio up with her, turned on all the lights, and began to rummage through cartons filled with the accumulated junk of twelve years of married life, not to mention the cartons she and Norman had brought to the marriage. One was stuffed with her crinoline petticoats. She used to wear as many as five at a time to make sure that her skirt was fuller than anyone else's. How important that had been at the time. Five crinolines at once; horsehair, taffeta, net; under her felt skirt, her quilted skirt, her Lanz dresses. She'd been saving her crinolines for Jen, sure that one day she would be invited to a Fifties Party, just as Sandy had attended a series of Roaring Twenties parties when she was a teenager, dressed in Mona's flapper outfits, ropes of beads around her neck, a velvet headband across her forehead.

Somehow, saving her crinolines for Jen to wear to a party seemed foolish now. She would get rid of them. Well, most of them anyway. No harm in saving one or two.

She opened a carton marked "Sandy's School Box." She'd get rid of everything except her high school yearbook. Bucky and Jen would have a good laugh over that someday. And her Five Year Diary, with its faded blue cover, frayed at the edges. She had started it as a sophomore in high school.

She opened it to the last entry.

Dear Darling Diary,
I am utterly, hopelessly in love with N. I am so much more mature now than I was last year when I thought I loved S. R. With S. R. it was all sex, sex, sex! Now, in my maturity I know that sex isn't everything. It certainly isn't love. N and I have so much in common. We want the same things out of life. I will wear his ZBT pin forever . . .

Utterly, hopelessly in love.

Had she really felt that way about Norman? Or had she just wanted to be so in love? She couldn't remember any more. She remembered loving Shep. But would it have worked out any better with him? Probably not.

Sandy, what are you saying?

The truth, for once . . . it wouldn't have worked . . . not twelve years ago and not now . . .

Sandy, I can't believe this.

Marriage to him would have meant a life very much like the one I lead with Norman.

No!

Yes, a house in the suburbs, kids, car pools.

But Sandy, what about sex?

Okay, so it would have been better but after a while, even with him, it would probably have become routine.

Routine? You sit there and call such great sex routine?

Okay . . . okay . . . so it was good, very good . . . but God, the jealousy, the mistrust, the lies . . . it wouldn't be worth it . . .

You don't think he'd have given up other women for you?

Maybe . . . I don't know . . .

You don't think he runs around because it's not good with her . . . with Rhoda?

Okay . . . so it's a nice idea . . . that he'd have loved me so much he wouldn't have needed anyone else . . . a nice idea but you'll pardon me for not believing it . . . I know him too well . . . on the airplane . . . in the restaurant . . . I think he'd be out with girls regularly, not to mention older women . . .

Older women too?

Look at me. I'm thirty-two, for God's sake.

No, already!

Yes, already.

That's hard to believe . . . to me you're still a girl . . .

To me too . . . but I don't want to be a girl any more . . . I want to be a woman . . .

So be one.

How?

How, she asks . . . I should know?

Hmph!

One more question.

Go ahead.

If he should call now . . . if he should say he's changed his mind . . . he wants to spend the rest of his life with you and only you . . . what then?

The truth?

The truth.

I'd probably run to him.

24

HER VAGINAL ITCH returned. She was scratching in her sleep again, waking up raw. She went back to Gordon's office and he ran some tests. His nurse called her two days later. "Mrs. Pressman?"

"Yes."

"Dr. Lefferts would like to see you tomorrow morning at nine."

"Why, is something wrong?"

"Doctor wants to discuss some test results with you."

Oh, God! Cancer. Her punishment. Her comeuppance. How long did she have? Six months? A year?

"Mrs. Pressman, can you make it?"

"What? Oh, yes, I'll be there."

"Sandy," Gordon said, from across his walnut desk, as he tapped his fingers together, "you have gonorrhea."

"What?"

"Gonorrhea."

"Oh, my God! I can't . . . I mean . . . how . . . who . . ."

"You're not allergic to penicillin, are you?"

"No, but Gordy . . ."

"The nurse will give you the medication before you leave. You have to take it here, then wait for twenty minutes."

"Gordy, for Christ's sake, stop talking like my doctor."

"What can I say, Sandy? That I'm surprised? All right, frankly, I am, but we've been running routine gonorrhea cultures on all our sexually active patients for the last year and you'd be amazed at how many cases we've detected in that time. And by the way, your itch has nothing to do with this."

"Could I have gotten it from you, Gordy?"

"No. Not unless I got it from Myra."

"I don't think she's been with anyone lately."

"Lately, what do you mean by that?" he asked, leaning forward.

"Nothing. I think she'd have told me if she was having an affair."

"But you said *lately*. As if you knew about something."

"No. That's not what I meant at all." Oh, Sandy, you fool. First with Hubanski and now with Gordon. *Think . . . think before you speak, Sandy!* Mona had warned when she was a child.

"I haven't been with anyone but Myra," Gordon was saying, "except for that night with you."

"And I hadn't been with anyone else but Norman."

"Well, if you didn't contract it from me, then it must have been from Norman."

"I just don't know."

"Have there been others since we were together?"

She nodded. "Two . . . but mainly one . . . but I doubt that I got it from him. The other is more like it."

"I don't follow you."

"It's complicated."

Gordon rested his elbows on his desk top and tapped his fingers together again. "In a situation like this it's pointless to try to figure out who's to blame. It's a circle. The important thing is for everyone involved to be notified and treated. I'll need the names of all of your sexual partners, Sandy . . ."

"Oh, Gordy, do we have to go through that?"

"It's the law."

Sandy hesitated. "I'd rather tell them myself. Couldn't you please let me do that?"

"You'll really tell them?"

"Yes. I promise . . . right away . . . today . . ."

"Well, I guess in this case I could make an exception."

"Thank you, Gordon."

"You're welcome, Sandy, and I want you to know that everything we discussed today is strictly confidential."

"Yes, I know."

She could still taste the penicillin mixture when she got home. Vile pink liquid. The nurse had stood over her saying, "Bottoms up, that's a good girl." And yet, something about it was funny. Funny because she'd been convinced it was cancer. And it wasn't. Who'd have thought of gonorrhea? Another exotic illness to add to her list. But a lot easier to cure than cancer. Still, which one would make Norman more angry? Cancer, probably, because that was long-term and would mess up his life. With gonorrhea you drank the gloopy pink stuff and life went on. But he'd never forgive her. Never. He'd kick her out. Unless he got it first. Unless he gave it to her. But if not, she'd fight back. Fight for the children. She'd make the judge understand that he drove her to it.

"Hello, Vincent . . . it's Sandy . . . Sandy Pressman . . . yes, fine . . . Vincent, I need to talk with you . . . it's very important . . . back to Maine? . . . no, I didn't know that . . . well, I need to talk with you *privately* . . . no, no . . . before Labor Day . . . now? . . . over the phone? . . . are you sure? . . . can I really talk freely? . . . I mean, no one's listening? . . . all right . . . Vincent, I have gonorrhea . . . the doctor just told me . . . of course I'm sure . . . and Vincent, I think it's likely that I got it from you . . . I know you didn't come but that doesn't mean you don't have it . . . how do I know where you got it? . . . all those Thursday nights of yours, probably . . . yes, Lisbeth is a possibility too . . . you should both be checked out and treated . . . and don't wait . . . you don't necessarily have to have symptoms . . . please believe me, Vincent . . . I didn't have any symptoms either . . . yes . . . yes, I will . . . you too . . ."

How she wished that Shep wasn't involved. That she didn't have to phone him now.

"Hello, Shep . . . it's Sandy . . . Shep, I need to see you . . . it's very important . . . no, not a motel . . . just a place to talk . . . oh, I don't know . . . anyplace . . . how about the Ice Cream Factory in Summit . . . fine . . . see you there at two . . ."

"A black and white soda," Sandy told the waitress.

"And a hot fudge sundae with coffee ice cream and nuts, no whipped cream," Shep said. "So how are you, Sandy?"

"Not good."

"What is it?"

"A lot of things, but mostly it's that I've just found out that I have gonorrhea." In the booth behind them four small children were jumping up and down singing, "I scream, you scream, we all scream for ice cream!"

"You have gonorrhea?" he asked.

"Yes, I saw the doctor this morning. I'm as surprised as you, Shep. I didn't have any symptoms."

"Where did you get it?"

"I don't know, possibly from you."

"Where would I have gotten it?"

Sandy didn't say anything. She just picked apart the paper napkin in front of her.

"Rhoda . . . you think I got it from Rhoda?"

Sandy shrugged.

"No, I'd bet my life on it."

"Someone else then."

"I haven't been with anyone else for at least six months."

Six months. Twice a year. Was that how he worked it?

"Six months is a long time," he said. "I'd have known by now. What about Norman? You might have picked it up from him."

"I've thought about that." Had it never occurred to him that she might have been with someone else?

The waitress served them their ice cream.

"Jesus . . . gonorrhea . . . I've never . . . even in Europe . . ."

"I'm sorry, Shep. I wish I could make it go away."

"It's not your fault, I know that." He patted her hand. "I'm just trying to figure out what to do, what to say."

"You've got to go to the doctor. He'll tell you what to do."

"Yeah, I guess, but Rhoda, she's going to hit the roof!"

"Will she leave you?"

"I hope not." He spread his hands out on the table and looked down at them. She loved his hands, rugged yet tender, nails clipped short, a spray of black hairs below each knuckle, a callus on each palm. She shuddered, remembering the way he'd caressed her. She wanted to feel his hands on her again. She had to fold her own hands in her lap to keep from reaching out, to keep from placing her hand on his.

"Look, Sandy . . ." he said, quietly, "this isn't your way of getting us back together, is it?"

He might as well have punched her in the gut. "You think I'm lying . . . that I'd make up . . ."

"I don't know what to think."

"I should have let the doctor tell you." She started to cry, fished in her bag for a Kleenex, and when she couldn't find one, used the paper napkin instead. "How could you possibly think that I would ever stoop to . . ." She blew her nose. *Remember, Sandy, a high fever . . . a raging virulent infection . . . oxygen . . . intensive care . . . okay, so I thought about it but I didn't do it . . . there is a difference . . .*

"I'm sorry," he said, "I had to be sure." He leaned over and kissed her cheek. "Thanks for telling me yourself, kid."

She nodded.

"Let's get out of here."

"Anything wrong with your ice cream?" the waitress asked as they got up.

"No, everything's fine," Shep told her.

"But you didn't eat it."

"Some other time." Shep pressed a dollar bill into the waitress's hand and Sandy could have sworn that as he did, he let his fingers brush against her breast.

Outside, before Sandy got into her car, Shep put his hands on her shoulders and looked down at her face. "I'll always love you. Think you can remember that?"

"I'll try."

"And if you ever need me . . ."

*　　*　　*

She drove home, changed her clothes, and rushed upstairs, to the attic. What to do now? Find another man? Make the best of it, like Myra? Keep busy? Yes, she'd always kept busy. First school, then marriage, then children. Busy busy busy. Until this summer. Had not being busy enough led to this . . . this strange Sandy? She attacked the cartons, tossing things into piles. She would give away all the baby clothes and the toys the children had tired of and everything she hadn't worn in two years or more. She would combine "Norman's Tufts Box" with "Sandy's School Box," saving just a few items to share with the kids someday.

Dammit! How come Lisbeth didn't get gonorrhea on her Thursday nights? Or Myra with her plumber? *Norman, I've got gonorrhea.* That's how she would say it. Simple and to the point. *And while we're at it, who is Brenda Partington Yvelenski?*

She ripped open the "Tufts" box. It was stuffed with Playbills and programs and menus. *Menus.* Who saved menus? She opened a few of them. Jesus! He'd circled what he'd had to eat. She tossed them into the trash box. Look at that, his old sweatshirt. *Pressman, '56.* She shook it out and held it up, examining it carefully. Wash it and give it to Bucky? No, throw it out, along with his track shoes, still caked with mud, and his baseball cap. He'd probably forgotten all about them by now. Besides, he expected her to sort out his junk. Junk was her job. She pulled out a tiny needlepoint pillow she'd made for him one Valentine's Day, their initials worked into a heart. She sniffed it. Musty.

She dug back into the carton and this time came up with his fraternity caricature, showing a crew-cutted Norman, all big eyes and furry brows, wearing a white lab coat. The caption read: *Dr. Frankenstein, I presume?* Why Dr. Frankenstein? Had he set out to create a monster? Had he succeeded? Was she it?

Oh, shit! She'd forgotten to pick up the barbecued chicken she'd ordered at the deli. She left the contents of the "Tufts Box" scattered on the attic floor and ran downstairs. Banushka barked, then whined, straining to get off his run when he saw her. "Okay, I'll take you with me if you promise to be a good boy." She opened all the windows in the Buick. Banushka was less likely to get car sick if he rode with his head hanging out, the wind in his face.

She drove to South Avenue, to Larry's Delicatessen, where, in addition to the chicken, she picked up a pound of cole slaw, a double portion of noodle pudding, two baked apples, and a slice of bologna for Banushka which she would give to him when they got home. No use looking for trouble. And as long as she'd brought him with her she might as well take a chance and drop in at the vet's since his office was just down the street. With a little luck she'd be able to get #4 on Norman's list out of the way now.

Sandy was surprised that there were only two other cars and a motorcycle in the spacious lot adjoining the animal hospital. Ordinarily it was packed. She parked and carried Banushka into the new brown brick building. On the side, next to the glass doors, chrome letters in satin finish spelled out *Leonard E. Krann, DVM Practice limited to Canines and Felines.* She entered the building and gave the receptionist a breezy hello, as if she didn't know coming in without an appointment was against the rules.

"Yes?" the receptionist said, giving Sandy an icy stare.

"I've brought my dog for his shots."

"Do you have an appointment?"

"No . . . but . . ."

"Without an appointment . . ." she began.

Sandy didn't wait for her to finish. "But, you see, we're moving soon and we really have to."

The receptionist shook her head and flipped through her appointment book. "We could see your dog on September twenty-fourth at one-thirty."

"But I'm here now and it makes sense. Banushka gets car sick and . . ."

Dr. Krann passed by. "Hello, Sandy."

"Hello, Dr. Krann." Funny that he called her *Sandy* while she called him *Doctor,* even though she knew Emily, his sallow-faced wife, from Giulio's and from the A&P, where they'd chat at the meat counter on Thursday mornings, even though she'd heard that the Kranns had applied for membership to The Club. "I was just passing by and hoped you could squeeze Banushka in for his shots because we're moving soon."

"You're moving?" He sounded concerned.

"Yes, to Watchung."

"Oh," he laughed. "I was afraid you meant *away.*"

Did he really care that much? Did one dog more or less make such a difference? "No, but with all there is to do . . ."

"Sure, I understand. I'll be with you in just a minute."

"But doctor," his receptionist protested, "we were going to leave early today."

"You go ahead, Virginia, I'll take care of this myself."

"That's very kind of you," Sandy said.

"My pleasure. Bring Banushka into the back room. I'll be with you as soon as I finish up out here."

Sandy found Dr. Krann, slim, boyish, and usually quite shy, very attractive. At first she'd been bothered by his left eye, which wandered, and she'd had trouble looking directly at him. But now, having learned to concentrate on his right eye, she was at ease with him. She carried Banushka, who was already tense and shaking, into an examining room and sat down, holding him on her lap. "Poor little fellow." She stroked his soft fur and talked to him reassuringly. "It's all right. Soon your ordeal will be over for another year and when we get home I have something yummy for you." Banushka looked up at her, cocking his head to one side.

"Well, here we are." Dr. Krann walked into the room, washed up at the sink in the corner, dried his hands with a paper towel, and approached the examining table.

Sandy hated to set Banushka down on that cold slab of metal. Dr. Krann smiled at her. Sandy smiled back. "Nice dog," he said.

"Yes." *You'd never guess from my seemingly calm exterior that I'm in big trouble, would you, Dr. Krann? That I have to go home and tell my husband that I have gonorrhea?*

"Could you hold him still, Sandy."

"Oh, sure." Sandy had to look the other way as Dr. Krann prepared Banushka's injections. She'd never been able to look when the kids were getting their baby shots either. But the pediatrician had had a nurse to hold them still.

"There we go, that wasn't so bad, was it?" Dr. Krann asked Banushka.

Sandy let out a deep breath. The palms of her hands were covered with sweat.

"Have you had a nice summer?" Dr. Krann asked.

"Yes, how about you?"

"Emily and I were in Europe for two weeks. We just got back."

"Oh, that must have been exciting. I've always wanted to go."

"It's something everyone should do once. There's a lot of history there."

"So I've heard. Well, thanks very much," Sandy said, opening her purse. She pulled out her checkbook. "How much do I owe you?"

"Twenty-eight."

He held Banushka as she wrote out the check. Not only was she sweating but her hands were shaking too. She felt a lump in her throat and thought for a minute that she might start crying. *Hang on . . . hang on . . .* "I really appreciate this," she said, trying to keep her voice from breaking. "And next time I'll phone ahead for an appointment."

"Are you all right?" he asked, his right eye looking directly at her, his left jumping from the wall to the door and back again.

"Yes, of course, why?"

"Nothing . . ."

"I'm just not a very good doggie nurse."

"If you wait a minute, I'll grab my helmet and walk you to your car."

"That's not necessary . . ."

"It's okay. I'm finished for the day." He returned, carrying a stars and stripes helmet. No! Sandy thought. Not Leonard Krann, DVM, with a practice limited to Canines and Felines, with a wife who has problem hair, with two small screaming, snot-nosed children. Not Lenny Krann, future Club Member. No!

He saw her to her car, jumped on his motorcycle, revved up the motor, and took off, waving to her as he did.

My God! Could it be?

No! Steve had told her stars and stripes helmets were very big last year. The moon landing and all that.

Still . . .

25

SHE HAD THE table set and the food attractively arranged on a platter when Norman came home. "You didn't cook again?" he asked.

"I was very busy and it was so hot."

"Carry-out food two nights in a row?"

"Last night I wasn't feeling well. Besides, what's the difference?"

"I counted on pot roast tonight. I'd really like to get back on schedule, Sandy."

"All right, as soon as the kids come home I'll try. I did take Banushka to the vet though."

"What did he say?"

"He said Banushka is a beautiful dog . . . very strong and healthy . . . he could be a show dog he's so perfect . . ."

"Really?"

"Not exactly in those words."

"Well, at least you managed to accomplish one thing today."

"Yes, at least I did."

She waited until after dinner, until they were both seated in the den, Norman reading the paper, Sandy with her needlepoint spread out on her lap, the TV tuned in to some variety show, a summer replacement, before saying what she had to say. "Norm, I'd like to talk to you."

"Go ahead."

"Will you put down the paper, please, this is important . . ."

"I can read and listen at the same time."

"Norman, I've got gonorrhea."

"Uh huh . . ." He turned the page.

She raised her voice. "I said I've got gonorrhea!"

"What are you talking about?" Now he put the paper down and looked across the room at her.

"I'm talking about gonorrhea . . . the clap . . . you must have read about it in one of your *AMA Journals*."

"I know all about gonorrhea."

"Well, I'm telling you that I've got it."

"You've got gonorrhea?"

"Yes!"

"Says who?"

"Says Gordon, who the hell do you think?"

"It must be a mistake. They must have switched slides or something."

"No!"

"Sandy, if this is your idea of a joke."

"Would I joke about something this serious?"

"Where would you have gotten gonorrhea?"

"From you." Liar, liar, from Vincent X. Moseley, most likely, if Shep was telling the truth and if Rhoda doesn't play around and if Gordon really hasn't been with anyone else and if Myra hasn't lately and if *you* didn't.

"The hell you did! I haven't been with another woman since before I met you."

"How about a man? You can get it from them too."

"Are you calling me a fag?"

"I'm just stating the facts." *Almost.*

"If you've got gonorrhea, you got it from somebody else," he said, raising *his* voice as her words sank in.

"And I say that *you* got it from somebody else and gave it to me." Better to accuse than admit.

He stood up and paced the floor, smashing his right fist into his left palm. "I can prove that I haven't been with anyone."

"How, how can you prove that?"

He turned abruptly and pointed at her. On the TV screen John Davidson was singing to a woman named Loretta. "One of us is lying and I know it's not me! Not that I haven't had the chance. Just last weekend when you were away . . ."

"Last weekend, well, I'd certainly like to hear about that."

"Not one, but two, get it, two women at The Club propositioned me." He waggled two fingers in her face.

"Who . . . who were they?"

"You'll never know. I didn't take them up on it because I consider marriage a contract, not like you, you fucking bitch! I should have known. You've probably been screwing around for years."

"And what about you? You and Brenda Partington Yvelenski!"

He turned white. "What do you know about her?"

"Plenty."

"How did you find out?"

"That doesn't matter."

"It matters to me."

The audience was applauding, John Davidson was smiling his beautiful, dimpled smile.

"You've been in my Tufts box?"

"Yes." What did that have to do with it?

"What right did you have to go into my Tufts box?" The TV camera cut to an Alka-Seltzer commercial.

"I was sorting out your junk. And what right did you have to give her five thousand dollars without discussing it with me?"

"You never missed it."

"That's not the point."

"I suppose you read the letters?"

What letters?

"Answer me!"

She just looked at him.

"Answer me, I said!"

"Yes, the answer is yes." *But not to that question.*

"Then you know all there is to know." He walked across the room and switched off the TV.

I don't know anything, she wanted to say but she was already in too deep to back off.

"So you know that I couldn't have given you gonorrhea . . . so that leaves you . . . so who was it, Sandy . . . who'd you spread your legs for?"

She didn't answer.

"Tell me," he shouted, lifting her out of the chair by the shoulders. "Tell me, you bitch!" he said, shaking her. He was losing control now. She couldn't remember ever having seen Norman out of control. She found his anger frightening, but at the same time exciting. Exciting because she was the cause of it.

"Cunt!" He smacked her across the face, catching the corner of her mouth. Her hand automatically went to the place, holding it, trying to ease the pain. She tasted blood. "Who was it?"

"It doesn't matter," she said, as tears came to her eyes.

"Aha! So you admit it, you've been screwing around."

"Yes, I admit it! I've been with somebody else."

"I ought to beat the shit out of you."

"You touch me again and you'll live to regret it."

"Who was he?"

"I don't have to tell you. I don't have to tell you anything." She turned and ran, ran upstairs, and then upstairs again, to the attic, locking the door behind her.

Norman followed, yelling, "Goddamned whore. Goddamned fucking whore." And when he reached the door to the attic and found it locked, he kicked it, shouting, "Come out of there! Come out right now!"

"Go away," Sandy hollered. "Go away and leave me alone!" She heard Norman clomp back down the stairs. And then it was quiet. What was he doing? Would he get the gun, shoot the lock off the attic door, then shoot her? Or himself? Or both of them? *Murder-Suicide*

Local Businessman Shoots Wife, Self

Norman Pressman, owner of Pressman's Dry Cleaning Stores, shot and killed his wife, Sondra Schaedel Pressman, last night, before taking his own life. Friends and relatives described Mr. Pressman as a quiet man. "In fact, phlegmatic," said Mrs. Pressman's sister, Myra Lefferts, of Short

Hills, the owner of a showplace with eight and one-half baths.

One of them was supposed to leave. Sandy knew that. She'd read enough books, seen enough movies. She could hear Myra advising her. Pack your bags and come over here. We'll call a good lawyer, the best in the state. We'll take the bastard for everything!

But Myra, the children. What am I going to do about them? They'll be back soon.

For the time being you'll stay with me. Then we'll help you find a place of your own and you'll start a new life. Nobody has to take what you just took. Forget what I told you two weeks ago. Get out now!

But I want to end the marriage on my own terms, when I'm ready.

If you're not ready after this, then you'll never be ready and you deserve what you get.

Are you saying I'm a masochist?

I'm saying you're a meshugunah!

She thought she heard the front door slam. She ran to the window and looked down. There was Norman, walking Banushka, as if it were just any other night. She went to the "Tufts Box," her heart beating so loud she could hear it.

She turned the box upside down, dumping the rest of its contents all over the floor. Tiny color slides spilled out of dozens of Kodak boxes. She swallowed hard, then sifted through four years of junk until she found the packet of letters, eight of them, all in blue envelopes, addressed to Norman at the Plainfield plant, in purple ink. The return address read B.P.Y. Newburyport, Massachusetts. She checked the postmarks. Yes, they were in order, beginning in October, 1969, not even a year ago, and going through May, 1970. She turned them over in her hand. Did she even want to know?

Yes.

Yes, she certainly did!

October 18

Dear Norman,

So many years have gone by since we last saw each other yet I feel sure that you will remember me as I remember you. I made a lot of mistakes, Norman, and I know how deeply I must have hurt you. I don't expect you to forgive me or to understand. I loved you, not Stash. How can I explain? Let me try. I guess what happened was that I saw my life with you and I got scared. You had everything so well thought out and I didn't want to think about the future at all. I wanted to live only for the moment. So I rebelled and ran away with Stash, who didn't have a thought in his head. Does any of this make sense to you? I hope so.

Stash and I had three children in four years. He made some money in the used car business but then gambled it away. I finally left him, two years ago, and went to California. I worked as a waitress most of the time. Stash has never sent a penny to me or the kids. I've heard that he's in New Mexico now, involved in some land deal. But I'm not complaining. I've never been one to complain, as you know.

I came back east six months ago and am hoping to open a small restaurant in Newburyport. Remember the weekend we spent here? I guess that's why I've always wanted to come back. That weekend with you was the happiest of my life. But enough looking back. You can't look back, can you? You have to go forward. And that's what I'm trying to do, with a little help from my friends. To be blunt, I'm asking you for a loan of up to $5000. I will pay you back with interest, of course, I hope within two years. Less if things go well.

On a more personal note, what happened to us, Norman? You were going to be a great biologist and save the world. Instead you clean people's clothes. (You see, I've kept up with you!) Not that I am knocking your chosen profession. I certainly haven't accomplished what I set out to do either. Now, instead of becoming a great actress or writer, I am happy if I can manage to feed my family. But please do not feel sorry for me. I am strong and determined. At least I haven't changed that way.

With love and affection always,
Brenda Partington Yvelenski

My God! Was she writing about Norman, *her* Norman? A great biologist? Saving the world? When? How? By the time Sandy had met him he was a senior business major. He'd never even mentioned biology to her.

November 9

Dear Norman,

Thank you for your kind letter. I can understand that you want more information before committing yourself to an investment in my restaurant. It will be small, serving only 20–30 at a time. It is located on the main street, next to the bank. I plan to decorate with butcher block tables, wicker chairs, local artists' work, and plenty of plants. We will have a limited menu. (Remember how we used to save menus, circling what we'd had to eat?) I am a fine cook and my children are wonderful, willing helpers. I hope to hire two or three waiters. We won't have a liquor license at first, but customers will be encouraged to bring their own wine.

Norman, on a more personal note, I'm glad you're happily married and enjoying your two children. I'm sure Sandy is exactly the wife you always wanted. Even during that long, cold winter when we loved so intensely I had my doubts about us. You were already so sure of what you wanted out of life and I wanted, needed, to be free. Strange how things work out.

With love and the happiest of memories,
Brenda

Exactly the wife he'd always wanted? Not lately, Brenda!

November 24

Dear Norman,

Thanks so much for your letter and check. The $5000 is more than appreciated. My parents have come through as well and are lending me $2000 and my cousin, Irene, who married a stockbroker in Spokane, is lending me $2500, as is my brother, Rog, who is a butcher in Providence. Now I can go to the bank and make all the arrangements. I hope to open by Valentine's Day which I think will be a fitting holiday considering all the love that has gone into this project, not the least of all, yours.

On a more personal note, thank you for the picture of Sandy and the children. They look just right for you. I wish you had included a picture of yourself, as well. Norman, if it matters at all, please know that I have never loved anyone the way I loved you. And please know that I will always love you and if ever things aren't going well with you . . . I hope you know what I am trying to say.

With all my love and gratitude,
Bren

The love of her life? Norman? God, had Brenda been the love of *his* life too? Had he married *her* the way she had married him? For safety . . . for comfort . . . for convenience. Were she and Norman really alike after all?

December 16

A CHRISTMAS WISH TO YOU AND YOURS
A NEW YEAR FULL OF BRIGHTNESS
Brenda Partington Yvelenski

Andrew, Robin, and Yvette

All of this was printed on a color photo, showing three beautiful children and Brenda herself, a chunky woman of about thirty-five with a pretty, round face, framed by long dark hair. Beneath the photo she had added,

Thinking of you on this day . . . Remembering the holiday season we spent together. Was it really so long ago? It seems like yesterday to me.

Love always
B

January 5

Dear Norman,

I am going to be in New York on the 12th to shop for supplies for the restaurant. You can't beat the wholesalers prices there. I hope I can see you then. I want so much to thank you in person. I'll be at the H.J. Motor Lodge in mid-Manhattan. Please call me.

My love and devotion,
Bren

Had he gone? January 12, they'd been back from Jamaica ten days. Norman was still tan, thanks to his new sunlamp, and he had no herpes on his lips. Jesus, if he'd gone . . . if he'd . . .

January 18

Dearest Norman,

It was just wonderful seeing you again. You are every bit as attractive as you were way back when. I enjoyed our lunch so much. I only wish it could have been more. You know what I mean. Yes, I can understand your feelings about Sandy and I think it is admirable of you to choose to remain faithful to her. I certainly have no desire to break up your happy marriage. I guess I just wanted to renew our relationship on a "special occasions" basis. However, I will respect your wishes and will not contact you again except to let you know where to reach me. I am already on a crash diet and plan to lose 25 pounds before summer.

Much love, always
Brenda

Admirable intentions. How like Norman. Maybe if he had let go this time, given in to his emotions just once, she could have told him about Shep. Maybe then he would have understood and they could have worked things out together.

Sandy, you're supposed to feel proud that he cares so much he wouldn't you-know-what with another woman . . .

Maybe, but I'd rather know he's human . . .

Sandy, I can't believe this. Any other woman would get down on her knees and kiss the ground he walks on.

So sue me . . .

February 9

Announcing the opening of Brenda's Bistro
Main Street
Newburyport, Mass.

Serving dinner from six to nine
Reservations, please

Brenda Partington Yvelenski, Owner/Chef
(With a little help from her friends)

And finally . . .

May 10

Dear Norman,

I've been so busy I haven't had a chance to write. Business at the Bistro is excellent and we are looking forward to summer, our heaviest tourist season. Also, I have met a very nice man, Ken Sweeney, who has a house here. He is semi-retired, with business ties in Boston. He is slightly older (61) but we really enjoy each other's company. I am enclosing a check in the amount of $2750. I plan to pay off your loan by November. Again, thanks so much for your help, your support, your confidence in me. I will never forget you.

Affectionately,
Bren

How easy it should be to hate this overconfident, independent woman! How easy to hate this Brenda, who wanted to renew her relationship with Norman on a "special occasions" basis.

Sandy, you sound jealous.

I'm pissed, not jealous.

You could have fooled me!

Oh, yes, she wanted to hate Brenda Partington Yvelenski. But it wasn't so easy after all. Brenda sounded too decent, too human, and more love poured out of her letters than Sandy and Norman had shared in twelve years of marriage. That hurt more than anything else. She had a sudden desire to call Brenda, to ask her what Norman had *really* been like way back then. Because she could see now that there must have been another Norman. A Norman who dreamed of becoming a biologist . . . of saving the world. A Norman who loved intensely. Could that Norman still be locked inside the Norman she knew, just as another Sandy was inside her, struggling to get out?

Her Norman had opted for his parents' way of life . . . was becoming his father just as she was following in Mona's footsteps. Oh, God, do we all turn into our parents in the end?

Norman was banging on the attic door again, calling, "Sandy, come down, come to bed."

"Just leave me alone."

"You can't stay up there all night. Come down. I won't hurt you, I promise."

"Go away!"

"Sandy, please . . ."

"No!"

Sandy turned out all but one of the attic lights and crawled into Bucky's Snoopy sleeping bag. She slept fitfully, thinking about this man who was her husband. This man whom she hardly knew.

26

IN THE MORNING Norman was gone. To work? To his lawyer's office? To Reno? She didn't know. She checked his closet. All of his things were in order. She ran a hot tub, looking at herself in the mirror for the first time since last night's main event. Her lip was swollen. She should have put ice on it then. Now it was too late. She sank into the tub, trying to soak away the pain.

What was she supposed to do about her life?

Where were the rules when you needed them?

Norman came home from work carrying a pizza. A peace offering? "I didn't think you'd want to cook tonight."

Absolutely right.

"And I didn't think you'd feel like going out either."

Right again.

"I went to the doctor this afternoon. He had to massage my prostate to get a culture. You have no idea how uncomfortable it is for a male to have his prostate massaged."

Try having a baby some day.

"He didn't see any sign of gonorrhea but given the circumstances felt I should take the medication anyway . . . just in case . . . to be safe. I'll turn on the oven." He studied the knobs. "Which one—bake, broil, preheat, or time-bake?"

She almost laughed. "Bake, three-fifty."

"You don't look bad."

Thanks very much.

He shoved the pizza into the oven, closed the door, and, still facing it, said, "I've thought it over carefully and I've decided to let you stay. There's no point in messing up the kids' lives. I assume that you've learned your lesson and that it won't happen again." He paused. "Say something, will you?"

"I don't know if I want to stay," she said. "I don't know what our lives will be like if I do."

"I don't know either and I don't know if I'll ever be able to trust you again . . ."

She stood up. "Well, then . . ." She started to walk toward the door.

"Sandy . . . wait . . . don't go . . . please . . ." he said, turning away from the oven at last. "I need you . . . and I'm willing to try . . . I'll make every effort to trust you . . . if you promise . . ."

How like Bucky he seemed now. How like a little boy. Did he really need her or was he just saying it?

"And I'm willing to get a double bed for the new house."

"A double bed?" Now she could see how scared he really was. Scared that she'd actually leave him. For the first time in years she wanted to put her arms around him. To comfort him.

"Yes. You've always wanted one, haven't you?"

"But Norm, you . . ."

"I said I'm willing to try and I'm sorry if I hurt you last night." He looked at the floor, not at her. "But you have to remember that you hurt me first."

Okay. She could understand that. Could try to, anyway. "You should have told me about Brenda. I read her letters last night."

"Reread them, you mean."

"No, I read them for the first time."

"But you said . . ."

She shook her head. "I found the canceled check . . . that's how I knew."

"What were you doing in the gun cabinet?"

"Dusting."

"Come on, Sandy."

"All right . . . I was thinking about shooting myself."

"Because of the gonorrhea?"

"Because of us . . . me, you . . . I don't know . . ."

"Sandy, what would that have solved?"

"For me, everything, but, as you can see, I decided against it."

He let out a deep sigh. "I don't know what you want from me, San. You once said *love*. Well, I love you. I love you the only way I know how. I'm sorry if it's not enough for you." His voice caught.

She began to cry, softly. "Can we make it work? Can we, Norm?"

"I don't know. I think if you'll be reasonable this time, we can. I think if you stop thinking, stop questioning everything, and just settle back and relax, we can. If you accept me the way I am, yes. Otherwise, I just don't know, but I find the idea of divorce repulsive."

Divorce.

"Tomorrow's our anniversary. You don't throw twelve years of your life away just like that," he said, snapping his fingers. "I think we should turn over a new leaf. Maybe I shouldn't have pushed you so hard this summer. Maybe I should have let you sit home alone day after day. I thought I was doing what was best for you. I've always tried to do what's best for you."

That's news to me.

"So what do you say, San?" he asked, nuzzling her.

"The pizza's burning."

27

"HAPPY ANNIVERSARY!"

Myra had arranged a family dinner at The Club to help them celebrate. Twelve years. Sandy looked around the table as they toasted her and Norman, thinking, *What am I doing here?*

Myra sat opposite Sandy in faded bluejeans, a T-shirt, and a sleek new haircut, her San Francisco look. "And Sandy," she'd said earlier, when they'd gone to the Ladies Room by themselves, "Gordy and I smoked our first grass out there. Everyone at the convention had it and it was great. I'm telling you, we've never enjoyed each other so much . . ."

I know, Sandy wanted to say, *I saw pictures.*

Gordon sat next to Myra. He looked slightly embarrassed. From the intimate details of *her* life, Sandy wondered, or his own?

Connie sat next to Gordon, and Kate, next to her, each of them twenty-five pounds lighter, with an adorable new nose and acting *vivacious,* just like their mother. The wonders of plastic surgery!

Mona, next to Sandy.

Enid, next to Norm.

Myra was saying, "And Gordy and I flew to Aspen on our way back from San Francisco and we bought a fabulous condominium and we're all going to learn to ski next winter."

"Wonderful," Norman said. "I've always wanted to ski."

Not you, Sandy thought. Them.

"Let's hope nobody breaks a leg," Mona said.

"Oh, Grandma, you always think the worst about everything!"

"Somebody has to."

"And . . ." Myra went on, "that's not all. We're thinking of going into boating next summer. We've been looking at yachts all week. They're so cute. Just like little houses, with three bedrooms and two baths and double ovens. What size are we looking at, Gordy, fifty feet?"

"Something like that."

"We're thinking about boating out to the Hamptons or up to the Cape . . . and did you hear that Gordy's taking a partner next month so he won't have to work so hard . . . and we're going to have more time together . . ." She leaned over and kissed him. Gordon blushed. "And you're all invited on our yacht next summer."

"Thank you, but I prefer land," Enid said.

"Yes, we hear you're going to Florida," Gordon said to her.

"Maybe. My son thinks I should retire." Enid gave Norman a martyred look. "But I don't know."

"You've worked hard for a long time, Mom," Norman said.

"Oh, I'm sure you'll love it there, Mrs. Pressman," Myra said. "Gordy's parents have been there for years and they're very happy."

"It's full of old people," Enid said, "waiting to die."

"No, that's not so at all," Myra told her. "There are a lot of retired people but they're not necessarily old."

"And who knows," Mona said, "maybe you'll meet a nice man."

"I don't see you with one," Enid shot back.

"But I'm not in Florida," Mona said, winking at Sandy, letting her know that she and Morris Minster were still going strong.

Enid turned to Mona. "Never mind Florida . . . I suppose you hear they sold the house to a realtor . . . practically gave it away . . . and the railing on the stairway alone is worth a small fortune . . . imported . . . I tell you, Mona . . . it's one disappointment after the other . . ."

"Be happy they're well, that's what counts."

Enid sighed. "Who's to say? If I had it to do over again I would do it a lot differently, I'll tell you that."

"So who wouldn't?" Mona asked.

Yes, Sandy thought. Who wouldn't? I might be sharing my anniversary dinners with Shep, and Norman might be sharing his with Brenda, no matter what our parents had to say about it. No . . . wait . . . that's unfair . . . I can't go on blaming Mona forever . . . I'm the one who married Norman . . . nobody held a knife to my throat . . . stop thinking, Sandy . . . it hurts too much to think . . .

"Sandy, you're not touching your food," Mona said.

"Who can blame her?" Enid asked. "You should only try cutting this drek they call roast beef, and cold soup just like last time."

"What happened to your mouth, Aunt Sandy?" Kate said. "It looks swollen."

"Another herpes, San?" Myra asked.

"No, it's . . ." She had applied her makeup carefully, hoping that no one would notice.

"We didn't want you to know," Norman said, "but Sandy had a little accident two days ago. She fell down the stairs."

Very good, Norman. Very imaginative.

"Sandy, sweetheart!" Mona looked concerned.

"I didn't fall down the whole flight," she told them, trying to laugh it off. "Just the bottom three. I tripped."

"You went to the doctor?" Mona asked.

"Yes, of course."

"You're sure you're all right?"

"Yes. Fine." She caught Gordon looking at her, skeptically, and repeated, "I'm fine, really."

Enid offered an after-dinner toast. "May the next thirteen years be just as happy."

"Twelve," Sandy said.

"So be happy an extra year."

"How about a little something for our anniversary, San?"

"You already gave me a gold bracelet."

"But you haven't given me anything yet."

"I didn't know what to get."

"I'll settle for a little something. Remember our wedding night, San?"

"Very well."

"And our honeymoon?"

"Uh huh."

"We were really hot stuff then, weren't we?"

"I guess."

He rolled on top of her. "Got your diaphragm in?"

"No."

"I'll get it for you." He padded off to the bathroom and returned with the blue plastic case.

"Norman, why didn't you ever tell me you wanted to be a biologist?"

"I was just a kid then. By the time I'd met you I'd changed my mind . . ."

"I wish you'd told me anyway . . . about that and about Brenda . . ."

"It was a long time ago."

"You must have been very hurt when she ran off."

"I don't want to talk about it."

"Sometimes you have to talk about things even if they do hurt."

"Look, there was no way I was going to marry Brenda."

"Why not?"

"Because she was too . . . too . . ."

"Too what?"

"Too different."

"Because she was a shiksa?"

"She was a shiksa, she was a townie, and if you want to know the truth, I sent her the five thousand dollars because I've always felt guilty."

"She's the one who ran off."

"And when she did I was relieved. I knew I'd never marry her."

"But you loved her."

"What's love, anyway?"

"It's a feeling."

"I told you, I was a kid then. None of it matters now."

"What was it like when you saw her in New York?"

"I didn't sleep with her. You already know that."

"But you wanted to?"

"I thought about it."

"Maybe you should have."

"Maybe."

"Norman, why did you marry me?"

"Why does anybody get married?"

"I'm asking you."

"Because you were the right girl for me, the girl I wanted to spend the rest of my life with."

"And now?"

"I like things the way they are. That is, the way they were, until recently."

"We don't really know each other, Norm. Doesn't that scare you?"

"Sometimes."

"We should get to know each other better."

"How?"

"I'm not sure. I think we have to get to know ourselves, first."

"Okay."

"Okay, what?"

"I'm ready for you, San." He ran his hand down her body.

She inserted her diaphragm.

She came twice.

Well, why not? Who was it helping when she didn't come? Not Norman. Not herself. Not the marriage.

After, instead of rolling into his own bed he stayed close to her and asked, "Was it good with the other guy?"

"It was okay."

"So who was he, San?"

"You don't know him."

"Was it *as* good with him?"

"Different."

"You always come twice with me."

"Yes."

"Did you with him?"

"No." *How about a five-course meal, kid?*

"I want you to know that I understand why it happened," he said and she could feel his relief. "I really do. You married me when you were just a girl. You'd never slept with anyone else and you were curious. I guess I'm glad you got it out of your system now so long as it never happens again. Because that would be the end. I couldn't tolerate it happening again."

"Norm . . ." She took his hand.

"Uh huh."

"If I shave off my pubic hair do you think you might, you know?"

"Did *he* do that to you?"

"Yes."

"And you liked it?"

"Yes."

"And he didn't gag?"

"No."

"I see, but if you shave won't that make it feel like whiskers?"

"I don't know. I think you have to develop a taste for it, Norm, like lobster."

"Maybe so . . . maybe so . . ."

"And without hair to get caught in your throat."

"Yes, I see what you mean."

"Didn't you and Brenda . . ."

"No."

"Oh."

"Tell you what, shave it off tomorrow and we'll give it a try."

"Fair enough."

"Night, San, glad we got it all worked out."

"Night, Norm, glad we got started."

28

THE NEXT MORNING Norman got up and sprayed the bedroom with Lysol. He showered and shaved, kissed Sandy's cheek, and left for work. Sandy lay in bed thinking, about Norman, about herself, about the marriage, until she heard the sound of the motorcycle. Was he back? Was he? She hurried to the window in her nightgown. Yes, there he was. In his usual place. When he saw her in the window he dropped his jeans around his ankles and began. In the middle of his act she called, "Who are you? Take off your helmet for a change."

He stopped.

"Are you Dr. Krann?" she asked.

He pulled up his jeans.

"I want to know who you are!"

He ran to his bike, jumped on it, and took off.

Damn! She'd probably never know now. Whoever he was she had the feeling he wouldn't be back. Just as well, she told herself. The kids were coming home from camp today. They'd be moving in a few weeks. She'd be busy again. Much too busy to think about him or anyone else.

SMART WOMEN

To the smart women in my life . . .
my friends

PART
1

MARGO SLID OPEN the glass door leading to the patio outside her bedroom. She set the Jacuzzi pump for twenty minutes, tested the temperature of the water with her left foot, tossed her robe onto the redwood platform, then slowly lowered herself into the hot tub, allowing the swirling water to surround her body.

The late August night air was clear and crisp. The mountains were lit by an almost full moon. The only sounds were Margo's own breathing and the gentle gurgling of the water in the tub. She inhaled deeply to get the full aroma of the cedar as it steamed up, closed her eyes, and felt the tensions of the day disappear.

"Margo . . ."

The voice, coming out of the stillness of the night, startled her. She looked around, but all she saw were the barrels of overgrown petunias and geraniums surrounding the hot tub. She never remembered to pick off the dead flowers, but that didn't stop them from flourishing.

"Over here . . ." the voice said.

He was standing on the other side of her weathered wood fence. She could barely see him.

"What are you doing?" she asked sharply.

"Just wondering if you'd like to have a drink. I'm Andrew Broder. I'm staying in the house next door."

"I know who you are," Margo snapped. "Didn't anyone ever tell you it's impolite to spy on your neighbor?"

"I'm not spying," he said.

"And that eleven is too late to come over for a drink?"

"Is it?" he asked.

"Yes, it is."

"I'm a night person," he said. "It feels early to me."

"Well, it's not. Some of us have to get up and go to work in the morning." She expected him to apologize and then to leave. She looked away. Certainly she was curious about him but no more so than any of her friends' ex-husbands. Last Saturday she had seen him struggling with grocery bags. As he had walked from his truck to his house one had torn and everything had come crashing out, including a carton of eggs. Margo had watched from her upstairs deck, where she'd been reading. He'd stood there quietly, shaking his head and muttering. Then he'd cleaned up the mess, climbed back into his truck, and an hour later had returned with two more bags of groceries.

And on Sunday she'd heard him laughing with his daughter, Sara. She'd thought how nice it is for a father to enjoy his kid that way. And then she'd felt a pang because she never heard her kids laughing with Freddy any more. She didn't even know if they did laugh together.

"Look," he said, and Margo realized that he was still standing by the fence. "Francine said that . . ."

"Francine?"

"I guess you call her B.B. . . . she said that if I needed to borrow sugar I could ask you."

"Is that what you want then, sugar at eleven o'clock at night?"

"No," he said. "I told you, I thought we could have a drink." He held up a bottle.

"What is it?" Margo asked. "It's dark. I can't see that far."

"Courvoisier. I've got the glasses too."

Margo laughed. "You're certainly prepared, aren't you?"

"I try to be."

"The gate's unlatched," she said.

And then another voice went off in her head. *Margo, Margo . . . what are you doing?*

I'm not doing anything.

Bullshit.

Look, he's not a killer, he's not a rapist, I know that much.

You know more than that. You know why you shouldn't let him in.

It's just for a drink.

I've heard that before.

I'm just being neighborly.

Some people never learn.

He opened the gate and walked across the small yard to the hot tub. He sat down at the edge and poured them each a drink. "To neighbors," he said, lifting his glass.

"It's dangerous to drink in a hot tub," Margo told him. "The alcohol does something . . . it can kill you." She dipped her tongue into the glass, tasting the brandy, then set it down. Her body was submerged in the foaming water and the steam had made her black hair curl and mat around her face.

"You look different up close," he said.

"Up close?"

"I've seen you a few times, walking from your car to your house."

"Oh." So, he'd been watching her too.

"You look like the girl on the Sun Maid Raisin box."

"I'm hardly a girl."

"Her older sister then."

"Is that supposed to be a compliment?"

"I like raisins," he said.

Margo tried to remember how the girl on the raisin box looked, but all she could picture was a floppy red bonnet.

"I've never been in a hot tub," he said. "What's it like?"

"Hot," she told him. "Some people can't take it."

"I'd like to give it a try," he said.

"There are several hot tub clubs in town, but Boulder Springs is the best. You should call in advance. They get booked up."

"I was thinking more of now," he said.

"Now? In my hot tub?"

"I wouldn't mind," he said, pulling his sweatshirt over his head.

"Hey . . . wait a minute . . ."

He kicked off his sandals, loosened his belt buckle, and

dropped his jeans. He wore bikini underpants. Margo was suspicious of men who wore boxer shorts. Freddy had worn boxer shorts, had insisted that they be ironed. "Wait a minute . . ." she said again, as he stepped out of his underwear. She hadn't looked directly at him as he had undressed, but she'd seen enough to know that he was tall and lean and very appealing. She'd seen that while she'd been watching him last weekend. She'd seen that while he'd been fully dressed. "What do you think you're doing?"

He slid into the tub, facing her. "I thought you said *okay* . . ."

"No, I didn't say that."

"You want me to get out?"

"I didn't want you to get *in*."

"Oh, I misunderstood."

"Yes, you did."

"But now that I'm here, is it okay? Can I try it for a few minutes?"

"I suppose a few minutes can't hurt."

When the Jacuzzi timer went off he climbed out and set it for another twenty minutes. But before it went off again he told her he was feeling light-headed. Margo urged him to get out quickly, before he fainted. He did, and just in time. As it was she had to wrap a blanket around him, revive him with a glass of Gatorade, and help him back to his place. It wasn't easy getting him up the steep flight of outside stairs leading to the apartment over the garage.

"I warned you," she said, as he slumped onto the sofa in his living room.

"It was worth it," he told her.

"You'd better take a couple of aspirin and get some sleep."

"Can I try it again tomorrow?" he asked.

"I don't think so. It doesn't seem to agree with you."

"I'll get used to it."

"I've got two kids, you know."

"I've got one."

"Mine are teenagers."

"Mine's twelve."

"Mine have been away all summer, visiting their father. They're coming home tomorrow."

"I'd like to meet them."

"Don't be too sure."

"You're very defensive about them, aren't you?"

"Me, defensive about my children?"

"You have beautiful breasts," he said.

Margo looked down and flushed. Her robe was open to the waist. She pulled it closed. "Another piece of useful information," she said. "Hot tubbing is not a sexual experience."

"I'll try to remember that," he said.

"Goodnight," she told him.

"Goodnight, Margo."

The next afternoon, while Margo was driving to Denver to meet her children at the airport, she thought about last night and her strange encounter with Andrew Broder. She never should have let him into her hot tub. It was going to be tricky living next door to him for the next three months now. Her impulsive behavior, though she was well aware of it, continued to cause her problems.

Didn't I warn you?

Okay . . . okay, so you warned me.

Margo knew that B.B. was divorced, but unlike other divorced women, B.B. never complained about her former husband. Never said a word about how cheap he was or how miserable a father. Never talked about how he ran around with girls young enough to be his daughter or the fact that he had no sense of humor or that he was colder than a fish. Never laughed bitterly about the lack of style in his lovemaking. B.B. never shared the details of how or why her marriage to Andrew had failed and Margo didn't feel close enough to ask. Until last May, until the day that B.B. had called Andrew a fucking bastard, Margo had never even heard B.B. say his name.

It had probably been a mistake to arrange for him to rent the apartment in the Hathaway house. B.B. should not have asked for her help in finding him a place to live. But what's done is done, Margo thought.

She glanced at herself in the rearview mirror, wondering what her children would think of her new layered haircut. For years she had worn her dark hair shoulder length, parted in the middle, and blown dry, but this summer she had felt ready for a change.

"Look," Stan, the hair stylist, had said, assessing her, "you might as well take advantage of what you've got . . . good skin, nice eyes, and naturally wavy hair."

That's it? Margo had thought. *After forty years that's what it comes down to?*

After her haircut she had vowed to let her hair grow back and never cut it again. But now she had to admit, it did show off her eyes.

"We should have named her Hazel," her father used to joke, "for those big eyes."

"Who knew she was going to have such eyes," her mother would say.

"You have unbelievably ugly eyes," James had said, making her laugh. James had been her first lover and something about Andrew Broder reminded her of him. It could have been the way he looked directly at her or the way he laughed, heartily, without holding back.

Margo had met James when she was seventeen. He was a tall, lanky college freshman, wildly funny, yet sweet and tender, a perfect combination. It was his wry sense of humor that kept them going during their first awkward attempts at making love and from then on their lovemaking was filled as much with fun and laughter as with passion, which wasn't all that bad, Margo realized later. In fact, there was a lot to be said for it.

James had died of pancreatic cancer two and a half years after they met. She had not even known that he was sick. Her mother had come across the obituary. *James Schoenfeld, twenty, following a brief illness.* Even though Margo and James weren't going together anymore, hadn't seen each other for sixteen months, his death had so affected her that she had not made love again until she and Freddy were married.

At the time Margo could not stop thinking about the night she and James had broken up. She could not stop thinking about how she had flirted with another boy at the fraternity party, had actually slipped him a piece of paper with her phone number on it. James had consoled himself by chug-a-lugging a six-pack of Miller's. Then he'd passed out on the floor. Margo had had no choice but to let the other boy, Roger, drive her home. The next afternoon James had come over, looking pale and acting sheepish, and he had apologized for his behavior. They'd gone for a walk to the pond, but she had not let him kiss her. "It's over," she'd said. "I'm not going to see you anymore."

"Why?" he'd asked. "That's all I want to know. Why?"

"I don't know," she'd said. "It's just something that I feel . . . or don't feel . . ."

James had turned and walked straight into the pond, fully dressed, his hands over his head. She had stood on the grassy bank, yelling and screaming and laughing until tears stung her eyes. Maybe she did love him, she'd thought. But there were so many boys to love. She wasn't ready to love just one.

Her mother urged her not to confuse sadness with guilt. It was not her fault that James had died. Her father cradled her in his arms, stroking her hair. Her sisters, one older, one younger, stood in the doorway to her bedroom, silent.

Margo went to the funeral by herself. After paying her respects to James's parents and his brother she asked who the small, long-haired girl was, the one who was weeping hysterically, and his brother said, "That's Rachel. She and James were going together."

Margo nodded and bit her lip. James had replaced her. Well, what had she expected? She approached Rachel. "I'm Margo," she said. "I just wanted to tell you how sorry I am."

Rachel stopped crying and looked at Margo. "He told me about you," she said. "About how you were his first girlfriend. It was a long time ago, wasn't it?"

Not so long, Margo thought.

"We were pinned," Rachel said. On Rachel's black dress was the Phi Ep pin that Margo had once dreamed of wearing.

She still had dreams about James. James walking into the pond. She would call, "Come back, James. Let's start over . . ." but it was always too late. She would awaken with tears on her cheeks.

Freddy had been as different from James as any young man Margo had met. Perhaps that was why she had married him.

She had been married to Freddy for fourteen years and had never been unfaithful, although she had certainly thought about it. After Freddy, there was Leonard, and after Leonard, her boss, Michael Benson. Then, a series of brief affairs, some lasting months, some weeks, some just the night. There had been twelve of these men, from a physiology professor at Colorado University, to a Buddhist at Naropa, to more than one construction worker. And then, this summer, for five days, there had been Eric.

Margo kept a list of her lovers at the office, in her top desk drawer, the one that locked. She wondered if other women did the same. She wondered what her children would think if she died suddenly and they had to go through her papers. There were seventeen names on her list. Seventeen men. Not so many lovers for a divorced woman of forty, she thought. She knew some women who barhopped every weekend, picking up men for the night. They could wind up with fifty lovers in a year. She'd been divorced for five years. Multiply that by fifty and she could have had two hundred and fifty lovers by now. She laughed aloud at the idea of two hundred and fifty lovers. It seemed to her both wildly funny and grotesque, and then, terribly sad and she bit her lip to keep from crying, the idea was so depressing.

She switched on the car radio and rolled down her window. A piece of brush blew across the highway, rested briefly on the hood of her car, then flew off. The end of summer, Margo thought.

It had been a full summer. She'd worked long hours on a new project with Michael Benson, a complex of solar condominiums in town. She'd taken only one break, a week in Chaco Canyon, where she had gone to be alone, completely and absolutely alone for the first time in her life. It was to be a test of self. To prove—she wasn't sure—that she could survive on her own, she supposed. But on her second day out she had met Eric, twenty years old and irresistible. Eric, she decided later, was to be the last of her impulsive sexual encounters. Because afterwards she always felt empty. Empty, lonely, and afraid.

She would wait the next time she felt tempted and make an effort instead to find a steady man. In the meantime she would concentrate on her work, which was going well, and on her kids, who were coming home.

She had been up early this morning to cook their favorite dish, a tangy chicken in rum sauce. She hoped it would be a happy homecoming, hoped the new school year would be an improvement over the last one. She was going to try. She was going to try to give them more time, more understanding, to be there when they needed to talk, to be less judgmental, to be the warm and gentle earth mother she had always wanted to be, yet never seemed able to pull off. This would be her last chance with Stuart. He would graduate next spring, then go off to college.

And with Michelle, she didn't know. She didn't think she could take another year of hostility. Maybe when the plane landed she would find that Michelle was not on it. That Michelle had stayed in New York with Freddy and Aliza. What would she do then? Jump on the next plane to New York and drag Michelle back? She wasn't sure. If only Michelle could understand that you don't quit just because of rough times. That you work through your problems not by shutting out the people who love you most, but by letting them in to help and comfort you.

Margo turned off the Valley Highway, then followed the signs to the airport. She was twenty minutes early. Good. She'd have time for a quick cup of coffee before the plane landed. Time to relax for a moment before her reentry into motherhood.

Later that night, after the welcome home dinner, Margo showered and put on the robe that her friend Clare had given to her last week for her fortieth birthday. God, the feel of the silk against her nakedness. Yards and yards of pure silk, the color of a young girl's blush.

"When you put it on in the morning you're supposed to glow," Clare had said. "That's what the saleswoman told me, anyway. So what do you think?"

"I think it's not the kind of robe you put on in the morning," Margo had said, "unless it's the morning after . . ."

They had laughed over that.

There were rumors around town that Clare was part Navajo, rumors that Clare enjoyed more than anyone. And when she played it to the hilt she did look like some gigantic, exotic half-breed, with her dark, silver-streaked hair, two slashes of color accenting her high cheekbones, deeply tanned skin, and ropes of turquoise and coral wrapped around her neck. Had Margo met Clare ten years earlier she might not have taken the time to get to know her. She might have put Clare down as an oil heiress from West Texas, with an accent so offensive you couldn't possibly get past the first sentence.

"When I celebrated my fortieth birthday, last year," Clare had said, "I bought myself a sheer black nightgown and a feather boa."

Margo was reminded that she still had a drawerful of sheer black things, left over from her time with Leonard, but she hadn't worn them lately. Hadn't even thought about them. Too bad.

Leonard had been one of the reasons Margo had left New York three years ago. She'd been running away from a no-win affair with him, running away from Freddy and his new bride, and finally, running away from herself, hoping to find a new self in the mountains, and if not exactly finding one, then creating one.

She'd decided on Boulder because of her interest in solar design and was lucky enough to land a job with a small architectural firm, Benson and Gould, based on her portfolio, a letter of recommendation from her boss in New York, and an interview that had gone very well. Later, she'd found out that Gould was spending more than half his time in the Bahamas, that Benson had a neurotic fear of responsibility, and that they had been overjoyed when she'd accepted their job offer.

Margo moved to Boulder in mid-August and, with her half of the cash from the sale of the co-op on Central Park West, bought a house on a dirt road, tucked away against the mountainside. A funky, upside-down kind of house, with the kitchen and living room on the second floor, to take advantage of the view of the Flatirons, and the bedrooms on the first, with a hot tub outside the master, which is what really sold her. The realtor, a woman called B.B., assured Margo that the house could only go up in value.

Two months after Margo moved in, B.B. introduced her to Clare, who was looking for an architect to renovate her gallery.

Now Margo walked down the hall to say goodnight to her children. Michelle was sitting up in bed reading *Lady Chatterley's Lover*. "How do you like it?" Margo asked.

"I'm only reading it because I have to . . . it's on my summer reading list," Michelle said defensively.

Margo laughed. "Not the book . . . this . . ." She twirled around the room, showing off the silk robe, keeping time to the music coming from Michelle's stereo. It sounded like Joan Armatrading, but Margo couldn't be sure. Michelle was very into female vocalists singing about the female experience.

"God, Mother . . . what *is* that thing you're wearing?"

"It's a robe. Clare gave it to me for my birthday. Isn't it gorgeous?"

"It's a weird gift for one divorced woman to give to another. She could have given you a painting from her gallery. We have a lot of bare white walls."

"I think she wanted to make it a personal gift."

"Yeah . . . well, it's personal all right."

"So how do you like it?"

"It's okay, I suppose, if you're into silks and satins."

"I meant the book."

Michelle looked up at Margo, her mouth set defiantly, ready to do battle. "I told you . . . it's assigned reading."

"I know that. But you can still either like it or not like it." Margo warned herself to stop. This conversation was going no place.

Michelle closed the book and rested it on her lap. She gave Margo a hostile look. "It's an interesting book . . . in an old-fashioned way."

In an old-fashioned way, Margo thought. That was hard to take. She remembered when she'd read *Lady Chatterley*. She had been in college and she'd found the sex scenes so steamy she'd locked herself in the hall bathroom and stood under the shower for an hour. "D. H. Lawrence lived in the southwest . . . in Taos. Did you know that?"

"Of course I know that, Mother. But this particular book is set in England."

"Yes," Margo said, "I know." She approached the bed and tried to drop a kiss on Michelle's cheek, but Michelle squirmed away.

"Please, Mother . . . don't be disgusting."

"Goodnight," Margo said, trying to sound pleasant, trying not to let Michelle see that she was getting to her.

"Goodnight," Michelle answered, opening her book again. "And Mother . . . you really should do something about your breath. Have you tried Lavoris?"

"I had chili for lunch."

"Well, you don't have to advertise."

Margo sighed and left the room.

She did not understand how or why Michelle had turned into this impossible creature. Margo would never voluntarily live with such an angry, critical person. Never. But when it was your own child you had no choice. So she kept on trying, kept hoping for the best, kept waiting for the sweetness to come back.

She passed the bathroom that separated her children's bedrooms and stopped in front of Stuart's closed door. She knocked.

"Yeah?" Stuart called over the latest album from the Police.

"Just wanted to say goodnight," Margo said.

"Yeah . . . okay . . . goodnight . . ."

Margo had been speechless when she had first seen Stuart at the airport that afternoon. It wasn't just the haircut, but the clothes. A Polo shirt, a sweater tied over his shoulders, a tennis racquet in one hand, a canvas duffel in the other. He looked as if he'd stepped right out of some Ralph Lauren ad in the Sunday *Times*. She'd had to suppress a giggle. She wasn't sure if she was glad or sorry that her son had turned into a preppie over the summer.

"Where'd you get all the new clothes?" Margo had asked him, driving back from Denver.

"Dad took him shopping . . . to East Hampton," Michelle said.

"I can talk for myself, Mouth," Stuart said. "And I don't think there's anything wrong with taking a little pride in the way you look. Even Mother has a new haircut."

"I noticed," Michelle said.

Before Margo had a chance to ask Michelle what she thought of it, Stuart said, "I want to get my college applications in early. Dad said he'd take a week off in October and we'll do the tour and interviews together."

Margo felt a pang. She'd always thought she would be the one to take him to his college interviews. She had saved a week of vacation for just that purpose.

"I'm thinking of applying to Amherst, early decision."

"Why Amherst?" Margo asked.

"You know Dad's friend, Wally Lewis?"

"Yes."

"He went there . . . and he said he made contacts at school that have lasted a lifetime."

Margo felt nauseated. This was too much. "Really, Stuart," she said, "you're beginning to sound exactly like your father."

"What's wrong with that?" Stuart asked. "He *is* my male role model, you know. Besides, it's time to think about my future. I've grown up a lot this summer, Mother."

Margo went upstairs to the kitchen, and poured herself a glass of brandy. She wished she didn't feel so alone. She wished she had an ally in her own home. "Here's to you, kid," she said, toasting herself. "You're going to need it."

2

WHAT A CASE her mother was, running around in that robe that looked as if it belonged on some ancient movie star, Michelle thought. And expecting Michelle to admire it or something. God! Michelle did not understand what was wrong with her mother. But ever since last winter she had been impossible. Whatever Michelle said Margo took in the wrong way. So naturally she wasn't going to tell Margo the truth about the robe.

On the plane, flying home today, Michelle had hoped that this school year would be better. She had vowed to try—no more towels on the bathroom floor, no more unwashed dishes left in the sink, no more sarcasm. She had hoped that Margo would like her better this year and treat her as a human being, recognizing the fact that she had feelings too. But after just a few hours together they were right back to where they had left off before the summer.

Michelle tried to pinpoint the exact time of the change, but she couldn't. It wasn't the end of one of her mother's love affairs, which was always an intense time around the house, with Margo weeping all over the place, then putting on a big, phony smile for the sake of the children. Also, at the end of an affair Margo tended to appreciate her kids more and to show them a lot of attention and affection.

Like after Leonard.

Leonard had been her mother's first boyfriend after the divorce. The only trouble was, he was married, with three kids, two girls and a boy—Anya, Deirdre, and Stefan. Dumb, asshole names. They used to phone all the time. His wife, Gabrielle, put them up to it. They used to phone and cry and say, *Please give us back our Daddy.* They said it to Michelle and she was only eleven then. How was she supposed to understand what was going on? His kids were younger. They called every week, sometimes twice a week. *Please give us back our Daddy. We miss him. We need him.* Michelle would have been glad to give him back. But he wasn't living with them. He had a place on Gramercy Park. *Your Daddy doesn't live here,* she told his kids. *Call him at his office.*

One time his wife, Gabrielle, came to their apartment, took a gun out of her purse, waved it around, and threatened to kill Margo. It turned out that the gun, which had scared the shit out of them, wasn't real. But it had looked real. And that had been it. The next day Margo decided to leave New York and move to Boulder.

Leonard came out to Colorado one time. *Just passing through,* he had said. *On my way to San Francisco. Just wondered how you were getting along?* They were getting along just fine, thank you, Michelle thought. And that had been the last they'd seen of Leonard.

No, it wasn't the end of an affair. Besides, Michelle kept mental notes of who her mother was sleeping with, so that she would be prepared in case of a disaster, but for the past school year there hadn't been anyone special. No one bringing his kids over for Sunday supper, no hour-long phone calls in the middle of the night, no one appearing in the kitchen unexpectedly in the morning. As far as Michelle could tell, her mother had just been sleeping around this year and not that often either. So it wasn't sex. And it wasn't money or work either. There was a time, right after the divorce, when money and work were Margo's number one problems, but not now.

Michelle rolled over in bed and felt the beginnings of a lump in her throat. She was scared out of her mind that if she couldn't make peace with Margo, Margo would ship her to New York, to Freddy and his Sabra wife. Well, let Margo try it. Michelle would run away. Then Margo would be sorry she'd been such a bitch lately.

She hated it when people told her she looked just like her mother. People were always telling kids they looked just like this parent or that one. It was all such bullshit! If Michelle could look like anyone she knew it would not be her mother, it would be B.B., this big time realtor in Boulder. When B.B. walked into a room, people noticed. Michelle wished that people would notice her that way. A lot of the time Michelle felt invisible.

When they had first moved to town Michelle used to babysit for B.B.'s bratty kid, Sara. B.B. was going out with this movie producer from L.A. and they had some of the most intense fights. They would come storming into the house around midnight and B.B.'s face would be all puffy from crying and twice she had black eyes and she would race into her room and slam the door and then he—his name was Mitch—would pay Michelle and drive her home and he never said anything, except goodnight and thank you very much and B.B. will phone you to make arrangements for next weekend. He wore brown loafers without socks winter and summer and left his shirt unbuttoned so that you could see the hair on his chest, which was black and curly and extremely disgusting.

Michelle had never told her mother about B.B. and Mitch and their fights. She was afraid that if Margo knew she wouldn't let Michelle sit for them anymore. And she never told B.B. or Mitch about the time that Sara bit her on the shoulder because she made Sara turn off the TV and go to bed. And everyone knows the human bite is far more dangerous than the bite of an animal.

Michelle saw B.B. driving around town all the time. She drove a BMW 528i. She had dark red hair, like an Irish setter's, hanging down to her shoulders. Her skin was very white and she was tall and thin and Michelle wondered if maybe she was anorexic, like Katie Adriano, this girl in her class who was always vomiting. Probably B.B. wasn't because she ate out a lot and anorexics don't like restaurants.

B.B. had a slight overbite, but on her it looked good. Michelle knew about teeth because her father was a dentist. Frederic Sampson, D.D.S.—a Professional Corporation. Michelle liked the idea of her father being a professional corporation. It made her feel secure, as if her father owned General Motors or something.

But she hated her father for having insisted that she spend another summer at Camp Mindowaskin. "You have to keep in touch with your own kind," he had told her. "You can't grow up thinking everyone is like . . ."

"Like what?" Michelle had asked.

"Like the people in Boulder."

"What's wrong with the people in Boulder?"

"Nothing is wrong with them, exactly . . . but there's more to life than . . ."

"Than what?"

Her father had sighed heavily.

Her experience as a camp waitress had been a disaster. This was her last summer there, no matter what. She was going to be seventeen, for God's sake. She was old enough to make her own decisions about how to spend her summer. And she was sick of those little bitches calling her The Pioneer just because she lived in Colorado. She might have turned out like them if her parents hadn't been divorced and her mother hadn't moved her away.

And it wasn't any better after camp, when she went out to Bridgehampton to spend two weeks with her father and Aliza. Two weeks of being talked at by her father, when all she wanted was for him to love her the way she was. At dinner the conversations centered around tennis and why, after nine years at camp, Michelle still couldn't serve. *Oh, love me, Daddy . . . please love me . . . never mind my serve. Tell me that you're proud that I'm your daughter. That I'm just right . . . that no matter what you'll always love me . . .*

But that was not the way it was. He loved Aliza now. He was interested in Stuart and his college applications, but not in Michelle. She was nothing to him. Nothing but a pain in the ass. She reminded him of Margo. She heard him say so to his friend, Dr. Fritz. "Every time I look at her," he'd said, "I see Margo."

"You've got to fight those feelings, Freddy," Dr. Fritz had told him.

"I'm trying," her father had said. "But it's not easy."

Michelle had been eleven when her parents were divorced. At the time she had wanted to die. But she got over it. Then, less than two years later, her mother had told her they were moving away.

"Moving where?" Michelle asked.

"To Colorado," her mother answered.

"Colorado?"

"Yes . . . to Boulder."

"Boulder . . . you mean where Mork and Mindy live?"

"Mork and Mindy who?" her mother said.

Michelle had laughed. Her mother was so out of it.

All her friends in New York thought she was really lucky to be moving to the town where Mork and Mindy lived. They said maybe she'd get a job working on their show. They said maybe she'd even get to be a regular and then they'd be able to see her on TV every week. She promised to get Mork's and Mindy's autographs for every one of them.

But when they got to Boulder, Michelle found out that Mork and Mindy hardly ever came to town. They filmed most of their shows in California. She didn't blame them. Boulder was a big zero. It was just this little college town in the middle of nowhere. It couldn't compare to New York City. And Michelle hated her mother for ruining her life. But she got over that too. And now she even liked it here, especially in winter, when the mountains were covered with snow.

That robe her mother was wearing tonight was such a joke! The idea of it made Michelle laugh into her pillow. But then the lump in her throat started again and this time it wouldn't go away, no matter how hard Michelle swallowed. She didn't understand the lump in her throat any better than she understood her mother. She didn't understand why she cried herself to sleep every night either.

3

B.B. CONCENTRATED ON the sound of her breathing and the rhythm of her feet as she ran along the road. She did three miles each morning before breakfast. Then she showered, dressed, and was at her office by nine. She ran not just for the physical exercise, but to clear her head. It was a time for solving problems, a time for making decisions. Her body was as trim and firm as it had been when she was twenty, but she felt better now. She supposed one day she would have to face growing old, the way her mother was facing it now, but it seemed very far away. She breathed deeply, reminding herself not to gulp air. Sometimes she gulped and became bloated. She checked her watch as she rounded the corner. She'd gone two in eighteen-four. Not bad, B.B., she told herself.

She hadn't always been called B.B. She'd been named Francine Eloise Brady by her Jewish mother and her Irish father in Miami, in 1940. All her life she had been Francie to her family and friends and Francine to everyone else. Then she married Andrew and had taken his name—Broder. She thought she would be married for the rest of her life, but in twelve years it was over.

She left Miami a month before the divorce was final. She left with Sara, who was six years old, with two suitcases, and with thirty-two thousand dollars in cash, which she had earned selling real estate. She left in the Buick at four in the morning and drove west, away from Florida, away from the ocean, away from reminders that she'd once had another life, a life she could not get back.

She headed for Colorado because the year before she had seen an article in *Architectural Digest* about restored Victorian homes in Boulder. She remembered the color of the sky and the snow-capped mountains in the distance, which seemed as far from anything she had known as possible. When she arrived she checked into the Boulderado Hotel and two days later she bought her own small Victorian house on Highland. A week after that she went to work for the agency through whom she'd bought the house. And after a year she had opened her own agency. *Francine Brady Broder—Elegant Homes.* People around town began to call her B.B. because of her double last names. She didn't mind. She thought it had a snappy sound to it.

She ran up her driveway and paused at the car, checking her pulse. Lucy came up to her and licked her legs. B.B. patted Lucy on the head, then went inside to the kitchen.

"Hi, Mom . . . table's all set," Sara said. "Did you have a good run?"

"Yes, I could have kept going. I didn't even feel tired."

"Did you know that female athletes sometimes have trouble getting pregnant?"

"Really?" B.B. said, washing her hands at the kitchen sink.

"Yes," Sara said, popping an English muffin into the toaster. "I read about it. They get too thin and their periods stop. All that exercise isn't good for their reproductive organs." Sara drained her glass of orange juice and poured another. "So you should be careful, just in case."

"In case what?"

"In case you want to have more children."

"I'm forty, Sara. I'm not about to have any more children."

"You never know," Sarah said. "Jennifer's mother is forty-one and she just had a baby."

"Well, I'm not going to have any more babies."

"Okay . . . fine. I just thought you should know."

"Thanks for the warning. Do you want scrambled eggs or fried?"

"Fried . . . so the yolks don't run."

"Hand me the frying pan, would you?" B.B. said, putting up the kettle.

"Do you remember your first day of junior high, Mom?" Sara asked.

"Yes . . . I was so scared I couldn't eat a bite of breakfast and my mother made me carry a buttered roll in my book bag. I flushed it down the toilet in the Girls' Room."

She laughed. "I'm not that scared. Besides, all my friends from Mapleton will be with me and Jennifer's in my homeroom."

"You're braver than I was."

After breakfast B.B. brushed Sara's hair, which was thick and honey-colored, like Andrew's. "A braid or a ponytail?" B.B. asked.

"A braid," Sara said.

When B.B. finished her hair, Sara collected her new notebook and pencils. They walked to the front door together. "Goodbye . . ." B.B. said, "I love you."

"And I love you," Sara answered.

"For how long?" B.B. asked.

"For always and forever."

"That's how long I'll love you too."

B.B. gave Sara a hug, then went back to the kitchen and put the breakfast dishes in the sink to soak.

Until last spring B.B.'s life in Boulder, aside from Mitch, had been peaceful and rewarding. Then, in May, the letter from Andrew had come. B.B. had arrived at her office a few minutes later than usual that day because she had taken extra time dressing. She had invited Clare and Margo to join her for lunch at The James to discuss an intriguing real estate deal. A twenty acre parcel of land outside of town had come on the market and if she could interest Clare in putting up half the cash, she was ready to make an offer. It was the perfect site for passive-solar cluster housing, a concept she knew appealed to Margo. She was prepared to offer Margo a piece of the action in exchange for her architectural services. She admired Margo's work. It had a class feeling, even when it was just a remodeled garage.

Miranda, B.B.'s secretary, had brought in the morning mail before noon and B.B., thumbing through it, had stopped when she'd come to the letter from Andrew, marked personal.

They never wrote. All communication between them regarding Sara was handled through his attorney in Miami and hers in Boulder. So what was this?

She slit the letter open with a silver and turquoise opener, a gift from a satisfied client. She read it quickly the first time, then slowly, to make sure she understood.

Dear Francine,

I plan to spend the next school year in Boulder, writing another book. That way Sara and I can have more time together, which we are both looking forward to.

I expect to leave here the second week in August and to drive cross-country, arriving in Boulder somewhere around the 20th. I hope that we can work out the arrangements easily when I arrive. I will need to find a small apartment or house, with enough room for Sara. If you have any suggestions I would be grateful.

Yours,
Andrew

She felt herself grow hot, then cold. A pounding began in her temples. And although she rarely sweat, she felt a dampness under her arms.

She stood and walked around her office, watering her African violets, straightening the Fritz Scholder posters on the walls. She went back to her desk and read the letter a third time. She lifted the phone to call her lawyer, then changed her mind and hung up. She folded the letter and dropped it into her purse. She could not believe that he was serious.

She took five shallow breaths and did a Lion, one of the Yoga exercises she learned last year. Then she grabbed her purse and went to meet Margo and Clare at The James.

4

MARGO HAD BEEN surprised by B.B.'s invitation to lunch last spring. Margo and B.B. were not close. Margo could never get beneath the surface, could never connect with B.B.'s feelings, so she had settled for a friendly relationship rather than a true friendship. Clare was really the link between Margo and B.B. and while the three of them lunched together every now and then it was always informal and arrangements were made at the last minute.

It had been a soft May day, a perfect day to eat outdoors and as they were seated at a table in the courtyard of the restaurant Margo caught the scent of lilacs. They were served by a waitress who was both pleasant and efficient, a welcome change from the sullen crowd usually employed by The James.

B.B. explained why she had asked them to join her as soon as their salads were served and Margo was flattered that B.B. had chosen her to design the cluster housing and grateful for the opportunity to participate in the joint business venture. If the deal took off it could mean big money. Margo got by on her salary and commissions, had even managed to save a little, but she wasn't exactly rolling in it. Freddy's child support payments helped, but she couldn't count on them after the kids went off to college, nor did she want to.

Several times during lunch B.B. put her hand to her head and closed her eyes, but Margo did not find that unusual. B.B. often seemed to be someplace else, even when she was talking to you, even when it was business.

They lingered over their coffee until B.B. checked her watch and said, "I've got to get back to the office." She paid the check and the three of them walked out of the restaurant. But before they reached the corner B.B. put her hand to her head again and swooned, as if she were about to keel over. Too much wine, Margo thought.

"Are you all right?" Clare asked, grabbing her.

"No," B.B. said quietly. And then she broke away from Clare and flung her purse into the street, shouting, "No, goddamn it, I am not all right!" The contents of her purse spilled out, a bottle of Opium smashing at Margo's feet, lipsticks rolling under cars, a hairbrush, a notebook, a pocket calculator, an envelope, all scattered on the ground. "I wish he were dead!" B.B. yelled.

"Who?" Margo and Clare asked at the same time.

"My ex-husband, the fucking bastard!"

Margo was stunned. Until that day she had never seen B.B. react emotionally to anything. And that was the first she had heard of Andrew Broder.

Five days later Clare had called Margo, asking if she knew how to make chicken soup, because B.B. had not eaten anything but tea and Jell-O since climbing into bed on the afternoon of their lunch.

"She says the only thing she wants to eat is the kind of chicken soup her mother used to make when she was a little girl. Jewish chicken soup. She says her father told her it would cure anything except warts and he wasn't sure it wouldn't cure those too. Do you know how to make it, Margo?"

"I haven't made chicken soup in years," Margo said, "but I could call my mother. I think the secret is in the kind of chicken you use."

"Let's try it," Clare said. "Otherwise I'm afraid she's going to wind up in the hospital."

That night Margo phoned her mother in New York. Her

mother was on her way to the ballet at Lincoln Center, but she was delighted that Margo wanted to make chicken soup and she explained how to do it, step by step, reminding Margo to use only a pullet, enough dill, and not to forget the parsnip.

On Saturday morning Margo shopped early. She came home and set the ingredients on her kitchen counter. The house was quiet. Stuart was at work, churning out ice cream, and Michelle was still asleep. Margo washed her hands at the kitchen sink, dried them with a paper towel, rolled up her sleeves, and soon the aroma of her childhood filled the house.

When Michelle came up to the kitchen, rubbing the sleep from her eyes, she sniffed around and asked, "What *are* you doing, Mother?"

"Making chicken soup."

"Chicken soup?"

"Yes. B.B. isn't feeling well. It's for her."

"You never make soup for me when I'm not feeling well."

"I thought you don't like homemade chicken soup, Michelle. I thought you said the little particles of fat floating on top make you nauseous. That's why you always ask for Lipton's when you're sick."

"I like it fine when it's cooked with rice," Michelle said. "The way Grandma used to make it."

"Which Grandma?" Margo said. "Grandma Sampson or Grandma Belle?"

"Grandma Belle," Michelle said. "Grandma Sampson used to make vegetable soup for me and she always strained it so I wouldn't gag on the vegetables."

"Oh, that's right," Margo said and she laughed.

"So what's wrong with B.B.?"

"She's depressed. Her former husband is coming to town unexpectedly."

"You mean the Brat's father?"

"Sara's not a brat, Michelle."

"You don't know because you never babysat her."

"Well, that's true. But she's older now."

"I doubt that makes much difference."

"Michelle, you're so hard on people. Why can't you give them a chance?"

"Me . . . hard? Come off it, Mother." She grabbed a carrot from the refrigerator and stalked out of the kitchen.

"Is that all you're having for breakfast?" Margo called.

"Carrots are extremely nutritious."

Late that afternoon Margo tasted the soup. She wasn't sure if she had put in enough dill, but it certainly wasn't bad. She was pleased. She had sworn off everyday cooking when she'd left Freddy, but now she found that cooking could be fun if nobody pressured her. And her kids had learned to cook too.

That night Margo and Clare arrived at B.B.'s house with supper. Margo brought the chicken soup and Clare brought a salad, a French bread, and a bottle of white wine. B.B. was sitting up in bed, wearing a white eyelet robe, her hair pulled back and tied with a ribbon. She looked as fragile and beautiful as Camille on her death bed. She made Margo feel shlumpy in her jeans and plaid shirt. Everything in B.B.'s house was as white and delicate as she was. There were fresh flowers in every room, even the bathrooms. Her house made Margo want to go home to clean, scrub, and redecorate.

B.B. laughed over the chicken soup. "It's delicious," she said. "It's just like my mother's." She finished her first bowl and asked for another. "I'm going to get out of bed tomorrow," she told them. "And on Monday I'm going back to the office. I may even go to see Thorny Abrams . . . just for advice."

Thorny Abrams was one of Boulder's many shrinks. Margo had worked on a solar addition to his house last year. His wife, Marybeth, could never make up her mind about anything, so plans for the addition had to be reworked seven times. Thorny would say, *It's up to Marybeth.* Marybeth would look forlorn and say, *You know I can't make decisions, Thorny.*

"And Richard Haver is looking into the law for me," B.B. continued. "It may be that I don't have to let Andrew have Sara at all. We've got an agreement, you know . . . and it calls for two weeks at Christmas, Easter vacation, and one month every summer. That's it. So if he comes to town and isn't allowed to see Sara, then surely he won't stay." She looked from Margo to Clare. "I mean, why would he stay under those circumstances?"

A week after that B.B. had phoned Margo, asking her to meet for a drink after work at the Boulderado.

"I'll get right to the point," B.B. said as soon as they had ordered Perriers. "Do you know if the Hathaway apartment is available?"

"I haven't seen anyone in it lately," Margo told her. "They usually rent it to university people for the summer."

"I'd like you to find out if it is available," B.B. said, "and if it is, I'd like you to secure it in the name of Andrew Broder, for three months beginning the third week in August, at say three hundred and fifty dollars a month."

"You're going to find him a place to live?" Margo asked.

"I've decided that's the best way to deal with it," B.B. said.

"It sounds tricky to me. Are you sure you want to get involved? Why don't you let him find his own place?"

"Because if Sara's going to spend any time with him I want her in a decent neighborhood. If I leave it up to him he'll rent some place off Twenty-eighth Street."

"But you're in the business . . . surely you could . . ."

"Do it for me, Margo . . . please . . ."

"Okay. If you're sure that's what you want."

"It is . . . yes . . . it's what I have to do."

Margo knew that there were times when you could feel so desperate that just making a plan helped. It gave you a feeling of control. Following her separation from Freddy, Margo had experienced that kind of despair, until she'd mapped out a plan for the next year in her life, and then, even though she eventually changed her mind, that sinking feeling disappeared. So that evening before dinner Margo called on her neighbor, Martin Hathaway, to see about the apartment.

"What were you doing talking to Mr. Hathaway, Mother?" Michelle asked later at the dinner table.

"Do I need an excuse to talk to Mr. Hathaway?" Margo said. God, she sounded as hostile as Michelle. If you lived with it long enough it became contagious.

"I thought you said he was a sniveling old fart," Michelle said.

"Did I say that?" Margo asked, trying to laugh.

"On several occasions," Michelle said. "And it's true, Mother . . . he is a sniveling old fart."

"I was discussing the apartment over his garage," Margo said.

"What about it?"

"Well . . . B.B.'s ex-husband is coming to town . . . I told you that, didn't I?"

"Yeah . . . so?"

"So, she's trying to find him a place to stay."

"Go on . . ."

"She asked me to find out about renting the Hathaway apartment for him."

"For how long?" Michelle asked.

"About three months."

"Let me get this straight," Michelle said, holding her fork in the air. "You're saying that B.B.'s ex-husband is going to live here . . . next door to us?"

"Yes," Margo said.

"God, Mother!" Michelle said, plunking her fork down on the table. She stood up, grabbed a deviled egg and shouted, "I just can't believe you!" She shoved the egg into her mouth, charged out of the room, and stomped down the stairs.

Margo stood up and called after her. "Why don't you ever say what you mean, Michelle? Why won't you communicate?"

But Michelle did not answer. Margo sat back down at the table, feeling very tired. "Why won't she communicate?" Margo asked Stuart. "Why won't either of you communicate?"

"Give me a break, Mom," Stuart said. "I'm eating my supper."

5

PROBABLY SARA SHOULD have told her mother about Daddy's plan to come to Boulder. Then Mom wouldn't have been so surprised by his letter. On the day that the letter arrived Clare had been at the house when Sara got home from school.

"Where's Mom?" Sara had asked.

"She's in bed," Clare said.

"What's wrong . . . is she sick?"

"She's having a bit of a crisis," Clare said.

At first Sara hadn't understood because Clare was talking very West Texas and when she did every word melted together, making it sound as if Mom had a *Bitova Cry Cyst*, which sounded serious. "What should we do . . . should we call a doctor?"

"No," Clare said. "There's not much you can do. It takes time, that's all."

"It's not catching, is it?" Sara asked.

"No," Clare said.

"That's what I thought," Sara said. "How long do you think it will last?"

"It has to run its course," Clare told her. "Don't worry. She's going to be fine."

That afternoon Sara heard her mother crying and saying things like *He has no right . . . he can't do this to me.* And then, *I've always known I couldn't trust him and this proves it, doesn't it?* So Sara knew the crisis had to do with her father.

She called Jennifer for advice, but Jennifer told her to just stay out of it. That parents have to learn to solve their own problems. Then Jennifer reminded her to eat lightly because of Arts Night. Sara and Jennifer were both in the dance program at school.

Sara was disappointed when her mother said she couldn't get out of bed to go to Arts Night and disappointed again when Clare said that she wouldn't be able to take her either because she had to go to some business dinner in Denver. So Clare asked Margo Sampson if she could take her and Margo said yes. Sara did not want to go to Arts Night with Margo. She hardly knew Margo. She would rather have gone with Jennifer's family, but everything was arranged before she had a chance to say a word. Margo came by with her kids, Stuart and Michelle, and took Sara to Beau Jo's for pizza. Stuart ate a whole pizza by himself, with pepperoni and extra cheese. Margo, Michelle and Sara shared a large vegie supreme with whole wheat crust. Sara picked the onions and the mushrooms off her slice and Michelle picked off the olives. Margo said, "Maybe vegie supreme was the wrong choice."

When Sara was younger and Michelle babysat her, Michelle never let Sara stay up late like babysitters are supposed to do. Sara's first babysitting job was coming up soon and she was going to be really nice and let the kid stay up as late as he wanted, even if he fell asleep on the floor.

Sara didn't finish her pizza. She was afraid she'd get gas.

When Sara came home from Arts Night she tiptoed into her mother's room. Her mother was asleep. Her mother's necklace, the one that Clare had given to her for her fortieth birthday, lay on the bedside table. It spelled out FRIENDSHIP in tiny gold letters. Sara thought it was very pretty.

Mom opened her eyes. "How was Arts Night?"

"Pretty good," Sara said. Her mother's eyes were all puffy from crying and her face had red blotches on it. "Are you feeling any better?"

"A little . . . but my head still hurts."

"Do you want a cold cloth?"

"That would be nice."

Sara went to her mother's bathroom and held a blue washcloth under the faucet until it felt very cold. Then she squeezed it out and brought it to her mother. Mom lay back against the pillows and Sara placed the cloth on her forehead. "Better?"

"Much."

Sara sat on the edge of the bed holding her mother's hand. She loved the feel of her mother's hands. Her skin was so soft and her fingers were long and thin, with perfectly polished nails. She wore two delicate gold rings, one on the ring finger of her right hand and one on the middle finger next to it.

As Sara tiptoed out of her mother's room she saw the letter from her father lying face up on the dresser. She read it quickly, while pretending to be arranging Mom's perfume bottles in a row. It was a friendly letter. It didn't say anything bad.

Mom's crisis lasted five days and when she finally got out of bed and went back to work she was really tense. When Mom got tense she yelled at Sara. Then Sara would start biting her nails, which only made her mother yell some more. For weeks after that Sara's stomach felt queasy and she took Pepto-Bismol every day. She was glad when it was time to leave for summer camp. She figured that by August her mother would be used to the idea of having her father in town.

6

ANDREW HAD CALLED B.B. on August 20 to say that he was in Hays, Kansas, and expected to arrive in Boulder by eight P.M. It had been six years since she had heard his voice. Six years since they had seen each other. She was a wreck all day, knowing that he was on his way. She gulped too many vitamin C's and washed them down with too much cranberry juice. Her stomach tied into hard little knots, giving her spasms of pain. She had just rye toast and camomile tea for supper. Then she showered and tried to get dressed, but she couldn't decide what to wear. So she sat on the edge of her bed in her robe for an hour, gnawing on the insides of her cheeks, until they were swollen and sore.

Finally, she got off her bed and dressed in jeans, sandals, and a baggy white sweater. She let her hair hang loose. She wore no makeup. What did she care how she looked to him anyway?

It was a matter of pride, she decided, spraying her wrists and the back of her neck with Opium, out of habit. She wanted him to be sorry he'd lost her. She wanted him to love her still, to desire her, so that she could reject him again. Punish him. Cause him pain. The way he had caused her pain. Damn him! She had worked it out so carefully. She had convinced herself that she would never have to see him again. At least not until Sara graduated from high school or college or got married. And each of those events were years away. One of them might be dead by then.

Once last spring, after a lengthy session with her lawyer, who had told her that legally she could not keep Andrew out of town, she had become so filled with rage that she had gone to her room after dinner and had screamed, surprising herself as well as Sara.

Sara had rushed into her room, her face ashen. "Mom . . . Mom, what's wrong?"

"Get out!" B.B. had yelled.

"Is it about Daddy coming to live in Boulder?"

"He's trying to ruin my life!" B.B. had cried. She'd picked up a shoe and hurled it across the room. It smashed the little stained glass window above her desk. "That goddamned father of yours is trying to ruin my life!"

"No, he's not Mom . . . really, he's not . . ."

"Oh, what do you know?" B.B. had cried. "You're just a baby."

Now Andrew was on his way and there was nothing B.B. could do about it. She walked through her house, adjusting the pillows on the sofas, picking a wilted flower out of the arrangement on the piano, running her fingers along the oak dining table. Everything looked perfect. Everything was in order. She'd done a good job. And she'd done it on her own. She didn't need anything from him.

She opened the front door and stepped outside. The sky was cloud-covered and the wind was picking up. There was a rumble of thunder in the distance and flashes of lightning over the mountains. She sat on her front porch swing, with Lucy at her side, swallowing hard each time she heard a car.

And then a battered Datsun pickup, the color of infant diarrhea, pulled into her driveway. He never did have any taste. He parked and got out of the truck. Lucy stood and began to bark. B.B. hushed her. He had grown a beard, darker than his sunstreaked hair, which was shaggy now. He was wearing jeans, a gray sweatshirt, and running shoes. During their marriage she had selected his clothes. He'd had nine cashmere sweaters with a color coordinated shirt for each. He was the best-dressed reporter on the Miami *Herald*. She used to stand inside his closet, surrounded by his things—shoes lined up, jackets and trousers carefully arranged, ties hanging in a row—and she would get this warm, safe feeling. He was her man. Now he looked like some aging hippie. The kind of man Margo went out with. Boulder was full of them.

"Hello, Francine," Andrew said.

At the sound of his voice, she felt the tea and toast come up, up from her stomach to the very edge of her throat. She had to fight to get it back down.

"I'm known as B.B. here," she told him. "For Brady Broder."

"I'll try to remember," he said.

She did not look directly at him.

"You're looking good," he said. "I like your hair that way."

"Thank you," she said. "You're looking . . . different."

He laughed and ran his hand through his hair. His laugh used to be enough to make her laugh.

"Is Sara asleep yet?" he asked.

"She's spending the night at a friend's."

"Oh. I guess I thought she'd be here. You did tell her I was coming tonight, didn't you?"

"No, as a matter of fact, I didn't. I thought it made more sense to wait." She was pleased at how steady her voice sounded. Pleased and surprised.

He paused, kicking a stone away from his foot. "Okay. I'll see her tomorrow then."

"Tomorrow she's going to Denver to do some back-to-school shopping."

He didn't say anything.

She did not take her hand away from Lucy's head. At that moment Lucy was her security, her connection to reality.

"Well," he said. "I guess that will give me a chance to settle in."

She thought she saw a tightening of that vein in his forehead, the one that stood out when he was angry or thinking hard. She had planned to invite him in, to offer him a drink, to show off the lovely home she'd made for Sara. But now she wanted to get this over with as quickly as possible. "Shall I show you the way to your place?" she asked.

"I'd appreciate that."

She stood up. Lucy walked down the steps with her and began to sniff him.

He let Lucy smell his hand, then he patted her on the back. "Nice collie."

"Her name is Lucy."

"I know."

"You know?"

"From Sara."

"Of course," she said. "From Sara." She hated the idea of Sara talking with Andrew. Telling him about her dog, about her life in Boulder. What else did he know? What else did they talk about behind her back?

"You can follow me," she told him. "It's just a few blocks."

"Okay."

She got into her BMW. She held onto the steering wheel tightly, trying to steady her hands. She started the car, then began to count backwards from one hundred, in Spanish. *Ciento, noventa y nueve, noventa y ocho.* Often, when she couldn't fall asleep at night, that's what she'd do. Usually it calmed her. She kept sight of him in her rearview mirror and drove slowly, up to Fourth, left on Pearl, right on Sixth, across Arapahoe, up the hill to Euclid, right on Aurora to the Dead End sign, then up the dirt road to a driveway shared by Margo and the Hathaways. It was just a mile and a half from her house.

He parked alongside her car. "I've got the keys right here," she said, fishing them out of her canvas bag. He followed her up the outside stairs leading to the apartment over the garage. But at the door she had trouble getting the key into the lock, her hands were shaking so badly.

"Here . . . let me . . ." he said, his fingers brushing hers.

"No! I can do it. Just give me a minute."

"Okay. Sure. Just trying to help."

"I don't need your help," she told him. She managed to unlock the door. She stepped inside and switched on a light in the living room. He was right behind her. "This is it," she said. "Living room, bedroom, bath, and kitchen."

"It looks fine," he said. "Exactly what I'd hoped for. Thanks for finding it for me."

"They keep it up nicely," she told him. "It's just been painted and the sofa's been recovered. We got them down to three-fifty a month. You've got a three-month lease." She sounded professional now, the reassuring realtor.

"Renewable?"

"You'll have to discuss that with the Hathaways. I didn't draw up the contract myself." God, what gall, she thought. A renewable lease. Did he think she would go out of her way to make sure he could hang around? In three months she wanted him out of town, out of her life. She walked across the room. "Here are the keys," she told him, dropping them on the dining table. "I'm sure you want to get unpacked and I've got to run anyway. If you need anything, like a cup of sugar, my friend Margo lives next door."

"I wish you'd stay for a while," he said. "We've got to talk."

"I don't want to talk," she told him.

"Look, Francie . . . I just want you to understand that I'm not trying to hurt you by being here."

She choked up and turned away from him.

"I'm here for just one reason," he continued, ". . . to be near Sara. That's all there is to it."

"Maybe for you," she managed to say. "Maybe that's all there is to it for you. But what about me? Did you stop to think about me?"

"Yes, I did."

"I'll bet," she said.

"You never did have much faith in me, did you?" he asked.

"With good reason."

He grabbed her roughly, forcing her to face him. "I've spent six years paying for what may or may not have been my fault. I'll never get over it completely. But I've learned to deal with it . . . with my guilt . . . with your hate . . . with losing Bobby . . . and then you, taking Sara away. Six years is enough."

"Enough for you," she said.

"Enough for any of us," he said softly.

He held her for a moment, the way he used to, and when she looked up at him, her eyes filled with tears, he kissed her. Afraid of what might happen if she let herself respond, she broke away and wiped her mouth with the back of her hand. "What are you doing?" Her voice was hoarse. "What do you want?"

"I don't know," he said. "Seeing you again . . . remembering . . . I just don't know."

He walked across the room, his hands brushing his hair away from his face. She leaned back against the empty bookcase. Neither one spoke.

Finally, he broke the silence. "Can I have Sara this weekend?"

"You can have her on Sunday from ten until six."

"That's not much of a weekend."

"It's enough for now."

He sighed. "Look . . . either we're going to work this out by ourselves, sensibly, or we're going to work it out through our lawyers, and if necessary, through the courts."

"I can't believe you're standing here saying these things. That after six years you think you can walk into my life and destroy everything I've put together."

"You haven't given me any choice."

"You haven't changed. You're as selfish and irresponsible as you always were."

"And you're just as inflexible."

She strode across the room to the door, opened it, paused, then turned back to him. "One thing . . . don't expect anything from me while you're in town. As far as I'm concerned you don't exist!"

"That's right . . . bury your head in the sand the way you always have . . ."

She ran to her car. A flash of lightning lit up the sky, followed by a roar of thunder. She turned on the ignition, raced the engine, and tore out of the driveway, tires screeching. It began to rain heavily, then to hail, pounding the roof of her car. But she hardly noticed for the pounding inside her head.

Men, B.B. thought. You had to learn to use them the way they used you, the way they had been taught to use you. She'd learned that a long time ago. She'd learned that when she was fourteen and her father had died of a heart attack in the bed of a stock clerk from his store. She was a redhead, like B.B., and young, with two babies and no husband in sight. She was Irish, like him. Kathleen Dooley. Her father had been screwing Kathleen Dooley for more than six months when he died. But B.B. didn't know it at the time.

Her mother did though. After the funeral her mother had confided that she'd known it all along. "It was the Irish in him," her mother had said. "He couldn't help himself. He loved us, Francie, more than anything, but some men, especially the Irish, have it in their genes. They can't resist, even when they want to. They're like male dogs, chasing a bitch in heat."

Francine tried to picture her father as a dog, chasing Kathleen Dooley into the stockroom of the store, Brady Army Surplus, barking his head off, nipping at her legs.

"I want you to know, Francie," her mother continued, "that I forgave your father. The first time it happened he came home and cried in my arms. I told him, *I don't want to know about it, Dennis. You have to work late one or two nights a week . . . it's okay . . . just spare me the details.* And then I put it out of my mind. That's what you have to do when things get unpleasant. You have to put them out of your mind. You have to concentrate on other things. And then you don't feel unhappy or angry."

"You weren't angry that he was fooling around?" Francine asked.

"He should have died in his own bed. That's all I'm angry about."

"I'd have been angry," Francine said.

Her mother shrugged. "Marry Jewish. That's my advice. They make the best husbands. Look at Aunt Sylvie . . . look at all the happiness she has with Uncle Morris. A beautiful home, you could call it an estate and not be exaggerating . . . furs, even down here in Miami, where you don't need them . . . jewels . . . cruises every year . . . and for their children, only the best. So remember Francie, when the time comes, be smart. It's just as easy to fall in love with a nice Jewish boy, one with a future, one who'll take care of you."

"Maybe I won't get married at all."

"Bite your tongue," her mother said. "Of course you will. Learn from my mistakes and learn from Kathleen Dooley too. She wasn't so dumb. Use what God gave you to get what you want, but try not to hurt anybody along the way."

So Francine had used what God had given her. Her beauty. She knew she could have any boy she wanted. Just like that! Because boys were stupid and all they cared about was how you looked. In high school she had more boyfriends than anyone else. She was popular with a capital P, her mother told Aunt Sylvie, and Aunt Sylvie said, "Sure, why not? With that Irish nose and red hair . . . she looks like a shiksa. Momma would roll over in her grave if she could see her."

After high school Francine enrolled at Miami U. She spent her first two years living at home and commuting, but then her mother urged her to move into a dormitory to get a taste of college life, and so she did. That very same year she met Andrew Broder, a graduate student in journalism from Hackensack, New Jersey. She liked his seriousness, his shyness, his sense of humor, and the fact that he was exactly one head taller than she was so that when he held her in his arms her lips came up to his neck.

He was awed by her beauty and she used it to tantalize him because this was the man she was going to marry. It took her a while to convince him that he wanted to get married. But finally one balmy night she climbed into his bed, naked, and she let him touch her all over. She let him hold her close and rub up against her until he came, leaving her thigh wet and sticky.

They were married a week after she graduated, on the grounds of Aunt Sylvie and Uncle Morris's estate, under a chuppa covered with roses. She wore a white batiste cotton dress, nipped in at the waist, with a square neck, and a wide-brimmed garden hat instead of a veil, and she carried a single white rose.

Before the ceremony Uncle Morris took her into the house, into his private den, and slipped an envelope into the bosom of her dress, inside her strapless bra. "Twenty-five hundred smackers," he told her, his hot pudgy fingers squeezing her small left tit.

"Thank you, Uncle Morris," she said politely.

"You're a gorgeous girl, you know that, Francine?"

"Thank you, Uncle Morris."

"I wouldn't mind shtupping you myself. You know what I mean?"

"I know that you're teasing me, Uncle Morris."

"Teasing, shmeasing . . . don't be too sure. Look, if he doesn't come through, this guy you're marrying . . . come and see me. Understand?"

"I'm not sure . . . but thank you very much for your generous gift and for giving us the wedding." She pecked his cheek, then ran out of his den, her heart pounding. He had felt her up! Uncle Morris had felt her up on her wedding day.

Sex. That's what they were all after. You had to give it to them though. At first, just enough to keep them interested. Then, enough to make them think you really enjoyed it. You had to, otherwise they wouldn't marry you. And once you were married, you had to keep doing it, twice a week, at least.

But that part, the doing it part, wasn't nearly as nice as the hugging and kissing, Francine discovered on her honeymoon. Andrew seemed to think it was though, so she never told him what she thought. He would moan at the end, then collapse on top of her, as if he were dead. At first, she worried that Andrew would die the way her father had, but as the week went on, she saw that it was nothing more serious than exhaustion. "Oh, Francie . . . my beautiful darling . . . you're so wonderful . . ." he would whisper.

For the next two years they lived in Georgia at Fort Benning and she got a job working as a receptionist in a real estate office. The business fascinated her and she began to study for her broker's license.

They continued to have sex twice a week. On Wednesdays and Saturdays. It hardly took any time at all. She still preferred the kissing and the hugging, but the trouble was, if she started kissing Andrew, he got it all wrong and thought she wanted more, thought she wanted to do it. And she didn't know how to tell him she didn't. So she stopped kissing and fooling around, waiting for him to take the initiative. That way she always knew how it was going to end.

After two years they went back to Miami and he got a job on the *Herald* and she passed the Florida realtor's exam and went to work for Pride Properties. She took six months off when Bobby was born and four when Sara was born and when she went back the second time she was named second vice-president in charge of residential properties.

By then Andrew had his own byline and was talking about taking a leave of absence. She tried to convince him not to do it. They had too many responsibilities.

"Fuck responsibilities! Let's blow it off and go to Fiji."

"Andrew, sometimes you scare me with your crazy ideas."

"Then New York," he'd said. "Let's go to New York for a year."

"It gets cold in New York," she'd told him. "This is the best place to raise children. They can be outside all year round."

"I'm going out of my mind here, Francie," he'd said. "I've got to have a change."

"This just isn't the right time for a change, Andrew. Take up tennis or something. You'll feel better."

Instead of tennis, Andrew bought a little sailboat, spending most of his weekends out on the bay, teaching Bobby to sail. Which would have been fine, except that now he wanted sex more often, and in different positions, and with the lights on. She went along with some of it. She had no choice. She didn't want to leave him, or worse yet, for him to leave her. His need for constant excitement worsened. He was no longer satisfied with a nice vacation in Jamaica, lolling about on the beach. He wanted to raft rivers, to explore jungles, to live on the edge. She tried to remain calm.

"It's just a mid-life crisis," her mother had told her.

"But he's only thirty-four," Francine had said.

"So, he's an early bird. Just as well to get it out of the way now . . . one less worry for later."

Oh, why did he have to go and ruin things? Why couldn't he just have continued to be a good husband, going to work, playing with the kids, not getting in the way?

The year Francine was named first vice-president of Pride Properties, Aunt Sylvie died of stomach cancer and a year later, right after the unveiling, Uncle Morris married her mother. "I'm happy as a lark, Francie," her mother said. "All in all, I think Aunt

Sylvie would be pleased, don't you? And if she wouldn't, what can I say? Life is for the living."

Andrew began to talk about taking a leave from the paper to write a book.

"What kind of book?" Francine asked.

"I don't know yet."

"When you know we'll discuss it," she told him.

But they never got around to discussing it because two months later Bobby was killed.

7

SARA WAS HELPING her father clean out his truck. IT was a mess from his long drive cross-country. Her father chewed pack after pack of gum on the road. He said it helped him to stay awake. So his truck was full of Juicy Fruit wrappers and when you were riding in it, with the windows open, the wrappers blew all over the place.

Sara's mother still hadn't accepted the idea of Daddy living in Boulder. If she had she wouldn't be making such a big thing out of Sara seeing him. And Sara wouldn't have to sneak over to his place, the way she had today. She would just be able to say, *I'll be at Daddy's after school. I'll be home by six.*

And then Mom would say, *Okay, Sweetie . . . see you then.*

Daddy's place wasn't much—just this little apartment over Mr. Hathaway's garage, at the end of a long dirt road, which was bumpy and eroded from the summer rains and hard to manage on her bicycle. Twice she had fallen off and scraped her knees.

Sara was helping him fix up the apartment, trying to make it feel more like a home. Last Sunday they had shopped for a cast iron frying pan because her father said it was impossible to cook eggs evenly without one. They had also bought some plants and three posters. Daddy had hung Sara's favorite poster, three coyotes wearing roller skates, over the sofa in the living room. The sofa pulled out into a bed and that's where Sara was going to sleep when she had overnights. Daddy promised that soon she would come for the whole weekend. But for now she should just be patient and not discuss the subject with her mother.

Sara was allowed to visit her father only on Sundays, from ten until six. But what her mother didn't know wouldn't hurt her. Besides, that was such a dumb rule. For the first time in six years her father was living nearby. And until next week, when school started full time, she had every afternoon free and her father did too. So why shouldn't they spend their time together? After all, that had been the whole idea.

Sara's father had come up with the plan last April, while Sara was visiting over spring break. They were sailing in Biscayne Bay that day and Daddy seemed really lonely. "I wish I could see you more often," he had said.

"I wish I could see you too."

"I wish you could live with me for a while."

"That would be nice."

"Really?" Daddy asked. "You mean it?"

"Well, sure . . . but I can't."

"Why not?"

"I can't leave Mom . . . she needs me." Sara hoped that her father wouldn't say that he needed her too, because then she wouldn't know what to do.

Her father understood. And that was when the idea first hit him. Since Sara couldn't leave Boulder to be with him, he would come there to be with her. And that way she would be able to see him whenever she wanted. At the time it had seemed like a very good idea.

Later, Sara wasn't so sure.

Sara's parents never talked on the phone or wrote letters, like some of Sara's friends' parents who were divorced. But they never fought either, which Jennifer said was the pits. Jennifer's parents were always fighting about money and visiting rights and each other's lovers, especially since Jennifer's mother had a new baby from her lover.

Sara's mother didn't have a lover now, but she used to have one named Mitch. He had made her mother cry all the time. Sara had hated him.

Sara had this fantasy that when her parents saw each other again they would realize that they still loved each other and would get married a second time. Then both her parents would live not only in the same town but in the same house. That could happen. Jennifer knew this family who had been divorced for seven years and then the parents got married again. But Jennifer wasn't sure that was a good idea because if they didn't get along the second time you had to go through a whole other divorce.

Sara had been only six when her parents were divorced. Before the divorce they'd lived in a big house in Florida. Sara had a room with a door to the patio so she could wake up early and go swimming in the pool. Except she wasn't allowed in unless someone was there to watch, even though she was a really good swimmer. But it was silly to think that just because someone was watching, you were going to be okay. Even if it was Daddy. Because Bobby had been with Daddy when the accident happened.

There were no pictures of Bobby in their house. It was as if there never was a Bobby. Sara said that she was an only child. That's the way her mother wanted it. Sometimes she felt like saying, *I had a brother, but he died.* But she didn't say it. It would have upset her mother too much. Besides, it all happened a long time ago.

Sara had a picture of the four of them. Mom, Daddy, Bobby, and herself, but she kept it hidden away under the false bottom of her jewelry box. Bobby was only ten when he died, younger than Sara was now. If he were still alive Bobby would be a teenager. Sara wondered what it would be like to have a teenaged brother. Would they be friends or would they fight all the time?

When Daddy's book was published he sent her a copy. Inside he had written, *To my darling Sara, I hope some day you will understand. I love you very much, Daddy.* Sara was just nine when the book was published and she didn't understand all of it, except that it was about a family something like theirs, but not exactly. And in it there was an accident and the youngest child was killed. A boy.

Daddy called him David. On the back of the book there was a picture of Daddy before he grew his beard. He was sitting on the sea wall wearing his favorite jacket, the denim one with the torn pocket.

Sara's mother caught her reading the book one time and threatened to take it away from her, but Sara had cried, so her mother let her keep it. She told Sara that she never wanted to see it again. So Sara kept it hidden in the bottom of her closet, in her game box.

Sara was still stuffing the gum wrappers from her father's truck into a trash bag when a blue Subaru drove down the dirt road and pulled into the driveway. Sara was really surprised when Margo and her kids got out. She wondered what they were doing here.

Her father, who was hosing out the back of the truck, stopped when the car pulled into the driveway and called, "Hello . . ."

"Oh, hello," Margo said.

"Who is that?" Sara heard Michelle ask Margo.

"Andrew Broder," Margo told her.

"B.B.'s husband?" Michelle asked.

"Former husband," Margo said.

Daddy walked over to their car. Sara climbed out of the truck and followed him.

"How are you today?" he asked Margo. Sara was surprised that her father knew Margo.

"Okay . . . how about you?" Margo said to her father.

"Much better," her father said.

What did he mean? Sara wondered. Had he been sick?

"Were you sick?" Michelle asked.

"No," Sara's father said, laughing. "I passed out in the hot tub a few nights ago."

The hot tub? Sara thought. What hot tub?

"Our hot tub?" Michelle asked him.

"Yes," her father said. "I guess the heat was too much for me."

"Andrew," Margo said, "I'd like you to meet my children, Stuart and Michelle. Kids, this is Andrew Broder."

Her father wiped his hands on his jeans, then he and Stuart shook hands. Michelle kept her hands in her pockets.

Then her father turned to her. "And this is my daughter, Sara."

"We already know each other, Daddy," Sara said, embarrassed.

"Oh, right," her father said. "I forgot . . . it's a small town."

"I used to babysit Sara," Michelle said.

"A long time ago," Sara said, to set the record straight. "When I was just a little kid."

"You mean a little brat," Michelle said.

"You weren't the greatest babysitter," Sara said.

Then Margo laughed a little and said, "Well, Sara . . . how was your summer?"

"Very nice. I went to camp near San Diego."

"Yes, I know," Margo said. "Your mother told me you were going."

"And I started junior high this year," Sara said, more to Michelle and Stuart than to Margo.

"Wow . . . junior high," Michelle said.

"Which school . . . Casey?" Stuart asked.

"Yes."

"Watch out for Mr. Loring. I've heard he fails half his class every year just for smiling."

"Really?" Sara asked. "For smiling?"

Michelle snorted. "I'm going inside."

"Same here," Stuart said. "Nice to meet you, Mr. Broder."

"Andrew," Sara's father said.

"Andrew," Stuart repeated, shaking her father's hand again.

"I'll be in in a minute," Margo called after her kids.

Then Margo and her father just stood there, looking at each other. "Well . . ." Margo finally said, "those are my kids."

Sara did not move.

"How about a movie tonight?" her father said to Margo.

"No, not tonight," Margo said.

"Tomorrow night?"

"I don't know," Margo said. "We'll see." She looked over at Sara.

"Maybe I could go with you, Daddy. I could ask Mom . . ."

"That would be nice," her father said. "Say, could you run inside and get me that vinyl spray cleaner for the front seat of the truck?"

"Now?" Sara asked.

"Yes, now."

Sara knew he was trying to get rid of her. What did he have to say to Margo that he couldn't say in front of her.

"Please . . ." he said.

"Okay . . . okay . . ." Sara said and she ran up the path leading to the Hathaway house. Probably her father wanted to tell Margo something about how Sara wasn't supposed to be visiting today and that Margo shouldn't mention it to Mom.

When Sara returned with the vinyl cleaner her father and Margo were standing close, talking. When they saw her, they stopped.

"I've got to go in now," Margo said. "But maybe I will go to the movies with you some night . . . if something good is playing."

"Let me know when you think something good is playing," her father said.

"*Return of Frankenstein* is at the Fox," Sara said.

Margo started to laugh. Then her father laughed too.

Sara didn't see what was so funny, especially since *Return of Frankenstein* was a really scary movie.

8

B.B.'s OFFICE WAS in a stately federal house on Spruce. She had restored it over the past few years and had rented the second floor to a State Farm insurance agent. The house itself was listed in the guidebooks as an historic site, dating back to 1877, and B.B. was as proud of it as she was of her home.

But now it was being painted inside. The painter had convinced B.B. to go with an oil rather than a waterbase paint. It would last longer and look richer, he'd said. She had gone along with him and that had turned out to be a mistake. The strong odor was causing everyone in the office to feel headachey and nauseous and her secretary, Miranda, could not stop wheezing. B.B. assured them all, as well as the insurance agent upstairs, that the painting would be finished by Friday and that she, personally, would make sure the house was aired out all weekend so that on Monday, when they came back to work, the odor of the paint would be gone.

It had also been a mistake to agree to have the house painted during the first week of school. She should have arranged to keep her afternoons free, to make plans with Sara to go into Denver to the museum, or shop—anything. She did not like the idea of Sara hanging out after school. Now that she had started junior high B.B. would have to keep a careful eye on her. Sara would be exposed to drugs, to sex, to kids without values. And it was up to

B.B. to make sure that Sara did not stray. It made her dizzy to think of all the problems that lay ahead.

She picked up a WonderRoast chicken on her way home from the office and was preparing butternut squash when Sara came in. "Where have you been?" she asked. "It's after six."

"Out . . . riding my bike with some of the kids from school. What's for dinner?"

"Chicken and squash."

"Butternut?"

"Yes."

"Mashed?"

"Yes . . . the way I always make it . . . with cinnamon."

They sat down to dinner a few minutes later. "Um . . . it's good," Sara said.

"I'm glad you like it."

They ate quietly for a while. B.B. was distracted, thinking about the office. Perhaps she should have gone with strong colors in the reception area instead of off-white.

Then Sara said, "I didn't know Margo lives next door to Daddy. I was really surprised when I saw her there."

"You saw Margo?"

"Yes."

"When?"

"This afternoon."

B.B. lay down her fork. "What were you doing over there this afternoon?"

"Oh . . . I . . ." Sara's cheeks turned red and she began to chew on her fingernails.

Caught in the act, B.B. thought.

"I forgot my library book when I was there on Sunday and I was afraid it would be overdue so I rode my bike over to get it, but I didn't stay."

"I don't want you doing that again," B.B said. "Do you understand? You are never to go over there without my permission."

"But Mom . . . I was only there for five minutes, maybe less."

"I'm warning you, Sara. If I find out that you've disobeyed me you're going to be grounded. And then you won't be allowed to see your father at all." B.B. did not want to punish Sara for Andrew's foolishness, but what choice did she have? If she didn't hold the reins tightly who knew where it all might end. "And you are never to lie to me again."

"I didn't lie."

"You did and we both know it. You didn't leave your library book over there."

"I'm sorry. It's just that for the rest of this week we get out of school at noon so I have all this free time and so does Daddy."

"Use that time to get your room in order."

"It is in order."

"Go over your clothes and pull out everything that doesn't fit. I'll give you a box to stack them in."

"Okay."

B.B. got up to clear away the dinner plates. "So . . . did you introduce your father to Margo?"

"They already knew each other."

"Oh?"

"Daddy said something about passing out in Margo's hot tub."

"Really?"

"Something like that."

"Are you sure?"

"Not exactly."

Sara must be mistaken, B.B. thought as she washed the dishes. Children were always putting two and two together and coming up with five. But she would give Margo a call and ask her to keep an eye on things. Margo could be on the lookout for Sara sneaking over to Andrew's and it wouldn't hurt to ask her to keep an eye on Andrew too. Anything B.B. could get on him, any leverage to use in court, if it went so far, would help.

But when B.B. phoned Margo and asked her to do just that, just a simple favor, Margo turned cold and said, "You're asking me to spy on him?"

"Not spy. Just to keep an eye on things, especially Sara."

"I can't do that," Margo said.

"What do you mean, you can't?"

"It wouldn't be right. I wish you'd stop putting me in the middle."

"How have I put you in the middle?"

"By moving him in next door to me in the first place. And now, asking me to watch him. I don't want to watch him. I don't want to know any more about him than I already do."

"What do you know?"

"Nothing. Very little. He seems like a nice man. That's all."

"I hear he's already been in your hot tub," B.B. said softly, hoping that Margo would deny it and ask where she had gotten such a foolish idea.

"It was nothing," Margo said.

So, it was true. B.B. did not respond.

"Look," Margo continued, after a moment of silence, "I'm sorry I can't help you out. Try to understand."

"Of course," B.B. said coldly. "See you in Jazzercise." She put the phone back on the hook. God, you couldn't trust anyone, could you? She wondered if they'd worn bathing suits.

9

MARGO FOUND HERSELF thinking about Andrew Broder, found herself standing on her deck watching for his truck or hoping she might run into him on the Mall. If she did she'd say, *Oh, hello . . . would you like to get a cup of coffee?* And he'd say, *Sounds good to me,* and they would walk over to Pearl's and sit at the outdoor cafe and order espressos. She would be wearing her heathery pink poncho and he would say, *I like the way you look in that. It brings out the color in your cheeks.*

Fool, she told herself. Find another fantasy.

She wished that B.B. hadn't called, asking her to keep an eye on Andrew. When she'd told B.B. to stop putting her in the middle, B.B. had been pissed. Margo had heard it in her voice.

On Monday morning, at the office, Margo finished up the preliminary sketches for the cluster housing project and decided to drop them at B.B.'s office on her way to lunch. She told Barbara, the receptionist at Benson and Gould, she'd be back by one-thirty and if Michael phoned from Vail she had information for him on those Trocal windows. Then, as an afterthought, she picked up the phone on Barbara's desk and called home. The phone rang twice before Mrs. Herrera answered. "Mrs. Margo Sampson's residence . . ."

"Hello, Mrs. Herrera . . . it's me," Margo said.

Mrs. Herrera had been cleaning for Margo since Margo had come to town. She cleaned for B.B. on Tuesdays and Fridays and for another friend on Wednesdays. Today, Mrs. Herrera complained that with Stuart and Michelle back the house was a mess and it was going to take her at least two extra hours to clean it properly and was Margo willing to pay?

Margo told Mrs. Herrera that she was.

"Because I don't do this for fun," Mrs. Herrera said.

"I understand," Margo said.

"And last week I left you a list and you didn't buy one thing on it. How am I supposed to clean if you don't buy the supplies?"

"I'm sorry . . . I forgot."

"Mrs. B.B. buys two of everything so we never run out."

"You'll have all the supplies you need next week. I promise."

Margo hung up the phone and smiled at Barbara, who relished the weekly conversations with Mrs. Herrera. "I shouldn't have called home," Margo said.

"She would have called here if you hadn't."

"That's true." Margo slung her leather bag over her shoulder, waved at Barbara, and left.

Benson and Gould's offices were in a handsome red brick building on Chestnut, converted in 1973 from an old warehouse by Jeffrey Gould, before he discovered the Bahamas. When Michael Benson and Margo had been lovers they used to stay at the office until Barbara and Jeffrey had gone, lock the doors, and make love on the floor. Then Margo would go home and prepare dinner for her children. It had been a pleasant arrangement while it lasted. Twice married and twice divorced, with two sets of children, Michael was terrified of personal responsibilities, a trait that sometimes carried over into his professional life. By the time Margo introduced him to her children her feelings for him had fizzled anyway, so she was not hurt at his suggestion that they find other lovers and become friends.

Outside, the temperature was still in the eighties and Margo would not have minded if the weather stayed this way all year long. She walked a few blocks to Spruce, to B.B.'s office.

"She's already left for lunch," Miranda said, when Margo asked for B.B. "She's at The James, with clients. She should be back in an hour."

"I'll just leave these with you," Margo said, placing the folder on Miranda's desk.

"I'm sure she wouldn't mind if you dropped in and gave them to her yourself. She'd probably welcome the interruption. These clients are bo-ring." Miranda fanned the air in front of her face to make her point. Miranda had come to work for B.B. fresh out of C.U. two years ago and now she dressed like B.B., wore her hair like B.B., and was even beginning to sound like B.B.

"I'm in a hurry myself," Margo said. "So just give them to her when she gets back."

"Okay," Miranda said. "Sure."

Margo walked from B.B.'s office to the Mall. Before she'd arrived in Boulder her idea of a Mall was Saks, Bonwit's, and Bloomingdale's strung out around a huge concrete parking area, either in New Jersey or Long Island, and swamped with career shoppers, like her sister, Bethany. In Boulder, which had once been a supply center for the mining towns in the mountains, the Mall was an area of renovated buildings, some dating back to the late 1800s, housing shops, restaurants, and galleries. The streets were cobblestone and closed to traffic. Some of the old-timers complained that it was too tourist oriented, but Margo disagreed. It provided a downtown shopping area for the locals and made it fun to work in the neighborhood.

She went into the New York Deli, ordered two pastrami sandwiches on rye—you had to specify here or you might get it on whole wheat or, worse yet, white bread—and two iced coffees to go. Then she waited outside, lifting her face to the sun. When her order was ready she crossed the Mall and walked to the corner, to Clare's gallery. The gallery represented Margo's most creative renovation in Boulder. She had left as much of the original bank building intact as she could, including the tellers' windows, the winding staircase and the balcony, which had become a sculpture gallery.

Clare had come to Boulder like Margo, following her divorce from Robin Carleton-Robbins, a West Texas banker who had run off to the Amazon or someplace like that—Clare wasn't sure, it might have been the Nile—with one of his tellers. She was very young, Clare said, and smelled like doughnuts. Clare had come to Boulder with her daughter, Puffin, a classmate of Margo's children, and her millions, some of which she used to open her gallery, one of the few in town that was not a front for drug traffic. *Strictly legitimate,* Clare would say, proudly. *I don't wash anybody's money.* And she had never eaten a doughnut again and swore she never would.

At first Margo found it odd that a woman whose husband had run off with a bank teller would choose a bank building for her gallery. One day during the construction phase Margo had mentioned that to Clare and Clare had laughed her big, booming laugh and had replied, "It is odd, isn't it?"

Margo pushed open the heavy glass door to the gallery. "Lunch . . ." she announced.

"Be right with you," Clare called. "Just let me wash up. Have a look at the balcony while you're waiting."

Clare's fall show had opened on Labor Day weekend. It featured artists of the Southwest. The walls were hung with R.C. Gormans, Doug Wests, and Celia Ramseys. Margo went through the gallery to the vault, which served as Clare's office space. She dropped the lunch bag on Clare's desk, then ran upstairs where Clare's assistant, Joe, was setting up a barnyard exhibit of carved wooden animals. "They're wonderful," Margo said, eyeing a brown pig complete with teeth. "How much does that one go for?"

"Ninety-five," Joe said, "but if you're interested . . ."

"I know . . ." Margo said.

Clare would be leaving for Europe day after tomorrow. She went every September, after the fall show opened, and it was always a lonely time in Margo's life. The last time she and Clare had had a good talk had been on Margo's fortieth birthday. Clare had taken her to dinner at John's French Restaurant, had presented her with the silk robe, and had ordered champagne. Over dessert, a decadent hazelnut cake, Margo had confessed that what she wanted most for her fortieth birthday was a steady man. "One who'll be there in the morning," she'd said, feeling giddy from the champagne.

"I wouldn't mind one myself," Clare said, "but they're not easy to find and if we should happen to find them, then we won't be this close anymore."

"That's bullshit," Margo said, draining her champagne glass. "Why should we have to choose between a man and a friend?"

"I don't know. I suppose because it's hard to keep that kind of intimacy going with more than one person at a time. While I was married to Robin I never had friends . . . real friends . . . did you?"

"I had friends," Margo said, "but I never confided in them until my marriage fell apart."

"You see?"

"But it doesn't have to be that way." Margo poured herself another glass of champagne. She knew she was going to be sick, but she didn't care.

Clare came into her office and stretched out on the sofa. Margo handed her a sandwich and said, "I'm crazy about that pig . . . the one with the teeth."

"He's yours."

"I want to *buy* him."

"Consider it done."

"For a fair price."

"Of course."

"Michelle's always campaigning for a pet. Maybe this will satisfy her."

Clare laughed.

"I'm going to miss you," Margo said. "Who's going to listen to me while you're gone? Who's going to laugh at my jokes?"

"I'll be back in three weeks."

"Three weeks is a long time."

"I keep telling you . . . you should come with me."

"I will, one of these days."

"Keep in touch with B.B.," Clare said. "I'm worried about her . . . about how she's handling having her ex in town."

"She'll adjust," Margo said. "She'll have to."

Clare sighed. "That's what life is, isn't it . . . a series of adjustments."

"Did I tell you, I met him?"

"No . . . what's he like?"

"Friendly . . . seems nice enough . . ."

"Who knows, maybe he and B.B. will get back together."

"I doubt it," Margo said.

"Why? Didn't you ever think of getting back together with Freddy?"

"In the beginning, sure . . . during the hard times. I thought about how easy life could be if I didn't fight it. But I wasn't ready to give up. And I wasn't sure he'd want me back . . ."

"They all do . . . eventually."

"I don't think so. Anyway, I'm glad I held out. I would never have forgiven myself for running back just because it was safe. And I haven't been tempted in years. Besides, he's married, so I don't have to think about it." She balled up her sandwich bag and tossed it across the room into Clare's trash basket.

"I think about it sometimes," Clare said.

"About what?"

"About going back to Robin. We've been separated for four years and we're no closer to a divorce now than we were when he ran off with the Doughnut. It's hard for the wealthy to divorce," Clare said, laughing into her iced coffee. "There's all that money to divvy up, all that property . . . it could take years . . . maybe it's not worth it." She lowered her voice. "He's back."

"Robin?"

"Yes . . . he's in Dallas."

"Why didn't you tell me?"

"I didn't know until yesterday. He called. He wants to see me."

"What about the Doughnut?"

"That's over. It only lasted six months. He's been living in Cuernavaca, alone. A mid-life crisis, he says."

"God," Margo said, "I am so sick of men and their mid-life crises. What about us? When do we get ours?"

"I suspect we've already had them."

"Are you going to see him?"

"I don't know. I'll think about it while I'm in Paris."

"Don't do anything you're going to regret," Margo said.

Clare laughed. "If I didn't do anything I was going to regret I'd never do anything . . . and you know it."

"I want you to be happy," Margo said. "I don't want to see you hurt."

"You sound like a mother."

"I am a mother."

"I know," Clare said, "but not mine."

Margo left the gallery at one-fifteen and was rushing back to the office when someone called her name. She stopped. It was Andrew Broder, standing in front of the Boulder Bookstore, loaded down with packages. "Hello," he said. "How are you?"

"Okay . . . how about you?"

"I've become a shopper . . . as you can see. Do you have time for a cup of coffee?"

"I'm on my way back to the office," she told him. "But I'd love to, some other time."

"It's a deal," he said, shifting the packages in his arms.

Fantasy into reality, she thought, walking away. *Too bad it's too warm for my heathery pink poncho.* She started to laugh. She was still laughing when she got back to her office.

10

B.B. DID NOT get out of bed on the following Sunday morning. She lay under the covers in her rumpled nightgown, sleeping fitfully, floating in and out of dreams. She had told herself that she needed to catch up on her sleep, but she knew that she wasn't getting out of bed because there was no reason to, since Sara had gone off with Andrew for the day. She had watched from her bedroom window as Sara had raced out of the house at nine, carrying her Monopoly game. She had watched as they had driven off together in Andrew's ugly truck. It was a warm, sunny early September day and as she dozed B.B. heard children's voices laughing. But they were not the voices of her children.

At five, jolted awake by some inner alarm, B.B. jumped up and out of bed, took a shower, and dressed carefully so that when Sara came home she would be ready to take her out to dinner. She was sitting at the kitchen table, sipping tomato juice and reading the Sunday *Camera,* when Andrew pulled into the driveway. He and Sara got out of the truck and walked to the back door together.

B.B. hugged Sara and said, "Hi, Sweetie . . . I missed you. All set for dinner at Rudi's?" She ignored Andrew.

"I already ate," Sara said. "Daddy made hamburgers and french fries."

"You already had dinner?" B.B. asked.

"Yes, so I'm not hungry . . . maybe just some ice cream later."

Sara stood on tiptoe and kissed Andrew. "Bye, Dad . . . see you next week."

"The reason I wanted her back at six," B.B. said to Andrew, speaking slowly and softly, trying not to show the anger she was feeling, "was so I could take her out to dinner."

"I didn't know," Andrew said.

"Sara should have told you," B.B. said.

"But Mom . . ." Sara said, "you didn't say we were going out tonight."

"You should have known," B.B. said. "We always go to Rudi's on Sunday nights, don't we?"

"But Mom . . ."

"I don't want to hear another word about it," she said, her voice becoming harsh. "Just go to your room."

Sara's eyes filled with tears and she turned and ran down the hallway.

"Aren't you being tough on her?" Andrew asked.

"Don't tell me how to handle my daughter," B.B. said, slamming the door in his face.

B.B. went to her room, took off her clothes, got back into bed, and didn't get up until the next morning, not realizing until she began to run that she hadn't eaten anything yesterday and now she was so weak she could only go a mile.

This was no good. None of it was any good. She could feel herself losing control. Her hair was shedding in the shower. The bottoms of her feet alternately itched, then burned. She continued to lose weight.

The weight loss had started over the summer. She had assumed it was the worry of Andrew coming to town. She had always had trouble eating during times of stress. For weeks she had lived on only farina and dried apricots. To clear her mind she had started to run four, five, sometimes six miles a day. With Sara away at camp she had thrown herself completely into business matters and community projects. But instead of her usually innovative ideas, she drew blanks at meeting after meeting. People asked her if she was feeling all right.

In mid-July she had taken a week off to go out to San Diego to visit Sara at camp. She stayed at La Costa, sure that a week of pampering would relax her. On her first day there she took a tennis lesson from a craggy faced but still handsome pro who told her she was the most gorgeous thing he'd seen all summer. He was impressed by her sure, firm strokes as well. They spent the night together, but he was a disappointing lover, fast and hard, with no interest in foreplay. Afterwards he said, "Nice, babe . . ." the same way he'd said it on the court. Then he rolled over and was out cold, snoring and farting in his sleep. She was relieved when at five A.M., he left.

The next night, her fortieth birthday, she dressed in white chiffon and had dinner by herself in the main dining room. When she was a child birthday parties meant black patent leather shoes, ribbons in her hair, and Dixie cups and then, when she opened her Dixie and licked the ice cream off the inside of the lid, she would find a movie star's picture. One time she had found Lassie's picture and all the other children at the party begged her to trade with them, but she wouldn't. So they'd teased her, calling her Skinny and Red and Freckle-face, and she had cried, but she hadn't given up Lassie's picture.

After dinner she went back to her room and sat on the edge of her bed for a long time, feeling lonely and depressed, wanting to talk to someone, but not knowing who. She picked up the phone and thought about calling her mother, but she knew that as soon as she heard her mother's voice she would start to cry and then there would be questions. So she did not call her mother. She knew a million people, but she had so few friends. Clare was one of the few people she felt close to. With Clare she didn't have to say what was on her mind because Clare sensed it. She wished there were more people like Clare. She would have called Clare tonight but Clare was away too, visiting her mother on Padre Island. Should she call Margo? No, Margo wasn't really a friend. Margo was just someone she sometimes saw for lunch. She reached for the plaque Sara had made for her at camp. *Superwoman,* it said. Was that really how Sara saw her, as a superwoman? And if she was, then how come she felt so small, so insignificant now?

She supposed she could call Mitch, just for old times' sake. Maybe she would even invite him down for the weekend. After all, this was her birthday. She owed herself one. She picked up the phone and dialed his old number.

He answered on the third ring. "B.B.," he said, "wonderful to hear your voice again."

"I'm in San Diego . . . at La Costa . . ."

"Wonderful place, San Diego . . ."

"I thought you might drive down for dinner over the weekend . . . we could catch up on what's been happening . . ."

"Love to," he said, "but I'm all tied up. I'm doing a series, you know."

"I didn't know."

"Yes, one of the top twelve."

"That's great."

There was a long pause.

"And I'm living with someone . . . but surely you knew that."

"No, I didn't."

"Yes. She's a producer too. We have a lot in common. It's working out."

"I'm glad for you," she told him. And suddenly she remembered that the last time they'd been together she'd wound up with a black eye and a strained ligament in her left leg.

She hung up the phone, feeling humiliated, rolled over onto her stomach, held the bed pillow tightly, and wept.

After, she went to the bathroom and washed her face. It was puffy and splotched. *Look at you,* she said to her reflection. *Forty years old . . . half your life, maybe more than half, gone. Look at those lines around your eyes, around your mouth. You're aging, Francine. Oh sure, from a distance you could still pass for twenty-five, but up close, forget it. You're not fooling anyone.* Aging, she thought, was the least fair fact of life.

She took off her white chiffon dress. It was a mess now, wrinkled and without shape. She'd kept it tucked away for too many years. She'd bought it for a cruise she and Andrew had taken to celebrate their tenth anniversary. But Andrew had acted sullen and bored on the cruise, so she had flirted with the ship's captain, let-

ting him breathe into her ear on the dance floor, which had infuri-
ated Andrew.

When they'd returned to their cabin, Andrew had practically
torn the dress off her, pushing her down on the lower berth,
standing over her showing off his erection and telling her exactly
what he was going to do with it. But as soon as he entered her he'd
lost it, and blaming her, calling her the ultimate C.T., he had run
out of the cabin, still zipping up his pants. He'd returned at dawn
to apologize, telling her that he'd been drunk and had been sick all
night. *Forgive me, Francie,* he'd said. *It's just this goddamned
cruise . . . I can't take being cooped up this way.* She had told him
that it didn't matter, that she'd already mended her dress. But
when he'd tried to crawl into the berth with her, when he'd tried
to hold her, to kiss her, she had turned away and pretended to be
asleep.

She should have gotten rid of the dress a long time ago, she
thought, tossing it into the wastebasket.

How was it possible, she wondered, as she got into bed, that it
was working between Mitch and the producer when she had tried
so hard to make it work with him and couldn't? She had thought
they would marry and move to Beverly Hills where she would find
them a big, wonderful house with possibilities. She would open a
branch of Brady Broder—Elegant Homes. Sara would go to school
with all the right kids. She and Mitch would be part of a tight little
social group of producers, directors, writers, and actors. They
would all tell her that with her looks she should have been on the
screen. She would just pooh-pooh them, take Mitch's arm, smile
up at him and he would feel unbelievably lucky to have her for his
wife.

But Mitch never asked her to marry him. And she never asked
him. Instead, his moodiness turned ugly. She could never figure
out his hostile behavior. He was hostile even when they were making love. He would accuse her of either coming on too strong or
not strong enough. She had tried so hard to get it right. To do all
the things he said he liked in bed. She had studied sex manuals in
order to please him. But nothing was enough. He became increas-

ingly critical. Yet she was sure, if she was sweet enough, understanding enough, it would be all right.

He said she drove him to it, to his hostile, abusive behavior. To their battles. He said she was too controlling, too demanding. But what had she ever demanded? She couldn't think of a thing. Okay, so she liked making plans. And she had a lot of plans for them. But that had nothing to do with control or demands.

Why had she phoned him tonight? What had she hoped to hear? That he missed her? That he wanted her? That he had changed his ways? *Fool,* she told herself. *Goddamned fool!* She should have called her mother instead.

The next morning she went to the pool to swim laps. She was getting anxious about being away from the office. Maybe she would cut her week short and leave the next day. At home, surrounded by her things, by the routine of her life, she would feel better. And in just three weeks Sara would return and she would have a reason for living again.

She was in the middle of the pool when she collided with another swimmer. He had been swimming underwater and she hadn't seen him coming. He had kicked her in the head.

"I'm terribly sorry," he said, coming to the surface, sputtering. "Are you all right?"

"Yes, I think so. Are you?"

"I'm fine."

They swam across the pool to the ladder and climbed out. She felt slightly dizzy for a minute and he helped her to her lounge chair. "I'm a doctor," he said. "Let me have a look." He took her pulse, turned her head from side to side, then up and down, and pronounced her healthy. "But we should keep an eye on you today . . . to make sure."

He pulled his lounge chair next to hers. His name was Lewis Branscomb. He was a cardiologist from Minneapolis, a widower, fifty-seven, with two grown children and two grandchildren. He was balding and not terribly attractive, but he seemed to be in good shape. By the time they ordered lunch she decided that he was not unattractive either. And she had always enjoyed doctors.

They had a certain self-assuredness that she liked. She knew, before they finished lunch, that he would fall for her and she didn't discourage him.

They spent that night together, and the next, and he extended his stay for the coming weekend. He was good for her bruised ego. He was good for her state of mind. He was sweet and predictable and in bed he expected very little of her. Not like Mitch, who had insisted that she suck on him endlessly, until she was sure her jaw would dislocate.

Lewis told her that he had never had such exciting sex. That just watching her undress was enough to make him feel nineteen again.

"I can't stand the idea of losing you," Lewis said on their last night together. "Come with me to Minneapolis."

"I can't," she told him.

"Why not?"

"It's too cold there."

"I'd keep you warm."

"You're sweet, Lewis . . . but, no."

"I'll come to Boulder, then."

"Come for a visit in the fall, when the aspens turn color."

"What am I supposed to do until then?"

She didn't answer.

"If you marry me," he said, "you can call yourself Triple B."

She laughed. "That's not a good enough reason to get married."

"I'll try to think of a better one."

The next day, as they said goodbye, he gave her a gold bracelet, expensive and elegant. She liked this man. He had style. She liked the idea of having a lover far away. She could not handle someone new and nearby in her life right now.

She did not tell him that Andrew was coming to town.

Lewis phoned her in Boulder several times a week. He sent her cards with absurd messages, books he thought she might enjoy, cassettes, flowers. He had already booked a room at the Boulderado for the first week in October. He was anxious to meet her little girl, to see how she lived, to be with her again.

She did not tell him about Bobby.

He missed her terribly, he said. There was no one else for him. There never would be. And somehow he was going to convince her of this.

She did not tell him, when he phoned on Monday, that she had lain in bed the night before thinking about death, imagining herself hanging from a rope, or with her wrists slit and bleeding, or with half her head blown away by a bullet.

11

MARGO HAD CALLED Puffin twice since Clare left for Europe and both times Puffin assured her that she was fine. Clare's cousin from Padre Island stayed with Puffin every year while Clare traveled. Margo wanted to have Puffin over for dinner so she asked Michelle and Stuart to choose a night that was good for them.

Michelle said, "Oh, Mother . . . do we have to have her over for dinner? She's such a pissy kid."

"Maybe she's changed over the summer," Margo said. "You never know."

"She's lost about twenty pounds," Stuart said. "I saw her at school yesterday. She's very together looking."

"Well," Margo said, "Thursday or Friday would be best for me. Let me know in the morning. I'm going to the movies tonight."

"What are you going to see?" Michelle said.

"Apocalypse Now."

"I hear it sucks," Michelle said.

"I'm going anyway. I'll be back by eleven."

Margo went downstairs. She bushed her teeth, changed her shirt, tossed a sweater over her shoulders, then picked up the phone and dialed Andrew Broder's number.

He answered on the first ring.

She thought about hanging up when he did.

He said hello twice before she responded. "Hello . . . it's Margo."

"Margo?" he said, as if he had never heard the name.

"Margo . . . from next door."

"Oh, that Margo."

Very funny, she thought. "I'm going to the movies tonight . . . to see *Apocalypse Now* . . ."

"Mixed reviews," he said.

"I'm going anyway. I like Martin Sheen."

"Not Brando?"

"Brando too. It starts at seven-thirty. I'm leaving in five minutes. If you decide to come meet me outside." Before he had a chance to say anything else she hung up. She shouldn't have called. She brushed her hair and glossed her lips.

When she got to her car, he was sitting inside it. "I decided to come along," he told her.

"Good," she said, as if they had just closed a business deal. She fished her glasses out of her bag, put them on, and drove to the Fox.

"I like the way you look in glasses," Andrew said.

"I'm nearsighted," Margo explained. "I need them for driving and movies."

"But not for making love?"

She looked over at him. "Don't you ever think of anything else?"

"Yes, sure . . . all the time," he said. "I didn't mean anything personal. I was just wondering."

"Just for the record," she said, "I don't wear them when I'm making love."

"Some people do, you know . . . but I guess they're farsighted."

"I haven't ever thought about it," Margo said.

"I guess it's because I write," he told her. "An offbeat subject like that could make an interesting article. I could sell it to the *Optician's Quarterly*."

"Is there such a magazine?" she asked.

He laughed. "I don't know. There might be."

She laughed too. It was hard to be angry at him.

The movie was long and tedious. After an hour Andrew pulled two small boxes of raisins out of his pocket. He passed one box to her. She hadn't eaten raisins in years, not since she'd been sixteen and somewhat anemic. "Either iron tonic or a box of raisins a day," her mother had said. "Which will it be?"

"Raisins," Margo had answered. But after a week just looking at the red box had been enough gag her. "I'll take the tonic," she'd cried to her mother one morning. "I never want to see another raisin!"

Andrew reached for her hand. His warm fingers wrapped around hers as if they always held hands, as if they went to the movies regularly. And later, when she felt herself about to doze off, her head went automatically to his shoulder. He gave her cheek a quick, gentle caress and his fingers brushed her hair. In the darkened theater they shared a smile.

Afterwards, she drove home.

"You're supposed to ask me in for coffee," he said, when they pulled up in front of her house.

"Really?"

"Yes, it's in the Rule Book."

"Okay. Would you like to come in for a cup of coffee?"

"Yes," he said. "I'd like that."

"My children will probably still be up."

"That's fine."

"Just warning you."

"Stop apologizing for them, will you?"

"I'll try."

Michelle was already asleep, but Stuart was in the kitchen making himself a peanut butter sandwich.

"It's great on rye bread with lettuce and mayonnaise," Andrew told him.

"You've got to be kidding," Stuart said.

"No, you should try it."

"I like it this way, on gross white bread with grape jelly."

"Andrew went to the movies with me," Margo said, feeling an explanation was in order.

"Yeah?" Stuart said, as if he couldn't have cared less. "So how was it?"

"Long," Margo said.

"Your mother found it pretentious," Andrew said.

"Not all of it," Margo explained, as she put up the kettle. "I was moved by some of it . . . but the ending was . . . I don't know . . . I just couldn't get into it . . ."

"That's because you were asleep," Andrew said.

"No shit," Stuart said, laughing. "She really fell *asleep?*"

Margo felt self-conscious. She busied herself pulling out mugs and plates and slicing up a loaf of banana bread.

"So how do you like Boulder?" Stuart asked Andrew.

"Hard to say . . . so far it seems okay. I'm going to be starting work on a new book soon. It should be a good place to write."

"What kind of book?" Stuart said.

"Nonfiction."

"What subject?"

"An in-depth study of Florida's correctional system."

"You mean prisons?"

Why didn't Stuart just shut up and go to bed? Margo thought.

"Yes, but Florida's not unique," Andrew said, as if he needed to make Stuart understand. "The rest of the country has the same problems."

"No shit," Stuart said. Then he turned to her. "Say, Mother . . . Dad called. Michelle left one of her bathing suits at the beach house. Aliza just found it behind the bed. She said it was mildewed so she's throwing it out."

"Okay. Anyone else?"

"Yeah . . . some guy named Eric called. Said you met him over the summer in Chaco Canyon and he just wanted to say hello. He didn't leave a number. Said he'd call again sometime when he's in the neighborhood."

Eric. That was all she needed now. "Okay . . . thanks."

"Well . . ." Stuart said, balancing his sandwich and a glass of milk in one hand, "I'm going to bed. Goodnight."

"Goodnight," Margo said, relieved. "See you in the morning."

"Goodnight," Andrew said.

Margo loaded a tray with the coffee pot, the mugs and the dishes, the banana bread.

"Can I give you a hand with that?" Andrew asked.

"Yes, sure . . ." she said. He carried the tray into the living room and set it down on the coffee table. She turned the stereo to KBOD, classical, then joined Andrew on the sofa in front of the fireplace. It was too warm for a fire now, but in a month or so they'd have one every night. Oh, it would be so nice to share life again. To share it with a steady man. One who didn't get up to go racing home at two A.M. One who slept with his arms around her every night.

Stop it! she warned herself.

"Nice kid," Andrew said, bringing Margo back to reality.

"What?"

"Stuart . . . seems like a nice kid."

"Last year at this time he would have just grunted at you. Now he reminds me of Freddy."

"His father?"

"Yes."

"Sounds like the standard fear of every ex-wife."

"And ex-husband?"

"With us it was different."

She waited to hear more, not sure that she wanted to know how it was between him and B.B., not sure that she didn't.

Instead he said, "Tell me about your work."

"There's not that much to tell," she said. She didn't want to talk about her work tonight. She wanted the magic of the darkened movie theater. "I'm an architect," she said, "with a special interest in solar design."

"Where'd you go to school?"

"The first time, Boston U . . . fine arts. I was an art teacher for a while, at Walden, in New York."

"So what happened?"

"I don't know. After ten years and two kids of my own I wanted a change. So I took a leave and went to Pratt. When I got my degree I went to work for a small firm in the city. Then, after Freddy and I split up, I decided to try Boulder. And here I am."

"How long have you been divorced?"

"Five years. How about you?"

"Six. You didn't know that?"

"No, why should I?"

"I don't know. I assumed since you and Francine are friends . . ."

"Look, we're friendly, but we're not real friends. There's a big difference." Margo poured each of them a second cup of coffee. She wanted them to hurry up and get this business out of the way. Every time you met a new man it was the same thing. Tell me about your work. Where did you go to school. Divorce details. Problems with children. Every time. What a pain. "Just to set the record straight," she said, "I don't know anything about you, except that you write."

"What do you want to know?" he asked, not giving her a chance to finish. She was about to tell him that she didn't care. That he seemed like a nice person, an interesting person, a very attractive person and that under different circumstances . . .

"I was a reporter on the Miami *Herald* for a long time and then I quit," he said. "I went to live in Israel for a year, on a kibbutz, but it wasn't what I'd expected. And then I came home and wrote a book. That was a couple of years ago and since then I've been writing freelance articles, mostly investigative reporting. I like the way your mouth curls up. You're very pretty, you know that?"

"Please."

"Please what?"

"It's better if we don't get personal, I think."

"Why is it better?"

"You know."

"I don't."

"I'll write you a letter about it, okay?"

"Sure, okay. You want my address?"

"I know where you live."

"But I pick up my mail. My box number is three-five-nine."

"Three-five-nine," she said. "I'll remember that. I'd like to read your book."

"I'll bring you a copy."

"Okay. But right now I've got to go to bed. I get up early."

He stood up. "When are you going to have me over for dinner? That's what you're supposed to do when someone new moves into the neighborhood."

"Is that in the Rule Book too?"

"Absolutely," he said. "Page forty-two."

"I see."

"Of course, I could have you over too. I make a mean spinach lasagna, an outstanding chicken curry, and I'm working on a stuffed zucchini."

"Sounds delicious."

"So . . . when?"

"When, what?"

"When should we get together for dinner?"

"I'll have to think about it."

"I swim every afternoon at the University pool. Would you like to join me some day?"

"I'm not much of a swimmer. I get water up my nose."

"I'll get you nose clips."

"Then I'd look like a frog."

"What's wrong with frogs?"

"They're green and slimy."

"You're right," he said.

She walked him down the stairs and to the front door.

"I'm reading Proust," he said. *"The Captive."*

"I never got past the endless minutiae of *Swann's Way*."

"So you're not a romantic," he said.

"Says who?"

"If you were you'd like Proust."

"Not necessarily," she said, opening the front door. They stepped outside into the darkness. She kept forgetting to replace the burned-out bulb in the hanging lamp next to the door. "Why are you telling me all of this anyway?"

"I want you to know me, I guess. I want you to like me."

"I do like you. Now go home."

"How about a soak first?"

"No, not tonight."

"When?"

"I don't know. Maybe never."

"That would be a real shame."

She shrugged.

"Margo . . . I'd like to kiss you goodnight."

"No," she said.

"Can I shake your hand then?"

She put her hand out. He took it. His touch sent tingles up her arm, weakened her legs, sent a flash between them.

Adolescent. Romantic imbecile.

"Goodnight, Margo," he said.

"Goodnight, Andrew." She pulled her hand away just in time. In another second she'd have been in his arms, her mouth on his. Instead, she turned and walked back into the house, closing the door behind her.

Just like Leonard, the voice inside her head said as she was brushing her teeth.

Are you crazy? she argued. *He's nothing like Leonard.*

The same tingles . . .

That's just physical attraction. She spit out toothpaste.

You're telling me?

So I admit it. I'm attracted to him. But he's nice too.

You didn't think Leonard was nice?

Yes, I did . . . in the beginning . . . but it turned out he was neurotic.

And how do you know this one isn't?

I don't. How could I? We hardly know each other.

Ah ha! That's exactly what I've been trying to tell you.

Margo got into bed.

No more affairs going nowhere, she promised herself. From now on she was only interested in men who wanted to settle down. Men who were divorced or widowed or had never been married, although she preferred divorced. That way she wouldn't be fighting ghosts and he'd have had some experience with whatever marriage was and was not. He'd have kids at least as old as hers, maybe even older. She was not interested in merging families. She had only one more year, after this one, with kids living at home. Then it was to be her turn. She wasn't about to give up that kind of freedom for some guy with kids. And he would have had plenty of experience with women, her steady man, and with life, so that settling down with her would be a pleasant relief. Not boring, of course, and not routine. But he wouldn't need to prove anything either. They would see eye to eye on important subjects. He would be politically liberal, but no longer an activist. He'd have gotten that out of his system in the sixties. He'd welcome a nice place to live, a real home, but he wouldn't get crazy over it. He wouldn't be a collector, like Leonard, who couldn't get a divorce because he was afraid of losing his de Koonings, his oriental rugs, his Ming vases. They would share a simple life, with plenty of laughter, plenty of passion, but without crazy expectations.

That's how it would be with her steady man.

Andrew was probably in bed now, thinking about tonight. Thinking about her. If they had kissed, if she had gone next door with him, they would be in bed together now, their bodies naked, wrapped around each other. She would like to have kissed him. His lower lip was fleshy and inviting. She would have nibbled on it. It would have been nice to run her hands through his soft-looking hair, to kiss the back of his neck.

That's enough, Margo! Go to sleep.

Sleep . . . how can I possibly sleep?

Close your eyes, for a start. Then count sheep. Count lovers. Count anything. But get off the subject of Romeo next door before you start thinking you're Juliet, at forty.

12

MICHELLE HAD A rash on her legs. The doctor said she had probably gotten flea bites over the summer and they had caused this allergic reaction. He prescribed a white cream, which she was supposed to apply twice day. But most mornings she forgot because she was always in a hurry to get to school. So all during the day her legs itched and she scratched until they were bloody and sore.

School wasn't bad this year. She liked her English teacher. She liked her Chemistry teacher. She liked Gemini, a new girl in her class. She thought they might get to be friends. Real friends. She was even getting along with her mother, who had changed for the better over the summer. This year Margo wasn't on her case all the time and they hadn't had one major battle since Michelle got back from New York.

Puffin was coming to dinner tonight. Puffin was in her class too, but they had never been friends. Puffin was so spoiled, flitting around town in her Porsche. A princess from Texas. Michelle didn't see how her mother could be friends with Clare, Puffin's mother, but they were. "I don't judge my friends by their children," Margo had said one time, "any more than you judge your friends by their parents."

"But Mother," Michelle had argued, "she's a product of her environment. Clare must have made her the way she is."

"Clare has gone through many changes, Michelle," Margo had

said. "And Puffin will too. It's not her fault that her parents have so much money she doesn't know what to do. Shopping to her means going out and buying a Georgia O'Keeffe. Try to remember that."

"I still don't like her," Michelle had said. "I don't like her attitude toward life."

"You're entitled," Margo had said.

And so Puffin was invited to dinner. And then Margo decided to ask Andrew Broder too, the Brat's father, because he was new in town and seemed lonely. When Michelle heard that, she asked Margo if she could invite Gemini, who was also new in town. Gemini was a Pueblo Indian from New Mexico. She was living with the family of an anthropologist from C.U. who had met Gemini a year ago while he was doing research at her pueblo. He had convinced Gemini's family to let her come to Boulder because she was a gifted student and deserved the best educational opportunities. Gemini's mother and four older sisters were well-known potters—the Gutierrezes. Their pots sold for a fortune. Margo was always admiring them in the Indian gallery on the Mall.

Gemini was definitely headed for Harvard, Yale, or M.I.T. and she knew she'd get in any place she wanted, and with a full scholarship too, because she was a Native American and all the best schools were knocking themselves out trying to recruit Native Americans. A few years ago it had been blacks, but now nobody was that interested in them.

Gemini wasn't her real name. She chose it because it suited her new life in Boulder. Michelle and Gemini had a lot in common. They were both good students, they were both virgins, and they agreed that Stuart and his preppie friends were fools who, as Gemini put it, did not know the way of the world. Michelle wasn't sure what that meant, but she thought it had to do with having your priorities in order. Having your values straight. And Michelle certainly did, which was probably why Gemini had decided to hang out with her.

So there would be six for dinner. Michelle baked whole wheat bread and, for dessert, brownies. Margo made chicken marengo, her old standby, and Andrew Broder brought the salad and the wine. Michelle did not like the way he and Margo kept looking at each other.

Puffin did not talk, she exclaimed. "Oh, Margo . . . this chicken is simply fabulous!"

"Oh, Stuart, I think you look so nice with your short haircut!"

"Oh, Mr. Broder, I hope you like Boulder as much as we do!"

And Michelle did not like the way Stuart kept looking at Puffin. Puffin was such a flirt. It was disgusting. Gemini didn't say anything. She ate quietly, taking it all in. She got rice stuck to her hair.

Margo drank too much wine and got silly. God, Michelle hated it when her mother got silly. It was intensely embarrassing. Why couldn't Margo see that? Once, Andrew Broder reached out and covered Margo's hand with his own. Oh, it was coming all right. Her mother was getting *ga ga* over this guy. Michelle thought back to that night last spring, that night she had given Margo hell for renting the Hathaway apartment for B.B.'s ex-husband. If only Margo had understood that Michelle had just been trying to protect her. She had felt what was coming, even then. She had felt that her mother was going to get involved in somebody else's life again. God, she hated that word, *involved*. If only she had been able to make Margo understand that she had been thinking of her own good. Margo should have learned her lesson the last time, with Leonard. That was all Michelle had meant. But no, Margo courted disaster. That was a line from one of the books Michelle was reading for English class. She couldn't remember which one, but it was certainly fitting.

Puffin and Stuart drank wine too. Puffin was practically in Stuart's lap by the time Michelle carried in the brownies and ice cream. Of course her mother didn't notice. She was practically in Andrew Broder's lap. Gemini watched it all without a word. She got ice cream in her hair.

They all helped clear the dishes, but then Margo shooed the kids out of the kitchen. Too small for all of them, she said, so just she and Andrew Broder would clean up. Oh, Mother, Michelle thought, who are you fooling?

Puffin and Gemini stayed until eleven, then Puffin drove

Gemini home. After about fifteen minutes the phone rang and Michelle and Stuart picked up at the same time. It was Puffin, calling Stuart. They stayed on the phone for about an hour, Michelle thought. She wasn't sure because she fell asleep reading *Billy Budd.* She wasn't sure what time Andrew Broder left either. And she had meant to check up on that.

13

SARA WAS FINALLY going to spend the night at her father's. She couldn't wait to tell Jennifer her good news. But when she did, Jennifer said, "That's weird, Sara . . . because last weekend, when you begged to stay over at your father's, your mother exploded, right?"

"Right," Sara said. "But this weekend she's had a change of heart, I guess."

"Well . . . take whatever you can get . . . that's my motto. And remember, Omar says *You have the courage of your convictions now and know how to express them to bring people around to your outlook.*"

Sara and Jennifer read "Omar Reads the Stars" every day. It was a column in the *Daily Camera* and as far as they were concerned, the only reason to look at the newspaper, except for "Dear Abby," who was sometimes interesting.

"You think that's why she's letting me go then . . . because of the courage of my convictions?"

"Could be," Jennifer said.

Sara was not about to ask her mother. She would just take what she could get.

Last weekend her mother's friend, Lewis, had come to town to see the aspen. They turned color every year at the same time, the first week in October, making the whole mountainside look like a forest of gold. Lewis brought Sara a sweatshirt that said *Minnesota is for Lovers.* Sara didn't tell him they had the same sweatshirt for sale at the C.U. bookstore, only that one said *Colorado is for Lovers.* She pictured Minnesota on top of the map of the United States that she'd had to memorize the first week of school. Her history teacher had let them color it. Sara had colored Minnesota turquoise.

Sara did not know if her mother and Lewis were just friends, if it was some kind of business deal, or if Lewis was a new lover. She worried that Lewis would be like Mitch because her mother had met him in California too. But he wasn't. He was kind of old and friendly and he showed her pictures of his grandchildren. She didn't think Lewis was her mother's new lover. For one thing, he didn't stay at the house. He stayed at the Boulderado Hotel. And for another, they didn't hold hands or anything like that.

Still, it was her mother who had suggested she stay overnight at Jennifer's last Saturday. Sara had begged to stay at her father's instead and that's when her mother had exploded.

"Why are you doing this to me?" she had screamed.

"Doing what?" Sara had asked.

"Do you want to hurt me, Sara . . . because that's what it feels like when you talk that way."

"What way?"

"I won't have this behavior, Sara. I mean it."

"All right . . . I'll go to Jennifer's."

So naturally, after all the noise her mother had made, Sara was surprised to find out that this Saturday she was allowed to go to her father's for an overnight. She got up early and tiptoed around the house, careful not to annoy her mother, afraid that if she did her mother would ground her and not let her spend the night at her father's after all. Her mother threatened to ground her all the time now. Sara didn't even know what she was doing wrong. She tried to figure it out, but she couldn't. Her mother didn't get up in time to say goodbye and that was pretty weird because Mom was always up early to go running. So Sara left her a little note, saying she had gone to Daddy's, that she'd already fed Lucy, and that she hoped Mom would have a very nice weekend.

On Saturday afternoon Sara and her father went bicycle riding.

When Sara asked where he'd gotten the bicycles he said he'd borrowed them from Margo. On Saturday night they went to the movies to see *10*, which was partly funny and partly gross.

On Sunday they were wrapping cheese and bread and planning their hike into the mountains, when someone knocked at the door. It was Margo.

"I brought back the book," she said, handing it to Sara's father. It was *his* book, the one he'd written. Sara recognized the cover, without even seeing the title or Daddy's name. "I can't begin to tell you how moved I was . . ." Margo said.

"I'm glad," Daddy said. "But you weren't supposed to return it. It's for you." He walked over to his desk and pulled a felt tip pen out of a mug. "Here . . . let me sign it . . ."

Sara couldn't see what her father wrote inside Margo's book, but whatever it was, when Margo read it, she got all mushy and she looked at the floor, as if she were about to cry.

"I wrote you a note too," Margo said, shaking the book. A small blue envelope fell out and Daddy and Margo both bent down to pick it up off the floor. As they did they bumped heads. Then they both laughed.

"Sara and I are going on a hike this afternoon," Daddy said. "Would you like to join us?"

Margo stood up, smoothed out her skirt, and looked over at Sara for what seemed like a long time. Sara just stared right back at her. Finally Margo said, "Thanks . . . maybe some other time. I've got a lot of catching up to do today."

Sara felt relieved. She didn't understand why her father would have invited Margo to join them anyway. Sunday was *their* special day. She was glad that Margo couldn't go with them.

That night, when Daddy drove Sara home, he told her he'd had the best weekend and that he hoped she would come to stay for a week sometime soon.

Sara said she would like that a lot.

When she went into the house, Mom was really angry. She was almost always angry on Sunday nights now, but this night she was angrier than before. And Sara had to answer a million questions.

"What did you do today?"

"We went on a hike. We had a picnic."

"What did you eat?"

"Cheese . . . I think it was Cheddar . . . and French bread and a grapefruit."

"Did you go alone . . . just the two of you?"

"Yes."

"Did you see Margo?"

"Just for a minute. She brought a book back to Daddy's house. But I didn't see what book," Sara added quickly.

"And what else?" Mom said. "What did you do on Saturday night?"

"We went to the movies."

"What did you see?"

"*10.*"

"*10!* That's not a movie for children."

"I liked it. It was funny."

"He has no sense, no sense at all."

"It's okay, Mom . . . really. I understood everything in it."

"That's not the point."

Sara nibbled at her fingernails.

"Please, Sara," Mom said, "stop biting."

Mom looked out the window for a minute and Sara held her breath, hoping that that was the last of the questions. But when Mom turned around again she said, "Did he have clean sheets for you?"

"Yes. They had stripes."

"What do you do when you're not at the movies or hiking?"

"We talk," Sara said.

"About what?"

"I don't know. We just talk . . . like everybody does."

"About me?"

"No. We never talk about you." Sara wasn't sure she should have added that, but she thought it would please her mother. Also, it was mostly true.

"Why not?" Mom asked. "Why don't you talk about me?"

"I don't know. We just don't."

"Are you afraid to talk about me in front of him? To tell him how much we love each other?"

"No," Sara said, "I'm not afraid."

"Good."

"I just wish you wouldn't ask me so many questions every time I come home from Daddy's."

"Why?"

"I just wish you wouldn't . . . that's all."

"I don't understand that, Sara. I really don't," Mom sad. "When two people are as close as we are it's only natural for one to ask the other about what's going on. Aren't you curious about how I spent my weekend?"

Actually, Sara wasn't.

"You should be curious and interested," Mom continued, "because you love me and you care about me. Don't you . . . don't you love me Sara . . . and care about me?" Now Mom had tears in her eyes and her voice had turned to a whisper.

So Sara said, "Yes, Mom. Did you have a nice weekend?"

"No," Mom said. "I was very lonely. I missed you very much."

"What did you do?" Sara asked.

"Nothing."

"Didn't you go out with your friends?"

"No."

"How come . . . last weekend when you went out with Lewis you had fun, didn't you?"

"That was different. Besides, Lewis lives in Minneapolis."

"I know, but you have lots of friends here. You used to go out with them all the time. So how come you don't now?"

"I guess it's because I miss you too much, Sara. I just can't get myself together when you're gone."

"You should try, Mom. Jennifer say that when she goes to stay with her father her mother has a really good time. That's how it's supposed to be when you're divorced." Sara didn't get it. Her mother never complained about being lonely when Sara slept over at Jennifer's.

"Well," Mom said, blowing her nose, "that's not how it is with me. But I did go out for a few hours. I went to a party at Clare's house. She's back from her trip."

"Was it a nice party?" Sara asked.

"Yes. Clare's parties are always very nice. I met Clare's ex-husband there. They're thinking about getting back together."

"Do you think you and Daddy will ever get back together?"

"Would you like us to?" Mom asked.

"Well, if you did, then you wouldn't be lonely."

"That's right. And I wouldn't have to share you, would I?" Mom smiled, a funny lopsided smile, and Sara couldn't tell if she was serious or not.

Sara felt very tired. She yawned. "I'm going to get ready for bed now."

When her mother tucked her into bed she smoothed the hair away from Sara's face, kissed her forehead, and said, "I love you, Sara."

"And I love you."

"For how long?" Mom asked.

"For always and forever," Sara said, closing her eyes.

"That's how long I'll love you too," Mom said, turning out the light.

When her mother was gone, Sara rolled over in her bed. She felt frightened. One minute her mother was full of anger, the next she was telling her how much she loved her. Sara didn't know what to expect anymore. She felt like a top, spinning and spinning, waiting to fall, but not knowing where or when she would.

14

B.B. HAD WORN a new dress to Clare's party, purple with a red sash. From across the room she looked sensational, she thought, catching a glimpse of herself in the mirrored wall of Clare's bedroom. But up close, her face looked drawn and thin and she had had to use makeup to hide the black circles under her eyes.

She was glad that Clare was back in town. Surprised at the news about her ex, or whatever he was, since they weren't formally divorced, but curious too. Clare had always said that she and Robin had had an almost perfect marriage, until he'd gone crazy and run off with the Doughnut. An almost perfect marriage. She and Andrew could have had that too. Clare had asked her once what had gone wrong with her marriage and she had thought about telling Clare about the accident, about Bobby, but she found she couldn't. She couldn't risk opening the wound again, couldn't expose herself to the pain, so she'd said, *Oh, the usual . . . we married too young . . .* and Clare had nodded.

Robin Carleton-Robbins looked like the photos she'd seen of him at Clare's house. Tall, angular, with dark eyes, a slight stutter, and a soft accent. He seemed shy and unsure of himself at the party. Clare had told everyone that he had come to town for a visit with Puffin, but B.B. knew the truth. That Clare and Robin were thinking about getting back together.

Maybe that's what she should do too. Try to make a go of it with Andrew. It wouldn't be easy, she knew, and she had mixed feelings about taking Andrew back. On the plus side, she would no longer have to worry about sharing, or even losing, Sara. And Andrew was still attractive. She was sure she could get him to trim his hair and shave his beard. And she would buy him some decent clothes at Lawrence Covell's. Andrew was a successful author now, about to write his second book. He should look like one. Not that she had read his book, or ever would, but she knew that it had been well-reviewed. On the minus side, Andrew was still Andrew. She was never going to be able to change him or trust him. And he would never adore her, never want her the way that Lewis did. And between her and Lewis there was no destructive history. No pain. So she just didn't know.

Her mother had phoned several days ago, hinting that she was the reason that Andrew had come to town.

"Are you giving him a chance, Francie?" her mother had asked. "That's all I want to know."

"A chance at what?"

"Getting back together."

"What makes you think he wants to get back together?"

"Why else is he in town?"

"To be with Sara."

"That's not all of it . . . believe me," her mother had said.

"Do you know something, Mother? Did he say something to you before he left?"

"I know what I know."

"What's that supposed to mean?"

"That a woman shouldn't be by herself."

"Mother . . ."

"Let me finish, Francine. You're a big-time businesswoman and I'm proud of you. I couldn't be more proud. But in the long run a woman has to have more . . . a woman has to have a man."

"Mother . . . I don't . . ."

"You don't want to hear it because you know it's true."

"I don't want to talk about it," B.B. said.

"What do you want to talk about, Francine . . . the weather?"

"Yes. How's the weather down there?"

"Gorgeous."

"And how's Uncle Morris?"

"Wonderful. Playing eighteen holes a day and watching his weight. We're both on low sodium. My pressure's been up lately. How's Sara?"

"Just fine."

"When will I see her . . . Thanksgiving? Christmas?"

"Maybe Christmas. We're going to Minneapolis for Thanksgiving."

"Minneapolis? What's in Minneapolis?"

"A friend."

"Since when do you have a friend in Minneapolis?"

"Since summer."

"I see."

If Andrew was interested in getting back together he was going to have to make the first move and he was going to have to make it before Christmas, because Lewis had already asked her to join him in Hawaii for the holidays and she was seriously considering his offer.

B.B. stood in front of the massive stone fireplace in Clare's living room. It was a dramatic two-storey glass house, on top of Flagstaff mountain, with an overall view of Boulder, especially dazzling at night when the city was lit. It had been put on the market three years ago by the family of a wealthy alcoholic Buddhist who had driven off the mountainside one night and Clare had bought it, through B.B., a week later.

She looked around at the party guests. Oh God, there was Clint, the politician who called her Red. He spotted her and waved. She looked away. He got the message. If he ever said a word to anyone about her, she'd deny it.

She had met him at a party at the mayor's house several years ago. She'd had too much to drink and had flirted with him. He was going to run for Congress in the next election, he'd told her proudly, letting his hand rest on her ass. He was young and very good-looking and when he offered to drive her home, she accepted. He took her to his place and fucked her quickly on the living room floor. She couldn't remember much about it except that while he was pumping her he'd whispered in her ear in Spanish.

She'd seen him a few times after that. Once she'd had a flat and had taken it into Big-O to be repaired and he had been there, buying a new set of tires for his Jeep. He had greeted her warmly. "Hey Red . . . how're you doing?"

"Excuse me?" B.B. had said.

"It's me, Clint . . . don't you remember?"

"No," she'd told him.

"The mayor's party . . ." he'd said, reminding her.

"Oh, yes. The mayor's party. Nice to see you again."

She had read about him in the *Daily Camera* recently. He wasn't running for Congress, but he was a candidate for the state legislature and had a good chance of making it.

And there was Margo, across the room, talking to Caprice, who owned an antique shop in town. Margo was wearing the suede suit that B.B. had helped her select. Margo looked up, saw B.B., said something to Caprice, then headed toward her.

"Hello . . ." Margo said. "How are you?"

"I'm all right," B.B. answered.

"How do you like the suit?" Margo asked, turning around for B.B.'s inspection.

"Maybe you should have gotten the next size," B.B. said. "It looks a bit tight across the chest."

"Really?" Margo said. "It's very comfortable . . . I'm sure it will give as I wear it."

"I suppose so."

"Have you met Robin yet?" Margo asked.

"Yes. Now the only ex-husband who's missing is yours."

Margo laughed. "It's not likely that Freddy will come to Boulder. He thinks it's the end of the universe."

"Speaking of ex-husbands," B.B. said, "I hear you're pretty chummy with mine."

Margo looked into her wine glass. "We run into each other . . . we live next door . . ."

"He can be quite charming, can't he?"

"I suppose so."

"But thoroughly unreliable."

"I wouldn't know."

"Have you, by any chance, seen Sara this weekend?"

"I saw her for a minute," Margo said. "She seemed to be having a good time."

"I don't like her spending too much time over there."

"I know how hard it is," Margo said. "Every time my kids fly east to visit Freddy I'm convinced I'm never going to see them again."

"How would you feel if Freddy moved into town and expected to have the kids every weekend?"

"I wouldn't mind the every weekend part as much as I would having him in town. But I'd adjust. I'd have no choice."

No choice. That's what Clare had told B.B. at lunch earlier in the week. "Face up to it," Clare had said. "He's here . . . Sara wants to see him . . . there's no point in setting up an impossible situation. Let her go . . . let her spend the night . . ."

"Why should I give in to his demands?" B.B. had asked.

"Because they're reasonable. Because if you don't it's going to tear you apart. I can see it already. I can see it in your eyes. What do you have to lose by letting her spend the night?"

"Everything," B.B. said.

"I know you love her," Clare had said, "but you can't control her whole life."

B.B. had nodded, biting her lower lip. "All right. I'll let her spend Saturday night."

"Good," Clare had said. "That makes sense. And you'll come to my party. I want you to meet Robin."

"Do you really think getting back together can work?"

"I don't know. But in four years I haven't met anyone I'd rather be with . . . and God knows, I've tried." Clare had laughed then. Her laugh echoed through the restaurant. "Let's have some outrageous dessert. How about sharing a piece of coconut cake."

"I'll have one bite," B.B. had said.

15

"SO HOW WAS Clare's party?" Michelle asked Margo on Sunday night. They were having cheese omelets with parsley and sautéed potatoes.

"Very nice," Margo said. "I met Clare's ex-husband."

"He's not ex," Stuart said. "They were never officially divorced."

"Well, whatever . . ." Margo said.

"And?" Michelle asked.

"And what?" Margo said.

"What was he like?"

"Shy, but pleasant," Margo said.

"Pleasant is such a blotto word, Mother. It has no meaning . . . none whatsoever."

"I didn't get to know him," Margo said. "I barely said hello."

"Puffin hates his guts," Stuart said. "He ran off and left them, you know . . . with some bimbo who worked in his bank."

"At least Clare had plenty of money," Michelle said. "Some women and children are left without a penny."

"That's why you have to prepare yourself for whatever life dishes out," Margo said to Michelle, "so that you're never economically dependent on anyone else."

"Let's face it," Stuart said. "It doesn't matter if you're a man or a woman. What's important is money. You can knock it if you want to, but you can't change the hard facts. Money is power and money is living well and living well is the best revenge."

Margo laid down her fork. "Where did you hear that?" she asked quietly.

"From Aliza!" Michelle said.

"Aliza?" Margo asked. "Aliza's an Israeli . . . Aliza's a Sabra, for God's sake. I can't believe . . ."

"You just don't know, Mother," Michelle said. "Aliza is such a princess! Everything is *designer* in her house. She even has designer dishes. She's into spending Daddy's money as fast as he makes it."

"Come off it, bitch!" Stuart said. "He likes it too. They have their heads together. They're not trying to prove anything like some people. Why shouldn't they live well? They've earned it, you know . . . he's worked hard all his life and her parents were both in a concentration camp . . ." He turned to Margo. "Did you know that, Mother . . . that Aliza's parents were both in Treblinka during the war?"

"Yes, I've heard that story."

"And that's supposed to make it okay?" Michelle fumed. "That she spends money like it's going out of style . . . and all because her parents were in a concentration camp?"

"She doesn't buy anything more than Mother!" Stuart shouted.

"Mother . . . Mother . . . oh, I just can't believe this," Michelle said dramatically, hitting her head with the back of her hand. "Mother doesn't buy anything. Well, hardly anything. When's the last time you bought a new dress, Mother?"

"I think it was . . ." Margo began, her head swimming.

"And it wasn't a designer dress, was it?" Michelle asked.

"Well . . . I might have had . . ."

"You see!" Michelle said, "Mother doesn't waste hundreds and hundreds of dollars on every dress. Mother is aware . . . Mother has values."

"You want to wear hospital rags for the rest of your life, that's up to you," Stuart said.

"What's wrong with my scrubs?" Michelle asked, smoothing out her green shirt.

Margo listened intently, trying to figure out where all of this was going. Was Michelle suddenly her champion? Had Stuart really turned into Freddy or was this just another phase like spewing facts from the *Guinness Book of World Records,* like being unwashed, like experimenting with marijuana? A phase that would pass. But if it didn't. She just didn't know.

If only she hadn't had her children with the wrong partner. She had suspected that Freddy was the wrong partner for her even before she married him. But she'd married him anyway.

The first time Margo had gone sailing with Freddy, they'd capsized in Sag Harbor Bay. She'd lost her Dr. Scholl's, her favorite sweater, and her prescription sunglasses.

At the time, her older sister, Bethany, who was visiting along with her children, said, "Maybe he can't do anything right."

"He forgot to lower the centerboard," Margo explained. "That's all."

"Yes, but if he's the kind who forgets the centerboard . . ."

"There was a squall," Margo said. "He was trying to bring us in."

"Worse yet," Bethany said, "to panic during a squall."

"He *didn't* panic. He forgot. There's a difference."

Margo's younger sister, Joell, who was then twelve, said, "At sailing camp the first thing we learned was control. C-o-n-t-r-o-l."

"Thank you," Margo said, "but I already know how to spell it."

"*And* to remain calm," Joell said. "You're hardly ever calm, Margo."

"It's not easy to be calm around here," Margo said, "with everyone telling you what you should do and what you shouldn't do and judging you every single minute of every single day!"

"Margo, darling," her mother said, "who's judging? We all think Freddy is a lovely boy . . . lovely . . . and he's going to be such a fine dentist . . . I'd trust him with my teeth completely. Don't get so huffy, sweetheart . . . you're just upset because you're about to be married."

"Upset because you're marrying the wrong boy," Bethany whispered in her ear.

That night Margo met Bethany coming out of the bathroom. "Suppose that were true," Margo said, "about marrying the wrong boy."

"Then get out of it now . . . while you still can. Don't make the same mistake as me. I'm telling you, it's not all it's cracked up to be."

"Are you saying you don't love Harvey?" Margo asked.

"I love Harvey, in a way . . . it's hard to explain. I wish I'd waited, that's all. And I'd hate to see you flushing yourself down the same drain. Before you know it you'll be stuck with babies and a house and responsibilities and you'll grow to hate it just like me."

"Bethany, I'm shocked. I always thought you and Harvey had a perfect life."

"Nobody has a perfect life, Margo."

"But I couldn't get out of it now, even if I wanted to . . . the invitations are out . . . there's a roomful of gifts . . . we have a lease on the apartment . . ."

"Those aren't good enough reasons to get married."

"It will be all right," Margo said.

The next morning, at the breakfast table, her mother, sensing Margo's anxiety and convinced that it had to do with the sailing mishap, said, "Darling . . . you and Freddy will laugh about this for the rest of your lives. Now eat some toast, at least. At a time like this you need your strength."

Her father, trying to turn it into a joke, said, "So who pays for the new sunglasses . . . him or me?" Then he laughed and everyone else at the table joined in, even Bethany.

And so Margo had married Freddy and they'd flown off to the Virgin Islands, to Bluebeard's Castle, for their honeymoon. While they were there they'd met another honeymooning couple, Nelson and Lainie Berkovitz, from Harrisburg, and one day on the beach Lainie had cried to Margo, had cried and confessed that she and Nelson just weren't able to do it, that it wouldn't go in and she didn't know what they were going to do or how they were going to go home and face their families with her still a virgin.

Margo suggested some of the jelly that she smeared inside her diaphragm and Lainie agreed to give it a try. Late that afternoon Lainie knocked on Margo's door and Margo squeezed some jelly into a paper cup for her. Lainie thanked her very much, then went back to her room where she hoped to convince Nelson to give it another try because by then Nelson was feeling very depressed.

Margo and Freddy laughed about poor Lainie and Nelson and felt smug because they were able to do it with no trouble at all. Of course Freddy did not know that Margo was experienced, that she had slept with James, who had died.

They came back from their honeymoon and settled into an apartment in Forest Hills and sixteen months later Stuart was born and a year after that, Michelle. When Michelle was two they moved into Manhattan, to a spacious apartment on Central Park West where they lived for the rest of their marriage.

Margo did not know exactly why she and Freddy were divorced, except that she couldn't stand it any more, couldn't stand Freddy or her life or any of the endless shit, and felt that she was headed down a long road going nowhere and that she had to get out in order to save herself.

By then Freddy was an oral surgeon with an outstanding practice and a fine reputation and Margo's parents were confused and concerned about her plan to divorce. They urged her to see a marriage counselor, but Margo's mind was made up. She wanted out. Besides, Freddy had already found an apartment on the East Side and was invited to one dinner party after another, where he was seated next to attractive divorcées who thought he was some good catch.

Stuart had been twelve and Michelle eleven when Margo and Freddy separated. Stuart had withdrawn, saying it was their problem, not his, and that he was not going to get caught in the middle. Michelle had screamed at Margo, "I hate you, you fucker . . . I hate you for ruining my life. Daddy says it's all your fault. That you're just an immature baby who doesn't know when she has it good."

"If you hate me, then go and live with Daddy!" Margo screamed back. Oh, it wasn't working out the way it was supposed to. None of it. Margo felt lonely and frightened and disoriented and was on the verge of tears from morning until night, although she still made it to work every day. "Just go and live with Daddy if you think he's so great!"

But Michelle had cried, "I won't live with Daddy. And you can't make me. I hate him as much as I hate you. I hate you both and I hope you die tomorrow because I don't give a shit about either one of you. You hear me? I don't give a shit about you or about him! You're both fucking assholes!"

Michelle carried on for more than a month. Then one day she approached Margo. "I've decided to get on with my life," she said. Margo had breathed a sigh of relief and had tried to get on with her own.

Seven months later she had met Leonard. It had been the middle of winter in New York and freezing. She had worn fleece-lined boots and wool socks to the party and had carried a pair of sandals to change into once she was there. The party had been given by Lainie Berkovitz, who had been divorced from Nelson for six years. Lainie was earning thirty-five thousand dollars on Wall Street. Lainie, who couldn't do it on her honeymoon, was doing it regularly now with her live-in mate, Neil, an investment banker. Margo imagined that Lainie and Neil got into bed at night and had long, involved discussions about money.

Leonard was Neil's friend and a tax lawyer. At the time Margo had had no idea that he was married. He had approached her, offering a cracker spread with caviar.

"Thanks, but I don't like caviar," she'd said.

"Everybody likes caviar," he'd told her.

"Not me."

He had sat down next to her, had eaten the cracker himself, and had made small talk for more than an hour, letting his arm brush against hers, letting his hand rest on her knee. She'd felt warm and excited and very desirable and when she'd excused herself for a minute to use the bathroom, he'd followed her down the hall, to Lainie's bedroom, and had locked the door behind them. They had kissed without speaking, then had fallen onto Lainie's bed, on top of the coats that were piled there. He'd unbuttoned her silk shirt and kissed her breasts. She'd raised her skirt and kicked off her panties and had felt something soft and furry under her ass. Mink, she'd thought, as she came.

She and Leonard had met every day for a week and at the end

of that time he'd told her about his wife and children. About how he kept a small apartment in Gramercy Park that he used week-nights, but that on weekends he went home, to Pound Ridge, to his family. He wanted a divorce, he'd explained, but Gabrielle wouldn't give him one, although he was sure she would eventually. Margo believed him.

Their affair had lasted more than a year and had ended, finally, because Margo realized that it wasn't the family he couldn't leave, but his collections. And then, of course, there was the incident with Gabrielle and the gun.

Leonard had flown out to Boulder once, to try to convince Margo to return to New York, but by then she had begun her new life, her children were set in school, and she was involved with her boss, Michael Benson. Even though she was wise enough this time to know that she and Michael weren't going anywhere, he did help her understand there were other fish in the sea and for once she was able to look at Leonard objectively and she didn't like what she saw, an infantile man who wanted it all, on his own terms, without giving an ounce to anyone.

Margo took a sip of coffee and was surprised to find that it was already cold. She heard music coming from her children's rooms and hoped that they had started their homework. She stood up, cleared away the dinner dishes, and picked up the phone. Margo was concerned about Clare. She had been in a frenzy at the party last night, the sleeves of her long silk kimono flapping like the wings of a bird trapped in a glass house. Last weekend, before Clare had flown to Dallas for a reunion with Robin, Margo had tried to warn her. "People don't change," she had said. "They may try, they may pretend for a while, but then they revert."

"Look," Clare had said, "if Robin hadn't run off with the Doughnut we'd still be together."

"But he did run away with the Doughnut," Margo had reminded her. "That's the whole point."

Margo dialed Clare's number and Clare answered the phone on the third ring.

"It was a wonderful party," Margo said.

"Really . . . I couldn't tell . . . I was a wreck."

"I know."

"Tell me it's going to be okay . . . that I'm not making a terrible mistake," Clare said.

"I can't tell you that."

"Suppose you're right . . . suppose he runs off again . . . with or without a Doughnut . . ."

"We all make mistakes," Margo said. "You can always get out of it."

"You're only allowed so many mistakes," Clare said.

"No . . . you're allowed as many as you need," Margo told her. "There's no limit."

"You're sure?"

"Yes . . . look at me!"

Clare laughed. "I want it to work. God knows, I really want it to work. Maybe I shouldn't have had a party . . . maybe it was too soon. He used to love parties, but last night he was like a frightened child."

"Give it some time," Margo said.

After they'd hung up, Margo made herself another cup of coffee. She took it into the living room and settled on the sofa with the Sunday *Camera*. But she found herself thinking about Clare's party again. It had been strange seeing Clint there. She had once had a fling with him. He had whispered to her in Spanish while they were making love. She hadn't understood a word he was saying, but she had thought of whispering back to him in Yiddish, if only she could remember some of her grandmother's favorite expressions. The idea of speaking Yiddish to him had made her laugh. He had been offended, thinking she was laughing at him. Last night Clint had been putting the make on Margo's friend Caprice, who owned the antique shop where she had bought her rolltop desk. She wondered if she should have warned Caprice about Clint. But what would she have said?

Margo was tired of Boulder parties. She longed to stay at home on Saturday nights, working on her quilt, sharing a quiet evening with someone special. She thought about Andrew Broder and how, when she had returned the book to his house that morning, he had invited her to go hiking with him and Sara. Margo had been tempted, but when she'd seen the look of surprise and hurt on Sara's face she'd decided against it. She wasn't about to come between a man and his daughter.

She didn't see him again until Wednesday night, when he called, asking if she'd like to take a drive. It was clear and brisk outside and she zipped up her vest as she walked to his truck. They drove up to the Red Lion Inn, found a table in the back, and ordered brandies. She thought about telling him that she couldn't see him again. That she felt she had to stop before it was too late. That Boulder was a small town and since she and B.B. lived here, worked here, and were raising children here, she simply could not risk getting involved with him.

But as soon as they sat down he took her hand, looked directly into her eyes, and said, "I've missed you. Where've you been?"

"I've been working on a fund-raiser for the Democratic Professional Women's Organization."

"I didn't know you were active politically."

"I'm not. I mean, I might be, but I can't work up any enthusiasm for Carter. This is just a luncheon I was asked to co-chair. And Michael was out of the office for a few days . . ."

"Michael?"

"Michael Benson . . . one of the partners in the firm."

"Oh, I thought maybe there was competition."

She didn't laugh. She swished the brandy around in her glass. "And I've been thinking too . . . about us."

"So have I. Your note was beautiful. Thank you."

She had written a note about his book, telling him that it was tender, funny, sad. She shouldn't have written anything.

"The book is based loosely on the accident," he said, "but I guess you knew that."

"The accident . . . what accident?"

"When Bobby was killed."

"Bobby?"

"My son. He was ten."

"Oh God." Her throat closed up. She looked away from him. Tears came to her eyes. She'd had no idea.

"You've known Francine since you came to Boulder and you didn't know about Bobby?"

She shook her head.

"Jesus!" He ran his hands through his hair. A vein in the center of his forehead stood out. "Does anybody here know?"

"I doubt it," Margo said softly. "I would have heard." She wished she'd known sooner, wished she'd known all along.

"I was driving," Andrew said. "She blames me. And for a long time I blamed myself. Writing the book was a cathartic experience. My way of dealing with it . . . of facing up to it."

Margo thought of B.B.'s cool exterior, the vacant eyes.

"It tore us apart," Andrew said. "She's never forgiven me."

Suppose Freddy had been driving, had had an accident, and Stuart or Michelle had been badly injured, had been killed. Would she have been able to forgive him? God, what an impossible situation.

"I don't know what to say," she told him, covering his hand with hers. Suddenly she understood so much.

"I was sure you knew," he said. "I was sure everyone knew."

"No wonder B.B. didn't want you to come here."

"I came because of Sara."

"Stop, please . . ." Margo said. "I don't want to hear anymore. Not now. Not tonight."

"Sorry. I usually don't go on about it."

"I'm glad you told me. I just need a little time to digest it."

"One thing," Andrew said. "I don't feel sorry for myself anymore and I don't want anyone else feeling sorry either. Got it?"

"Got it," Margo said.

They sat quietly for a long time, nursing their brandies.

And then Margo began to talk. She told him about her marriage to Freddy, about the divorce guilt and how it affected her relationship with her children, about her fears of not being a good enough mother, of screwing things up with Michelle, of blaming herself for a million little things that she knew, at some other level, were not really her fault.

She told him about James and how James reminded her of him. She told him about Ruby, who had been her neighbor in Forest

Hills, and how their first babies had been born just two days apart. About how, one summer day, while they were pushing their infants in their carriages, Ruby had asked, "If you had to choose between your husband and your baby who would you choose?"

"I can't answer that," Margo had said. "It's a crazy question."

"I'd choose my husband," Ruby had said. "We could always make another baby."

Margo had looked down at Stuart's sweet sleeping face. I'd choose my baby, she'd thought, and find another husband.

She babbled on and on, anxious to share the intimate details of her life.

By the time they got back to her house it was after midnight and Stuart and Michelle were asleep. She invited Andrew in for a soak and he accepted.

"You're not going to pass out, are you?" she asked as he stepped into the tub.

"Not tonight," he said.

"Fifteen minutes . . . that's all you get," Margo told him, setting the timer.

"I'll try to make the most of it," he said.

They sat on opposite sides of the tub, facing each other, not speaking, not touching.

When the buzzer went off Margo stepped out of the tub, wrapped herself in a robe, handed Andrew another, and told him that he could go home through the gate in her fence.

He grabbed her by the shoulders then, spun her around, and kissed her. She didn't resist. It was a long, warm, wet kiss and from it she knew how it would be to make love with him. But before it could go any further she broke away, saying, "Not yet . . . not yet . . ."

"Why?"

"I don't know . . . I'm not ready."

"When . . . tomorrow, the next day?"

"I don't know."

"Don't you ever act on impulse?" he asked.

"I'm one of the most impulsive people you'll ever meet," she told him. "And right now I'm fighting it harder than I've ever fought anything."

"Why fight?"

"I need to think about it."

"Goddamn it, Margo. You're acting like some fifteen-year-old tease."

"I don't know if I can handle this, Andrew."

"Does anyone ever know?"

"Some people . . ."

"That's bullshit and you know it. What is there to handle?"

"You . . . us . . . the complications . . . the consequences . . . please, Andrew . . . go home and let me think."

"I hope you know what you're doing," he said.

"I hope so too."

He kissed her one more time, then gathered his clothes and left. She watched him walk away. Then she went into the house and climbed into bed.

Well, Margo . . . the voice began, *I'm proud of you!*

I figured you would be.

You really thought things through tonight.

I've just postponed it, that's all . . . because I really like this man . . . hell, I'm crazy about him.

Think, Margo!

I am thinking. I've been thinking.

She tossed back her covers and sat up.

Margo . . . the voice warned.

I'm a fool. There may never be another night like this one. He could be dead in the morning. I could be. The bomb could fall. The world could end . . .

She got into her robe, slipped her vest on over it, stepped into her sandals, tiptoed out of the house, and went next door, pausing for a minute at the foot of the staircase leading to his apartment. Then she ran up the stairs and knocked on his door, timidly at first, then stronger.

He opened the door. He was wearing his jeans but no shirt and no shoes.

"I was wondering if I could borrow a box of raisins," she said.

He closed the door behind them, took her in his arms, and kissed her. She threw her vest on the floor. Her robe fell open and she felt the warmth of his skin next to hers. He took her hand and led her into the bedroom. They made love for hours and finally, worn out and exhausted, fell asleep in each other's arms, their bodies covered with sweat, the sheets damp and sticky. When they awoke it was close to five and she put on her robe and crept back to her house. She got into her cold bed and thought, I am in love.

And then she fell asleep.

16

MICHELLE WAS SO pissed at Margo! How could she let him move into their house, into their *home,* without discussing it, without bothering to find out how she and Stuart would feel about it, without a second thought?

One morning in November, while they were in the kitchen, Margo had announced it. "Andrew is going to move in next week." Just like that.

Michelle had been gulping orange juice at the time and had choked on it. Margo had had to whack her on the back. "His lease is up and since we're together all the time anyway . . ." Margo went right on talking, never mind that Michelle's throat was closing up, that she couldn't breathe, that she might die right on the spot.

"Does this mean congratulations are in order?" Stuart asked, stirring two sugars into his coffee.

"If you want to congratulate us on being happy, sure . . ." Margo said.

"That's not what I had in mind," Stuart told her.

"Well, we're not talking marriage at this point," Margo said. "We're talking living together."

Michelle got her breath back. Living together! *Him,* living here. As if he belonged. It was one thing for Margo to have a boyfriend, one who slept over sometimes, one who was around a lot. It was another thing completely to have her boyfriend move in, to take his showers there, open their refrigerator whenever he wanted, put strange foods into it, shit in their toilets, to be around *all* the time. "Is he going to pay," Michelle asked, "or just live here free . . . just live off us?"

"I don't see that it's any of your business, Michelle," Margo said.

"It's *all* my business, Mother. This is *my* house too . . . remember? And as I recall my father pays child support that goes toward our house payments and our grocery bills and so I have every right to know what kind of arrangement you've made with your boyfriend."

"He's going to contribute the same amount of money that he was paying next door."

"Which is?"

Margo sighed. "Three hundred and fifty dollars a month."

"And what about food?"

"He'll pay for his share of the groceries. We'll divide our bill by four. Anything else?"

Margo was really tense now. Michelle could tell by the tightening of her mouth, the crease in her forehead. Her mother looked old when she got tense. Michelle had no trouble visualizing her as an old old woman, her face all lined, her mouth puckered and sunken, her flesh loose and hanging from her bones, her fingers arthritic, like Grandma Sampson's. And how many boyfriends would she have then?

"Yes," Michelle finally said, answering Margo's question. "There is one more thing. What about the Brat? Because if you think she's going to stay in my room when she comes over, you can guess again. And I mean it, Mother!"

"Well, she certainly can't stay in my room," Stuart said. "I need my privacy."

"We all need our privacy," Margo said.

"So what about it, Mother?" Michelle said.

"We're working on it," Margo said.

"Working on it? What does that mean?" Michelle asked.

"It means we're thinking about it," Margo said. "Sara has to feel welcome here. Andrew is her father."

"But it's not *his* home," Michelle said. "It's ours! The Brat has her own home in Boulder . . . with her mother."

"You are acting selfish and unreasonable, Michelle," Margo shouted, "and I'm getting sick of it!"

"You should have thought about all of this before you decided to let him move in, Mother. You could have waited. Stuart will be gone next fall and I'll be gone a year later. You could have waited until then to let him move in."

"No, I couldn't have waited," Margo yelled, "because this is also *my* home, and *my* life, and I'm tired of waiting." Margo's voice choked up and she started to cry. Michelle knew she would. She was such a baby.

"We're going to be late for school," Stuart said.

"I'm ready," Michelle told him.

"Then let's go."

They left Margo with her head on the breakfast bar, sobbing. Serves her right, Michelle thought.

17

MARGO WAS IN love and no one was going to spoil it for her. Not Michelle and her hostility, not Stuart and his blasé attitude, not B.B., not Sara, not anyone.

It wasn't as if they'd made the decision to live together on the spur of the moment. They had been inseparable from the first night they had made love, running back and forth from her place to his, having dinner together, laughing and talking into the night, feeling exhausted but exhilarated the next morning.

Andrew had brought up the subject of living together on the night that Steve McQueen had died. They had lain in bed talking about how fragile, how unpredictable life was and Andrew had asked, "Would you go to Mexico for laetrile treatments?"

"No," she answered. "Would you?"

"Yes, I'd try anything."

"If it comes down to that, I'll take you."

"Even though you're not a believer?"

She wrapped her arms around him. "Even though . . ."

They had made love tenderly.

Later, Margo was curled beside Andrew, her head on his chest, her finger tracing an imaginary line from his belly to his neck and back again. She loved the smoothness of his skin and the soft hair that ran from his chest to his belly, then spread out so that his lower half was covered with a downy fur. It was hard to be near him and keep her hands to herself. Like Puffin and Stuart, she thought. But Puffin and Stuart were new at the game and Margo and Andrew weren't.

He had stroked her face. He loved her cheekbones, he'd told her. He loved to kiss them and touch them and nibble at them. She'd never been aware of her cheekbones, but now, when she looked in the mirror she noticed them first and tried to see herself as he saw her.

"My lease is up in a few weeks," Andrew had said. "I can't renew it. Hathaway has rented the place for the whole winter. I could look for another place . . ." He hesitated.

Or you could move in with me, Margo thought.

"Or I could move in with you," Andrew said. "That is, if you'd have me."

If she'd have him! She tried to think reasonably, but she couldn't. She wanted to jump up and shout, *Yes, move in with me,* but a mature adult did not react solely on an emotional level. A mature adult thought things through, considered both sides of the issue. Finally she said, "There would be a million complications."

"I can only think of nine hundred thousand," he said.

She reached down and pulled up the quilt, then snuggled close to him again. "It would be nice to have you here every night, to wake up next to you every morning, but moving in together . . . I don't know . . . are you saying that you're going to stay in Boulder? Are we talking serious commitment?"

"We're talking about being together as long as it works . . . as long as we both want to be together."

"But suppose one does and the other doesn't?"

"Then we'd have to figure out what happened and why and make adjustments."

"Adjustments," she said, more to herself than to him. "You wouldn't just walk out . . . without discussing it?"

"No," he said. "And you wouldn't just kick me out, would you?"

"No . . . not unless you did something to make me hate you."

"Such as?"

"Being dishonest with me . . . or making love with someone else."

"Ah . . . so you're the jealous type."

"Monogamous. I couldn't live with you unless I knew it was a monogamous relationship, unless I could trust you."

"There's more to trust than sexual faithfulness."

"Oh sure, I know, but it's a good place to start. How would you feel if I made love with another man?"

"I probably wouldn't like it," Andrew said.

"You're supposed to say you'd hate it, that you'd kill him, or me, or both of us."

"But then I'd go to jail."

"I'd visit every Sunday."

"Assuming I spared your life."

"Right."

"Would you bring me raisins?"

"By the carton."

"Then it's a deal," he said.

"What is?"

"Living together in a monogamous, trusting relationship."

"For how long?" Margo asked. "I need to have some idea so that if we ever have a difference of opinion, which I realize is unlikely but still possible, I won't worry that it's all over between us."

"How does six months sound for a start?" he asked.

"Six months . . ." she said, mentally counting. "No . . . six months is no good because that would put us right in the middle of May and I can't take the chance that my life is going to fall apart this spring, because Stuart will be graduating and Freddy and Aliza will be coming to town. It would have to be until the end of the school year, at least."

"Okay . . . fine," Andrew said. "At least until the end of the school year and much, much longer, I hope."

"I hope so too."

They were quiet for a while, then Andrew said, "Margo . . ."

"Hmmm . . ."

"I love you . . . at least I think I do . . . and if I think I do that must mean something."

"I'm sure it means something," she said, "because I've been thinking that I love you, too, but I've been afraid to say it, afraid that you wouldn't respond, that you'd be embarrassed or say,

Well, I like you a lot, Margo, but love, that's a different story, that's . . ."

"Come here," he said, taking her in his arms, kissing her. "Right now there's not a doubt in my mind that I love you, that I'm going to keep on loving you."

"Sounds good to me," she said, climbing on top of him, kissing his face, his neck, his mouth. In a minute she knew it was going to be another night of very little sleep.

Afterwards, she said, "If you live here we'll be able to make love like regular people and still get some sleep."

"We'll never make love like regular people, Margarita," he said, "because regular people don't have this much fun."

Margo and Clare were at the Overland Sheepskin Company, looking at gloves. Although the temperature was in the low seventies, snow was forecast, with a thirty degree drop expected overnight. Tomorrow morning it would be winter if the weatherman was right.

"Andrew is moving in at the end of the month," Margo said as she tried on a fleece-lined glove.

"Are you sure you know what you're doing?" Clare asked.

"We feel that it's right for us. We seem to be . . ." She hesitated, looking at her hands in the gloves, then went on, ". . . in love." She could feel her cheeks redden and she smiled.

"After two months?" Clare asked.

"It's closer to three and anyway, don't you think we're old enough and wise enough to know quickly?"

"I'm not sure we're ever old enough to know," Clare said, "and wise enough is out of the question."

"Still . . . it feels right to us."

"It could be such a mess, Margo."

"I know, but it's not fair to us, to Andrew and me, to say we can't be together because . . . look, I wish I didn't know his ex-wife, but I do. I can't change that. Anyway, I hear she has a new man in her life."

"Yes. A doctor from Minneapolis. Robin and I had dinner with them a few weeks ago. He's a nice man and obviously adores her."

"Well, that's great. Is it serious?"

"I think it could be, on his part anyway. But it's a long way from Minneapolis to Boulder."

"I'm going to take these gloves," Margo said to the saleswoman.

"You're sure it's not just sex?" Clare asked as they left the store and headed back to work.

Margo laughed.

There had been moments, at the beginning, when Margo thought it might be just the sex, because neither of them ever tired of it and because it worked so well between them. Margo had read all the books. She knew about the limits of limerance and the three-to-six-month life of the typical affair. But she also knew that if you never tried, you would never find out what it might grow into.

Okay, so they'd only known each other a couple of months, but still, there was so much promise. This was what she'd had in mind when she'd left Freddy. And certainly, one of the reasons she had left was that they had brought their resentments to bed with them. How could you feel loving toward someone who was constantly putting you down? How could you respond in bed to someone you wanted to smash with a baseball bat? For a long time after Margo left Freddy she thought it might not be possible to find the kind of love she had imagined.

Okay, so it was too soon to be able to trust completely, to feel secure all the time. There were still moments of panic, of doubting, but she got through those moments, often with Andrew's help.

Ten days after Andrew moved in, Margo invited Clare and Robin to dinner. Puffin came too, of course, since she and Stuart had also become inseparable. Clare had met Andrew a few times in town, but they hadn't had the chance to get to know each other. And Robin was meeting him for the first time. Robin seemed more relaxed than at Clare's party and Margo was pleased at how well dinner was going when Michelle turned to Andrew and said, "Did you know when we first moved to town my mother joined Man-of-the-Month Club?" Michelle paused for a second, making sure everyone had heard what she'd said and that she had their attention. Then she went on. "First there was her boss, Michael Benson . . . then there was that asshole physiologist from the University, who always had to have the last word . . . then there was Bronco Billy . . . remember Bronco Billy, Stuart?" But Michelle didn't wait for Stuart to answer. She kept going. "Bronco Billy used to clean his fingernails with his pocket knife . . ."

"Eeeww . . . gross . . ." Puffin said, listening intently.

"Then there was . . . oh, what's his name . . ." Michelle said, "the one with the bad arm . . ."

Margo swallowed hard and fought back tears. Why did Michelle want to hurt her this way? Clare and Robin had stopped eating. Clare gave Michelle a look of such contempt that it should have shut her up, but it didn't.

"Oh, I remember now," Michelle said. "His name was Calvin and he was a lawyer . . . and after him there was Epstein, Mom's token Buddhist . . ."

"That's enough, Michelle," Margo said quietly. She wanted to take Michelle and shake her by the shoulders, wanted to slap her face, scream, *Why . . . why are you doing this?*

"But, Mother . . ." Michelle said, wide-eyed, "I'm just getting started."

Before Margo had a chance to respond, to really blow it, Andrew placed his hand over hers and said, "Oh, those were just alternate selections, Michelle. They don't count. I'm a main selection. There's a big difference. Besides, I thought you knew, Margo's quit the club." He smiled at Michelle and then at Margo, letting her know that it was okay, that he could take it. And Margo, relieved and deeply grateful for his understanding, for his sense of humor, smiled back. The awkward moment passed.

"Well, Andrew," Michelle said, "at least you're a useful one . . . *you* can cook."

"Thanks, Michelle," Andrew said.

Everyone laughed self-consciously, then went back to eating the lemon chicken with snow peas.

*   *   *

"A Buddhist named Epstein?" Andrew asked later, when they were in bed.

Margo laughed. "He wasn't born a Buddhist."

"I never knew Buddhists fucked."

"Oh yes . . . quite a bit."

"How was it . . . was it different . . . did he chant while you were making love?"

"Not that I noticed," Margo said.

Then they both laughed and when they stopped they made love.

18

MICHELLE HAD SET out to test Andrew as soon as he'd moved in, because it was better to find out now if he could take it, and if he couldn't, to get rid of him quickly, before she got to know and even like him. So she'd given it to them good at the dinner party, figuring if they couldn't handle a little scene like that then they didn't have a prayer of staying together. And really, if she could scare him away so easily then it was better for Margo to know, even though she might be angry for a little while. Eventually she'd get over it and thank Michelle for making her see the light.

Also, Margo had been a bitch about the dinner party. She wouldn't let Michelle invite Gemini.

"Look," Margo had said, "this dinner is for Clare and Robin to get to know Andrew."

"What about Puffin? She's invited too."

"Puffin is Clare's daughter."

"God, Mother, you're always telling me who's related to who around here, as if I've got an acute mental disorder."

"If Stuart had another girlfriend, someone who was not my best friend's daughter, she would not be invited to dinner tonight. Now try and get that through your head, Michelle, and if you feel that you can't behave in a civilized way, then don't come to the dinner table . . . all right?"

Michelle might not have come to the dinner table except that during English class, while Ms. Franzoni was telling them they could become members of a book club for only one dollar and get four books free, she had dreamed up her Man-of-the-Month-Club number.

And it had worked beautifully. She'd waited until just the right moment to face Andrew and tell him about Margo's lovers. Michelle had expected to ruin the dinner, had expected Clare, Robin, and Puffin to get up and leave the house, had expected her mother to dissolve into tears, and then, just maybe, to be slapped around a little by Andrew so that Michelle could call her father and tell him that Margo had a live-in boyfriend who was into child abuse. Upon hearing this news her father would order Andrew out of the house . . . *or else*. Michelle wasn't sure what the *or else* would be, but her father would think of something, she was sure.

Michelle had been surprised that Andrew had taken it so well. You just never knew.

That night, after the dinner party, after Clare and Robin and Puffin had gone home, Andrew and Margo had put on their vests and had gone for a walk. Michelle was in bed reading *Franny and Zooey* when Stuart burst into her room. "What the fuck were you trying to pull tonight?"

Michelle did not answer. She kept her book in front of her face and pretended to go on reading. Pretended that she didn't even notice that Stuart was standing over her, his face red, his breath coming hard.

But then he swatted the book out of her hands and sent it flying across the room. "I said, what the fuck were you trying to pull tonight?"

She could feel Stuart's anger and it frightened her. But the best way to handle it was to stay calm. So she said, "Oh ho . . . aren't we getting violent?" She scrambled across her bed and reached down to the floor to retrieve the book.

Stuart yanked her back by the arm. "It's about time someone got violent with you, you little bitch!"

She was sure he was about to smash her. She tried not to cower, she tried to stare him down, and after a minute he punched her panda bear instead.

"I just don't want Mom to be hurt again," she explained. "I don't want to go through another Leonard."

"Leonard was years ago," Stuart said. "Why don't you just leave her alone for once. She's happy. Or is it that you can't stand to see her happy?"

"I'm the one who has to suffer through it every time one of her love affairs fizzles. Me . . . not you!"

"It's her life, Michelle, so just butt out of it."

"It's my life too. And when she's miserable, I'm miserable."

"You better cut the cord, Michelle, before it's too late. Besides which, she's not miserable, she's in love."

"Oh, sure. Now. Today. But what about next week, next month, next year? You'll be gone, so what do you care? But I'll still be around."

"You worry too much," Stuart said. "You're getting to be just like Grandma Sampson."

"I am not! But somebody around here has to think ahead. And since when do you care about her anyway?"

"I've always cared."

"Yeah . . . well, you'd never know it."

"I keep my feelings to myself."

"I'm glad to know you have feelings, Stuart. That's a real revelation."

"Hey, bitch . . . I'm the one who defends you every time somebody makes a rude remark about you and your Indian maiden."

"What do you mean?"

"Wake up, Michelle . . . everybody's saying you've got a thing going with Gemini."

"That is the most intensely stupid remark I've ever heard."

"Hey, look . . . it's nothing to me if you're gay."

"I am not gay!"

"Or bi . . ."

"I am not bi!"

"Then don't get so defensive. I just thought you should know what everybody's saying."

"Some people don't recognize friendship because they've never experienced it. All *you* know is sticking it up Puffin."

He grabbed her by the arm again, roughly, his fingers digging into her flesh. "I swear, Michelle, I'll kill you if you ever say anything like that again!"

She pulled away. "Get out of my room, you fucking asshole!" He turned and left. As he did she threw her copy of *Franny and Zooey* at him, but it missed, hitting the wall instead. She looked at her arm. His fingers had left red marks on it. She began to cry into her pillow. Life was not turning out the way she had planned. Everything was screwed up. How could they say those things about her and Gemini? Gemini was the best friend she'd ever had. Gemini even understood her poems, calling them outstanding examples of contemporary thought.

A couple of times Michelle had thought about showing her poems to Margo. But at the last minute she'd always changed her mind. Margo was too busy. Margo wasn't interested in Michelle, especially now that she had a live-in boyfriend.

One day Margo would be sorry. Sorry that she'd had a daughter and hadn't bothered to get to know her. Sometimes Michelle thought about slitting her wrists, the hot blood flowing out of her body. She pictured her family finding her on the floor, dead. They would blame themselves, each of them feeling guilty forever. Plenty of poets killed themselves. Even modern poets like Sylvia Plath and Anne Sexton. The only trouble with killing yourself, or with dying in general, was that you wouldn't be around to find out how everyone took it. It would be different if you could come back and say, *Well, all right, now you have another chance and this time you better treat me right.*

Anyway, Michelle wasn't about to kill herself. There were other ways to get even with people. Like when her poems were published and Michelle was interviewed on the *Today Show* and Jane Pauley said, *Tell us, Michelle . . . did your mother encourage you to write?* Michelle would say, *My mother? My mother was too busy with her boyfriend to even notice.*

Michelle got out of bed and walked across the room to her desk. She picked up a pencil, opened her special notebook, and jotted down a few lines. She yawned then, feeling incredibly tired. She closed her notebook. She would finish her poem in the morning. She got back into bed and fell asleep.

19

SARA COULD NOT believe it. Her father, who had come to Boulder to be with her, had moved in with Margo Sampson. And Sara was never going to forgive him. Never! Now all of her plans, her secret plans, were spoiled. Because she had been thinking that maybe she would tell her father about her mother's screaming fits and that Daddy would say, *Well, Sara, in that case, why don't you come and live with me?* And she would.

Jennifer said that Sara was more than disappointed. Jennifer said that Sara was depressed. And Jennifer should know. One time Jennifer had been so depressed she'd had to see a shrink three times a week. That had been a long time ago, when they were in fifth grade. Jennifer said that she would help Sara through her depression. Jennifer was the one who had clued her in on what was going on between Margo and her father in the first place.

It was on the Saturday night before Halloween and Jennifer had come to Daddy's house with her. The three of them had played a marathon game of Monopoly and then Daddy had cooked them baked ziti, which Jennifer refused to eat until Daddy explained that it was just spaghetti in a different shape. After dinner Margo had come by and she and Daddy had gone for a walk while Sara and Jennifer had watched a movie on TV.

That's when Jennifer had asked, "Are Margo and your father lovers?"

"I don't think so," Sara said. "Do you?"

"Yes," Jennifer told her, "without a doubt."

"How can you tell?"

"I've had experience with my own parents."

"I don't think you're right," Sara said. "They're just friends is all."

"You're so naive, Sara," Jennifer said. "If you don't believe me you can smell the sheets."

"Smell the sheets?"

"Yes."

So she and Jennifer went into her father's bedroom and pulled back the blanket and Jennifer bent down and sniffed the sheet. "What'd I tell you?" she said. "They're doing it all right."

Sara sniffed the sheets too, but she didn't smell anything strange. Still, it gave her a funny feeling to think about her father doing it with Margo. She had noticed that one time Daddy and Margo were holding hands, but still . . .

There was just one way to find out for sure. On Sunday night, when her father drove her home, she asked him. "Are you doing it with Margo?"

"Doing what?"

"You know . . . sex."

Her father took a deep breath and tightened his grip on the steering wheel. "What makes you ask?"

"I'm curious."

"Well, it's true that Margo and I are very good friends."

"But are you doing it?"

"Sometimes, yes."

Sara squeezed her eyes shut for a minute.

"Does that bother you?" her father asked.

"I guess not," Sara said, biting her nails. "I just like to know what's going on." Damn her mother! If only her mother had been nicer to Daddy then he wouldn't be doing it with Margo. He'd be back home, where he belonged. "Margo's not as pretty as Mom, is she?"

"They're very different," her father said.

"But Mom is prettier, don't you think?"

"This isn't a contest, Sara."

Even if her father wouldn't admit it, Sara knew it was true. Her mother was the prettiest woman in Boulder. Everybody said so. It would be nice to look like her mother, Sara thought. But she didn't. She looked more like her father's family, like a Broder. Sometimes she couldn't remember what her father looked like underneath his beard, so she'd take out her photos, the ones she kept hidden away, and she'd study them. In the photos Sara could see that she and her father had the same eyes. Bobby had had them too. Sleepy-looking eyes that changed from gray to green, depending on the light. And she had her father's thick hair which Jennifer called *dirty blonde,* but which her mother called *honey,* and she had her father's teeth, which was why she had braces and couldn't eat raw carrots anymore. She wondered what Bobby would look like if he hadn't died. He'd be about the same age as Stuart Sampson. Maybe they'd be friends.

"Do you like Margo better than Mom?" Sara asked.

"Sara, honey . . ." Daddy said, "your mother and I are divorced and have been for a long time."

"I know that! Don't you think I know that? What I mean is do you like Margo more than you liked Mom when you first met her?"

"I can't answer that."

"Why not?"

"Because it's not fair to compare how I felt at twenty-two and how I feel at forty-two. It's very different."

"But suppose you were just meeting Mom now, for the first time. Wouldn't you think she was beautiful?"

"Yes, I suppose I would."

"I thought so," Sara said.

When her father pulled up in front of Sara's house he turned off the engine and faced her. "You're beautiful too, Sara. Your beauty comes from inside, like Margo's."

"I'd rather look like Mom than like Margo," Sara said.

Daddy took her in his arms and talked into her hair, so softly that she could hardly hear what he was saying. "Just because Margo and I are close friends . . . are lovers . . . doesn't have anything to do with the way I feel about you. You know that, don't you?"

"I guess," Sara whispered back.

"Because I love you very, very much and nothing will ever change that."

Sara let him hold her that way for a long time. She liked being close to him. She liked the way his hair smelled from that shampoo he bought at the health food store. She liked the feel of his denim jacket, which was so old it was soft against her cheek. She liked being absolutely alone with him. She wished they were the only two people in the whole world. She wished that Margo and her mother were both dead.

It was that night, after she'd said goodbye to her father, that she'd gone inside and had made the terrible mistake. She never should have told her mother that Daddy and Margo were sleeping together. And maybe she wouldn't have if her mother hadn't started in on her right away.

"God, you stink when you come back from his place, Sara. Doesn't he ever make you take a bath or brush your teeth? And look at your hair. I'll bet you didn't brush it once all weekend, did you? Now get into the shower and scrub everywhere, or else I'll come in and do it for you!"

"I'll do it later," Sara said. "First I want to call Jennifer."

"You'll do it now!" her mother shouted, grabbing her by the arm and dragging her toward the bathroom.

"Get off my case!" Sara shouted.

"Don't you talk to me that way."

"Daddy and Margo are lovers. Did you know that?"

There, she'd surprised her mother all right. She could see the change in her face. Well, it served her mother right.

"What did you say?" her mother asked.

"I said that Daddy and Margo are lovers," Sara repeated, more quietly this time.

"Where did you ever get such an idea?"

"I asked Daddy and he told me."

"Do you know what that means, when two people are lovers?"

"Yes. It means they're fucking."

Her mother slapped her across the face, stunning her. Her mother had never hit her before, not even on her bottom when she'd been little. Sara could feel the sting long after the slap. Tears came to her eyes. But she wasn't going to cry. Instead she thought about how good it would feel to slap her mother back. But a wild look came into her mother's eyes and Mom began to make these strange sounds, like a puppy yelping. Then her mother took off, running down the hall. Sara heard a door slam shut and the yelping turned to screams. The screaming grew louder and louder until there was just one horrible, continuous sound.

Sara covered her ears with her hands and prayed, *Please God, let her stop . . .*

20

B.B. DID NOT KNOW what to do. And she felt afraid. Sometimes the screaming just started in the back of her throat and came out, surprising her. She had to work harder at controlling it. Control was the key to success. If she could not control the screaming, if she ever let go completely, she would never stop, she was sure. And then she would lose everything. Everything she had worked so hard for. Everything that mattered.

She almost lost it in Jazzercise, the day after Sara told her that Andrew and Margo were lovers. That morning, after her run, while she and Sara were in the kitchen having breakfast, B.B. had said, "I hope you didn't think I was angry at you last night. It's just that I have so much on my mind. We're so busy at the office. I didn't mean to slap you. You understand, don't you, Sweetie?"

"Sure," Sara had said.

"And Sara, about Margo and your father . . ."

Sara looked up from her bowl of cereal. "What about them?"

"Well . . . I just want you to know it's nothing but a convenience."

"How do you mean, a convenience?"

"You see, a man needs a woman for sex and since he's living right next door to Margo and since he's new in town and doesn't know anyone else, it's convenient for him to be having sex with her."

"Doesn't a woman need a man for sex too?"

"Yes, of course . . . that's what I'm saying. Margo and your father are both lonely people, and somewhat neurotic, and so they . . ."

"What do you mean, neurotic?"

"Oh, nothing . . . nothing . . . just forget it."

"No," Sara said, laying down her spoon. "I want to know."

"It's hard to explain," B.B. said. "Margo and your father are two people who aren't especially steady or reliable . . . they flit around a lot, like bees . . . the first convenient flower is the one the bee sits on . . ."

"Bees don't sit," Sara said. "They cross-pollinate."

"Right. So you see what I mean."

"Are you saying they don't really like each other?" Sara asked.

"Oh, I'm sure they like each other, but it's just a diversion. It's not an important relationship or one that's going to last."

"Is it like you and Lewis?" Sara asked.

"No. Lewis and I have an important relationship."

"Are you going to get married?"

"It's much too soon to talk about marriage. We've only known each other since last summer and he's only been to Boulder twice."

"But you're lovers, right?"

"Well, yes. But we're good friends first."

"That's just what Daddy said about Margo and him."

"Really . . ."

"Daddy thinks you're very pretty," Sara said. "Did you know that?"

"Did he say so?"

"Yes. It would be nice to have him come home, wouldn't it?"

"Home? Do you mean back here with us?"

"Don't you think that would be nice?" Sara asked.

"Is that what he wants? Is that what he told you?"

Sara shrugged. "Not exactly."

B.B. felt tense, confused. After breakfast she offered to braid Sara's hair, but Sara said, "No thanks. I'm going to wear it loose today." B.B. walked Sara to the front door. "Bye, Sweetie. I love you."

"And I love you," Sara mumbled.

"For how long?"

"For always and forever." Sara did not look at B.B. as she said it.

"That's how long I'll love you too," B.B. said, hugging Sara, feeling her warmth, not wanting to let her go. Sara stood there stiffly, allowing B.B. to embrace her, but not responding.

God, B.B. thought, suppose Sara decided to go and live with Andrew? Suppose they went to court and Sara told the judge that her mother screamed all the time, that she had even slapped her face once, that she was afraid of her? Surely any judge would allow a child to live with the other parent in that case. And Andrew would be there, ready and willing to take Sara away.

B.B. watched Sara run down the front steps, jump on her bicycle, and head off to school. Then a sadness washed over her, a sadness so unbearable she had nothing to compare it to, except for the day that Bobby died.

They had reached her at the Millar house that afternoon, which she had been showing to a family from Pennsylvania, assuring them they could get it for under three hundred thousand dollars, if they didn't waste any time, and that all they would have to do was paint inside and clean up the landscaping. They had told her over the phone and she had politely excused herself, had driven to the hospital, and hadn't felt anything, hadn't reacted at all until she had asked to see Bobby's body. They had tried to dissuade her. But she had insisted and when they took her to him, when she held him in her arms for the last time, when she refused to let go so that they'd had to pry her loose, she had finally screamed and cried and cursed Andrew.

It had been his fault. She knew it. Never mind that the witnesses, the police reports, later Andrew himself, told her that the other car had crossed the dividing line, had crashed into their wagon. She knew that he had been talking over his right shoulder, the way he always did, to the boys in the back, probably telling them a joke, probably laughing, oblivious to the road. The boys in the back had been banged up, a bruise here, a cut there, nothing serious. Only one had required stitches. And Andrew had cut his head, had been in shock, had been hospitalized overnight.

But Bobby was dead.

Dead on Arrival.

Ten years old and still wearing his Little League uniform and his new cleats.

Now, at the idea of losing Sara, B.B. felt as if she were surrounded by grayness, a thick cloud, separating her from the rest of the world.

Later, when she was in her office dictating a letter to Miranda, the tears came unexpectedly and once she began to cry she could not stop. She put her head on her desk and sobbed uncontrollably. Miranda left the room quietly and returned a few minutes later with a glass of water and two small yellow pills.

"Here, B.B. . . . take these . . . you'll feel better."

"What are they?"

"Valium. I keep them in my desk for emergencies."

"No," B.B. said, waving them away. "I don't take tranquilizers."

"I know you usually don't, but in this case . . ."

"No," B.B. said again. "I don't need them."

"All right," Miranda said, tucking them into her pocket. "Is there anything I can do?"

"No. It was just a touch of the blues. It's over now."

Miranda nodded. "You're supposed to meet a client at ten-thirty, at the Russo house. Would you like me to cancel, or ask someone else to show them around?"

"No, I'm all right. And I'll go directly to Jazzercise from there, so I'll be back here around one-fifteen."

"Shall I get you something for lunch?"

"A container of strawberry yogurt would be nice."

"Sure," Miranda said, "no trouble."

B.B. was late getting to Jazzercise because the clients, two women from Detroit, insisted on inspecting every square inch of the Russo house even though they weren't serious buyers. B.B. could tell from the moment she met them. They were just tourists, looking for a cheap way to spend the morning, trying to see the *real* Boulder. And she'd told them so. Had even called them bitches.

They'd been surprised by her outburst and threatened to report her to the Board of Realtors. But she'd just laughed, telling them to go ahead, telling them that she was the chairperson of that Board. She'd laughed so hard she'd had to run back inside the house to use the toilet. She'd laughed until tears were rolling down her cheeks, but when she looked at herself in the mirror her face looked contorted, as if she were crying. *Control . . . control* she reminded herself as she drove to Jazzercise. She had never been rude to a client before. Never. Well, she could always explain it as a bad day. It happened to the best agents. That it had never happened to her until now proved that she was more patient than most and that's why she was on top. Still, she could not stop her hands from shaking.

She came into Jazzercise in the middle of the second number. She stood in the back instead of at her usual place down front, between Margo and Clare. Jazzercise always relaxed her, relieved her tensions in a way that was different from running or yoga. The beat of the music, the burning sensations in her muscles, the stretching and toning. Yes, she felt better already. Just being here was therapeutic.

After class there was the usual scramble for the showers. Clare waved at her from across the crowded locker room, then disappeared into a shower stall. Margo's locker was next to B.B.'s. Margo was humming the tune of the final number as she pulled off her leotard and tights. Humming and smiling to herself.

B.B. watched as Margo undressed. Margo's breasts were big and round with full pink nipples. In a few years, if she wasn't careful, she'd look like a cow, B.B. thought, enjoying the idea. She'd seen Margo naked a million times, but today was different. Today B.B. saw Margo as Andrew's lover. Andrew kissed this woman's lips, Andrew caressed this woman's breasts, Andrew lay on top of her or under her or alongside her and thrust his penis into her.

"What is it?" Margo asked.

"What do you mean?" B.B. said.

"You've been staring at me for the longest time."

"I hear you're sleeping with Andrew," B.B. said. Oh, she shouldn't have said anything, shouldn't have gotten started, but she couldn't help herself. Maybe Sara had made it all up, maybe Margo would deny it.

Margo's face turned red. "How did you . . ."

"Sara told me," B.B. said.

"Sara," Margo said. "How did she . . ."

"Andrew told her."

"Andrew."

So, it was true. B.B. grabbed her towel and headed for the showers.

Margo caught up with her. "Look, I . . ."

"He's just using you," B.B. said. "Can't you see that? You're nothing to him but a convenient hole."

"I don't think we should discuss it," Margo said.

"Why not?" B.B. asked, her voice rising. "Everyone else is." She turned around. "Well . . ." she said to the women in the locker room, "aren't you all discussing it? Aren't you all talking about Margo and Andrew fucking their heads off?"

"Please," Margo said.

"You're such a fool," B.B. told her. "I never thought you'd turn out to be such a fool!"

Margo pushed ahead of B.B. and stepped into the shower. B.B. pulled aside the shower curtain and shouted into the steamy stall, "Does he still cry out when he comes? Does he call you his beautiful darling?"

Margo jerked the shower curtain out of B.B.'s hand. It had grown very quiet in the locker room, the only sounds were the water running in the showers and B.B.'s own voice. "What are you looking at?" she shouted at the silent women watching her. "Haven't you ever seen a naked body before?"

They turned away and busied themselves dressing.

"B.B.," Clare said softly. "Come on . . . let's get dressed and go have a cup of coffee."

Clare drove to the Mall. They went to the New York Deli, chose a table in the back, and B.B. sat facing the wall. "Well," she said, biting into a piece of toast, "I certainly made a scene, didn't I?"

"Yes," Clare said, "you certainly did."

"I didn't mean to, you know . . . it just happened."

"I know." Clare squeezed B.B.'s shoulder. "It's all right."

B.B. shook her head. "I can't believe the things I said."

"Look," Clare told her, "we all blow it sometimes. You should have seen me when Robin ran off with the Doughnut."

"He's sleeping with Margo. Did you know that?"

Clare nodded.

"I guess everyone knows."

"I don't think so. Not until you announced it in the locker room. Anyway, what difference does it make?"

"It's the idea of them together. It's just so tacky."

"Do you still love him, is that it?"

"No, but I don't want anyone else to either, especially not Margo, especially not right under my nose." She paused. "I guess that's selfish, isn't it?"

"Margo doesn't want to hurt you," Clare said.

"Then she shouldn't be sleeping with my husband."

"He's your ex-husband."

"So he's really not cheating on me . . . is that what you're saying?"

"That's right," Clare said.

"Well, he'll be gone soon," B.B. said, swirling the tea bag around in her cup. "His lease is up at the end of November. I'll just have to hang on until then."

B.B. wrote a note to her Jazzercise instructor, apologizing for her outburst in the locker room and explaining that she was transferring to the Monday-Wednesday class for personal reasons.

She toyed with the idea of making an appointment to see Thorny Abrams. Clare thought she should. But B.B. felt she could handle the situation herself, that the worst was over. It had been the shock of hearing the news about Margo and Andrew from Sara that had set her off. So instead of calling Thorny Abrams, B.B. called Cassidy, her masseuse, and set up an appointment for the following afternoon. During the massage, when B.B. told Cassidy she was going through a difficult time, Cassidy suggested that B.B. consult with Sensei Nokomoto, the acupuncturist.

Acupuncture could do wonders for the mind as well as the body, Cassidy explained, by regulating the pulses. B.B. agreed to give it a try.

She spoke with Lewis almost every night. Talking with her was the highlight of his day, Lewis said. He had seen a beautiful ring, gold with three diamonds. Could he interest her in becoming engaged? And had she decided about Christmas in Hawaii yet?

"So many questions all at once," B.B. said, laughing, not answering any of them.

"You're my fantasy woman," he told her.

"What happens when you find out I'm real?" she asked.

"I'll love you even more."

"Promise?"

"Promise."

For a few moments each day her spirits lifted. But as soon as she hung up the phone she plunged deeper into grayness. It was so hard to go on pretending to be all that Lewis and the rest of the world expected her to be. Sometimes she wanted to tell him to forget it, to forget her, that it was just a game. But she couldn't let go that easily. It was comforting to have him there, on the back burner. It wasn't fair to go on using Lewis, she knew, but wasn't he using her too, inventing her to serve his own needs? In the long run don't we all use each other, she wondered, isn't that the way we make it through the day?

When Andrew phoned a few weeks later, asking to see her, B.B. was not entirely surprised. Although she hadn't mentioned it to anyone it was possible that Andrew was simply using Margo to make her jealous, to make her beg him to come back. This was a possibility she could not ignore since both Sara and her mother had hinted at the idea of a reconciliation.

She hoped that Margo hadn't told him about her outburst in Jazzercise and that Sara hadn't told him about her screaming fits because she'd been doing so much better lately. She had seen the acupuncturist three times and it was true that her pulses had been out of sync. She was following the diet he had prescribed and could feel the poisons leaving her body. She rarely felt out of control now, but when she did she was careful not to show it. She would lock herself into her bathroom and shred Kleenex, or she would go for a long run.

She agreed to meet Andrew on Thursday afternoon, at four, while Sara was taking her piano lesson at Mrs. Vronsky's. She hadn't seen Andrew in more than a month, since the evening he'd dropped Sara off while she had been outside walking Lucy.

She came home from the office early to shower and change her clothes. She dressed in white. He had always liked her in white. She wondered if he liked Margo in white too. God, she didn't see how he was fucking Margo. She knew there had been other women in his life. After all, it had been six years. But the others were just faceless creatures who satisfied his physical needs.

When he rang the bell she was in the kitchen arranging crackers in a basket. She'd already put out the cheese, a sharp Vermont Cheddar she'd picked up at Essential Ingredients on her way home, along with a bottle of Blanc de Blanc.

"Hello, Andrew," she said, opening the front door. "Come on in." She felt calm, in control.

He stepped inside and followed her into the living room. "Nice," he said, looking around.

"Would you like a quick tour?"

"I'd like to see Sara's room."

"Of course." She led him upstairs and down the hall to Sara's bedroom with its white wicker furniture, its canopied bed, its blue and white ruffles and pillows and curtains.

"Pretty," Andrew said, "and so neat."

"I expect Sara to keep her room in order and she does."

She showed him the guest room and the hall bath, but not her own room, then led him back downstairs to the sun porch and the kitchen. He kept nodding and muttering, *nice*. The pots of geraniums on the kitchen window sill flourished in the late fall sun. Her copper pots and pans, gleaming, hung on a rack from the ceiling. The spices were arranged in alphabetical order.

He followed her back to the living room and sat on the sofa. B.B. sat on the love seat, opposite him. "Wine?" she asked.

"Please."

She poured a glass for him and then one for herself. She cut a slice of Cheddar, laid it on a water biscuit, and passed it across the glass table separating them.

"Thanks."

"Didn't my mother knit that sweater for you?" she asked. It was dark green with cables.

"I think mine did," he said. "Your mother made me a blue one that's similar."

"I remember this one," she told him. "It always looked nice on you . . . made your eyes very green . . . still does."

He took a bite of the cheese and cracker, followed by a long drink of wine. He seemed uncomfortable. Probably because they were on her turf. She tucked her bare feet under her and sat back seductively. She wanted him to want her. She wanted him to compare her to Margo and see that there was no comparison. If he would take the first step, she would take the second. She would prove to him that Margo was second best.

"Well," he said, clearing his throat, "the reason I asked to see you . . ."

She tossed her hair away from her face, sipped her wine, and waited.

". . . is that the lease on the Hathaway place is up at the end of this month."

"Oh, right," she said. "It was just a three-month lease, wasn't it?"

"Yes, although I'd hoped it was renewable."

"You can't always get a renewable lease around here. Hathaway probably rents to the same people every winter." She paused and sipped her wine. "So, you'll be heading back to Miami at the end of the month?"

"No, I'm going to stay here, at least until the end of the school year . . . maybe longer. And that's what I wanted to talk to you about."

He was either going to ask her to find him another place or he was going to ask if he could move in with her, B.B. thought. And she was not going to give him a definite answer now. There was too much at stake.

"I'm moving in with Margo," he said.

"What?" she asked.

"I'm moving in with Margo at the end of the month. I wanted to tell you now since that's where Sara will be staying when she's with me and I hope we can make arrangements for her to spend at least one week each month."

"No. Never." She stood up. "Why are you doing this to me?"

"It has nothing to do with you," he said.

A pounding began in her left temple. "Haven't you already hurt me enough?"

"I'm not trying to hurt you."

"I'll never let Sara stay there. Those children are horrors." Her voice sounded as if it was coming from very far away. "I don't understand why you're doing this."

"Because I want to be with Margo."

She picked up her wine glass and threw it at him. He ducked. The glass hit the piano and shattered. She reached across the table for his glass, but knocked over the bottle of wine instead. The wine dripped down onto her Navajo rug. "Look at that . . . look at what you've made me do."

"Where's a sponge?" he asked.

"Never mind a sponge. Don't you think I know what you're after? You're out to destroy me. You killed Bobby and now you're trying to take Sara so that I'll have nothing left, nothing to live for. You won't be satisfied until then, will you?"

His mouth opened as if to speak, but she couldn't hear what he was saying.

"What?" she screamed. "What did you say?"

He shouted at her. "You're making this more difficult than it has to be."

"Who sent you . . . my mother? The two of you planned it together, didn't you? She wants me out of the way because I know the truth. That's it, isn't it?"

"You're inventing things, Francine."

"Don't call me that."

He came toward her and tried to put his hand on her shoulder, but she pulled away. "You better calm down before Sara gets home," he said.

"Don't tell me what to do! You and my mother both think you

can run my life, but you're wrong. You can't. So get out . . . out of my house and out of my life." She picked up a stone carving as if to throw it, but before she could, he was gone. He had turned and said something as he'd slammed the door, but she had missed it. The cloud was forming, making her head feel fuzzy.

She ran into the kitchen and turned on the cold water tap. She stuck her head under the faucet, letting the icy water wash away the grayness. When her scalp felt numb she turned off the water and shook out her hair. Then she went back into the living room. She washed the rug with club soda, swept up the broken glass, Windexed the glass tabletop, and plumped up the pillows on the sofa. She carried the cheese and crackers to the kitchen, where she dumped them into the trash can. She brushed off her hands. There. She had removed every trace of him. It was as if he had never been there, as if this afternoon had never happened.

21

FROM THANKSGIVING UNTIL Christmas Margo worked late into each night stitching the commemorative quilt she had designed and appliqued for her parents' fiftieth wedding anniversary. She had constructed a series of connecting circles in primary colors. The center circle represented her mother and father, the next three, Margo and her sisters, the small circles, the five grandchildren. The idea for the quilt had come to her more than two years ago when she had been afraid that her mother would not live to see her next birthday, let alone her fiftieth wedding anniversary. In some childlike way Margo believed that by working on the quilt she could keep her mother alive. Now, she was determined to finish it before they left for the west coast and the anniversary bash that Bethany was throwing at her home in Beverly Hills.

Long after Stuart and Michelle had gone to sleep Margo and Andrew would sit in the living room, in front of the fireplace, Andrew reading, Margo stitching, the stereo turned to KBOD. During this time Margo felt a peacefulness she had never known. She would sometimes look up at Andrew, just to be sure that he was still there, and he would smile at her or reach out and touch her hair or squeeze her hand. As it grew later and her eyes became tired she would lie in his arms as the fire died and think, this is the way it's supposed to be. Sometimes they would make love on the rug and Margo would bite Andrew's shoulder as she came, to keep from crying out. Then they would creep downstairs, climb into bed, and fall asleep, his arms wrapped around her.

For five years Margo had slept in a bed by herself. And even during her marriage to Freddy she had really slept alone, although he had been there, in his half of the bed, with a can of Mace on the bedside table, ready to protect her. But he had not slept with his arms around her, had not made her feel warm and safe and well-loved. There had been no tender kisses in the middle of the night as she'd rolled over in her sleep. No wonder she was sleeping so well these nights.

Margo hadn't told her family about Andrew until he had moved in and then only because she felt she had to since the kids might mention something. She knew, once she told them, there would be questions.

"What a surprise!" her sister Bethany said. "How long have you known each other?"

"Since August."

"Since August . . . I see."

Margo could tell that Bethany did not approve of living together after only three months.

"And what does he do?" Bethany asked.

"He's a writer," Margo said.

"One of those Boulder types?"

Bethany did not like Boulder types. Every time she came to visit she walked along the Mall and disgustedly pointed out aging hippies to Margo. *They must all come here to retire,* she once said. *Not all,* Margo assured her. *Some go to Santa Fe.*

"He's new in town," Margo said. "He's from Florida."

"Oh, Florida," Bethany said. "I wonder if he knows Harvey's older brother. They moved to Florida a few years ago. You remember Ike and Lana, don't you?"

"I think so, but it's been a long time."

"Well, you'll see them at the party. You'll see everyone at the party." She paused and Margo pictured her sitting on her bed, the phone tucked between her ear and shoulder as she picked last week's polish off her nails. "You're bringing him, aren't you?"

"He doesn't have a tux," Margo said.

"Can't he rent one?"

"He'd rather not."

"Is he one of those avant-garde types?"

"Not really."

"Well . . . if he won't feel out of place, it's okay with me."

"I thought everything's so casual out there anyway. How come the party's formal?"

"It's an affair, Margo. And even if we are living out here, I'm still a New Yorker at heart and to me affairs are always black tie."

"Oh."

"I hope you can convince Stuart to bathe in honor of his grand-parents. The last time I saw him you could smell him a mile away."

"Oh, that's all changed," Margo said. "You can't get him *out* of the shower now. He's got a girlfriend."

"Really?"

"Yes."

"Well, you just never know, do you?" Bethany said, laughing, "You sound happy, Margo."

"I am."

"I'm glad. I was thinking the other day about how I warned you not to marry Freddy . . . remember?"

"Yes."

"But it wasn't so much Freddy I was talking about. It was mar-rying and having babies too soon. Before you were ready. I had a lot of my own problems in those days. But now, after so many years, Harvey and I have worked it out. It's not passionate, but it's nice. Is it passionate with you and Andrew . . . is the sex really good?"

"Yes," Margo said.

"I guess the second time around you make sure of that," Bethany said wistfully. "I know I would."

Within the hour, before Margo had had a chance to call her parents, her mother called her.

"Margo, darling . . . Bethany just told us the good news . . . that you have a *significant other*."

"Significant other?" Margo said.

"Yes. Isn't that what you call it out there? That's what Joell calls it. She has one too, you know. And to tell you the truth, it sounds so much better than saying she has a boyfriend. So much more grown up. Don't you think so?"

"Yes," Margo said. "I guess it does."

"So darling, tell me . . . he's a real mensh?"

"He's a very nice man. I'm sure you'll like him."

"So it's serious?"

"Well, yes. We're trying it out for six months."

"For six months?" her mother said. "What does that mean . . . for six months? I never heard of such a thing."

"Not necessarily *just* for six months," Margo said, trying to explain. "It could be for much longer. We hope it will be. We'll stay together as long as it works."

"Works?" her mother said. "What does *works* mean?"

"You know," Margo said, wishing she could get out of this conversation. "If we continue to get along and continue to care about each other . . ."

"Where's love?" her mother asked. "Don't people fall in love anymore?"

"Yes, of course," Margo said. "We're in love."

"Then it's settled. After six months you'll get married."

"We haven't discussed marriage yet."

"You should discuss it, darling."

Later, when she and Andrew were in bed, Margo said, "My mother refers to you as my *significant other*."

Andrew laughed. "Come over here and I'll show you *how* significant your other is."

Margo moved toward him.

"Feel that . . ."

"Wow . . . that's exceptionally significant."

Margo had been living in Boulder for just three months when her father had phoned. She had known right away it was going to be bad news. She had heard it in her father's voice.

"Dad," Margo had said, "what is it . . . what's wrong?"

"It's Mother," he'd said. "She's in the hospital . . . just tests . . . she didn't want me to tell you."

"What kind of tests?"

"Well, it looks like it could be . . . she found some little lumps . . . under her arm . . . it's probably nothing . . . but just to be sure, the doctor put her in."

"I'll be there as soon as I can," Margo had said.

She had flown east the next morning, after making some hasty arrangements with Michelle's English teacher, a young woman she had met and liked who had told her that she often stayed with her students while their parents traveled.

She had taken a cab directly from LaGuardia to New York Hospital. As she'd rounded the corridor, looking for Room 412, she could hear her sisters' voices. Her father was there too, all three of them standing at her mother's bedside. Her mother had been sitting up, wearing a pink lace bed jacket. Her hair, which was usually teased around her face, was brushed back, making her eyes look bigger and her face very small and white. But she had been trying to make the best of it, of whatever was about to happen, by laughing and joking. She had always told Margo that humor was the only way to get through life.

"Margo, darling . . ." her mother said, holding out her arms. "You didn't have to fly in for this. It's just a few tests. Abe . . . why did you have to go and tell her?"

"I'm glad he did," Margo said, kissing her mother's soft cheek. She smelled from Shalimar, her favorite perfume. "I want to be here with you."

The nurse came in then, to take her mother's blood pressure. She was a big black woman, with steel-gray hair and oversized glasses. "This is my daughter, Margo," her mother said.

"The one who's from Colorado?" the nurse asked.

"That's right." Her mother began to sing, doing her John Denver imitation. "Rocky Mountain high . . . aye aye aye aye . . . Rocky Mountain low . . . ooh ooh ooh ooh . . ."

The nurse laughed. "You're such a card, Mrs. Kaye."

"You should only know," Margo's father said.

Later, when Bethany, Joell and their father went down to the cafeteria, Margo's mother lay back against the pillows and said, "So tell me darling . . . how are you, how are the children?"

"We're all fine."

"You like it out there?"

"I think I will. It's still too soon to say for sure."

"I'll never understand why you had to move so far away."

"You know it's not that far. Did you study the map I sent? Did you see that Colorado and Arizona, where Aunt Luba lives, come together? And that Colorado's not nearly as far as California?" Her mother shared Steinberg's view of the world.

"You couldn't have just gone to New Jersey?" her mother asked.

Margo laughed. "No. I had to make a clean break, had to start a new life . . . you know that. But never mind me . . . tell me about you."

"What's to tell?" her mother asked. "If it's malignant they'll operate. I told them, *Go ahead, take it off. Abe will love me with one breast as much as with two.* And if they have to take them both off, that's all right too."

And they had. A double mastectomy. And even then they hadn't been sure they'd gotten it all. But they'd hoped that with radiation followed by chemotherapy . . .

It was Margo's father who needed the comforting. "Without Belle, I don't want to live."

"She's going to be all right," Margo said, trying to reassure him.

"But suppose she's not? Suppose they didn't get it all?"

"We can't plan ahead, Dad," Margo said. "We're just going to have to wait and see."

"She's my life," he whispered, tears in his eyes. "I love you girls, I love my grandchildren, but she's my life."

Oh, to be loved that way, Margo had thought. To be loved so completely. Would she ever know such love, such devotion? She doubted it. Maybe people just didn't love as intensely anymore. Maybe they were afraid.

"Look at this," her mother said, two days after surgery. "Flat as a pancake . . . just like a boy . . ."

And a few days after that, "This morning I had a visit from a beautiful young woman, Margo. She reminded me of you. She had a double herself, not that you'd ever know it, and she told me all about the possibilities. So what do you think . . . falsies at my age and maybe reconstructive surgery?"

"Why not?" Margo said.

"You know something, darling . . . even when they tell you it's cancer, you don't give up . . . you keep making plans. I keep telling myself I'm going to beat it. I suppose it's because I'm an optimist."

"You are going to beat it," Margo said. "And at a time like this an optimist isn't such a bad thing to be."

"Of all my children, Margo, you're the one who's most like me. I don't know if that's good or bad."

"I think it's good."

Her mother smiled. "Deep down I think so too."

Margo had called Freddy. "I'm in New York," she'd told him. "My mother's in the hospital."

"Nothing serious, I hope," Freddy said.

"A double mastectomy."

"I'm sorry to hear that. I'll send flowers."

"You don't have to send anything . . . I just thought you'd want to know."

"I said I'll send flowers." There was a long pause. Then Freddy said, "So how are you doing out there, in the middle of nowhere?"

"I think it's going to work out very well."

"I could go to court, Margo. I could go to court and get an injunction against you for taking the kids so far away. You're going to ruin my relationship with them. Some day they'll blame you."

"I thought you agreed that if it was necessary for my work . . ."

"I made a mistake. I never should have agreed to let you take them."

"I couldn't concentrate on solar design in New York, Freddy . . ."

"Don't feed me any of your crap, Margo."

"Let's not get started," Margo said. "This is a hard time for me."

"When isn't it a hard time for you? You thrive on hard times."

"Okay. If you say so. How's Aliza?"

"Aliza's fine."

"Good."

"Who's with the children?" he had asked.

"Michelle's English teacher."

"Is she a responsible person?"

"Would I have left her with the kids if she wasn't?"

"Probably."

"Goodbye, Freddy."

"Goodbye, Margo. And I am sorry about your mother."

She had hung up the phone feeling all the old anger, all the old resentments. She had not been the wife that Freddy had expected. He still blamed her for having had her own needs and he was still able to make her feel guilty. Freddy had wanted a Stepford Wife. Margo had once told him so in the heat of a bitter argument over the menu for a dinner party. She had hurled a copy of the novel across the room, catching him on his left shoulder. "A plastic princess who doesn't think!" Margo had yelled. "That's what you want, isn't it? A plastic princess who'll give elegant little dinner parties and fuck whenever you feel like it!"

"Right," Freddy had said, rubbing his shoulder. "That's exactly what I want."

At home Stuart and Michelle were full of questions about Grandma Belle. Margo tried to be honest, but at the same time, not to worry them, assuring them that the doctors would do everything possible and telling them that Grandma Belle was in very good spirits.

"Is she tap dancing, yet?" Michelle asked.

"No, not yet. But I'm sure she will be soon."

Margo's mother had taken up tap dancing at the age of sixty-two. She took three lessons a week, inspired by Ruby Keeler's performance in a revival of *No, No, Nanette*. And she was good. She used to love to dance for the grandchildren, before Bethany moved to the west coast and Margo moved to Boulder. Margo did not tell Michelle that she was afraid Grandma Belle would never put her tap shoes on again.

*   *   *

Margo was not sure that she should bring Andrew to the anniversary party. Too much too soon, she feared. But when Bethany offered them the use of her condominium on the peninsula at Marina del Rey, how could she refuse? A week alone with Andrew. A week of making love with no one else around.

It had been Andrew's idea to drive to L.A. They would drop Stuart and Michelle at the airport in Denver and hit the road by themselves. It had sounded romantic at the time. No kids, no responsibilities, no phone calls from B.B., accusing Andrew of ruining her life and of filling Sara's head with his fucked-up values. Margo urged Andrew to hang up when B.B. became hysterical, but he would not. He believed it was better to let her vent her feelings. Sometimes when Margo answered the phone, B.B. would lay it on her. "He has no sense. Can't you see that? All he's after is a quick fuck and a place to live. He doesn't give a shit about you or anyone else."

The evening Andrew had returned from B.B.'s house in mid-November, after telling her that he was moving in with Margo, Margo had asked, "How did it go? How did she take it?"

And Andrew had answered. "I don't know. She seemed hyper at first, almost flirtatious, and then she became hysterical."

"She'll get used to the idea. Don't worry."

"You're such an optimist," he said. "You always think everything will work out."

"It will."

"That's not realistic, Margo. Some things don't work out. Some things get screwed up and stay screwed up."

"I know," she said. "I've had my share of disappointments."

"I'm not talking about disappointments." He lay down on the bed, covering his eyes with his hand. "I don't know if this is going to work."

"What?"

"Me, living here. I might be making it harder on Sara instead of easier. Maybe I should leave, go back to Miami."

"I thought we made a deal," Margo said, her throat tightening.

"You'd come with me."

"I can't come with you . . . not now . . . you know that. I have responsibilities here."

"Fuck responsibilities."

"I can't and neither can you. What would Sara think if you walked out on her?" *Don't do this. Don't leave now when it's just beginning. I don't know if I'll ever allow myself to try again if you do.* But she could not say her thoughts out loud.

"Maybe I shouldn't have come here in the first place."

"Maybe not, but you did . . . and I'd like to think . . ." Her voice trailed off. *I would like to think you love me,* she thought, turning away.

He got off the bed and put his arms around her. "I'm sorry," he said. "It's not you. I'm glad I found you. You know that."

"It'll be okay," she said into his shoulder. "There's a lot to get used to, that's all."

Margo found herself avoiding B.B. She stayed away from The James at lunch, meeting Andrew at the library instead or eating alone at her desk. She no longer browsed in the Boulder Bookstore at noon or met friends at the Boulderado for a drink after work. Anyway, she was too busy for friends. But surely after the holidays, after the mad rush to get everything in order, both at work and at home, so that she and Andrew could enjoy their trip, she would have more time. Unless what Clare had said about having a steady man was true. That it was hard to keep that kind of intimacy going with more than one person at a time. And in the past two months Andrew had become everything—friend, lover, confidant.

Margo had been disappointed to hear that B.B. had put the land for the cluster housing project back on the market. Clare had told her.

"She feels that she can't work with you," Clare had said. "Not anymore. And she doesn't want to start in with another architect."

"But to put the land back on the market . . ."

"This is very hard on her," Clare said. "It's not just knowing that Andrew has moved in with you . . . it's the way you flaunt your happiness."

"I don't mean to flaunt it," Margo said.

"I know that, but it's there. You shine . . . you sparkle . . ."

"I try to think of her feelings . . . to put myself in her place . . . really. But she's making it so hard. She's so hateful, so off the wall. Does she want him back, is that it?"

"I think it's more that she doesn't want anyone else to have him. Look, Margo . . . you're both my friends. I can't take sides. I can't choose between you."

"I don't want you to," Margo said.

Margo kept reminding herself that B.B. had lost a child. She almost said something to Clare one day, but caught herself in time. If B.B. wanted Clare to know she would tell her herself. She tried to imagine how she would feel if she had lost a child, but the idea was so horrible she could not. Once, when Stuart was small, he had been very sick, running a fever of 105, and the doctors could not find out what was wrong with him. He lay in his bed for days while they awaited test results and Margo had slept on the floor next to him, rubbing his small body with alcohol every hour. She had known she might lose him and had felt utterly helpless. Well, B.B. had lost a healthy ten-year-old son. Margo tried to remember that, tried to sympathize, not allowing herself to hate.

But when they ran into B.B. and Lewis at the airport at the start of the holidays and B.B., cool as could be, introduced Andrew to Lewis, ignoring Margo and her children, Margo was pissed. And she was still feeling hostile when she and Andrew got back into the car to begin their drive to L.A.

If only B.B. hadn't been at the airport, Margo thought, there wouldn't be this tension in the car now. Andrew tried, singing along with country-western music on the car radio, but it was forced gaiety and they both knew it. After "Mamas, Don't Let Your Babies Grow Up to Be Cowboys," Andrew said, "Back in Hackensack, New Jersey, when I was about nine, I wanted to be a cowboy more than anything."

"Did you ride a horse?" Margo asked.

"Nope . . . a bicycle."

"It's hard to be a cowboy without a horse," Margo said, forcing a laugh, "although you certainly drive like one."

Andrew turned pale and slowed down. "I didn't mean to go over sixty."

"I didn't . . ." Margo began, "that is, I wasn't . . . oh, shit . . . I'm sorry . . ."

"It's okay," Andrew said.

But it wasn't okay. None of it was okay. She had reminded him of Bobby and the way he'd died. Bobby's death was always there, always with Andrew, and she was going to have to learn to accept it, along with his occasional bouts of melancholy. At first she had assumed his moodiness had to do with something she'd done or said, but now she knew that wasn't the case. Any reminder of Bobby brought on a sadness, a withdrawal. She had tried to talk to him about it, but he hadn't responded. The few times she had pressed he had become even more withdrawn. She remembered the night he had told her about Bobby. *I don't feel sorry for myself anymore and I don't want anyone else feeling sorry for me either.* Okay, she would not feel sorry for him.

During the rest of the trip to L.A. they were quiet, taking turns driving and dozing, twenty-four hours, straight through. Not exactly the romantic interlude they had planned.

AT FIRST MICHELLE had not wanted to go to the anniversary party. She'd wanted to fly straight to New York instead of spending five days in Beverly Hills at Aunt Bethany's house. If it hadn't been for hurting Grandma's and Grandpa's feelings that's exactly what she would have done. She always got headaches when she was around Aunt Bethany. Aunt Bethany never shut up. Michelle tried to follow her endless stories, but the harder she tried the more her head hurt. Little Lauren, who was Aunt Bethany's *mistake,* said that her mother was lonely living in Beverly Hills and that's why she talked so much. Maybe Little Lauren was right.

Margo and Andrew dropped Michelle and Stuart at the airport in Denver. It had been Andrew's idea to drive to L.A. and, of course, Margo did whatever Andrew wanted. Well, that was their business. As long as she and Stuart didn't have to spend twenty-four hours in the backseat of Margo's Subaru listening to the love-birds, who cared? Every time he called Margo *Margarita,* Michelle gagged.

God, it was so strange bumping into B.B. at the airport. Michelle thought that B.B. was going to pass out when she saw them. She hung onto this guy, Lewis something or other, as if he were her lifeline. He was older, but not bad. He had a nice smile. B.B. looked really sophisticated. She had her hair pulled back, showing off gold earrings, and she was carrying one of those expensive bags you see in *New Yorker* ads.

Michelle could not understand what Andrew saw in her mother after having been married to someone like B.B. Although, Michelle had to admit, B.B. was not the friendliest person around. When she introduced Lewis she said, "Lewis, this is Andrew, my former husband." And that was it. She acted as if the rest of them didn't exist.

But Margo offered her hand, saying, "I'm Margo Sampson and these are my children, Stuart and Michelle." Michelle was really proud of her mother then. If only Margo hadn't been wearing her faded jeans and that baggy sweater.

There was this awkward moment when no one said anything, and then everyone spoke at once. Finally they parted and walked off in opposite directions.

"God," she said to Stuart when they were on the plane, "I'll bet that really shook up Andrew."

"What?"

"Meeting his ex-wife and her new boyfriend."

"He's tough," Stuart said, yawning.

"Don't you wish we were going to Hawaii instead of Aunt Bethany's? Hawaii sounds so exotic." When she looked over at Stuart for some reaction she saw that he had fallen asleep. She didn't see how anyone could sleep on a plane, but Stuart was out cold and they had barely taken off.

She clutched her canvas purse. Gemini had loaned her gobs of jewelry to wear to the anniversary party and she was worried that if she lost it she would never be able to repay her. Michelle was going to do herself up for the party. Maybe she would meet someone exciting there. Not a poet or a true intellectual, because Aunt Bethany wouldn't know anyone like that, but possibly a movie star. Since Uncle Harvey was some big deal at one of the studios she was sure there would be some movie star types at the party. Not that she was interested in movie stars, because they wouldn't know the way of the world, but just for the night it might be interesting.

She took out her copy of *The Book of Daniel* and began to read. She wished her parents had done something dramatic with their lives, like Daniel's had.

23

GOING TO FLORIDA for two weeks was supposed to be a privilege. That's what Sara's mother told her. Sara didn't think it was such a privilege. Her mother had gone to Hawaii for the holidays to a place called Maui. Now that sounded like a privilege. Her mother should have invited her to go too. Not that she'd have gone, but she should have been invited. And her father! She'd spent every Christmas vacation with him since the divorce. But this year he was in Los Angeles with Margo. And he hadn't invited her either. It was just like Jennifer said. You couldn't trust parents. They were only interested in you when they didn't have anyone else. As soon as they had lovers, forget it.

"They'd probably get rid of us completely, if they could," Jennifer had said.

"What do you mean, completely?" Sara asked. "Do you mean they wish we were dead?"

Jennifer laughed her head off. "No stupid. They'd never go that far. Then they'd feel guilty for the rest of their lives. They're really subtle about it. What they do is, they send us away to school, except they act like it's for our own good instead of theirs. They say stuff like, *Wouldn't you like to go away to school next year . . . someplace where you could get a really fine education. You'd get to meet lots of interesting new people . . . people from all over the world . . .*

"And you say *No.*

"So they say, *But think of it in terms of expanding your horizons . . .*

"And you still say *No.*

"So then they say, *Well, we think you should give it a try, at least for one year . . .*

"And you say, *I won't go and you can't make me.*

"And they say, *It's already settled. We've paid the tuition and you leave on August fifteenth.*"

"Nobody is trying to send me away to school," Sara said.

"Yet," Jennifer said. "They wait until you're going into ninth grade or even tenth. That's how they did it with my sisters. And I know they're going to do it with me too. I'll bet you anything I'm going to be sent to the same school my mother went to when she was a girl."

"Where is it?" Sara asked.

"In Virginia. I'll be able to have my own horse."

"That doesn't sound so bad."

"The horse is the only good part of it."

So Sara went to Florida and spent the first week of her vacation with Grandma and Grandpa Broder. They wanted to hear all about Daddy and Margo.

"What does Margo look like?" Grandma Broder asked.

"She's all right. Not as pretty as Mom."

"A nice figure?" Grandpa Broder asked.

"Okay," Sara said. "Not as skinny as Mom."

"You like her . . . she's nice to you?"

"She's okay."

"You didn't bring a picture of her?" Grandma asked.

"No." Why should she have brought a picture of Margo? Who cared what Margo looked like anyway? It was just a passing fancy. That's what her mother told her. Sara really liked that expression—a passing fancy. It was just a convenient place for Daddy to live while he wrote his book. So why were her grandparents making such a big thing out of it? Unless they knew something she didn't. Oh, she hated grownups and all their secrets!

It was the same at Grandma Goldy's and Uncle Morris's the

next week. They wanted to hear all about her Thanksgiving trip to Minneapolis. She didn't tell them anything except that Minneapolis had been so cold her lips had been blue the whole time. And she told them that Lewis was seventeen years older than her mother. But they already knew.

Sara did not want to spend her vacation answering questions about her parents. She wanted to swim and play with the other kids who were down visiting their grandparents. If they were going to talk at all then Sara wanted to talk about *her* life. And she wanted them to tell her what a wonderful kid she was and how they hoped her parents appreciated her and that if ever her parents weren't paying enough attention to her she could fly right back to Florida.

"You're getting little bosoms," Grandma Goldy said, the first time Sara put on her one-piece Speedo. "Pretty soon you'll have all the boys after you, just like your mother."

Sara wanted to shout that she was nothing like her mother. And that the boys weren't even interested in her. They all liked Ellen Anders, who was always in trouble in school and who took Quaaludes every weekend.

24

B.B. FELT WONDERFULLY removed in Maui, with just the sun and the sea and Lewis, adoring her, making her feel young and beautiful, making her feel that her whole life was ahead of her. She remembered Andrew once saying, *Fuck responsibilities!* Well, maybe that's exactly what she would do.

She'd been proud of herself at the airport. She had really been in control. The night before she had phoned Andrew, had shouted at him.

"What do you want?" he'd asked.

She'd thought about saying, *I want you back,* but that was too demeaning and she wasn't even sure it was true, so she'd said, "I want you out of my life. I want you off my turf. Sara is mine."

"She's ours," he'd answered.

"No, not here. Here she belongs to me." Then she had slammed down the receiver.

She phoned their house at odd hours, when she thought they might be talking about her or making love. She hated the idea of them in bed together, snuggled close, Margo's head on his chest. She hated the idea of him telling Margo stories about their marriage, sharing the most intimate details of their lives. Sometimes she would phone in the middle of the night, then hang up. She didn't want to phone. She didn't want to show them that she cared, that knowing they were together hurt, but she couldn't stop herself. If only he would go away. If Margo loved him so much let her go with him. Love . . . the idea of it made her laugh.

She and Lewis made love every afternoon. Sometimes she would keep her eyes open and stare at the lovely designs on the ceiling of their villa. Sometimes she would become confused and think that Lewis was her father. There was something about his hands, something so familiar. She came close to calling him Daddy several times, but caught herself in time. Lewis was older than her father had been when he had died. She couldn't remember exactly how old her father had been then. She could remember only that her mother had told her he had died in some girl's bed. Some girl with red hair. Poor and Irish. But maybe her mother had made that up because her mother had been having an affair with Uncle Morris, hadn't she? She remembered her father accusing her mother of doing it with her own sister's husband. But none of it mattered. Because Daddy had loved *her* best. She had been his darling, his Francie. And now Lewis loved her the same way.

One afternoon, after making love, B.B. said, "I never tell anybody anything . . . you know that? I'm a very secretive person."

"You're the most together person I've ever known," Lewis said.

"You think so?" B.B. asked.

"I know so," Lewis said.

"I have a cloud that sometimes forms around my head, making everything fuzzy."

"You should see an ophthalmologist when you get back. Sounds like you need glasses." He kissed her fingers then, one by one.

B.B. laughed, could not stop laughing. She laughed until her body ached. Lewis didn't know. Lewis had no idea. And she was not going to spoil it by telling him about herself, by taking the chance that if he knew what she was really like he would stop loving her.

"I may never leave here," she said one day, as she oiled her legs.

"B.B., darling, if that's what you want I can make arrangements. Let's look for a place, a glass house on the ocean. What do you say?"

"Oh, Lewis, would you honestly do anything to please me?"

"Yes," he said seriously, sitting on the edge of her lounge chair. "Yes, I would."

"There's so much about me you don't know."

"If you want me to know, you'll tell me. Otherwise, it doesn't matter."

She had not yet told him about Bobby.

She wondered if she could spend the rest of her life pretending. Pretending to be happy. Pretending to be the most together person he had ever known. It was so hard to pretend. It took up almost all of her energy. Sometimes she felt so tired from pretending that she just wanted to let go, to slip away quietly, to let the warm ocean water cover her and carry her away.

"Marry me," Lewis said. "Marry me right now."

25

ANDREW SAT ON the deck of Bethany's condominium peering through a pair of binoculars that he had found in the kitchen cupboard. Margo assumed he was watching the parade of long, graceful sailboats leaving the marina. She lay back on a chaise, letting the sun warm her. No more serious sunbathing for her, though. She had more than enough lines around her eyes and mouth from years of careless sunning, when the most important goal of the summer was to have a good tan. She tried to warn Michelle to use a sun block routinely, especially in Colorado, where the high altitude made you even more vulnerable, but Michelle wouldn't listen. Michelle didn't believe she'd ever be forty.

"Have a look," Andrew said, passing Margo the binoculars. "It's tits and ass from here to Venice Beach."

Margo held the binoculars to her eyes. God, he was right. The beach was filling up with bodies—long, lean, gorgeous bodies—tanned, oiled, and wearing the skimpiest bikinis she had ever seen. She handed the binoculars back to Andrew without commenting.

"Put on your suit, Margarita," he said, "and let's hit the beach."

She went upstairs to the bedroom and got into her bathing suit, a black strapless one-piece with a diagonal pink stripe. As she appraised herself in the full-length mirror waves of insecurity washed over her. How could she possibly compete with all those leggy young things on the beach, their long hair flying in the breeze? Andrew was such an attractive man and his slim athletic body was very appealing. He would attract all those young girls on the beach, all those girls who wanted older men, so they could pretend they were fucking their daddies.

It's not how you look, dummy, she said to her reflection. *It's what's inside that counts.*

Bullshit. It's how you look, nothing more, nothing less.

But looks don't last.

Exactly. And you're a good example of that, aren't you? Look at the flab on the inside of your thighs.

Come on, I'm not flabby. For forty I'm in great shape.

Oh, sure. But if you really worked at it, if you ran, say, four or five miles a day, if you followed a strict macrobiotic diet, if you plunged your face into a basin of ice water three times a day like Paul Newman . . .

It's best not to think about aging. It's best to just accept it. Besides, it's not as if he's never seen my body . . .

But he's never seen it in a bathing suit, never compared it to a beachful of gorgeous California girls.

"Margo," Andrew called. "What are you doing?"

"Coming . . ."

Look, Margo said, trying to convince herself, *European women wear the tiniest bikinis no matter how old they are, no matter what their bodies look like, and they exude a kind of sexiness that women here aren't expected to have after a certain age. It's all in how you see yourself, in how you move.*

"Margarita . . ." Andrew called again.

"Here I am," she said, running down the stairs. She had pulled a t-shirt on over her bathing suit. She was furious at herself for feeling insecure.

They walked along the ocean's edge, holding hands. When they got down to the Venice Pier, they sat on the beach, watching a family with three children. The young mother, pregnant again, the father, building sand castles with the smallest. Suddenly it occurred to Margo that she and Andrew had never discussed the possibility of having children together.

"Have you ever thought about having more kids?" Margo asked

tentatively. She picked up a handful of sand and let it trickle through her fingers.

"I used to think I'd marry again and have more kids, but not anymore. You can't replace a child you've lost. And anyway, I don't want to go through it all over again. I'm glad your kids are older. That makes it easier." He paused. "You don't want more, do you?"

"No." She leaned over and kissed him. "It would have been nice to have a baby with you though."

"How do you know?"

"I just do." Margo choked up and turned away.

"What is it?" Andrew asked.

"I don't know," she managed to say. "Just the idea that we always have our kids with the wrong person."

"Not always."

"A lot of the time."

"It works out okay in the long run."

"Now you sound like me," Margo said. She bit on her lip to keep from crying.

"Too many people have the mistaken idea that when they love someone they'll make a baby that will be just like that person . . . and it's not true."

Margo looked away.

"Do you want another baby, Margo . . . is that it?"

She shook her head. "No, I don't want to start all over again either, especially now, especially knowing what I know about raising kids. I'm just being sentimental, that's all, wishing we had met in college, married young, had our kids together."

"We still would have had a lot to get through, and who's to say we would have come through it together?"

"I suppose you're right," Margo said. "But look at my parents . . . fifty years and they still love each other. Not just a comfortable kind of love, but *in* love. I just wish we had met sooner so we could have had a chance at that."

"You want fifty years together?" he asked.

She nodded.

"You've got them."

*   *   *

Margo felt nervous and upset dressing for the anniversary party. She popped two Rolaids into her mouth, hoping they would ease her queasiness.

"What's wrong?" Andrew asked. He had already finished dressing and was relaxing on the bed, watching her. He liked to watch her get dressed, he said. He liked the way she used her lipstick, then blotted almost all of it off, sliding a layer of clear gloss over it, making her mouth slick and inviting.

Margo crossed the room and sat beside Andrew. She touched his cheek, then his hair. "Look," she said, "this might be too much for you. It's not just a question of meeting my parents and my sisters. It's everyone all at once . . . aunts, uncles, cousins, old family friends . . . people I haven't seen in years, people I haven't seen since my own wedding. Are you sure you want to expose yourself to that?"

"It's probably easier to do it all at once," he said.

"You're brave," she told him. "I'm not sure I wouldn't opt to stay here and read a book."

"What's the worst that can happen?" Andrew asked.

She stood up, smoothed out her long skirt, and looked out the bedroom window. The sun was beginning to set over the ocean, turning the sky pink and the water golden. "They can ask you when we're getting married," she said, turning to face him.

"I'll tell them we haven't picked the date," he said easily. He got off the bed, came over to her, put his arms around her, and kissed her ear. "Would you?" he asked. "Would you get married again?"

"Maybe," she said. "Would you?"

"Maybe . . . if the right person came along."

"I'll remember that," she said. And then he kissed her mouth and she kissed him back and they both looked at the bed, rumpled and inviting, but knew that there was not time now. That they would have to wait.

26

AT THE ANNIVERSARY party Michelle sat at a little table by the side of the pool, watching Grandma and Grandpa dance. Grandma was wearing white chiffon and she looked like she was floating. You'd never know she'd had cancer, Michelle thought, sipping some kind of fruit punch with rum. You'd never know that she'd had both her breasts removed. God, what an idea. Michelle was still waiting for hers to grow. She was almost seventeen and her breasts were still the same size as when she was thirteen.

There weren't any movie stars at the party. Just a lot of family and friends who had flown in from all over the place and who did a *My, haven't you grown since the last time I saw you* number on Michelle and Stuart and the cousins.

Margo and Andrew were slow dancing, their bodies pressed very close. Every now and then Andrew kissed Margo near her ear and she looked up at him and smiled. Michelle finished the rum punch.

Aunt Joell, who had just turned thirty, was dancing with her boyfriend, Stan, who was divorced and had three kids. Aunt Joell ran this big travel agency in New York and said she was never going to have kids because they ruined your life. Imagine talking that way about having kids! How would she know? Did Michelle and Stuart look like they were ruining Margo's life? Not at all. On the contrary, Margo was very glad she had them. Otherwise she would be lonely and depressed. It was going to be very hard on Margo when both she and Stuart went off to college. Michelle wanted to have a child some day. But she wasn't sure she'd get married, unless there was some guarantee that her marriage would turn out like Grandma Belle's and Grandpa Abe's. That would be different.

The music stopped, then started again. Andrew walked across the dance floor and stopped at Michelle's table.

"How's it going . . . are you having a good time?"

"Yeah . . . sure."

"Want to dance?"

"Me?"

"Yes."

"I don't know how to do these dances."

"I saw you dancing with your grandfather. You looked like you were doing fine."

"That was different."

"Come on, Michelle, live a little."

"Well . . ."

He took her hands and practically pulled her to her feet, then out to the dance floor, which was a patio covered by a striped tent. He didn't try to hold her close or anything, but he looked directly into her eyes and smiled. "You look very pretty tonight," he said.

"I do?"

"Yes."

"Well, I tried, for Grandma and Grandpa. Gemini let me borrow all this jewelry." Michelle did think she looked kind of exotic. She had outlined her eyes with a silver green pencil and she was wearing a gauzy blouse with a Navajo sash tied around her waist.

"You look exotic," Andrew said. "You have good cheekbones, like your mother."

Michelle felt funny dancing with her mother's boyfriend. She had read an article about stepfathers putting the make on young girls at home. So as soon as the music stopped she ran for the house.

"Wait a minute . . ." Andrew called, coming after her.

She stopped outside the French doors.

"Look, Michelle . . . there's something I want to say to you . . ." he began.

She hoped he was not going to embarrass her. She fiddled with her Navajo sash, pretending that it was not tied properly.

"Michelle . . ." he said, "I know you weren't happy when I moved in . . . and I don't blame you . . . but I hope in time you'll accept me . . ."

He paused, as if he expected her to say something, but she didn't.

"I'm not going to try to be your father," he continued. "You already have a father. I know that. I guess what I'm trying to say is that I'd like to be friends."

"I've got to go in now," she said and she opened the French doors and stepped inside.

Later, Grandma put on the gold tap shoes that Grandpa had given to her for their golden wedding anniversary and she did a number to "You Are My Lucky Star," with double pullbacks and everything. Then they opened their gifts. The best one was the quilt that Margo had made. Grandma cried when she read the card, especially the part about the quilt being called *Circles of Love.* So did Margo. Even Andrew had tears in his eyes. And Michelle felt this gigantic lump in her throat and wanted everyone to love each other as much as they did then . . . forever.

27

IT WAS THE END of January and freezing. Sara wore her fisherman's sweater over her yellow turtleneck and sat close to the fire in the living room. She had a Spanish test coming up. Her mother was quizzing her, asking her all the words that began with the letter *N*. Last week they'd had *M* words and the week before that *L* words. So far Sara had an average of 100 on her quizzes. She wasn't sure if her good grades were the reason her mother had finally let her sleep over at Margo's house or not.

Her mother hadn't even told her she was going until last Thursday night, while they'd been sitting at the table, finishing their Jell-O. Sara liked to let the Jell-O melt on her tongue. When her mother told her about going to Margo's overnight she had been so surprised some of it had drooled out of her mouth and had landed on her white sweater. "How come?" Sara had asked. "How come you're letting me stay there? I thought you said you'd go to court first." Sara knew she shouldn't ask her mother questions, that she should just accept it, but she couldn't help herself.

"If you don't want to go you don't have to," her mother said.

"It's not that."

"Then what?"

"The way you keep changing your mind," Sara said. "I never know what's going on."

"Lewis convinced me that since your father didn't have you for Christmas he should have you one weekend a month."

"One weekend a month!" Sara said. "That's nothing."

"Why aren't you ever satisfied?" her mother shouted. "Don't you know what it means to me to let you stay there overnight? Have you any idea? Do you ever think of my feelings . . . because I have feelings too."

"Yes, Mom. I do try to think of your feelings."

Her mother stood up and paced the kitchen. Back and forth, back and forth, making a fist with one of her hands and smacking it into the other.

Sara started to feel all tangled up inside. She pushed her dish of Jell-O away and fooled with the crumbs from her Carr's biscuit.

Her mother whirled around, pointing a finger at her. "Ever since you've come back from Florida you've been acting like a selfish little bitch. What happened . . . didn't you have a good time there?"

"It was all right," Sara said. "I told you when I came back it was all right. There were just other things that I would rather have done over vacation." Like go to Hawaii, Sara thought. But she didn't say it.

"Your grandparents would have been very disappointed."

"All right!" Sara shouted. "So I went, didn't I? I stayed with them, didn't I?"

"Go to your room, Sara. And don't come out until you can control yourself."

"No! I don't feel like going to my room."

"Goddamn it, Sara! Do as I say."

"You're the bitch," Sara muttered, not caring if her mother heard her or not. "Come on, Lucy . . ." she said. Lucy followed her to her room. Sara slammed her bedroom door and flopped on her bed. "I hate her, I hate her, I hate her," she cried into Lucy's soft fur.

She knew she shouldn't argue with her mother. It only made things worse. But sometimes she got so sick of Mom she just felt like letting her have it. Mom was crying and carrying on in the living room, yelling about how she was a good person, how she had always been a good person, had always tried her best, and this is what she got for it. And why had God punished her . . . her of all people . . . why . . . ?

Sara did not want to hear anymore so she turned on her clock radio. It was small and white. Her father had given it to her for Christmas. Let her mother act like a nut, she thought. Who cares?

Suddenly Sara heard her mother running down the hall, but before she could figure out what was happening her mother threw open Sara's bedroom door, grabbed her clock radio, and hurled it across the room.

"Didn't I tell you to turn it down?" Mom yelled. "What's the matter with you, Sara . . . are you deaf? I told you at least four times."

"I didn't hear you," Sara said, jumping off her bed.

"Of course you didn't! How could you possibly hear me with that thing blasting? Blasting and making my head feel as if it's splitting in two?"

Sara ran across the room and picked up her clock radio. Its case had cracked. "You broke it!" she cried. "You broke my new clock radio. I hate you! You shouldn't be a mother!"

Her mother turned and left the room and in a minute Sara heard the front door slam, then the car start, and the tires screech. She ran to the living room window in time to see her mother's car racing down the street.

She felt dizzy then and sat on the piano bench, lowering her head between her legs. That's what you were supposed to do when you felt dizzy, to keep from fainting. Grandma Broder was always doing it. Her mother shouldn't be driving, she thought. You weren't supposed to drive when you were upset. You were much more likely to have an accident.

Sara waited half an hour. She pictured her mother's car smashing into a tree. Mom's head would have gone through the windshield of the car and would be covered with blood. Her eyes would be open, staring straight ahead, which meant that she was dead. Sara started to shiver. She went to the phone in the kitchen and dialed Clare's number, which was posted there for emergencies.

Clare answered.

"Hello . . . this is Sara. My mother's not home and I wondered if maybe she's at your house, or else, if you know where she is."

"I haven't seen her," Clare said. "Didn't she tell you where she was going?"

"No . . . see, we had a little disagreement and then she left and . . ."

"How long has she been gone?" Clare asked.

"About half an hour."

"Are you all right, Sara? Should I come over?"

"That's okay," Sara said. "You don't have to."

"I think I will," Clare said. "I'll be right there."

"Well, if you really want to."

On Friday afternoon her father had picked her up after school and brought her over to Margo's house. Sara had found out from Clare that Mom was meeting Lewis in Colorado Springs for the weekend. So that was why she had decided to let Sara go to stay with her father. Why hadn't Mom just told her the truth? Sara wondered if Lewis knew about her mother, about how she sometimes acted crazy.

Sara felt funny going to Margo's house, even though her father lived there now. Stuart and Michelle were out of town for the weekend, at a ski race, and Sara was glad. She knew Michelle didn't like her, would never like her, and that there was nothing she could do about it. Well, she didn't like Michelle either, so they were even. She didn't want to sleep in Michelle's room, but she had no choice.

Margo said, "This will be your room for the weekend. If you need anything just ask . . . okay?"

Sara would rather have stayed in Stuart's room. Stuart reminded her of Bobby, of what it might be like if she still had an older brother. She wished she had brought Lucy with her. Lucy would have helped her feel more at home, but Mom had said absolutely not and she'd hired a dog sitter for the weekend.

Michelle's room was filled with plants and posters. Sara was not allowed to tape posters to her wall. Her mother thought posters were tacky. Michelle's bed was covered with a brightly striped quilt. Sara lay down on it. The mattress was very hard. She looked up at the ceiling and counted the beams. There were seven of them. After a few minutes she got off the bed and opened her knapsack. There was no point in unpacking since she was just staying two nights, although Margo said she'd emptied a dresser drawer for her. Sara pulled a book out of her knapsack and lay down on the bed again. She tried to read, but she couldn't concentrate. She put the book down and crossed the room to Michelle's dresser. She opened one drawer at a time, poking around. Everything in Michelle's drawers was folded and stacked. Sara was surprised. She'd figured Michelle would be a slob. Only her socks were tossed into one drawer and weren't in pairs.

Sara found Michelle's diary under a pile of sweaters. She wanted to read it, but she was too scared. Probably Michelle was the kind who kept strands of hair in her diary so that she'd know if anyone ever tried to open it. Sara could not take that kind of chance. She put it back exactly where she'd found it. Then she tried on a couple of Michelle's sweaters. There was one she especially liked, a fuzzy blue one with a V neck.

She went through the bathroom cabinet too. You could find out a lot about a person by doing that. She'd done the same thing at her grandparents' apartments. But they'd had zillions of bottles of pills and Michelle had only one. *Michelle Sampson: one tablet twice a day for stomach cramps.* So, Michelle got stomach cramps too, Sara thought. Now that was interesting. Sara pictured Michelle sitting on the toilet, doubled over, with tears in her eyes from the pain, feeling as if her insides were about to come out.

Sara put the pills back into the cabinet and continued to look around. Michelle used Secret deodorant, washed her hair with Sassoon Salon Formula shampoo, and had a box of Tampax Regular. Sara hadn't started her period yet, but when she did she was going to use Tampax brand tampons too.

Sara had a weird feeling the whole time she was at Margo's

house. She knew that Margo was trying to be nice, trying to make her feel welcome, but still, there was something about being there that made her uneasy. Maybe it was knowing that her father slept in Margo's room. In Margo's bed. Knowing that they did it. That they fucked. She didn't like to think about them doing that, but sometimes she couldn't help herself and then she'd get this funny feeling down there, between her legs, like an itch, and she'd have to rub and rub until the itch went away.

On Saturday afternoon she and Daddy took a drive to the National Center for Atmospheric Research. Everyone who came to Boulder wanted to see it. It was on Table Mesa and the view was spectacular—that's how the guidebooks put it. But Sara wasn't as interested in the view as she was in the deer who browsed beside the road.

On the way back to town Daddy said, "Is everything all right at home, Sara?"

"What do you mean?" Sara asked.

"Are you getting along okay . . . no problems?"

"What kind of problems?" Sara asked.

"I don't know . . . any kind."

Sara knew that her father expected an answer. But she could not tell him the truth. She could not tell him about her clock radio, although she wanted to ask him if he thought the store would give her a new one. She could not tell him without going into the details of how and why it had cracked. And so she said, "Everything's okay."

"You're sure?" he asked.

She nodded.

When she got home on Sunday night she was glad she hadn't said anything, because there, on her bedside table, was a brand new clock radio, exactly the same, but without a cracked case. It was tied up with a red ribbon and there was a note propped in front of it.

Dear Sara,
I'm so sorry I broke your clock radio. You know it's not like

me to lose my temper that way. It's just that I had a terrible headache. I hope you will forgive me. I love you, always and forever.

Mom

Sara didn't know what to say. Her mother was standing in the doorway. "Sweetie . . . will you forgive me?"

"Yes," Sara said. "But I wish you would just talk it out when you feel that way, instead of screaming and running off in the car and scaring me. You were gone for almost two hours."

"I didn't mean to scare you. It's just that sometimes I need to be by myself, to let it all out. You can understand that, can't you?"

"Yes," Sara said quietly. But she really meant, *No. No, I can't take any more of this.* She pictured her mother's cleaver, the one she was never supposed to touch, and the way it could split a chicken breast in half just like that—thwack—with one solid movement. That's what her parents were doing to her.

28

MICHELLE RETURNED HOME from the first ski race of the season with two blue toes. She had been skiing for years, but she had never raced. Stuart convinced her to go out for the team this year, but she had known from the moment it began to snow that she was going to regret it.

She'd been sitting up front in the school van, a wad of Doublemint in her mouth, praying she would not get car sick. The coach was driving and Michelle was sure that he could not see more than six inches in front of him.

She heard Stuart's voice from the back of the van. She heard Puffin giggling. The van skidded. If they crashed and Stuart got out before the gas tank exploded, engulfing the rest of them in flames, which one would he try to save, Puffin or her? Probably Puffin. He loved her. He had shouted about his love for her over the holidays. He had shouted it across Freddy and Aliza's pale gray living room. "Goddamn it, Dad, I love Puffin!" He had shouted it in the midst of a monumental blowup because Freddy would not let Puffin, who was flying to New York, stay at his apartment over New Year's weekend.

"You'll have a million more girlfriends before you finally settle down," Freddy had told Stuart.

"You don't understand, do you?" Stuart had yelled. "You don't understand that Puffin and I have a serious relationship and I will not . . . repeat, will not . . . have you acting as if it's some kind of puppy love."

"I don't know what's gotten into you, Stu," Freddy had said, "but I don't like it."

If the coach didn't slow down none of them was going to have to worry about love, puppy or otherwise. Kristen, the girl squeezed between Michelle and the coach, was dozing and her head wobbled, finally landing on Michelle's shoulder. Michelle inched away. She wished she were home on her bed, reading a Stephen King novel.

Suppose the van careened off the highway and plunged into the canyon? Suppose she and Stuart were both killed? Margo would fall apart. Andrew had had a kid who was killed in a car crash. Michelle had just found out about that. She had asked Margo if she could read Andrew's book. She was curious. She'd read some of his magazine pieces, but they were just bullshit articles about prison reform and politics. The book was different. After she'd read it she couldn't stop thinking about the characters. And when Margo had told her about Andrew's kid, Bobby, Michelle had locked herself in her room, bawling her eyes out for hours.

Michelle closed her eyes and tried to think pleasant thoughts, tried to erase the picture in her mind of the van turned upside down, their bodies splattered across the highway, their blood turning to red ice.

She tried instead to remember the good, warm feeling she'd had at Grandma's and Grandpa's anniversary party. The feeling that if only everything could stay this way forever, life would be perfect.

On Monday morning Margo took Michelle to the doctor. "Frostbite," he said, examining her toes, "but I don't think you're going to lose them. You're lucky it's not your big toe. Big toes are the most useful, you know."

"Do I have to quit the ski team?" Michelle asked. She was hoping he'd say yes. She had never been so scared as when she'd been whizzing down the mountain full speed, totally out of control, and then, near the end of the run, catching her ski on the tip of a rock and falling. Falling and falling, head over heels, sure she would never stop, or that when she did both her legs would be broken, or even worse, her neck, paralyzing her for the rest of her life.

"I know you don't want to quit," the doctor was saying, "especially in January, when the season is just beginning, but if I were you I'd stay off the slopes and give those toes a chance to heal. They'll never be the same. You'll probably always experience pain in cold weather, but . . ." He paused for a minute and looked at Margo, then back at Michelle. "How did this happen anyway? Weren't you wearing thermal socks?"

"I forgot to loosen my boots after the race," Michelle said. "I rode all the way from Wolf Creek to Boulder without loosening them."

"That was not good thinking," the doctor said. "I'm surprised at you, Michelle . . . you've always struck me as a good thinker."

"These things happen," Michelle said seriously.

So, she had frostbite on two toes. Well, that was certainly more interesting than a sore throat, which was what Stuart had.

"I've got to get to the office now," Margo said, dropping Michelle off at school. "You think you'll be okay?"

Michelle did not answer her mother. She got out of the car and slammed the door shut. She was so pissed at Margo! While she had been at Wolf Creek, close to killing herself, Margo had let the Brat sleep in *her* room, in *her* bed, and Margo had not even asked *her* permission. Had not even told her, probably would never have told her. But Michelle had known instantly. Those little flowered cotton underpants at the side of her bed. The kind Michelle had worn in junior high. And her room had smelled differently too. The Brat never took baths and even when she did you could still smell her feet a mile away because she never bothered to wash them.

"You let Sara sleep in here, didn't you!" Michelle had yelled at her mother, the minute she'd surveyed her room. "How could you? How could you have done such a thing?"

"I changed the sheets for you," Margo said, sounding guilty as hell.

"Changed the sheets! You think changing the sheets makes it all right?" Michelle ripped the quilt off her bed and sprayed her sheets with Lysol. Then she checked every one of her drawers and her closet to make sure that nothing was missing, that nothing was out of place. She would never forgive her mother for this. Never! Suppose the Brat had read her diary? Suppose she'd seen some of the books Michelle kept buried under her sweaters or the letters she had written but never mailed?

Margo was always yapping about respecting privacy. Well, this showed how much she respected Michelle's privacy. But Michelle had made it very clear that the Brat was never to go near her room again.

29

B.B. HAD NOT BEEN to Miami in almost seven years, but in the midst of a late February snowstorm she was on her way. The drive from Boulder to Denver had taken more than two hours and the plane had been an hour and a half late taking off from Stapleton.

She did not know why her mother had had to have a stroke in the middle of winter.

Clare had driven her to the airport. At least she was able to get an aisle seat on the plane. Dinner was served an hour after take-off. Chicken Kiev. The flight attendant smiled sweetly as she served it. The man squeezed into the seat next to B.B., a jowly, heavyset man in a three-piece polyester suit, ate everything on his tray. He sopped up the Kiev juices with his roll, smacking his lips together as he did. Afterwards he picked his teeth with his fingers.

B.B. nibbled on a cracker.

The phone call from Uncle Morris had come at five in the morning. Her mother couldn't move, couldn't speak.

"Not hungry today?" the flight attendant asked, eyeing B.B.'s untouched dinner tray.

"Not especially," B.B. said. "But I would like some coffee."

The flight attendant, who wore too much green eyeshadow, poured the coffee sloppily, spilling some on B.B.'s lap. "Oh, no . . . I'm terribly sorry," she said. "Here, let me help you." She tried to wipe up the coffee that was seeping into B.B.'s beige pants, burning her thighs. "If you'd stand up," she said, "I think it would be easier."

"Here . . ." the man next to B.B. said, passing his napkin.

"Club soda," the woman in the window seat said. "It works every time."

"If you'd just stand up . . ." the flight attendant said again, sounding annoyed, as if this had been B.B.'s fault instead of hers.

"I don't *want* to stand up," B.B. said.

"Well, I can't help you unless you do."

"Club soda," the woman in the window seat repeated. "Believe me, I know."

B.B. was trying very hard to hang on, to keep from crying out or screaming.

Her mother had gotten up to use the toilet at one A.M. and had passed out on the bathroom floor. Uncle Morris had been awakened by the thud. Thank God the bathroom floor was carpeted, he'd said on the phone.

The man next to B.B. leaned over and said, "You pay three, four hundred bucks and this is what you get. That's why they're all going out of business . . . know what I mean?"

B.B. nodded.

She had begged Andrew to stay at her house with Sara and not to take her to Margo's.

Now two flight attendants approached her, the one who had spilled the coffee and another. "When you reach your final destination and have your trousers cleaned, please send the bill to the airline," the older one told her.

"Yes . . . all right," B.B. said.

She had phoned Andrew at six that morning. Margo had answered the phone sounding sleepy. "Honey . . . it's for you," she had heard her say. "It's B.B."

Tears came to B.B.'s eyes and spilled over, running down her cheeks.

"Please accept our apologies," the senior flight attendant was saying.

"Yes, all right . . ." B.B. answered. "Just leave me alone, please."

"Of course." One looked at the other, then both flight attendants walked down the aisle away from her.

"My mother is just sixty-one," B.B. said quietly.

"Mine's eighty-four," the man next to her said, as if she'd been talking to him, "and senile . . . don't know a thing . . . don't recognize us . . . it's no good . . . who wants to live that long? When my turn comes I hope it's quick."

She did not answer him. She closed her eyes and kept them closed until they landed in Miami.

At the airport B.B. rented a car, a Dodge Dart, green, smelling of newness. She had not been to Miami since the accident. Bobby had been ten. He'd be seventeen now, tall and handsome, with a deep voice. Almost a man. Her mother should have died instead of having a stroke. Death was clear. The ones who were left knew what to do. Arrange for the funeral. Go through the motions of mourning. The other feelings, the ones that lived deep inside, the gnawing empty feelings of loss, of unbearable sadness, you kept to yourself.

B.B. had been packed and ready to go by the time Sara was up that morning. They'd had a quick breakfast together and B.B. had told Sara what had happened.

"Is Grandma Goldy going to die?" Sara had asked.

"I don't know. She's very sick."

"What's it like to have a stroke?"

"I don't know that either. I imagine it's like being inside a tunnel but you can't get out, no matter how hard you try."

Sara began to cry.

"Don't, Sweetie . . . it will be all right . . . come on now . . ."

Sara had come to her then, had let her hug her for the first time in a long time. "I don't want her to die."

"Neither do I, but it's not up to us to decide. You better get ready for school now."

Sara had looked out the window. "Do you think school will be open with all this snow?"

"I don't know. Why don't you put on your radio and find out."

"If it's closed I'll go over to Jennifer's . . . okay?"

"Okay."

"How long will you be gone, Mom?"

"I'm not sure . . . probably four or five days."

"And Daddy's coming here to stay with me?"

"Yes."

"Will you send Grandma Goldy my love?"

"Yes."

B.B. drove directly to the hospital. Uncle Morris was slumped in a chair outside the intensive care unit. He looked exhausted. He was seventy-eight, an old man, seventeen years older than her mother. She had a vision of Lewis at seventy-eight—seventeen years older than her. This is how he would look. Uncle Morris should have been the one to have had the stroke, not her mother. Then his children, her cousins, could have come running, eager to get their hands on his money at last. All but her mother's share, two hundred and fifty thousand dollars or half the estate, whichever amount was greater at the time of his death. Her cousins had hated the prenuptial agreement, had believed that their father's entire estate belonged to them.

"Francie . . ." Uncle Morris stood up when he saw her and they embraced.

"How is she?" B.B. asked.

"No change . . . still nothing . . . we don't know what's going to be. I only wish it had been me instead. She's still so young."

"Can I see her?"

Uncle Morris checked his watch. "Every hour, for ten minutes. That's the rule. But it's been more than an hour so go ahead."

B.B. entered the intensive care unit, whispered her mother's name to the nurse in charge, and was escorted to her mother's bedside.

"Hello, Mother . . . I'm here . . ."

Her mother did not respond. Her eyes were closed, as if she were sleep. B.B. stayed for a few minutes, then went back outside. She told Uncle Morris that he should go home, should get some rest, that she would stay and if there was any change she would call him.

"You're sure, Francine . . . you're not tired yourself, after your trip?"

"No, I'm fine. I want to stay here."

"All right then. I'll go have a nap, take a shower, maybe heat up some soup."

"Yes."

Uncle Morris kissed her cheek and walked slowly down the hallway. His bald head was tanned. B.B. had always liked the way bald men tanned on their heads.

In an hour she went back inside to see her mother. Her mother seemed so small, and although her skin was suntanned, a grayish color had seeped through. Her bleached hair, stiff with spray, stuck out like porcupine quills. B.B. took her hairbrush from her purse and gently brushed it back, away from her mother's face.

Her mother opened her eyes and looked at her.

"Mother . . . it's me . . . Francine . . ."

Her mother made a small noise, like a cat mewing, then her eyes closed again. Had she recognized her? B.B. couldn't be sure. She sat at her mother's side holding her hand until a nurse asked her to leave. It was eleven o'clock.

She walked down the hall to a pay phone and dialed her home phone number. It would be just nine o'clock there. The phone rang twice and then her answering machine clicked on with Andrew's voice saying, *You have reached 555–4240. If this is an emergency please phone 555–6263. Otherwise, please leave a message and someone will get back to you. Thank you.*

Damn him! She hung up and dialed the other number, Margo's number. Michelle picked up on the third ring. "Hello . . ."

"Is Sara there?"

"Who's calling?"

"Her mother."

"Just a minute . . ." B.B. heard Michelle calling, "Hey, Sara . . . it's for you . . . it's your mother."

"Hello, Mom . . ." Sara said, coming on the line. "Where are you? How's Grandma?"

"I'm at the hospital. She's asleep. What are you doing at Margo's?"

"Oh, it was really snowing and Daddy decided it would be better for all of us to be together since he's the only one with a four-wheel drive, in case of an emergency . . . you know . . ."

"Where's Lucy?"

"Lucy's here, with me."

"Don't let her drink out of their toilets."

"Why not?"

"Because I said so. Where are you going to sleep?"

"I'm not sure. Upstairs on the sofabed, I think."

"Watch out for those children, Sara. They're drug addicts."

"Not really, Mom."

"Listen to me, Sara. I know. Don't take anything they give you. Promise me that . . . promise me that you won't take anything."

"Okay . . . I promise."

"Let me talk to your father now."

"Hang on . . . I'll get him."

Andrew came on the line a minute later. "Hello, Francine . . . how's your mother?"

"Why did you take Sara there? I asked you not to, didn't I?"

"Because of the storm, but that's not important . . . how's your mother doing?"

"I'll decide what's important!"

"Look, don't worry, everything is fine here. Lewis is trying to reach you. He asked me to have you call him as soon as you can."

"I want to talk to Sara again."

"Yeah, Mom?" Sara sounded annoyed this time.

"Sara, I want you to make your father take you home tomorrow. It's not safe for you there. Do you understand?"

"Okay, Mom. I'll try."

"I love you, Sara."

"And me you."

"For how long?"

"You know . . ."

"For always and forever?" B.B. asked.

"Yes."

"Then say it, Sara."

"I can't right now."

"Why not?"

"You know."

"Because they're listening?"

"Something like that."

"Are you embarrassed to have them know you love me?"

"No, Mom."

"Then say it."

"For always and forever," Sara said, softly.

"For always and forever what?"

Sara didn't respond.

"For always and forever what?" B.B. said again.

"I love you for always and forever," Sara said quickly.

B.B. began to cry. "The flight attendant spilled hot coffee on my lap. My pants are all stained."

"I guess you'll have to wash them," Sara said.

"Yes," B.B. said, hanging up the phone. She had lost Sara too. She could feel it. Sara would be happier if she never came back.

B.B. awoke at dawn with a cramp in her foot and a kink in her neck. She had fallen asleep in the chair in the hallway outside the intensive care unit. It had been hours since she had seen her mother. But surely if there had been any change they'd have called her.

She went inside. Her mother was still asleep, or whatever it was that looked like sleep. B.B. sat beside her, looking down at her, feeling an intense anger building up. "Damn it, Mother! I was such a good girl. I always tried so hard to please you. I never did anything wrong, did I? Never got into trouble like other kids. Never let the boys touch me. I did everything right and now look! Look at what a mess I'm in. How come? I mean what's the point in being a good girl if this is what you get for it? My son is dead. My daughter doesn't care about me any more. My husband's living with another woman, right under my nose. My whole life is such a disappointment. Why didn't you tell me what to expect? Why did you lie to me, saying I had everything? I expected to be happy and now I can't remember what being happy feels like. I haven't felt happy since Daddy died."

She turned the gold bracelet she was wearing around and around on her wrist. "Did he really die in that girl's bed, Mother, or was that just some story you invented because you were playing around with Uncle Morris? I remember that time I walked in on the two of you and your blouse was unbuttoned, but you just laughed and said that Uncle Morris was tickling you. I believed you, Mother . . . I believed you because Uncle Morris liked to tickle me too. Did you know that? Did you know that he felt me up on my wedding day? That he said he'd like to shtup me himself . . .

"You told me when things get unpleasant I should just put them out of my mind and then I wouldn't feel unhappy or angry. Why did you tell me that?" She grabbed her mother by the shoulders, "Why are you just lying there like that? Why won't you answer me? Why am I being punished this way?" She shook her mother and shouted, "Why did you have to go and have a stroke? Haven't I had enough . . . haven't I?"

"Now, now . . ." a nurse said, restraining her. She led B.B. out of the intensive care unit. "We must pull ourselves together, dear. At a time like this it's important to . . ."

"Fuck off!" B.B. yelled, wriggling free.

"We're going to have to be quiet," the nurse said, "or we're going to have to leave."

"Don't talk to me as if I'm a three-year-old." B.B. turned and ran down the corridor to the emergency exit, then through the parking lot until she came to her rental car. She had to think, had to clear her head. She drove off, as the sky turned from black to gray. She drove for ten minutes, for twenty, for forty, until she came to the cemetery. She parked the car, leaving the door on the driver's side open, and ran past row after row of grave sites. *Turn right . . . turn left . . . across the hill, beyond the trees . . .* until she came to a small grave, covered with ivy. In the early morning light she looked down at the simple gray headstone with block letters carved into it.

ROBERT ALLAN BRODER
1964–1974
BELOVED SON OF ANDREW AND FRANCINE
BELOVED BROTHER OF SARA
REST IN PEACE

She lay down on the ivy and wept.

She did not know how much time had passed when a caretaker, young and black, kneeled beside her, tapping her shoulder. "You all right, lady?"

"Yes," she said, standing up.

"You all wet."

"Yes," she said, surprised. She had not been aware of the rain until then.

"You gonna catch cold, you not careful."

She walked away, her feet squishing in the soft ground. She walked back to the rental car. The seat was wet. She turned on the ignition, but she did not know how to turn on the windshield wipers. It didn't matter. She drove away. She drove across the Causeway. Just a flick of the wheel, she thought, just a flick would send the car jumping off the bridge, into the black water below.

30

MARGO HAD PALE, putty-colored paint in her hair. When school had been cancelled that morning because of the heavy snowfall, she had decided to stay at home and finish up the trim in the new room. It was a beautiful room, light and spacious, with two skylights, a window wall facing south, rough wood walls, and brick floors. Even she was surprised that they had been able to turn the garage into this handsome space in just four weeks. They had done the work themselves, with some help from a carpenter who owed Margo a favor. Andrew had worked full time, Margo had worked weekends and evenings, and Stuart and two of his friends, after lengthy negotiations over hourly wages, had worked after school each day. Even Michelle had participated, helping to set the brick floor in sand, and then applying eight coats of glossy sealer to it.

It had become clear to Margo when Sara stayed overnight for the first time, in January, that they did not have enough space in the house for a visiting third child. She had been thinking of converting the garage for a long time anyway, at first as a studio for herself, then, after Andrew moved in, as a hideaway for the two of them. But after Michelle's indignation over Sara having spent the night in *her* room, without *her* permission, Margo knew that what they needed most was a room that could serve as a kid's bedroom now and someday double as a workspace for her and Andrew.

"You're not going to give this room to the Brat, are you?" Michelle asked, as she and Margo were painting the trim around the windows.

Margo had anticipated that question and was surprised it had taken so long to come. "No, I think it should be Stuart's for the rest of this year and then, when he goes off to college, it should be yours. We'll give Stuart's old room to Sara so that when she comes over she'll have a place to sleep."

"All this trouble for one weekend a month?" Michelle asked.

"Andrew is hoping she'll come more often once she has her own space. And this will give all of us more privacy."

"So you're saying that next year this room will be all mine?"

"Yes ... if you want it."

"What about when Stuart comes home from college?"

"I guess he can have your old room."

"I think he'd rather have *his* old room."

"Well, we could certainly arrange that."

"But that would mean the Brat would wind up with *my* old room."

"I think we shouldn't worry about this now."

"Don't you ever think things through, Mother?"

"Some things."

"I like to think things through totally," Michelle said. "I like to know what's going to happen next."

"No one can know exactly what's going to happen."

"I like to try."

"You have to bend a little, Michelle. Otherwise life gets to be unbearably hard."

Michelle turned away. "Who paid for this room anyway?"

Margo felt herself stiffen. She was not comfortable discussing the financial arrangements between her and Andrew and she did not know why. "Andrew and I split the cost fifty-fifty."

"Does that mean that part of the house is his now?"

"No, but if I decided to sell I'd pay back his share."

"Suppose you get married ... what happens then?"

"We haven't discussed it."

"Do you think you will ... get married?"

"I don't know. Does it matter to you?"

"I wouldn't mind . . . then I wouldn't have to worry so much."

"Honey, it's my life . . . you don't have to worry about it."

"I do have to worry, Mother. Suppose next year you come home with someone else and I don't like him at all?"

"It's unlikely that I'll be coming home with someone else next year."

"But you can't guarantee that, can you?"

"No, but things are working very well between Andrew and me. You can see that, can't you?"

"Yes, but it's only been a couple of months."

"The first months are the hardest," Margo said.

"Not according to this book I read about *affairs.* It said that *affairs* last three to six months and then *poof,* the magic is gone."

"Well, since it's the end of February, it's already been six months and the magic is still intact."

Michelle gave her a long look, then said, "I'm going out to build a snowman."

Margo sighed and went upstairs to the kitchen. She put the kettle on and grabbed a wedge of Gouda. One minute Michelle seemed to be an old woman, taking on the worries of the world, the next, she was a child, building a snowman. Margo found the child easier to understand.

"It's fabulous!" Clare said, a few hours later, as she stood in the middle of the new room. She had stopped off at Margo's on her way back from driving B.B. to the airport to catch a plane to Miami. B.B. had called Andrew early that morning to tell him her mother had had a stroke and to ask him to look after Sara while she was away.

"I'd take it for myself if I were you," Clare said. "It's so much roomier than your bedroom."

"I know," Margo said, "but we don't want to give up the bathroom or the hot tub."

"I guess I wouldn't either. Especially the hot tub. I wouldn't mind a soak right now. It's been a long day."

Margo checked her watch. "Good idea."

Clare sprawled out on Margo's bed while Margo stepped outside to get the hot tub going. When she came back inside she closed the sliding glass doors and leaned back against them, blowing on her hands. "It's cold out there."

"You're telling me?"

"How did it go this morning?"

"Two hours to get down to the airport. We'd have missed the plane except it was delayed."

"How was B.B.?"

"Couldn't tell, really. She slept most of the way to Denver. Didn't say a word about her mother."

"She doesn't deal well with reality," Margo said.

"How can you say that?" Clare asked. "She has the best business sense of anyone I know."

"In her personal life, I mean." Margo went to her closet and pulled out two terry robes.

"I can't discuss B.B. with you, Margo. It's too hard. I feel disloyal. I know now what it must be like for kids caught in the middle of their parents' divorce, because I sure as hell feel caught in the middle. On the one hand I'm glad that you and Andrew are so happy. On the other, I hate seeing B.B. so unhappy."

"I don't want to see her unhappy either. But it's not as if I stole him away," Margo said. "They'd been divorced for years."

"I know . . . I know . . ."

"And she's got Lewis. He seems like a nice man."

"He is . . . but something's wrong . . . I can't put my finger on it, but it scares me."

"I think it will all work out. It just takes time. The tub should be ready now."

"Good, my bones are aching," Clare said. "Do you remember having had aching bones when you were younger?"

"I've only become aware of my bones recently," Margo said, laughing.

"See what I mean? Our bones are aging," Clare said, as she undressed, "like the rest of us."

"I refuse to believe it."

"So did I, but every day I look into the mirror and see more signs."

"I only look when I have to." Margo knew that wasn't exactly true, but she liked thinking of herself as a person with more important things on her mind than how she looked, except, of course, for that week in L.A., when she'd realized she no longer had the body of a young girl.

"If we had been ugly kids we'd be better off now," Clare said.

"Why . . . you think it's easier for ugly people to adjust to growing old?"

"Yes, I do. It's losing your looks that's hard. If you never had them in the first place you wouldn't miss them."

"I've heard that about money," Margo said, "but never looks."

"About money, I wouldn't know."

Margo knew that Clare never thought about money. It had always been there for her, like her eyes or her teeth. Clare's money made some people afraid, especially men. To Margo, money meant freedom from economic dependence, which is what kept her sister Bethany from leaving Harvey. But people with a lot of money never knew what to do with it. It complicated their lives. She did not want money, or the lack of it, to dominate her life again, the way it had right after her divorce.

They stepped outside, threw off their robes, and shrieked as they lowered themselves into the steaming tub.

"Has Andrew started the new book yet?" Clare asked after a few minutes.

"No, he's still doing research and he's been so busy with the new room, he hasn't even had time for that."

"I can't stand having Robin around and not working . . . it's driving me up the wall, although next week he's flying to Montana to look for land."

"Really?"

"Yes, he's got this idea that he wants to ranch . . . says he needs to get in touch with nature."

"You're not going to Montana, are you?" Margo asked.

"Can you see me in Montana?" Clare asked, laughing. She

stopped abruptly. "He's bored," she said. "He's never satisfied. I don't know what we're going to do."

Margo reached over and touched Clare's shoulder. "I'm sorry," she said. "I didn't know you were having trouble. I know how much you want it to work."

"What I want doesn't seem to matter. God, I wish he'd grow up, face up to responsibilities, make a commitment and keep it. You know what he says . . . that women spend their lives building nests and men spend theirs flying away from them—that women are interested in loving, but men are only interested in fucking. He says he doubts he could see a nipple without wanting to suck on it. I tried to point out that that's because his development was arrested at the infantile stage. He says plenty of men follow their cocks through life. I told him fine, but if you're going to follow yours and it takes you beyond our bedroom, forget it, because I won't be here waiting next time. And I won't. I wish I'd never let him back into my life."

"If that's the way it is, let him go, Clare. You were doing fine without him."

"I know . . . but I went and got my hopes up thinking it would work this time . . . that we'd both learned a lot. Why do smart women keep getting themselves involved with shmucks?"

Margo laughed. "I love it when you use words I taught you."

"You taught me *shmuck?*"

"Didn't I?"

"Margo, shmucks are not necessarily Jewish men found exclusively on the east coast. Shmucks can be found everywhere, sometimes where you'd least expect them."

"I feel really lucky to have found Andrew," Margo said. "I feel so lucky I'm embarrassed."

"You don't have to be embarrassed. You *are* lucky."

"That's not to say we're without problems."

"When you're without problems," Clare said, "you're dead."

That night after dinner Andrew and Margo and the three kids played Monopoly in front of the fire. Lucy sniffed at the board, at the Monopoly money, then settled down for a nap with her head in Michelle's lap.

"She likes you," Sara told Michelle.

"Animals always do," Michelle said.

"So how come you don't have any animals?" Sara asked.

Michelle looked at Margo.

"We have a pig," Margo said.

"You have a pig?" Sara asked.

"A wooden pig," Michelle said. "It's Mother's little joke."

"Oh, that pig," Sara said.

"I wanted a cat," Michelle said, "but Mother wasn't able to handle any extra responsibilities."

"That was three years ago, Michelle," Margo said. "And at that time . . ."

"Cats are easy," Sara said. "They take care of themselves. All you have to do is feed them. You want me to look around for one for you?"

"We'll have to discuss that," Margo said. "We don't want to jump into something . . ."

The conversation was interrupted by the telephone. "I'll get it," Margo said, relieved.

"Maybe it's Mom," Sara said.

It was Lewis, telling Margo that her number had been left on B.B.'s answering machine. Margo explained that B.B.'s mother had had a stroke and that B.B. had flown to Miami to be with her. She promised to have B.B. call him in Minneapolis as soon as she heard from B.B. herself.

"That was Lewis," Margo said to the group. "He wondered why he couldn't reach B.B."

"I thought it would be Mom," Sara said.

"It's your turn, Mother," Michelle said to Margo. "You're on Park Place."

B.B.'s call came half an hour later and after it Sara lost interest in the Monopoly game. She yawned several times, until Andrew asked, "Tired?"

"A little."

"Want to get ready for bed?"

"Where am I going to sleep?"

"You can sleep in my room," Stuart said, "and I'll try out the new room."

"You'll be cold," Margo told him. "We don't have the heaters in yet."

"I'll use my sleeping bag. It's good for ten below."

"That's okay," Sara said. "I'd rather sleep up here, on the sofabed. And I'll keep Lucy with me for company."

"What about our game?" Michelle asked. "Aren't we going to finish our game?"

"Could we finish it tomorrow?" Sara said.

"I'm not promising I'll play again tomorrow," Stuart said. "If I don't you can divide my properties."

"It's no fun that way," Michelle said.

"Why don't we leave the board set up on the coffee table," Margo suggested, "and we'll decide what to do about it tomorrow."

"This family never finishes anything!" Michelle said.

"We finished the new room," Stuart told her.

Margo and Andrew went downstairs and listened to the news on the radio. Margo wanted to tell Andrew about Clare and Robin, about how Robin said men follow their cocks through life. But Andrew seemed preoccupied. Margo was feeling very tense herself. Maybe she was getting her period. Andrew turned off the radio and the lights. They got into bed. But they did not make love.

In the middle of the night Sara called out in her sleep and Andrew rushed upstairs to make sure she was all right. When he came back to bed he tossed and turned for hours. Finally he took a magazine and went into the bathroom. Margo was cold without him and pulled on socks, but she still could not sleep.

The next morning, after Sara and Stuart had left for school, the phone rang. Margo was in the bathroom, dressing for work. She heard Andrew saying, "What . . . when?"

She came out of the bathroom, carrying her hairbrush, and

went to his side. He was sitting on the edge of the bed, the phone to his ear. His face was drained of color, his body tense. "What?" she asked.

Andrew shushed her. "Yes," he said into the phone. "Yes, thank you for calling. I'll be back in touch later."

"What happened?" Margo asked. "Is her mother worse?"

"It's not her mother," Andrew said, hanging up the phone. "It's her."

31

MICHELLE THOUGHT SHE might be coming down with something, probably the flu. Gemini had it and so did half her class. Her head hurt and her body ached. She woke up thirsty and gulped down two glasses of orange juice, then felt incredibly nauseous. "I'm sick," she announced in the kitchen, while everyone else was having breakfast. "I'm going back to bed."

She had fallen asleep when the phone rang, waking her. Maybe it was the clerk at school, calling to find out where she was. She lifted the receiver off the hook and heard Andrew saying, "Yes . . . you have the right number." Then some guy began telling Andrew this weird story—something about a cemetery and this woman lying on a grave in the rain. Something about a caretaker who had notified the police, giving them the number of her license plate because the woman had seemed dazed and he had thought she shouldn't be driving. When the police had finally caught up with her she had been sitting in her car, in the middle of the Causeway, with her hands over her ears. She would not speak. She would not communicate in any way. She seemed to be extremely disturbed. They took her to the nearest hospital, Mt. Sinai, where she was being held for observation.

When the guy on the phone had finished talking Andrew said, "I see." His voice was all trembly. Then the guy said something else, something that Michelle didn't get and Andrew answered, "Yes, I do understand, but I'd like to call my personal physician in

Miami and ask him to take a look at her first. I'll get back to you as soon as I can, within the next few hours."

"You're her husband?" the guy asked.

"I was," Andrew said. "We're divorced."

Suddenly it hit Michelle. They were talking about B.B. Michelle got a picture in her mind of B.B. sitting in her car on the Causeway, her hands covering her ears. And then the police, two of them, coming up to her car, knocking on the window, asking, *Are you all right, Ma'am?* But obviously she's not. One look and they can see they've got a case on their hands. They suspect drugs or booze or a combination. They search the car but don't find a thing except her purse, with her wallet and her driver's license. *Hmmm,* they say, *Colorado.* They compare the photo on the license to B.B. and agree that it is the same woman, even though her long red hair is sopping wet and her eyes have this wild, crazed look. She will not answer their questions. She will not speak at all. They try sign language, thinking she might be deaf. Still no response. They shake her, but that doesn't work either. She just sits there with her hands over her ears and will not respond.

Michelle had had thoughts about blocking out the world that way, but she had never carried them to such extremes. When she had been in ninth grade a boy in her class had suffered from extreme mental exhaustion—that's how the teachers had put it— and he had been sent off to some private hospital in the mountains. What Michelle remembered most about him was that when he smiled only one side of his mouth turned up. But how could someone like B.B., someone who was so beautiful, someone who had everything, go crazy? It didn't make any sense.

Michelle turned her pillow onto the cool side. She was sure she had a fever. She was shivering under the weight of her quilt. She would probably miss a whole week of school.

She wondered if her father would take charge the way Andrew had if something happened to Margo, if Margo, say, was found on I-25 with her hands over her ears. Probably not, Michelle decided. She and Stuart would have to do it on their own.

Her bedroom door opened and Margo walked in, smelling of

Chanel No. 19. She sat on the edge of Michelle's bed and placed a hand on her forehead. "You feel warm, honey. Have you taken aspirin?"

Michelle nodded.

"I've got to go to work now, but Andrew is here if you need anything. I'll call at noon to see how you're feeling."

"Who was that on the phone a few minutes ago?"

"Oh, that was nothing," Margo said. "Stay in bed and take more aspirin if you feel feverish. I'll try to get home early." She dropped a kiss on Michelle's forehead, then left.

Nothing, Michelle thought. B.B.'s gone bonkers and Margo calls that nothing! What about Sara?

Right before noon the phone rang again. School, Michelle thought. She picked up the phone, but Andrew was already on. This time it was Lewis, B.B.'s boyfriend. Michelle listened as Andrew told him the whole story. He finished by saying, "I've already been in touch with my doctor down there. He knows Francine. She was his patient. I'm sure that whatever he recommends . . ."

But Lewis interrupted. "I'm taking the next flight out. I'll be in Miami by tonight."

"That really isn't necessary," Andrew said.

"You don't understand," Lewis told him. "I'm taking charge of the situation. She's my wife."

"She's your what?" Andrew said.

"My wife. We were married in Hawaii on New Year's Eve. She wanted to keep it a secret for a few months, until we had a chance to make some plans."

Michelle held the phone away for a minute. She was breathing so hard she was afraid they would hear her. When she put the phone back to her ear she heard Andrew asking, "Does Sara know?" His voice was barely a whisper.

"No," Lewis said. "B.B. and I were planning to tell her the next time I came to Boulder."

God! Michelle thought. B.B. had married Lewis and they hadn't told anyone, not even Sara. How could they have done such a thing? Michelle would never forgive Margo if Margo got married secretly. Marriage was a family matter and the children had a right to know. Now somebody was going to have to tell Sara not only that her mother had gone off the deep end, but also that she was married to Lewis. What a mess, Michelle thought. What an intensely ridiculous mess!

32

SARA WAS SICK for two weeks, longer than anyone else in the house. The doctor had come twice and Clare had come over every day, bringing soup and Jell-O and dog food for Lucy, but then Clare had come down with it too. Everyone in the house was still coughing, but Sara's cough was the worst. Her cough kept her up at night and sometimes she felt like she couldn't breathe. Then she'd get scared and knock on Margo's bedroom door, asking her father to come sit with her. And he would, holding her hand until she'd fallen back asleep.

Now her father said it was time for her to go back to school. She didn't want to go. She cried and begged him to let her stay home a few more days. But he said it would do her good to get out of the house, to be with her friends again. He said it would help take her mind off her mother.

She could not stop thinking about her mother, imagining her in a hospital that was exactly the same as the place where they took Jack Nicholson in the movie *One Flew Over the Cuckoo's Nest*, which she had seen on HBO at Grandma and Grandpa Broder's house over Christmas vacation. It was a scary place, filled with weird patients and mean nurses. Her mother would not like it there. She would cry herself to sleep every night. Sara could see her, wearing an old hospital gown, lying on her small cot, her knees pulled up to her chest, her fingers twirling several strands of hair the way Sara sometimes did when she was tired or frightened.

Sara could hear her mother crying, *Help me, Sara . . . please help me . . .* And Sara wanted to help her mother, but there was nothing she could do. Sometimes, in the middle of the night, Sara would wake up crying.

She had cried too on the day that her father had told her that her mother had had a mental breakdown.

"Do you mean she's cracked up?" Sara had asked.

"Yes, I guess so," Daddy had said.

"But why?"

"Because sometimes life just gets to be so hard," Daddy explained, "that one more crisis sends you over the edge. It must have been very hard for your mother to deal with Grandma Goldy's stroke."

"But the last time Mom had a crisis it only lasted a week and she didn't have to go to the hospital."

"When was that?" her father asked.

"The day she found out you were coming here."

Daddy covered his eyes with one hand and shook his head back and forth, back and forth. Then he took her in his arms and stroked her hair as if she were a puppy and said, "Poor Sara . . . this has been very hard on you, hasn't it?"

"Sometimes." That was all Sara was going to say. She was not going to tell him how her mother had been screaming and crying and acting crazy for months. *Crazy.* That's what had happened. Her mother had gone crazy, although no one would say that word. Sara wasn't all that surprised either. She had known something was very wrong, but she had not known what to do about it. In a way it was a relief that it had finally happened and that it had happened far away. But Sara knew she should not be glad, even though she had secretly wished that her mother would go away and never come back. She had wished worse things too, but they were too terrible to think about. She began to cry again.

"It's temporary," her father said, misunderstanding her tears. "She'll get better."

"When?" Sara asked.

"No one can say for sure."

"A week? A month?"

"Longer than a week. Maybe even longer than a month."

"I want to talk to her," Sara said.

"She can't have phone calls now," Daddy said.

"Why not?"

"Her doctors think it's best that way."

"But when you're sick you want to talk to your family."

"Look, Sara . . . your mother . . ."

"Stop calling her *your mother,*" Sara shouted. "I hate it when you call her that!"

"I'm sorry," Daddy said. "I didn't know. What should I call her?"

"Francine. That's her name."

"All right," Daddy said, "from now on I'll call her Francine."

They were quiet for a few moments. Then Sara cried, "It's all my fault."

"No," Daddy said, "it has nothing to do with you."

"You don't know," Sara said.

"Don't blame yourself for Francine's problems. None of it is your fault."

"You don't know anything about it." Sara bolted from the room. Her mother would be angry if she said anything more and she would be angrier still if Sara stayed at Margo's house. She would never forgive her for that. Sara would have to get her father to take her home and stay there with her until her mother returned.

But then they had all gotten sick, one right after the other.

The day before Sara was to go back to school her father took her home to pack up some of her things. She had not been home in more than two weeks. Everything looked the same and yet it all seemed different. She ran her hand along the polished wood of the piano. Maybe she wouldn't have to take piano lessons any more. She didn't like piano lessons, but her mother said it was important to learn to play. Sara didn't see why, but Mom kept telling her she would understand when she was older. It had something to do with being popular at parties. Sara sometimes went to parties, but nobody ever played the piano. Twice this year when Sara had come home from parties her mother had stood her under a bright lamp and had looked into her eyes to see if her pupils were dilated. Mom thought all kids did drugs. She had also smelled Sara's clothes and her breath. Sara had been really angry. "You don't trust me, do you? You don't trust anyone!"

"It's hard for me to trust," her mother had said.

"You could at least try to trust the people you love."

"Try to pack up quickly, Sara," Daddy said, sitting down on the sofa in the living room with a copy of *Newsweek*. "There's a lot to do at home."

"This *is* home," Sara said, "and I don't see why we can't stay here. I don't see why you can't just move in until Mom gets better and comes back."

"Try to understand," Daddy said. "I can't live with you in this house. I don't belong here."

"Well, I don't belong there, in Margo's house," Sara argued.

"I know you feel that way now, but as soon as we fix up your room ..."

"I already have a room. A very pretty room. Right here."

"We're going to paint your room at Margo's," Daddy said. "What color would you like?"

"I don't give a damn about that room!" Sara shouted. "It's Stuart's room, not mine. It will never feel like my room even if you paint it purple."

She ran upstairs to her bedroom and slammed the door behind her. Her room looked perfect. Mrs. Herrera had been in to clean. Sara could tell because Mrs. Herrera always tilted the pictures on the wall so Mom would know she had dusted them. She did the same thing at Margo's house. It was weird seeing Mrs. Herrera cleaning there too. Yesterday she had taken Sara aside and had asked, "You're all right here? They're treating you okay?"

"Yes," Sara had said.

"If you want my opinion it should never have happened. They shouldn't have let it happen. You get what I'm saying?"

"I guess," Sara had said. But she wasn't really sure.

Sara turned on her clock radio. It reminded her of the night her mother had thrown it across the room, screaming at Sara, and Sara had screamed back, *You don't deserve to be a mother!* That was the night she had secretly wished that her mother would go away and never come back. Well, Sara's wish had come true. She felt the beginning of tears and swallowed hard. If she had been nicer to her mother, if she had said, *For always and forever* that night Mom had phoned from Grandma Goldy's hospital . . .

Sara went to her closet and took out a canvas duffel. She packed her clothes. Then she walked down the hall to her mother's room. It still smelled from her perfume. She opened the door of Mom's closet and looked at her clothes, all lined up, all the hangers facing the same way. She grabbed her mother's blue silk blouse and tucked it into her duffel. "Why did you have to go and have a mental breakdown?" Sara whispered. "I'll bet you didn't stop to think about me, did you . . . about what would happen to me if you had to go to the hospital for a long time. Now look, now I have to go and live at Margo's."

"All set?" Daddy asked, when she came into the living room carrying her duffel.

"I guess," she told him.

In the truck on the way home, she asked, "Who's going to water the plants?"

"Miranda has arranged for a house sitter."

"Oh," Sara said.

"Have you thought about what color you'd like me to paint your room?" Daddy asked.

"Purple," Sara said, staring out the side window.

Two days later she came home from school to find that Stuart's room had been painted purple. Margo said the room needed a nice rug and asked if Sara would like to go shopping with her. "You need some plants and posters too."

"I can tape posters to the wall?" Sara asked.

"I think it's probably better to tack them up because tape pulls off the paint," Margo said.

Sara nodded, thinking about the posters she would choose. She liked animal posters best, but she might get a couple of rock stars too.

She had to remember that Margo was only being nice to her because of her father. She could not allow herself to like Margo, not even a little, because that wouldn't be fair to her mother. No one ever mentioned her mother, except Daddy, and he didn't bring up the subject that often. He did tell her that he had talked with Lewis and that Lewis had been to Miami to visit Mom and had arranged for her to be transferred to a very nice private hospital, one with a swimming pool and tennis courts and arts and crafts studios. It sounded more like a camp than a hospital, Sara thought.

Sara was having trouble in school. She tried to pay attention, but her mind was always someplace else. The teachers knew that her mother was sick and in the hospital so they didn't hassle her. The kids knew that she had moved into Margo's house and from the way they looked at her she was sure they knew that her mother was on a funny farm. She remembered that when David Albrecht's father hung himself from a rafter in his garage everyone talked about it behind David's back. No one knew what to say or how to act in front of David, and David didn't either. That's how it was with her now.

At least Jennifer was not afraid to talk about it. She said, "Look, parents crack up all the time. It's no big deal. I'll bet you half the kids in our class have parents who've gone off the deep end. That's why Boulder has one hundred and nine shrinks."

Sara bit a sliver off her left thumbnail.

"Your mother had a lot on her mind," Jennifer said. "She's a very intense person. Probably a classic Type A personality."

"Type A's have heart attacks," Sara said. "I read it in my grandmother's *McCall's*."

"Yes, but they also crack up. It's like a warning that they should slow down. It's probably good that this happened. She's been acting weird all year, Sara."

"I know."

*   *   *

Sara was in bed, trying to read, but she couldn't make sense of anything. Jennifer had given her the book *I Never Promised You a Rose Garden.* It was about a girl who goes crazy. Jennifer thought it might help Sara understand her mother, but the girl in the book wasn't anything like her mother. The girl in the book had invented a secret world with a secret language and everything. Sara did not believe that her mother had created a secret world inside her head.

Lucy was asleep on Sara's legs. Sara liked watching Lucy sleep. She listened for sounds that would tell her what kind of dream Lucy was having. If Lucy sighed and seemed serene, then she was having a good dream. If she shuddered and whimpered and her body twitched, she was having a nightmare. Sara wondered if Lucy dreamed about dogs or people, if she dreamed in color or black and white.

Sara heard someone coming down the hall. She could recognize each of them by their footsteps. Margo's were soft and quick; Stuart's, in his Topsiders, were squeaky; Michelle clomped in her clogs or hiking boots. These were her father's footsteps and he was wearing his Nikes. "Dad . . ." Sara called.

"Yes, honey . . ."

"Could you come here for a minute?"

"Sure." He came into her room and sat on the edge of her bed. She put out her hand and he took it.

"I love you, Daddy."

"I love you too."

"For how long?"

"What do you mean, for how long?" Daddy asked.

"You're supposed to say, *For always and forever,*" Sara explained, "and then I say, *That's how long I'll love you too.*"

"Who made that up?" he asked.

"Mom. We say it every day."

"Maybe we could come up with something new and original," her father said.

"No! I don't want something new and original. I want you to say this one."

"Okay, sure . . . let's start again."

"I love you, Dad," Sara said.

"I love you too."

"For how long?"

"For always and forever."

"That's how long I'll love you too." Sara thought that saying it would make her feel better, but it didn't. It sounded babyish and stupid. And probably her mother would be angry that she had taught it to Daddy. It was supposed to be their special ritual. Sara looked down at her father's hands. She liked the way his finger-nails ended in half moons. "Do you think she misses me?" Sara asked quietly.

"I'm sure she does."

"Do you think I could write to her?"

"I think that's a very good idea," her father said.

She started her letter the next day, in English class. She slipped a piece of notebook paper into her American Poetry book and wrote:

DEAR MOM,

I'm sorry you're sick and I hope you feel better very, very soon. I had the flu. It lasted almost two weeks. But now I'm better. Lucy is fine. We had a lot of snow but now it's getting nice and I hope to go skiing next weekend. I wish you could . . .

"Sara . . ."Mrs. Walters called. "Sara . . . are you listening?"

"What?" Sara asked. "Me?"

"Welcome back to earth, Sara," Mrs. Walters said.

Everyone laughed. Sara could feel her face turn red.

"We were discussing what Robert Frost had in mind when he wrote the lines, *But I have promises to keep,/And miles to go before I sleep.*"

"I'm sorry," Sara said. "I wasn't paying attention."

"We know. Try to pay attention from now on," Mrs. Walters said.

"I will." Sara folded the letter and tucked it into her math book. It wasn't any good anyway. It sounded like the kind of letter you write because you have to, not because you want to.

"FRANCINE, YOU HAVE a letter from Sara."
  She would not speak.
"Would you like to read it?"
  She would not think.
"Would you like me to read it to you?"
  She would not feel.
"I'll leave it here, on your table, in case you change your mind."
  And no one could make her.
  She closed her eyes.

IT WAS NO longer an affair, Margo thought. IT WAS no longer just a live-in situation. It was a merging of families, a merging of histories. She had wanted Andrew. She had wanted him to share her life, but she had not given enough thought to sharing his. She should have considered the possibilities earlier in the relationship. She should have sorted out her feelings in advance, so that they would not come spilling out now, when she needed to remain clearheaded. She had never expected Sara to move in with them. She had had no time to prepare, no time to get used to the idea, yet she wanted it to work. She had helped Andrew paint Sara's room—which until a few weeks ago had been Stuart's room—a soft violet color, hoping to make Sara feel more at home. But she was not sure that Sara would ever feel at home here.

Every time Margo approached her Sara put up a barrier. She was polite to Margo, but she did not relate to her.

"Sara, I know this is a hard time for you," Margo had said once, "but if you ever feel like talking . . ."

"That's okay," Sara had said. "Where's Dad?"

Another time Margo had begun, "Sara, if there's anything I can do to help . . ."

"That's okay," Sara had answered, and then she had quickly changed the subject. "Do you have an old shopping bag? I need to take a project to school tomorrow."

"Sure, under the kitchen sink," Margo had said.

Sara reminded Margo of the windup mouse that Stuart had loved as a baby. He would watch it travel across the room, waiting for it to bump into a piece of furniture, shrieking with delight each time it changed directions.

Margo was not at all sure that she would make a good stepparent. She thought of Aliza and what it must be like for her, trying to build some kind of relationship with Stuart and Michelle. She warned herself to go slowly, to be patient, not to expect too much.

When Margo and Andrew had first talked about B.B.'s breakdown, Andrew had cried, blaming himself. Margo had held him in her arms, comforting him, telling him over and over that it wasn't his fault, that his guilt wasn't going to help B.B., wasn't going to help Sara, wasn't going to help any of them. He began to have nightmares. All through that long week when they'd been sick, he had dreamed about Bobby. He had cried out in his sleep, reliving the accident—the sound of the glass shattering, the bodies tossed at impact, the children screaming. Margo had urged him not to confuse B.B.'s breakdown with the accident. "This is her problem," Margo had told him, "and the answer to it is somewhere inside of her."

She'd sounded so reasonable then, so perceptive, so certain, she had almost convinced herself. But the feelings of guilt did not belong exclusively to Andrew. There were moments when Margo blamed herself for B.B.'s breakdown. If only she hadn't met Andrew, hadn't allowed herself to fall in love with him, hadn't invited him to move in with her. Everyone has a breaking point, Margo thought. Everyone.

On the night Margo had told her children about B.B.'s breakdown she'd said, "This is going to be very hard on Sara. I hope you'll both be understanding."

Michelle, who had come down with the flu that morning, spoke in a whispery voice. "You don't have to tell us how to behave. We can appreciate how it would feel to have your mother go bonkers. We came pretty close ourselves."

Stuart had shot Michelle a poisonous look.

"Well, we did," Michelle said, coughing. "Mother was just hanging on by a thread when Leonard's wife came over with the gun. Isn't that right, Mother?"

"It was a difficult time in my life," Margo said.

"You can't count on anyone or anything," Stuart said, his voice breaking. "Life is shit . . . this proves it."

"Stu," Margo said, going toward him. It was not like Stuart to break down, to show emotion, although Margo wished he would more often. "Is everything all right with Puffin?"

"What do you mean?" he asked.

"I don't know. I just thought . . ."

"This has nothing to do with Puffin." He had spun on his heels and left the room.

Two weeks later, when they had all recovered from the flu, Andrew came into the bathroom one night while Margo was brushing her teeth. He sat down on the edge of the tub and said, "Do you think I should take Sara home and stay there until Francine comes back?"

Margo dropped her toothbrush into the sink. "Is that what you want to do?"

"Don't get defensive."

"I'm not getting defensive. I'm just asking a simple question." She looked into the mirror at his reflection. He had dark circles under his eyes.

"What do you think I should do?" he asked.

"Stay here." If he left now Sara would never take them seriously, and neither would Stuart or Michelle.

"For better or for worse?"

"Yes." She picked up her toothbrush and rinsed out her mouth.

"It'll complicate your life."

"My life's already complicated."

"What about your kids . . . I don't want them to become resentful."

"My kids will handle it." She turned to face him.

"I like the idea of Sara seeing us as a family," he said, pushing his hair away from his face. "And she'll have a better chance of adjusting away from Francine's house . . . won't she?"

Margo nodded.

"There are too many memories over there."

"Don't worry," Margo said softly. "We'll make it work."

He stood up and she rested her face against his flannel shirt, which felt warm and soft and reassuring.

But now Margo realized it wasn't as easy as she'd thought it would be. Andrew was overwhelmed by a sense of responsibility toward Sara. And Sara, understandably insecure, had become clinging and withdrawn. Margo thought she should see a therapist, someone to help her through the trauma of her mother's breakdown. But Andrew believed she needed only love.

They did not agree on what Sara should be told. Margo felt she should be told the truth, about everything. That it was important to learn to deal with reality.

"Since when are you an analyst?" Andrew asked angrily.

"I'm not, but you don't want Sara to grow up like B.B., do you, denying reality?"

"Sara is nothing like Francine."

"Good. Then tell her about the marriage. Tell her about Lewis."

"There's no reason for her to know about that now."

"It happened, didn't it? It's real . . ."

"It's not my place to tell her . . . it's Francine's."

"Oh, sure. And it's Francine's place to explain about the breakdown too . . . right?"

"I'll talk to her about Francine and her illness, but I don't see any reason to discuss the marriage and I'm asking you not to either. I'm not even sure, when Francine comes out of this, that the marriage will be intact."

"Is that what you're hoping?"

"I'm hoping she'll come out of it . . . that's all."

"Suppose someone else tells Sara about the marriage?"

"Who?"

"Lewis."

"I'll ask him not to."

"I don't like secrets, Andrew. Secrets always backfire."

"Just this one time," Andrew said. "Please."

"All right," Margo sighed. "All right."

She felt a growing distance between herself and Andrew, which frightened her. She missed him. Missed the closeness they had developed. Intellectually, Margo understood. Emotionally, she was having trouble. She would not allow herself to compete for Andrew's attention with a twelve-year-old. How could she possibly resent the time he needed to devote to Sara? She was his child and she had serious problems of her own. Yet, at times, Margo did feel resentful and she was ashamed.

She needed to talk to Andrew about her feelings. But right now there was so much going on that they weren't talking about anything except Sara and B.B. and what to have for dinner. They fell into bed exhausted each night. They had not made love in weeks.

"Darling . . ." her mother said over the phone, "are you sure you haven't bitten off more than you can chew?"

"I'm taking each day as it comes," Margo said.

"It's a big responsibility, another child."

"It's temporary."

"You're sure?"

"No, I'm not sure of anything."

"You have to do what's right for you, and for your children."

"I'm trying, Mother," Margo said, choking up. "The funny thing is, all I ever wanted is what you and Dad have."

"No, darling . . . you wanted more."

"Are you saying that you and Dad don't have what I think you have?"

"We have closeness and respect and love, if that's what you mean, but none of it happened overnight."

Clare told her, "You look like hell, Margo. Are you sure you're not walking around with pneumonia or something?"

"I don't think it's physical," Margo said, but she had pains in her stomach and a rash on her neck.

"I could take Sara for a while if that would help," Clare said.

"No. She belongs with Andrew . . . with us."

"Is she giving you trouble?"

"No, not at all. She keeps to herself. I'm worried about her, but Andrew thinks she's okay."

"You should get a checkup, Margo. It's not going to help if something happens to you too."

"I'll be okay," Margo said.

At the office the next day, Michael Benson said, "Is there anything I can do?" They'd been discussing the Danish Plan— designed to limit growth in the city by restricting the construction of residential units for the next five years. Michael had said, "I don't think it's going to hurt us that much. We've established a reputation for creative renovations and that's where the business is going to be." He'd paused for a minute to look at Margo and out of nowhere she had started to cry.

"That bad?" he had asked.

"I feel overwhelmed, Michael. I feel like I've lost control of my life."

"I warned you, didn't I? I tried to tell you about my own mistakes."

"This isn't a mistake," she said. "I love him."

"Enough for all of this?"

"I hope so."

"You know, Margo . . . you're a really fine architect . . . a really talented person. You can't toss it all away for some guy."

"I'm not tossing anything away."

Several times, before B.B.'s breakdown, Andrew had talked about tossing it all away and going to the Virgin Islands. He would start a salvage business, working when he felt like it, living the easy life. Margo would turn away, angry and frightened, when he talked that way, partly because she wasn't sure there would be room for her in his carefree island life. But more than that, she still had responsibilities—to her children, to her work, to herself. She did not want to drop out, to sleep in some bare room on a mattress on the floor. As much as she wanted to be with him, she did not want to live that way.

Other times he would be full of plans for their future. After the kids were out of school they would travel—to New Zealand, to South America, to the Orient. Maybe he would write travel books, maybe she would do architectural photo essays. She would play along with him for a while, then she would say, "I like what I'm doing now . . . you know that, don't you?"

And he would hold her tightly and say, "I'm only talking maybes. Don't take it all so seriously."

Margo went to see her doctor.

"Are you tense?" he asked.

She laughed. "You might say so."

"A difficult time?"

"Yes, but I'm trying to work it out."

"Are you exercising?"

"I do Jazzercise," she said, thinking that B.B. had also done Jazzercise.

"Good," Dr. Kaplan said. "Go easy on the diet for a while . . . stick to bland foods. I'll give you a prescription for those patches of eczema. Looks like you've lost weight too."

"A few pounds . . . with the flu."

"You need rest, Margo. Are you getting enough sleep?"

"I sleep."

"A change of pace wouldn't hurt either. Are you getting out enough?"

"Come to think of it, probably not."

So, when they were invited to Early Sumner's house for dinner, Margo accepted without asking Andrew first. She knew that if she asked him, he would find an excuse not to go, not to leave Sara. But Sara seemed pleased that they were going out and invited Jennifer to spend the night.

Before the party Margo lay in the bathtub, soaping herself, thinking back to the night last fall when she had calmly made a mental list of the qualifications her steady man would have to have.

He would be divorced and have kids at least as old as hers, maybe even older. She was not interested in merging families. She had only one more year, after this one, with kids living at home. Then it was to be her turn. She wasn't about to give up that kind of freedom for some guy with kids.

She laughed aloud, unable to believe she had been so naive, and not very long ago. She, who had vowed to simplify her life, had certainly complicated it. Andrew was right about that. She rinsed herself off and unplugged the drain, but did not get out of the tub. She lay there watching the water run out. Suppose B.B. did not get well? Suppose Andrew decided he should have custody of Sara? Five more years with a child at home. A child at home changed everything. She would be forty-five when Sara graduated from high school, almost forty-six. She began to sing, "Me and Bobby McGee."

That song had once been her Bible. She had wanted her freedom so desperately then. But she hadn't understood the meaning of the lyrics. That freedom is a myth. That sharing with another person is more important.

She stood up and reached for a towel. Tears stung her eyes. Why couldn't life ever go smoothly? Why couldn't you live happily ever after just for a little while?

35

MICHELLE WAS HOME alone, devouring a box of Dutch pretzels and reading *The Bell Jar,* when someone knocked at the front door. She jumped off her bed and went to see who was there. It was Puffin. "Stuart's not home yet," Michelle told her. "I think he's at tennis practice."

"I came to see you," Puffin said.

Michelle was surprised. She and Puffin were not the best of friends.

"Can I come in?" Puffin asked.

"Sure."

Puffin followed Michelle down the hall to her room. She sat on Michelle's bed.

"Want a pretzel?" Michelle asked, passing the box.

"Thanks." Puffin took one and nibbled on it. Then she said, "Guess what . . . I'm pregnant."

"I can't believe it!" Michelle said, shocked. "How did you get pregnant?"

"You know . . ." Puffin said coyly.

"I mean," Michelle said, "weren't you using something . . . some method of birth control?"

"Well, yes, but we wanted to try it one time without a rubber, to see what it would feel like. So I picked a time I thought was safe."

"There is no safe time," Michelle said.

"I know that now."

"I thought you were on the Pill, or that you had a diaphragm."

"The Pill made me nauseous and the diaphragm's so icky. You have to . . ." She paused, lowering her voice. "You have to touch yourself to get it in and I very nearly fainted trying to pull it out."

"Does Stuart know?"

Puffin nodded.

"Well, what are you going to do about it?"

Puffin shrugged.

It was amazing, Michelle thought, watching Puffin, that Clare had produced this air-brained creature. Which proved that you never knew what you were going to get when you decided to have a kid. You tossed up the genes and took your chances. Margo and Freddy had been really lucky. She wondered what this baby of Stuart's and Puffin's might be like. She wondered if it might be anything like her. But finding out was out of the question. Puffin had to have an abortion. And it was up to Michelle to make her see that. "I don't think you're ready to have a baby, Puffin," she said.

"But I'd get ready. There's plenty of time to order the cradle and buy the clothes and all that."

"That's not what I mean. I mean you're not emotionally ready and neither is Stuart. If you two get married now it'll be a disaster. It'll be over before you're twenty." She sounded wise, she thought, but not pushy.

"You probably don't know this," Puffin said, "but I'll be eighteen in August. I'm a year older than my class. I repeated seventh grade."

"I didn't know," Michelle said, trying to figure out what that had to do with anything.

"I switched schools in seventh grade and the headmistress thought it would do me good to take the year over again. Since no one there knew me anyway it didn't really matter, although I did cry about it at the time."

"Look, if you think that was hard," Michelle said, "picture yourself at twenty, divorced, with a two-year-old kid. You and Stuart would wind up hating each other, blaming each other. It would be really bad, not just for you, but for the kid."

Tears came to Puffin's eyes. "I do remember how I felt when my parents were divorced. It was just terrible. And even now that they're back together, I hate it when they fight."

"You see?" Michelle said. "That's what I'm talking about. Teenage marriages hardly ever work."

"My parents weren't teenagers when they got married," Puffin said, walking across the room and looking out the window. "That dog, Lucy, is digging a hole in your garden."

"She likes to dig."

"What's it like, having Sara here?"

"We're surviving."

"I'm an only child. That's why I want to start young and have a bunch of my own."

"Have you thought about giving the baby up for adoption . . . I mean, if you're dead set against abortion?"

"Please don't call it a baby!" Puffin said, turning around. "Please just refer to it as my pregnancy."

"Okay," Michelle said. "Have you thought about an adoption for your pregnancy?"

"I would not be able to give up my pregnancy for adoption. Not to brag or anything, but no family could give it as much as mine. It would have trust funds from the day it was born. It would have everything. So adoption is out of the question. We're the kind who might adopt, but not give up for adoption. Do you see what I'm saying?"

"Well, then . . ." Michelle said, sighing, "it sounds as if abortion is the only answer."

"Won't you please try to talk Stuart into marrying me? We'd have plenty of money. He wouldn't have to worry about supporting me or the pregnancy. He could still go to college if he wanted to and we'd go with him."

"I can't do that."

"I guess I didn't think you would." Puffin zipped up her vest. "Will you come with me to the clinic?"

"If you want me to."

"Will you call and set up the appointment for me?"

"When do you want to go . . . tomorrow?"

"Whenever." They walked to the front door. "You know something, Michelle? I used to think you were too serious, that you never had any fun, but now I wish I was more like you. I wish that I knew all that you know."

Michelle put her arm around Puffin's shoulder and was surprised by how small she seemed. "I don't know everything," she said.

"Maybe not . . . but you know enough."

Michelle accompanied Stuart and Puffin to the clinic. Stuart had been pale and edgy that morning. He'd snapped at Sara at the breakfast table, telling her to keep her goddamned dog out of the kitchen. Sara had left the table in tears.

He did not say a word to Michelle while they sat, side by side, in the outer office of the clinic, waiting for Puffin to have her abortion. And when Puffin came out, smiling bravely, it was Michelle who hugged her first, asking if it had hurt. Puffin shook her head and held Michelle's hand. Stuart just stood there, like a zombie. Then he drove them to Puffin's house, where Michelle heated up a pot of soup. They sat with her all afternoon, watching over her as she dozed. When Clare came home they explained that Puffin had come down with a virus that was going around school.

"Not again," Clare said. "We just got over the flu."

"This one only lasts forty-eight hours," Michelle explained. "Maybe even less."

"Well, that's a relief."

That night Stuart came to Michelle's room. "Thanks for coming with us today."

"I'm glad I could help."

"You won't say anything to Mom, will you?"

"No."

"Good. Puffin wanted to tell the whole world, but I convinced her not to."

"Do you love her, Stu?"

"I thought I did, but now I don't know. The idea of spending the rest of my life with her scared the shit out of me. She had all these plans for us, like how we'd fix up our house and where we'd go on vacations."

"Do you feel bad about the baby?"

"What would I do with a baby, Michelle? I don't even know where I'm going to college."

After Stuart left Michelle thought about how, in Margo's day, you couldn't just go out and get an abortion. If you got pregnant then you had to get married. And it was that fear, that fear of pregnancy, that kept girls virgins. Except, of course, Margo had slept with this one boy, James.

Suppose Margo got pregnant now? Michelle thought. Even though she was forty, it was still possible. God, what an idea! Margo, pregnant. Would she have an abortion or would she and Andrew get all sentimental and decide to get married and have the baby? That would certainly change things. She had worried when her father had married Aliza that they might have babies too, but so far they hadn't. And Michelle was glad. She didn't think either of her parents should have more kids. They should just try to do a better job with the two they already had.

During Christmas vacation one of Freddy's friends had come over to visit. He had three screwed-up teenagers from his first marriage, but now he was married again and his new wife was pregnant. *This time I'm going to do it right,* he'd told Freddy. *I know a lot more about raising kids now. Forget the permissive stuff. What they need is authority.* Bullshit! Michelle thought. What they need is love.

Even if Margo and Andrew did get married there was no guarantee that they would stay married. Look at that fight they'd had on the night of Early Sumner's dinner party. They had come home around one A.M., shouting. Mainly it had been Margo doing the shouting. Andrew had just kept repeating, "You've got it all wrong. She was just being friendly."

"Friendly!" Margo had yelled, slamming their bedroom door so that their voices were muffled. "She had her hand on your thigh. You call that friendly?"

"What was I supposed to do?" Andrew asked.

"You could have removed her hand. You could have walked away from her. For Christ's sake, Andrew, you're a grown man. You know the difference between friendly and flirtatious."

"I'm here with you, aren't I?" Andrew said. "Doesn't that mean anything?"

"No . . . being here isn't enough. I need to be able to trust you."

"I didn't fuck her. I didn't even want to."

"That's not what I'm talking about. I'm talking about needing to trust you not to hurt me. I'm talking about needing to be able to depend on you emotionally."

So, something had happened at the party, Michelle had thought. Somebody, probably Early Sumner, had put the make on Andrew, and Andrew had responded, leaving Margo feeling hurt and betrayed, not to mention jealous.

Early Sumner was old, more than fifty, but she had an interesting face. It looked carved. She was very thin and always wore black leather pants, big shirts, and amber beads, each one the size of a golf ball. She gave a lot of money to the library and the museums. Once a month she would drop by school to see who might be free to do some odd job around her house. She paid five dollars an hour. She never chose any of the girls though.

Whatever had happened Margo had been steaming. Michelle kept listening even though she was frightened.

"Men, you're all the same," Margo was shouting. "You're all babies with big egos. You're all such pushovers."

"And you're all so goddamned insecure."

"Who's insecure?"

"What do you want from me?" he asked. "Don't you know what I've been going through? Don't you know what a hard time this is?"

"It's a hard time for me too," Margo said. "Taking on the responsibility of another child and all the family problems that come with it. Not a day goes by without a phone call about either B.B.'s mother or B.B. herself. Jesus, Andrew, I'm so sick of Goldy and her stroke and B.B. and her breakdown I feel like I'm going to have one or the other myself. I've been afraid to tell you how tense I am because I know you are too. But here I am trying to help Sara feel at home and trying to think of your needs and her needs and my children's needs and my work, and my own needs have gone right down the drain . . . and yes, I'm feeling a little resentful because I needed a night out so badly and this is what I get from you!"

Michelle felt a lump rise in her throat, a lump as big as one of Early Sumner's amber beads. She wanted to run down the hall, to fling open their bedroom door, and shake them by the shoulders, yelling, *Stop this stupid fighting. Stop it right now, before you ruin everything!*

She realized then, for the first time, that she did not want Margo and Andrew to split up. She liked them together. She liked having Andrew in the house, in spite of Sara. It made her feel good. It made her feel as if she were part of a family.

"Come on, Margo . . . come on . . . I'm sorry," Andrew said, softly now, so that Michelle could barely hear him. "I just wanted to have a good time, that's all."

"I wanted to have a good time too," Margo said, crying, "but you acted as if I wasn't even there. I felt invisible . . ."

Michelle understood what Margo meant. Sometimes she felt invisible herself. And she would have to pinch herself to make sure she still existed.

A few days later, when Sara and Michelle were the only ones at home, Sara knocked on Michelle's bedroom door.

"Yeah?" Michelle called. She was still reading *The Bell Jar.*

"It's me, Sara."

"Come in . . ."

"Hi," Sara said, standing in the doorway.

"Hi."

"Could I, uh, borrow one of your, uh, Tampax?"

"Yeah, sure. They're in the bottom cupboard in my bathroom," Michelle said, without thinking. She was at this really interesting part of the book, where Esther was just getting out of the hospital. But then it suddenly dawned on her that this was Sara's first period, so she looked up and said, "First time, huh?"

Sara turned red and nodded.

"You need some help?"

Sara shrugged.

"You know how to use Tampax?"

"Jennifer showed me once."

"Well, go try and if you can't get it up call me, okay?"

"Okay."

Sara was locked in the bathroom for twenty minutes. Finally, Michelle knocked on the bathroom door. "You okay?"

"I think I got it up, but I'm not sure. It feels like it's going to fall out."

"Try again, with another one. Put some Vaseline on the tip before you shove it up."

"Where's the Vaseline?"

"In the bottom . . . where the Tampax is . . ."

"Okay, I see it."

"You want me to come in and help you?"

"That's okay. I'll try it again."

Sara came out ten minutes later. "I think it's up there this time."

"You shouldn't feel anything. It should be comfortable."

"It's pretty comfortable," Sara said. And then she smiled shyly.

Oh, she was so pathetic, Michelle thought. So young and so pathetic. "The first time I got it," Michelle told her, "I was almost fourteen and I was at this sleep-over with six other girls and I didn't want to tell any of them it was my first time so I just kept shoving Kleenex in my pants until I got home and then I told my mother and she was so excited she cried and that night we went out to dinner to celebrate."

Michelle saw the hurt come into Sara's eyes. "Oh, I'm sorry. I didn't mean to make you feel bad about your mother."

"That's okay."

"Well, if you need any more help just ask me."

"Thanks."

Michelle went up to the kitchen then and baked a chocolate cake. When the icing cooled she wrote *Congratulations, Sara* across the top.

36

SARA STILL HAD not heard from her mother, but she had talked to Dr. Arnold, her mother's doctor. Sara had been scared that once she heard Dr. Arnold's voice she wouldn't be able to think of a thing to say. So she had rehearsed her first question over and over in her mind. And then, when Dr. Arnold came on the line, Sara had said it. "Exactly when will my mother be better?"

"That's hard to say," Dr. Arnold answered, as if Sara's question was just ordinary. "She's improving, but very slowly."

"Should I keep on writing to her?" Sara asked.

"Yes," Dr. Arnold said. "Your letters mean a lot to her."

"Then how come she doesn't write to me . . . or call?"

"She's not ready to communicate, Sara."

"What does she do all day?"

"Well, she's begun to go out for walks and that's a very good sign."

"What else?"

"She watches TV."

"Mom *never* watches TV. She says it ruins your mind."

"She's watching now."

"Which shows?"

"Whatever's on in the lounge."

"Like *Happy Days* and *M*A*S*H?*"

"Sure."

"Does she laugh?"

"No," Dr. Arnold said, "she doesn't laugh."

"Will you tell her that I'm coming to see her as soon as school's over, unless she's better before then?"

"I'll tell her. And when you come down I'll introduce you to my daughter, Mimi. She's your age."

Sara did not tell Dr. Arnold that she didn't want to meet Mimi. Mimi would feel sorry for Sara, knowing that her mother had had a mental breakdown. *Mental breakdown.* That was such a weird expression. Sara imagined all these little pieces inside her mother's brain coming apart and spinning around. They would have to be put back together, like a puzzle, before her mother would be well again.

Sara thought it was good that her mother's doctor was a woman. Her mother was always saying, *Never hire a man if you can find a woman who can do the same job. Women are so much more dependable, Sara. Women take their responsibilities seriously.*

Sara found out about her own responsibilities the night they came home from the movies to find that Lucy had raided the pantry. She had dragged at least a dozen boxes of food into the dining room, hiding them under the table. She had chewed up parts of each box so that cookies, crackers, cereal, and spaghetti lay all over the floor. "Looks like Lucy had a great time tonight," Stuart said, and he and Michelle laughed.

Sara laughed with them until Margo looked at her as if she was as guilty as Lucy.

"Clean it up, Sara," Daddy said.

"But . . ." Sara began.

"No buts," Daddy said. "Lucy is your dog. You're responsible."

And so Sara cleaned up the mess by herself.

If they were a real family, like the Brady Bunch, Sara thought, everyone would have helped her. But they were just people who happened to live in the same house. They had responsibilities, but no feelings.

Sara was learning more about them every day. She understood that Margo was responsible for Stuart and Michelle, that she was responsible for Lucy, and that Daddy was responsible for her. Which got Sara to thinking that if anything happened to her father she would be all alone. Margo wouldn't want her. Margo had only taken her in and painted her room purple to please Daddy. But Margo didn't really care about her. Sara had suspected as much, but she was still disappointed to find out it was true. She heard it from Margo herself on the night that Margo and her father had had their big fight.

Jennifer had slept over and they'd gone to bed right after *Saturday Night Live.* Sara was just about asleep when she heard a door slam. At first she wasn't sure what was happening. Then she heard Margo's voice, followed by her father's. They were shouting at each other. Sara lay very still, pretending to be asleep. She hoped that Jennifer was already asleep and would not wake up, would not hear Margo and her father arguing. There was a lot of talk about loyalty and betrayal before Sara heard her own name.

"Sara!" Daddy said. "What has this got to do with her?"

"Having another child in the house means added responsibilities," Margo said. "I can't pretend that she isn't here just because she's yours."

"I can pack my bags and leave," Daddy shouted. "If that's what you want, just say so. If it's too much for you having Sara here . . ."

"Don't yell at me," Margo said. "I need to be able to be honest with you. If I can't be honest about the way I feel . . . if I can't discuss it . . ."

"Do you want me to go?" Daddy asked.

"Do you want to go?" Margo said.

"Sometimes," Daddy said. "Sometimes I want to get the hell out of here and just sail off to Bali."

How could he? Sara thought. How could he want to sail away without her? Unless he meant that he wanted to sail away *with* her. Yes, maybe that was it. Oh, that would be nice. Just the two of them, sailing off to Bali, wherever that was. She wouldn't have to go to school or anything. And she wouldn't have to share him with Margo either.

"Sometimes I wish you would just sail away," Margo said, ". . . sail right out of my life the way you sailed into it."

Sara could tell that Margo was crying.

"But then I think of life without you," Margo continued, "and I know that isn't what I really want."

"What do you want?" Daddy asked. "What the fuck do you want?"

"I want the closeness back."

Sara felt a sharp pain in her stomach. She drew her knees up to her chest.

"Sara . . ." Jennifer whispered, "are you awake?"

Sara did not answer.

Jennifer yawned noisily and rolled over in her sleeping bag.

Soon the house was quiet again and when Sara heard the familiar sounds of Margo and her father making love she covered her ears with her hands.

Ever since that night Margo and her father were lovey-dovey again. He called her Margarita, like the drink. Sara hated it when they kissed in front of her. And one time she had caught her father sliding his hand down the front of Margo's shirt. But even that wasn't as disgusting as the Polaroid pictures. Sara had found them in the middle drawer of Margo's bathroom cabinet, tucked away beneath the plastic tray that held Margo's cosmetics. Sara had been trying out Margo's lipsticks and eyeliners when she'd noticed the envelope. She'd lifted it out, turned it over, opened it, and had pulled out five Polaroid pictures, all of them of Margo wearing some dumb-looking black underwear and showing off her tits.

The pictures had made Sara feel weak and dizzy and she'd sat down on the edge of the tub with her head between her knees to keep from passing out. After a few minutes the dizzy spell passed and Sara had carried the pictures to her room. She'd hidden them in her bottom drawer, under her scrapbook. If Stuart or Michelle gave her any trouble she would show them what kind of mother they had.

Not that they'd been giving her any trouble. Stuart more or less ignored her, but Michelle had been nice once. She had baked a cake in honor of Sara's first period. And later that same night Michelle had come to her room. "What would you do if your mother got married again?" she had asked.

"I don't know," Sara said, thinking that was a weird question since her mother was in the hospital and Michelle knew it.

"Would you like it if she did?" Michelle said.

"It would depend on who she married," Sara told her.

"What about Lewis?"

"He's okay, I guess. But I doubt that my mother would marry him. I doubt that she'd marry anybody right now. What about your mother? Do you want her to get married again?"

Michelle seemed really surprised by Sara's question. "My mother?" she asked.

"Yes," Sara said.

"Well . . . I used to hate the idea of my mother remarrying, but now I don't care that much, as long as she marries someone I like."

"What about my father?" Sara asked.

"Your father is okay."

"Do you think they will . . . get married, I mean?"

"I don't know," Michelle said.

Sara wrote careful letters to her mother. She did not write anything that she thought would make her mother feel bad. She did not even write about her first period because she knew how sad her mother would be to find out that she'd missed a really important event in Sara's life. She wondered what life would be like when her mother returned. She did not know what to expect from her mother. She was not even sure of her father anymore, except that deep down inside she did not believe that he would leave her and sail off to Bali.

Every night, before Sara got into bed, she took her mother's blue silk blouse out of her drawer and held it to her face. She forced herself to think first of something good about Mom and then something bad. Because she knew it was important to hang onto the truth.

To help her remember, Sara went home one day after school. The neighborhood was so different from Margo's. She missed the wide streets, the big old trees, and the Victorian houses. She sat on the swing on her front porch for a minute. The swing squeaked. It needed oiling. It always did after winter. Then she got up and rang the doorbell. The house sitter answered. He was a tall man with a gray beard and he had a yellow pencil tucked behind his ear. He seemed to know who she was.

It felt so strange to be home, mainly because it didn't feel like home anymore. Sara thought about throwing herself across her bed and just crying for as long as she felt like it, until her throat was sore, until she couldn't catch her breath. Instead, she took the photo album out of her mother's closet and left quickly. The house sitter told her she could come over any time, but that she should call first, to make sure he was at home.

Sara did not answer him.

That night, when her father came to her room to kiss her good-night, Sara was on her bed, thumbing through the photo album. Her father lay down next to her and pointed to a picture. "I remember the day that was taken. You had just come out of the bathtub and . . ."

"What's happened to all the pictures of Bobby?" Sara asked.

"I have some of them," Daddy said, "and Grandma Goldy and Grandma Broder have some too."

"How come Mom had to pretend that Bobby was never born?" Sara asked.

"So she could pretend that he never died," Daddy answered.

FRANCINE AND DR. ARNOLD walked along the garden path on the grounds of the hospital. "Is my mother dead yet?" Francine asked.

Dr. Arnold looked up at her. "No, she's partially paralyzed, but she's improving."

Francine nodded. "Is my daughter all right?"

"Yes." Dr. Arnold smiled at her.

"Do you know what's happened to me?"

"Do you know?"

"Sometimes I think I do and sometimes I don't."

Dr. Arnold reached over to a hibiscus bush and plucked off a flower. "I'm going to try to help you figure it out," she said, handing the flower to Francine.

Francine held it to her nose. "When I married Andrew I carried a single rose."

MICHELLE DECIDED NOT to go skiing with the family even though it was a beautiful day and she enjoyed spring skiing best. The snow would start off like icy corn, turn soft by noon, and wind up slushy. Her face would get sunburned and that night Margo would give her a combination skin cancer/aging lecture that she would ignore.

But as tempting as the idea was, the idea of spending the day alone in a quiet house appealed to her even more. Maybe she would ski next weekend, even though her frostbitten toes still hurt in the cold. It would be her last chance before Eldora closed for the season. Andrew's parents were coming to town next weekend and Margo had already informed her that she and Stuart were expected to be at the family dinner she was planning, a sort of Passover Seder, but without the religious ceremony, since Passover would be over by then.

Margo had also made it clear that the family dinner she was planning was for family only. Not even Puffin was to be invited, which wasn't exactly breaking Stuart's heart, since he and Puffin were on the verge of breaking up. But of course, Margo didn't know that. Margo didn't know anything, not even about the abortion. Maybe some day Stuart would tell her.

Michelle decided to do some work on her World Cultures paper. She sharpened six yellow pencils and began to make an outline when the doorbell rang. She ran down the hall to the front door with Lucy at her heels. She opened the door and this gorgeous guy was standing there. He was big and blonde and suntanned and when he saw her he smiled.

"Hi . . . is Margo here?"

"No, she's not. Not now, anyway." His eyes were as blue as the sky. "Can I help you?"

"I'm Eric. I met Margo last summer in Chaco Canyon. She said if I was ever in town I should come by, so here I am." He rested one hand against the house and leaned forward. He had a hole in the left thigh of his jeans and Michelle had to resist the urge to put her finger into it.

"Well," Michelle said, "she should be home by five. You want to wait?"

"Could I?"

"Sure . . . come on in."

39

MARGO WAS NOT really listening to the conversation between Andrew and Sara as they drove back from Eldora. She was thinking about the hot tub, about how satisfying it would feel to peel off her clothes and step, naked, into the steaming water. The perfect end to an almost perfect day. She had taken one bad spill, on a fairly easy trail, winding up with a faceful of snow and a brief pounding in her head, but after she'd rested for a few minutes she'd felt better. Andrew had been loving and concerned and had wiped off her face with his bandana. The fight on the night of Early Sumner's dinner party, as painful as it had been at the time, had cleared the air between them. They were no longer walking on eggs. They were talking and laughing and making love again. Sara seemed relieved too. And today, during lunch on the slopes, Sara had been friendly. She had even laughed, making Margo believe in the possibility of a positive relationship with her after all.

Now, as Andrew pulled the truck into their driveway Sara pointed to a motorcycle parked next to the house. "Who's here?"

"Probably one of Stuart's friends," Andrew said.

"No, Stuart's still skiing," Sara said. "He passed me on our last run and said he'd be home around six-thirty."

"Well, maybe one of Michelle's friends, then," Andrew said.

"She doesn't have any friends who ride motorcycles," Sara said.

Margo hated the idea of motorcycles. She'd known a boy in college who had been killed on a motorcycle. *Decapitated,* the head-lines had said. She'd had nightmares about that boy, whose name she could no longer remember. She had forbidden her own children to ride either mopeds or motorcycles.

As soon as Andrew unlocked the front door Sara tore up the stairs, calling, "I'm dying of thirst."

"Me too," Andrew said. "You want a drink, Margarita?"

"Grapefruit juice," Margo said. "I'll get the tub going." She went to her bedroom, stripped down to her longjohns, slid open the glass doors, and stepped outside.

"Oh, Mother! I didn't expect you so soon."

Michelle was in the hot tub. Michelle, who was so modest she would not even undress in front of Margo, was naked and in the hot tub with some boy. Margo froze.

"Hey, Margo . . ." the boy called. "How're you doin'?"

Jesus Christ! It was not just some boy. It was Eric. What the fuck was he doing here? What the fuck was he doing in the hot tub with her daughter? "What are you doing?" Margo asked.

"We're soaking," Michelle answered. "What does it look like?"

"I was passing through," Eric added. "You said that any time I was . . ."

"Yes, I remember what I said," Margo caught a whiff of mari-juana.

She had shared a joint with Eric last summer in Chaco Canyon, and afterwards, she had become paranoid. "Are you going to kill me?" she had asked timidly, as Eric had caressed her neck. She'd thought he was going to strangle her.

"No, baby," he had answered. "I'm gong to fuck you."

She had nodded, as if it were okay either way.

Now he was smoking with her daughter.

"Here's your juice, Margo," Andrew called from the bedroom.

"I'm out here," Margo called back.

Andrew joined her, took in the scene, and looked confused.

"This is Eric," Margo told him. "He was just passing through, so he decided to drop in." She could tell that Andrew still didn't get it. "Eric," she said, again. "From Chaco Canyon . . . from last sum-mer . . ." She and Andrew had once exchanged lists of their former lovers, discussing each of their sexual encounters late into the night.

"Oh," Andrew finally said, nodding. "Eric." He handed Margo the glass of grapefruit juice.

"This is Andrew," Michelle said to Eric. "My mother's boyfriend."

Margo cringed at the word. It sounded so childish.

"Hey . . . how're you doin', Andrew?" Eric said. "You guys want to join us?"

"No!" Margo answered quickly.

"Could you toss us the towels?" Michelle said.

Andrew handed each of them a towel. Eric stood and stepped out of the tub first. Margo turned away.

When Michelle and Eric had disappeared into the house, Margo jumped into the hot tub, still wearing her longjohns. "Can you believe this," she said to Andrew. "Can you believe what's going on here?"

Andrew eased himself into the tub. "I think you're overreacting," he said.

"Overreacting!" She pulled off her sopping longjohns and tossed them out of the tub. "I don't like it. I don't like it at all."

"They were just soaking," Andrew reminded her. "Aren't you the one who told me that hot tubbing is not a sexual experience?"

"Sure, that's what I told you, but that doesn't mean I believe it."

Andrew laughed.

"Did he have an erection when he got out of the tub?" Margo asked.

"No."

"Good."

Eric not only stayed for dinner, he stayed overnight. "He doesn't know anyone else in town," Michelle told Margo, as she took bed linens from the hall closet. "I'm going to make up the sofabed for him."

That night Margo lay awake for hours. Michelle had been lively and flirtatious during dinner and Margo had suddenly seen her as Eric must, a very desirable young woman. Finally she got out of bed, put on her robe and slippers, and tiptoed through the darkened house, needing to convince herself that she should not worry, that Eric was asleep on the sofabed, alone.

But Eric was coming down the stairs as Margo was going up. They startled each other.

"Where are you going?" Margo asked sharply.

"To the bathroom. I have to take a piss."

"There's a toilet upstairs. Didn't Michelle show you?"

"I must have forgotten."

Eric followed Margo up the stairs and she led him to the half-bath, turning on the light. "Voilà."

"Thanks."

He was wearing only Jockey shorts and they were torn. He had a beautiful body, Margo thought, remembering the feel of his skin, the weight of him on top of her. She cleared her throat. "I'd appreciate it if you didn't go prowling around the house in the middle of the night. The dog will start barking and wake everyone and tomorrow is a school day."

"Okay." He put his hand on her shoulder and looked into her eyes. "And Margo, I want you to know I appreciate your letting me stay the night."

"Everything is different now, Eric. This is my home. These are my children. Do you get what I'm saying?"

"Sure." He took his hand away. "In the canyon you were a woman. Here you're a mother."

"That's not exactly it," Margo said, "but it's close."

"Well, if you don't mind, I've still got to piss."

She could hear him splashing into the toilet as she tiptoed back down the stairs.

The next morning, without Margo's permission, Michelle rode off to school on the back of Eric's Honda. Margo watched from the kitchen window, her stomach in knots.

When she got home from work Eric was in the driveway, working on his bike. "What are you doing here?" Margo asked.

"Michelle invited me to stay for a few days, until I can find a place of my own."

"A place of your own? Here in Boulder?"

"Yeah . . . this town has good vibes. I got a part-time job today, working on a construction crew up in Sunshine Canyon."

Margo marched into the house and went directly to Michelle's room. Michelle was humming to herself and writing in her diary. "He cannot stay in this house," Margo said. "We have enough people living here."

"But, Mother . . ."

"No, Michelle. You should have discussed it with me first."

"You can't just kick him out. At least let him stay tonight."

Margo let out a heavy sigh.

"Please, Mother . . ."

"Tonight is absolutely the last night, Michelle. Andrew's parents are coming to town on Thursday."

"I don't see what Andrew's parents have to do with Eric. They're not staying here. They're staying at the Harvest House, aren't they?"

"Listen, Michelle . . . either you are going to tell him he has to be out by morning or I am."

"He was your friend first, Mother. He came here to see you . . . remember?"

"But I didn't invite him to stay with us."

"I don't understand why you're behaving in this intensely hostile way, unless it's because we used the hot tub without your permission. Is that it?"

"That's part of it," Margo said. "And you know how I feel about motorcycles."

"You're getting to be a neurotic worrier, just like Grandma Sampson."

"That's bullshit, Michelle. And you know it."

That night, when Margo could not fall asleep, she wandered through the house again, but this time, as she passed Michelle's room, she heard muffled sounds and knew that Eric was in there. She felt a sinking feeling in the pit of her stomach. She did not know what to do. If she opened Michelle's bedroom door and demanded that Eric leave at once, Michelle would never forgive her. Besides, she had always vowed that she would respect her children's privacy.

"Margo." She spun around. Andrew was standing behind her. "Come back to bed," he whispered, taking her hand.

"He's in there with her."

"I know."

"You know?"

"From the way they've been looking at each other it was inevitable."

Margo followed Andrew back to their bedroom and climbed into bed beside him. "I can't stand the idea of it," she told him. "A girl's first lover shouldn't be someone who has slept with her mother. Michelle is such an innocent. I wanted her first sexual encounter to grow out of love."

"Desire is the next best thing," Andrew said, holding her.

"No . . . it's not the same at all. I know him, Andrew. He's just a fucking machine. He doesn't care about her."

"There's nothing you can do about it now. Try to get some sleep. Talk to Michelle tomorrow."

"Tomorrow is too late. You wouldn't be taking it so calmly if it were Sara."

"Maybe not," Andrew said. "Why did you give him your address in the first place?"

"You know how those things are. You have a nice time, you think you might want to get together again . . ."

"Was he that good?" Andrew asked.

"He's a kid."

"You just said he's a fucking machine."

"He was all right. It was pure sex, Andrew, nothing more."

"I keep picturing the two of you together. I keep thinking that if you hadn't met me, if I hadn't been here when he came to visit . . ."

"That's a whole different story. Besides, I wouldn't have been interested. You're not jealous, are you?"

"About as jealous as you were the night we came home from Early Sumner's."

"That jealous?"

"I think so."

On the night of Early Sumner's dinner party Margo had been blinded by sexual jealousy. She had been furious—at herself, for feeling vulnerable and insecure, at Early Sumner and other women like her, for not knowing how to relate to men except in a flirtatious way, and most of all, at Andrew, for allowing it to happen.

Oh, she hated women like Early Sumner. But she also recognized her former self in them, her married-to-Freddy self, when going to a party meant an evening of flirtations that would go nowhere but which would bring immense pleasure for a few hours—eye contact across the dinner table, a brushing of arms, of thighs, tingles followed by fantasies. She'd put out vibes in those days. *Here I am . . . come and get me . . . if you can.* She no longer put out those vibes, but other women did. And she could not stop them from coming on to Andrew.

It's your life, the voice inside her head had said that night. *You're in charge. If this is how he's going to behave and it makes you unhappy, then get rid of him.*

I don't want to get rid of him.

Then what do you want?

I want him to want me as much as I want him.

Oh ho! That old song.

Is that so unreasonable?

Depends who you ask.

So what should I do?

Tell him how you feel. See how he reacts. Maybe he'll understand. Maybe next time he'll be more aware of your feelings.

You know something . . . for once you're making sense.

Margo . . . I always make sense.

The next day, at noon, Margo drove out to the building site in Sunshine Canyon. She wandered through the new house until she found Eric. "I want to talk to you," she said.

"Sure, Margo."

"Not here. In my car."

"Be back in a few minutes," Eric told another worker, who

raised his eyebrows in response. Margo knew what he was think-ing, but she didn't care.

"What are you doing, Eric?" she asked, opening the car door.

"Mainly laying the floors and the patios."

"That's not what I mean. I mean, what are you doing with Michelle?"

"That's not something I'm going to talk about with you, Margo."

"She's too young for you. Too inexperienced."

"She's seventeen, isn't she?"

"Yes."

"And I'm twenty-one. That sounds just right to me."

"Damn it, Eric! I won't have you pulling any Mother-Daughter number on us."

"What's with you, Margo? Are you jealous? Is that it?"

"Jealous?"

"Yeah, that's how it looks to me. Oh, sure, you've got yourself some guy, but he must be what . . . forty, forty-five? It's not the same, is it?"

Margo thought about smashing him in the mouth, kicking him in the balls, telling him what an immature asshole he was. But she held back her rage and said, instead, "You're so far off the wall I won't even attempt to respond."

"You're afraid I'm going to tell her . . . that's it, isn't it?"

"It would be destructive to tell her."

"Hey, look . . . I don't brag about my sexual experiences. I don't have to."

"So why, when you could have any woman in town, does it have to be Michelle?"

"I like her. She reminds me of you."

That night, after dinner, while Andrew and Stuart cleaned up the kitchen, Margo went to Michelle's room. "Honey . . . I'd like to talk to you."

"I don't have much time, Mother. Eric's coming by at eight. He found a room on Arapahoe. He wants me to see it."

"Don't you have schoolwork?"

"I already did it."

"You can't ride on the Honda at night."

"I know. We're borrowing the truck. Andrew said it was all right."

"Michelle, listen . . . there are some men who go through life taking whatever they want, without ever giving in return."

"There are women like that too."

"Maybe. But some men, like Eric, think that nothing else matters . . . that no woman can resist them and all because of their good looks . . ."

"Good is putting it mildly, Mother . . ."

"I never thought you would be so sexist, Michelle."

"Me? You're the one who's being sexist. You're the one putting him down just because he's so good-looking, without even giving him a chance, without even bothering to find out what's underneath."

"I know what's underneath."

"How . . . how do you know?"

"I sense it." She wasn't making herself clear. She wished she could come right out and say, *He slept with me, Michelle. We were lovers for a week. I know what I'm talking about.* But in this case honesty was out of the question. "Don't sleep with him, Michelle . . . please."

"My sex life is my own business."

"I don't want to see you hurt."

"Are you jealous, Mother? Is that it?"

"Jealous of what?"

"Us. Our youth. Eric says that women of your age sometimes resent their daughters' youth."

"I don't resent your youth, Michelle. I've had my own."

"Well, I'm glad to hear that, Mother." Michelle pulled a blue t-shirt out of her dresser drawer. "I've really got to get changed now. Don't worry about me . . . okay?"

"I'm trying not to."

"Remember when I was little and you used to read me that Maurice Sendak book, *Higglety Pigglety Pop?*"

"Yes . . ."

"Remember Jennie, the dog who was trying to get experience . . ."

"What about her?"

"Well, that's me, Mother."

"Michelle's after experience," Margo told Andrew later that night. They were in bed, reading.

Andrew ran his hand up her leg. "How about you and me having a little experience tonight?"

"You're not listening. You think it's all a big joke, don't you?"

"Mmm . . ." Andrew had his hand between her legs now.

"And speaking of jokes," Margo said, "our Polaroid pictures are missing. I only hope Eric didn't find them. He used our shower last Sunday."

"More likely Mrs. Herrera found them."

"If Mrs. Herrera found them she'll quit. She doesn't approve of me living with a man who's not my husband . . . a man who used to be married to Mrs. B.B. She thinks I'm a sinner. Those pictures will prove it."

"Come here, sinner."

"You have a one-track mind."

"It's not my mind," he said, "it's this."

"Oh," Margo said, "I see." And in a minute she forgot about the pictures.

40

ANDREW'S PARENTS CAME to town on the day that Clare left for Miami to visit B.B. Andrew and Sara had met the Broders at the airport, had spent a few hours alone with them, then had dropped them at the Harvest House. Now Andrew was on his way back to their hotel to pick them up and bring them to the house.

Margo sat in the living room, waiting. She had dressed in southwestern style—a denim skirt, her concha belt, a brightly colored vest, boots, and silver bracelets. She waited nervously, fussing over a tray of cheeses from Essential Ingredients and a bowl of chopped liver from the New York Deli. She had picked up a tulip plant at Sturz and Copeland, which she moved from the coffee table to the dining table, then back again. She wanted the Broders to like her, to appreciate her, to see that she was just right for Andrew. Freddy's parents had accepted her, but they had never thought she was good enough for their son. No woman would have been good enough for their son, which is why their son treated women like shit.

She had had a call from Freddy that afternoon, accusing her of using his support payments to care for another child.

"That's ridiculous!" she'd told him.

"You've taken in his kid, haven't you?"

"She's living with us while her mother is in the hospital."

"The looney bin, as I understand it."

She'd held the phone to her chest and inhaled deeply. She would not allow him to throw her into a frenzy.

"Do you think it's fair, Margo," Freddy had continued, "taking in his kid at the expense of your own?"

"It's not at the expense of my own."

"You have to devote time and attention to her, don't you?"

"It's not your business, Freddy."

"Anything relating to my children is my business. And I don't want my money used to take care of his child."

"Not a penny of yours goes toward the care and feeding of Sara Broder!"

"Good. I'm glad to hear that. Now that we've got that straight, what about graduation?"

"What about it?"

"Have you booked us a room yet?"

"I sent you a list of hotels."

"I'm trying not to remind you that if you had stayed in the city Aliza and I would not have to fly out to never-never land for Stuart's graduation."

"All right," Margo said. "I'll book you a room." She no longer blamed Freddy for his hostility regarding the distance she had put between him and the children. She had learned, from living with Andrew, what it's like to lose your children to the geographical whim of a former spouse. She had learned how it could tear a person apart and she was not sure the law should allow it under any circumstances.

If only Freddy had made the time for Stuart and Michelle when they had all lived together, if only he had made it clear that he had loved them and had not wanted to lose them. Life was full of *if onlys.*

Maybe divorce should be outlawed, Margo thought. Divorce screwed up as many lives as disease. She tried to imagine a world in which there was no divorce, a world in which she would have been forced to make some kind of life with Freddy. Probably she'd have taken a lover. More than one. Probably Freddy would have too.

Michelle came into the living room and eyed the tulip plant, the cheeses, the basket of crackers and pumpernickel bread. "It looks like you're expecting the queen, Mother."

"It does look that way, doesn't it?" Margo said, surprised at how easy it was to avoid unpleasantness. A year ago she would have become defensive at Michelle's remark and there would have been a major confrontation.

"Eric is coming over at six. We're going to an early movie."

"Don't you think you're seeing too much of Eric?"

"I don't have time for a lecture now, Mother," Michelle said, skipping down the stairs.

No, not now, Margo thought. She closed her eyes, picturing Andrew and herself on a sailboat, moving silently through the emerald green waters of the Caribbean. She could almost smell the salt air, taste the spray, feel the wind whipping through her hair. She had not been sailing since the day she and Freddy had capsized in Sag Harbor Bay, but she and Andrew often talked about a sailing trip. Maybe this summer . . . if they could get it together.

Stuart came barreling up the stairs and began to attack the food Margo had set out so carefully. "Please, Stu . . . wait until the Broders get here."

"I'm hungry now," he said, his mouth full of food.

"Then take something from the kitchen."

"Jesus, you'd think Andrew's parents were more important than your own kids."

Margo clenched her teeth.

Stuart laughed and pecked her cheek. "Just a joke, Mom. No one's more important than your own kids, right?"

"Right," Margo said.

Finally, the front door opened and Margo ran down the stairs to greet Andrew's parents.

The Broders were a handsome couple, in their early seventies, both slim, silver-haired, and perfectly groomed. Nettie Broder wore a pale pink ultrasuede suit with a strand of coral around her neck. Her lipstick was bright, with a purple cast, and when she smiled Margo noticed that it had smeared onto her front teeth. In Sam Broder, Margo could see Andrew in thirty years.

The same jaw, the same smile, but without the sparkle in his eyes.

Sam Broder had sold his Buick agency in Hackensack twelve years ago. He and Nettie had settled in Florida, not just because it was the place to go when you retired, but because Andrew and Francine had lived there, with the grandchildren. Now Bobby was dead and Francine had brought Sara to Boulder. So much for carefully conceived plans.

Margo wished again that she and Andrew had shared the last twenty years so that by now they would know each other so well, would love each other so deeply, that nothing could ever come between them.

Margo would have embraced the Broders, but she did not want to come on too strong. So she offered her hand and each of them shook it warmly. "Well," Margo said, "shall we go upstairs?"

"Upstairs?" Nettie asked.

"The living room," Andrew explained.

"The living room is upstairs?" Nettie said.

"Yes," Margo told her. "It's an upside-down kind of house."

"A split level?" Sam said.

"No, not exactly," Margo said.

"We looked at a house once with the living room halfway upstairs," Nettie said, "but you still had to go up another four steps to get to the bedrooms. Remember that house, Sam?"

"But that was a split," Sam said.

"Our bedrooms are on this level," Margo said.

"You don't mind sleeping on the ground floor?" Nettie asked. "You're not afraid someone will come in?"

"We're used to it."

Andrew started up the stairs and his parents followed.

"How about a glass of wine?" Margo asked, after they had settled on the sofa.

"Just club soda for me," Nettie said. She opened her purse, took out a compact and looked into the mirror. She quickly wiped the lipstick off her front teeth, then smiled awkwardly at Margo, and Margo realized that Nettie was not at ease either, in this house in which her son was living with a strange woman.

"So where's our little Sara?" Sam asked.

"She's taking a bath," Margo said. "She'll be up soon." Margo had insisted that Sara bathe before dinner. Sara had argued that she didn't need a bath, that she had taken a bath yesterday, but Andrew had backed up Margo, telling Sara no bath no dinner at John's French Restaurant.

"Andrew tells us you have two children," Nettie said.

"Yes . . . they'll be up in a minute too."

Nettie tapped her foot nervously. Sam sipped a glass of wine.

Margo heard the sound of the motorcycle turning onto the dirt road, then Eric banging on the front door and Michelle, calling, "It's for me . . . I'll get it . . ."

"My daughter," Margo said.

Nettie and Sam nodded.

Why didn't Andrew engage them in conversation? Margo wondered. Why was he just sitting there like a lump across the room? She still wasn't used to him without his beard. She had asked him what he looked like without it so many times he had finally shaved it off, surprising her. That night in bed, in the darkness, she'd felt as if she were with a stranger.

The next morning he'd said, "Well?"

"I miss it," she'd told him.

He'd laughed. "I can grow another one in a month."

At breakfast Michelle had said, "Why, Andrew . . . you're good-looking. Who would have guessed?"

"Guessed what?" Stuart had asked. He hadn't even noticed.

But Sara had taken one look at Andrew and had cried, "Why did you have to go and do that?" She had left the table in tears.

Now Margo wished that Andrew were sitting next to her, with his arm around her shoulder, showing his parents how close they were. But he was acting as if he hardly knew her, as if he were a visitor in her home, like his parents.

Michelle and Eric clomped up the stairs, both of them wearing hiking boots and work clothes. They looked like soldiers in the Israeli Army, Margo thought. All that was missing were the rifles slung over their shoulders.

Andrew said, "Eric, Michelle, these are my parents, Nettie and Sam Broder."

"Hey, how's it goin', Nettie?" Eric asked, pumping Andrew's mother's hand. "How're you doin', Sam?"

"This is your son?" Nettie asked Margo.

"No, this is Eric," Margo said. She paused, searching for the right words. "A . . . family friend."

Michelle did not approach the Broders. But she did say, "Hi, glad to meet you, welcome to Boulder and all that. How do you like it so far?"

"It's so windy," Nettie said. "I never felt such wind. I could hardly catch my breath."

"Yes, it can be windy in the spring," Margo said.

"And no ocean," Sam said. "Nettie and I like to be by the ocean."

"We have mountains," Michelle said.

"What can you do with mountains?" Nettie asked.

"Climb them," Michelle said.

Eric was munching on the cheese and crackers when he noticed the bowl of chopped liver. "What's this?" he asked.

"You don't know chopped liver?" Nettie said.

"Chopped liver . . . never saw the stuff, but I'm always willing to try." He took a blob, dropped it on the center of a cracker, and wolfed it down. "Interesting," he said, brushing off his hands.

Margo felt her face stiffen into a half-smile.

"Well," Michelle said, "we really have to go. Nice to meet you Mrs. Broder, Mr. Broder . . . see you on Sunday, if not before."

Margo poured herself a glass of wine and drank it quickly, as if it were water. Then she poured another.

"Some handsome boy," Nettie said, when Eric and Michelle were gone. "Is he Jewish?"

Margo coughed on her wine. "No."

"I didn't think so, never to have seen chopped liver. You don't mind that your daughter goes out with a boy who's not Jewish?"

"Michelle's not marrying him, Nettie," Andrew said, coming to life.

Anyway, he's circumcized, Margo thought about saying.

How would you know? Nettie would ask.

I know because I fucked him, Margo would say.

Oh, my God! Sam, did you hear what she said?

Yes, Nettie. She said that she fucked him. And that's how come she knows he's circumcized.

I fucked him three or four times a day for a week.

Three or four times a day, Sam would say. *That's a lot of fucking.*

I'm feeling faint, Nettie would say.

It's probably the altitude, Margo would tell her.

"Oh, here's our little Sara," Nettie said, as Sara and Stuart came up the stairs.

"Hi Grandma . . . hi Grandpa. This is Stuart."

"Margo's Number One Son," Stuart said.

"You have more than one?" Nettie asked.

"No, that's just an expression," Margo told her.

Nettie nodded. Then she appraised Sara. "That's how you're going out to dinner . . . in dungarees?"

"Blue jeans, Grandma. In Boulder you can wear them any-where. Look at Margo's skirt . . . same material."

"Well, if it's all right with your father . . ."

"It's fine with me," Andrew said.

"Did I miss Eric?" Sara asked. "Is he gone already?"

"They went to an early movie," Margo said.

"Oh, shit!" Sara said.

"Sara!" Sam said. "Such language."

"Sorry, Grandpa . . . I forgot you don't like me to use those words."

"What movie did my sister and The Acrobat go to see?" Stuart asked.

"He's an acrobat?" Nettie asked. "He works in a circus?"

Margo laughed.

"No, Grandma," Sara said, and she laughed too. "He can walk on his hands. That's why Stuart calls him The Acrobat."

"That's not all of it," Stuart sang.

"Stu . . ." Margo warned.

Margo wanted to like the Broders, for Andrew's sake. She had known beforehand there would be questions. She had tried to prepare herself, planning to answer them honestly, in a friendly manner. But she hated having to tell them about Freddy over dinner, about a life that she no longer lived. She sensed, from their questions, they were trying to find out what problems she might bring to their son.

After dinner they dropped Sara off at Jennifer's, then drove out to the Harvest House. On the way there Sam ran his hand along the backseat of her car and asked Margo, "You like these little imports?"

"Yes, I've had my Subaru for three years."

"I had a Buick agency, you know."

"Yes, Andrew told me."

"It's very hard for a person of my age, a person who remembers everything about the War, to see young people riding around in these Japanese cars."

"The War's over, Dad," Andrew said, pulling into the Harvest House lot.

"Please, Andrew . . . I may be seventy-four, but I still know which end is up."

"I like a roomy American car," Nettie said, as they walked toward the hotel. "We have a four-door Buick, cream-colored. Light colors are best in Florida . . . they reflect the heat."

Margo nodded.

They went into the lounge and found a table in the back, away from the singles crowd, which gathered around the bar. They ordered two Irish coffees and two plain.

"We've been to see Francine," Nettie said. "I didn't want to discuss it in front of Sara, but I thought you should know."

"She didn't recognize us," Sam said.

"Of course she did," Nettie argued. "She just wouldn't talk to us."

"She twirled a rubber band around her fingers," Sam said. "The whole time we were there she twirled a rubber band around her fingers. Like a little kid."

"She was nervous," Nettie said. "She's always been high-strung."

"She looked terrible," Sam said. "Her eyes all sunken in. She used to be such a beauty."

"She will be again. All she needs is a good haircut. As soon as she gets out she'll get her looks back," Nettie said. "But her mother, Goldy . . ."

"That's another story," Sam said.

"She's aged overnight," Nettie said. "God forbid, it could happen to any of us, but Goldy is only sixty-five."

"Sixty-one," Andrew said.

"Really?" his mother asked. "That's all?"

Andrew nodded.

"She can't get the right words out," Sam said. "You can see how she's struggling. But at least she knew us."

"Francine knew us too. I don't know why you keep saying that she didn't. She just wouldn't say anything."

"It's just one tragedy after another," Sam said.

"You knew Francine, of course?" Nettie asked Margo.

"Yes," Margo said.

"It's a shame, not just for Francine, but for Sara."

"Yes," Margo said again.

During Sunday dinner, as Sam and Nettie brought Andrew up to date on their friends and who had died, who had been hospitalized, and who had been diagnosed as having this or that disease, Margo found her mind wandering. She stared out the window at the Flatirons, which were still snow covered, while in town, on the Mall, tulips and daffodils were sprouting everywhere. She could see Michelle out of the corner of her eye glancing at her watch, wondering how much longer this dinner was going to last, how many more minutes before she could be with Eric again. And Sara wasn't eating at all. She was just moving the food around on her plate and making silly faces at Stuart, who was encouraging her to misbehave in front of her grandparents.

It wasn't until after dinner that Nettie and Sam took Margo aside and Nettie said, "Do you think he really loves you or is he just trying to prove something to Francine?"

Margo felt as if she had been punched in the stomach. She could taste the turkey, the sweet potatoes, the fresh green beans working their way up to her throat. She could not bring herself to answer simply, to say, *Yes, he really loves me.* Instead, she said, "I don't know what you mean."

"He's never gotten over her," Nettie said. "When she left and took Sara with her, he fell apart. We thought he'd never come out of it."

"You never saw a boy so in love as Andrew was with Francine," Sam said. "He worshipped her."

"We don't mean to hurt your feelings," Nettie said. "He's our son and we love him, but he won't be satisfied until he gets her back. That's why he came out here."

"You're not the first and you won't be the last," Sam said, "but none of them lasts more than a year. Isn't that right, Nettie?"

"That's right. And it's all because he still wants her. So unless you're willing to be second best . . ."

Margo shook her head from side to side, denying what they were telling her, wanting to shout, *It's not true. You don't know anything about it.* But she couldn't say anything, except, "Excuse me . . ." and then she ran down the stairs, locked herself in her bathroom, and threw up into the toilet.

41

FRANCINE WAS LYING on a lounge chair in the garden. Her eyes were closed. She was practicing one of the relaxation techniques she had learned in *Group*. She pictured herself in a hammock tied to two coconut trees on the beach, the ocean lapping gently in the distance. She was wearing a loose white dress and her feet were bare. The sun warmed her body as the hammock swayed in the breeze. She felt peaceful.

She was expecting a visitor. She was not sure she would be able to talk today, but she was going to try. She wanted to be well. And in order to be well she had to relate to people. She had to talk to them and listen to them and even care about them.

When she opened her eyes she saw Clare walking toward her. Francine stood up and smoothed out the wraparound dress she was wearing. Clare waved, then hurried toward her. Francine stood stiffly as Clare embraced her.

"I'm so glad to see you," Clare said, releasing her, but still holding on to her hands.

Francine nodded.

"How are you?"

Francine nodded again. She poured each of them a glass of lemonade from the pitcher sitting on the white wrought iron table.

"Thanks," Clare said, pulling up a chair and sipping her drink.

Francine sat on the edge of the lounge chair. She wore two rubber bands around each wrist, like bracelets. Dr. Arnold said it was all right to use them if they made her feel more comfortable.

"How is Sara?" Francine asked, tentatively.

"She's fine," Clare said.

"You've seen her?"

"Yes," Clare said. "I try to see her at least once a week. She's singing in the school chorus and she got her first period."

"Her first period," Francine said. "I didn't know." She pulled a pink rubber band off her wrist and began to wind it around her fingers. She hoped it would not snap. She hated it when her rubber bands snapped, surprising her. She did not like surprises. Whenever a rubber band snapped she had to knot it and then it wasn't strong anymore.

"Sara sent you this," Clare said, pulling a blue envelope out of her purse.

Francine took it and put it into her pocket. It was so difficult to make conversation. It hurt her throat and her head. "She writes to me every week, but I never write to her. I don't know what to say."

"She understands," Clare said.

Francine took a blue rubber band from her other wrist and twisted it around two of her fingers. "She lives with them, doesn't she?"

"Yes."

"Is she happy there?"

"She misses you but . . ."

"I know a joke," Francine said, interrupting. "How many psychiatrists does it take to change a light bulb?" She was supposed to wait for the other person to answer, to say, *I don't know* or *I give up,* but she never did. She always gave the answer herself. "One," she said. "But it takes a long time and the light bulb has to really want to change."

Clare laughed.

In *Group* they were learning to tell each other jokes. That was the only one she had learned so far. She did not find any of the jokes funny. She did not find anything funny. She watched a lot of TV, mainly sitcoms, trying to figure them out. Some of the patients laughed their heads off at *Laverne and Shirley* or *Three's*

Company, but Francine wasn't one of them. Dr. Arnold said that her sense of humor would come back in time.

"Part of my problem is I don't find anything funny," Francine said to Clare. "Except for this. I married a man over New Year's in Hawaii. I don't remember having married him, but apparently I did. Isn't that funny . . . to have married someone and not remember? Of course, I don't have to stay married to him if I don't want to."

"You married Lewis?" Clare asked, leaning forward in her chair.

Francine wound the blue rubber band around her thumb. "Yes."

"Are you sure?"

"Yes, I'm sure. I'm not that kind of crazy."

"I'm sorry," Clare said. "It's just such a surprise. Does Sara know?"

"No one knows, except for Dr. Arnold, Lewis, and my *Group.*"

Clare finished her lemonade.

"Here's something else," Francine said. "I had a son who died in an automobile accident when he was ten. They tell me I have to learn to accept that. Do you think a person can ever learn to accept that?"

"Is all of this true, B.B.?" Clare asked, a worried expression on her face.

"Yes, it's all true. I'm learning to deal with the truth. That's why I'm here. And from now on would you call me Francine? That's my real name."

42

MICHELLE WAS IN love and no one was going to spoil it for her. Not Margo and her hostile attitude, not Stuart, calling Eric The Acrobat, not Andrew's knowing looks, not even her best friend, Gemini, warning Michelle that Eric was a loser. It was embarrassingly obvious that Gemini, like the other girls at school, was jealous. Only Sara understood the incredible, the amazing truth—not only did Michelle love Eric, but Eric loved Michelle.

Michelle had always known that if she waited long enough her time would come. She was glad she hadn't gone with any of those creepy boys at school, glad that she had saved herself for Eric. She would ride to the ends of the earth on the back of his Honda, her arms wrapped around his waist, the wind in her face, the helmet over her ears so that she could hear only the thump of her own heartbeat.

He waited for her every day after school, surrounded by a group of girls who stood back in awe as Michelle approached. She would climb onto the Honda and wave goodbye, as Eric revved up the motor and sped off, whisking Michelle away to his room on Arapahoe, where he would make love to her until dinnertime. Then, he would deliver her home to her mother, her cheeks rosy, a secret smile on her face.

She had gone to the clinic for a diaphragm after their first night together. No accidents for her, like Puffin. She had questioned Eric about venereal disease since he had had so many partners, but he had sworn he was clean. He'd encouraged her to examine him. He had turned on the lights and told her to get down close to his penis and look it over carefully and she had. She had never seen a penis up close before. She had never touched one. She liked the way it sprang to life, like an inflatable toy. He had been gentle that first night, but she had been so scared she couldn't let go. It had hurt like hell. She'd felt no pleasure, except for the pleasure of the idea. She hadn't even loved him then. It wasn't until the next day that she'd loved him. And her love had grown steadily in the five weeks since they had met. Eric had changed her life. There could be no going back for her now.

And so, when he told her on May 15 at 5:28 in the afternoon that he had to be moving on, she passed out. She was in his bed at the time.

When she came to, Eric was hovering over her, fanning her face. "What'd you do that for?" he asked.

"The shock, I guess. Do you have to go so soon?"

"I have to get back home in time to find a decent summer job," he told her. "If I'm going back to school in September then I've got to go after the bucks now."

She had known from the beginning that some day he would have to leave. But she had hoped that it would not be until the end of the school year, and then, that he would ask her to come with him to Oregon for the summer, where she would get a job waiting tables in some quaint inn while he worked on a highway construction crew. They would live in a tiny room, with just a hot plate, or else in a trailer, and she would learn to sew so that she could hang curtains in the windows. In September she would come back to Boulder, finish up her final year of high school, and apply only to colleges in Oregon.

"I can come out to Portland as soon as school is over," Michelle said. "I don't have to go east this summer."

"No."

"Why?"

"Because I can't get involved with you."

"You don't call this involved?"

"I never made any promises, did I?"

"No, but . . ."

"I want you to have this," he said, reaching across to the bedside table, handing her a small cactus plant. "I want you to take care of it for me."

Michelle held the plant close, feeling its prickly spines. "If it blooms, I will bloom," she said, closing her eyes. "If it dies, I will die too."

"That's real poetic, Michelle," Eric said. "You have a definite flair for the dramatic. You ever thought of going on the stage?"

She did not remind him that she had given him the cactus plant in the first place.

She could not eat for a week. At night she would wake up suddenly, drenched in sweat, her heart pounding. She would climb out of bed and check the cactus. It was thriving. She wished she were a child again, so that she could run down the hall to her mother's room and climb into bed with her. Her mother would hold her close, until she was no longer afraid. But her childhood was over, whether or not she was ready to give it up.

"I knew from the beginning that this is how it would end," Gemini said. "I saw it in his eyes. He did not know the way of the world."

"What exactly does knowing the way of the world mean?" Michelle asked.

Gemini shook her head. "I don't know."

"What do you mean you don't know?"

"I made it up."

"You made it up?"

"Yes."

"All this time you've been telling me who knows the way of the world and who doesn't, you didn't know what you were talking about? It's not some ancient Pueblo saying?"

"No."

"But why?"

"I wanted you to think I was exotic and very wise."

"But you are!" Michelle said. "You didn't have to go and make something up for me to believe that."

"Are you angry?"

Michelle looked around her room, focused on the cactus, and said, "No . . . because even if you did make it up, it's true. Some people know the way of the world and some don't."

"But you loved him anyway," Gemini said.

"Yes."

"Even though he was no good for you."

"He gave me exactly what I wanted," Michelle said. "He gave me experience."

"But was it worth it?" Gemini asked.

Michelle's eyes filled up. "I don't know yet. If I live, then I guess so. If I die of a broken heart, then probably not."

"You're not going to die of a broken heart," Gemini said. "You're too smart for that."

"I don't think it has anything to do with being smart," Michelle said.

43

SARA COULD NOT believe that Eric had left town without saying goodbye to her. And after promising to wait until she grew up, until her braces came off her teeth, after promising to be there for her first teenaged birthday, which was coming in just a few weeks. She'd had it all arranged in her mind. How Eric would sit next to her at the table, and then, after she'd blown out the candles on her cake, the way he would kiss her. She could almost feel the softness of his lips on her face. She had believed him when he'd made those promises.

Michelle had been the one to tell them that Eric was gone. She'd said it one night at the dinner table. "Eric left town. He won't be back." She'd said it in a very small voice and everyone except Stuart had stopped eating and looked up at her.

"So, The Acrobat took off," Stuart said, biting into the skin of a baked potato, "without even so much as a goodbye. Nice guy."

Michelle shoved back her chair, stood up, and raised her glass of apple juice, as if to make a toast. Then she turned and threw it in Stuart's face. "Asshole!" she cried, running from the dining table. A moment later her bedroom door slammed.

"Jesus!" Stuart muttered, wiping off his face with his napkin.

Sara expected Margo to give Michelle hell. You didn't just throw a glass of juice in someone's face and get away with it. But instead, Margo said, "Really, Stu . . . was that necessary?"

"What?" Stuart asked. "What'd I do?"

Margo just shook her head. Then she turned to Sara's father. "I better go down and see how she's doing."

Sara opened her mouth to speak, but Daddy covered her hand with his own and she knew that she should shut up and stay out of it. After that she wasn't hungry anymore, so when no one was looking she passed the rest of her pot roast to Lucy, who sat under the table, waiting.

Every night after that Sara could hear Michelle crying herself to sleep. Probably Eric had made a lot of promises to Michelle too.

Ten days after he'd left town, two postcards arrived from Eric. Sara collected the mail from the box that afternoon and read both of them. One was addressed to Michelle. It had a picture of a beaver on the front with *Greetings from Oregon* printed above it. On the back, Eric had written:

> Dear Michelle,
> Just a line to say you're a great girl and that knowing you was a great pleasure. Hope to see you again some day.
>
> > Yours,
> > Eric

The other was addressed to Margo. It had a picture of the Columbia River on the front. On the back it said:

> Dear Margo,
> Thanks a lot for your hospitality while I was in Boulder. I'm sorry I didn't have a chance to say goodbye to all of you. Please tell Andrew, Stuart, and, of course, Sara, that I hope to see them again. You're a swell family.
>
> > Sincerely,
> > Eric

It would have been nice if he had sent a card just to her, Sara thought, but at least he had mentioned her by name.

Margo didn't seem all that interested in Eric's card, so Sara asked if she could have it.

"Yes," Margo said. "Just don't let me see it around."

Sara knew that Margo hated Eric, but she did not know why,

unless all mothers hated their daughters' boyfriends. She wondered if her mother would hate Griffen Blasch, this new boy in her class who was not exactly her boyfriend, but who she secretly liked, even though he was so shy he never spoke to her.

Not that what she felt for Griffen Blasch was anything like what she felt for Eric, but being in love with Eric was kind of like being in love with Matt Dillon or some rock star.

Sara took the postcard to her room and hid it in her bottom drawer, with the Polaroid pictures of Margo and her mother's blue silk blouse. She turned on her radio and tuned it in to KPKE Rocks the Rockies. They were playing "Love Is the Drug."

Later that night Sara walked into the bathroom and found Michelle standing over the sink, a pair of scissors in her hand. "Oh, I'm sorry," Sara said. "The door wasn't locked."

"It doesn't matter," Michelle told her.

"What are you doing?" Sara asked.

"What does it look like I'm doing?"

"It looks like you're cutting Eric's postcard into tiny pieces."

"That's exactly right," Michelle said as the pieces fell into the sink.

"But why?" Sara asked. "It was such a cute picture of a beaver."

Michelle just snorted.

The next day, after school, Sara went to Jennifer's house. They were upstairs in Jennifer's bedroom and Sara was holding Jennifer's hamsters while Jennifer cleaned out their cage. The hamsters felt soft and furry, but their feet squiggled as they tried to get away from Sara.

"Have you talked to your mother yet?" Jennifer asked, as she removed the newspaper from the bottom of the cage.

"Not yet," Sara said.

"She'll probably call for your birthday."

"Probably," Sara said. But she wasn't sure that her mother would even remember her birthday. "Margo and my father said I should have a party."

"What kind of party?" Jennifer asked. She lined the cage with clean newspaper and sprinkled cedar shavings onto it.

"A birthday party," Sara said.

"I know that," Jennifer said, taking the hamsters from her and returning them to their cage. "I mean, what kind of birthday party?"

"Whatever kind I want."

"A boy-girl party?"

"Whatever." The hamsters ran around in their wheel, making a whirring sound.

"Have a boy-girl party," Jennifer said. "I'll help you write out the invitations and we can plan it together."

"I don't know," Sara said. "My mother wouldn't want me to have a boy-girl party. She'd want me to invite six girls over for pizza and a movie, then we'd go back to my house for cake and ice cream."

"You're always thinking about what your mother would want," Jennifer said, "instead of what *you* want. You've got to start thinking for yourself, Sara. After all, it's *your* life."

Sara walked across the room and looked out the window. The sky was clear and very blue. A bunch of kids were roller skating on Mapleton.

"Listen to this . . ." Jennifer said, rattling the newspaper. "Omar says *Today is a big improvement over yesterday, particularly in connection with your love life, social activities, or various recreational pastimes. Give a party.*"

Sara turned around. "Omar says that?"

"Yes, right here," Jennifer said, tapping the paper.

"Hmmm . . ." Sara said, "maybe I will have a boy-girl party. And maybe I'll invite Griffen Blasch."

"I knew you liked him!" Jennifer said.

The baby started to cry then and Jennifer went into the nursery to get him. He was fat and adorable and Sara watched as Jennifer expertly changed his diaper.

It would be very nice to have a baby, Sara thought. A baby would need you. A baby would love you, no matter what. Now that Sara got her period she could have a baby if she wanted. If Eric came back when she was, say, eighteen and wanted to have a baby with her, she might. Then they would buy the blow-up house on Sixth, the house that was made of foam and looked like it belonged to some other planet, and she would go to C.U. and become a vet and Eric would open a motorcycle shop downtown and she would ride to her classes on the back of his Honda, the way Michelle had.

"Do you think your mother and Bruce will have another baby?" Sara asked.

"No, my mother only had this one because Bruce wanted the experience of being a father. My mother didn't need another kid. She already had the three of us. Maybe your father and Margo will have a baby. Then you'll find out what it's like when you're not an only child."

"I'm not an only child," Sara said. Jennifer passed her the baby. He grabbed a fistful of her hair.

"Stuart and Michelle don't count," Jennifer said, rubbing her hands with baby lotion. "They don't belong to either one of your parents."

"I'm not an only child," Sara said again.

"You are too, Sara."

"No. I had a brother, but he died." Sara was surprised at how easy it was to say. "He was ten. His name was Bobby."

"Baa Baa," the baby said.

44

FROM THE MOMENT Margo took her seat on the grassy field of Boulder High School she choked up and could not speak. The idea of her son graduating from high school seemed not only a monumental event in his life, but in her own as well. She had kissed Stuart's freshly shaved cheek that morning, telling him how proud she was to be his mother, telling him how handsome he looked in his cap and gown.

He had flushed and said, "I feel pretty weird dressed up this way."

Out of uniform, out of his chinos and alligator shirt, he looked much younger to her, like a boy dressed in a man's costume.

The last few weeks had been so filled with the pain of her children Margo had hardly had time to deal with her own. On the day that Stuart received five college rejections he had locked himself in his room and when he came out, hours later, although he had been accepted at one school and wait-listed at another, he had said, "This is the saddest day of my life since the divorce."

His remark had cut into her, bringing back all the old divorce guilt, and for a moment she could not respond. It was the first time Stuart had admitted the divorce had affected him at all.

"It'll be okay," Margo had said finally, trying to comfort him. "Believe me, Stu, it'll all work out."

"That's what you always say. That's what you told me when you and Dad split up."

"And I was right, wasn't I?" she asked. But, of course, she had no way of knowing.

"I'm a failure at eighteen," he said sadly, shaking his head.

"No," Margo told him, "that's not true. We make too much of college. It's not your whole life."

"Maybe not to you . . . but what about Dad? What'll he think?"

"He'll understand," Margo said, praying that he would.

"I got six-fifties on my Boards, I have a solid B-plus average, I play second on the tennis team. What more do they want?" He paused for a minute. "Tell me, Mom . . . tell me the truth . . . is something wrong with me?"

"No, there's absolutely nothing wrong with you."

"Then why?"

"I don't know, Stu. Probably there were just a lot of kids with even higher grades and scores. And that's what they looked at."

"Maybe I came on too strong during my interviews. But I didn't want them to see me as some hick from Colorado."

"Rejection always hurts," Margo said.

"What do you know about rejection?"

"Plenty." Let it go at that, she thought. Let him learn to deal with one kind of rejection at a time. Later he would find out that college was just the beginning.

That had been on April 15. By May 15 Stuart had settled on Penn. "It's Ivy League," he'd said, consoling himself. "And it's Dad's alma mater."

Still trying to please his father, she thought.

Freddy had been a dental student at Penn when Margo had met him, the summer following her junior year at Boston U. She had been waiting tables in Provincetown and taking painting classes during the day. He had been vacationing with two of his buddies. He had seemed so full of life to her then.

Now Freddy sat two seats away from her, at their son's graduation. He sat on the other side of Michelle and on his other side sat Aliza, dazzling in a navy Chanel suit, her hands fluttering to her head, protecting her newly blonde hair from the strong breeze, each of her long manicured fingernails painted a dusty shade of rose. Her hands did not look as if she ever washed a dish, yet Margo knew that she liked to cook.

The graduates, more than six hundred of them, began their long march—step, pause . . . step, pause . . . step, pause—to the same music as Margo had marched to at her own high school graduation. She watched for Stuart and at first sight raised her hand as if to wave, then, realizing that he would be embarrassed, lowered it. *Stand up straight,* she told him mentally. *That's it . . .*

Michelle reached out and touched Margo's arm. Margo turned to her. "He's on the wrong foot," Michelle whispered. "Isn't that just like Stu?"

Margo smiled. She had not been sure that Michelle would recover from the pain of loving, then losing Eric. But a few weeks ago when Margo had gone to Michelle's room to say goodnight, Michelle had been sitting up in bed, holding a small cactus plant to her chest.

"He never lied to me, Mother. Not once."

"Well, there's a lot to be said for honesty," Margo said.

"Do you think I'll ever get over him?" Michelle asked.

"I think you'll always remember him, honey, but eventually, when you're ready, you'll allow yourself to love again." Oh, she'd sounded so wise, so knowing. Did children ever suspect what shaky ground their parents were on when they advised and comforted them?

"Is that how it was with you, Mother?"

Did she mean after James . . . Freddy . . . Leonard?

"Yes," Margo said. "That's how it was with me."

Michelle nodded.

The graduates took their seats.

Andrew sat on Margo's left side and next to him, biting her fingernails, was Sara. Behind them, Clare, Robin, and Margo's parents. Margo was glad her parents had been able to come. She was reminded of her own grandmother's death a few months before her high school graduation.

Two endless speeches followed, one by the valedictorian and

one by a Congressional hopeful, a former graduate of Boulder High School. Endless speeches about going out into the world early in this decade, about the beginning of their adult lives.

Adult? Margo thought. No. Adulthood started somewhere around the age of forty.

Andrew squeezed her hand.

Margo thought back to that cold November night when, snuggled close in her bed, Andrew had first proposed the idea of living together and they had agreed to give it a try.

For how long? her mother had asked, when Margo had told her of their plans.

For as long as it works, Margo had said.

The idea of it seemed so simplistic now that Margo laughed out loud. Both Andrew and Michelle looked over at her, probably thinking she'd found something funny in the politician's speech.

Until the end of the school year, at least, they had promised each other. Well, graduation was the end of the school year, wasn't it? And tomorrow Andrew was flying to Miami . . . and Margo could not erase his parents' message from her mind.

On the morning that Andrew had been driving his parents back to the airport for their return flight to Miami, Margo had gone out to a five-acre building site in Sunshine Canyon to walk the property with Michael's clients, a couple from Cincinnati who had plenty of money, whose children were grown, and who wanted to change their lifestyles.

Michael had been in Aspen at the time, skiing with a woman he'd met through a personal ad in the *New York Review,* a woman who was willing to relocate if she found the right man.

The couple from Cincinnati wanted a southwestern style house, like the ones they had seen in Santa Fe over Christmas, with white plaster walls, rough wood ceilings, and Mexican tile in the kitchens and bathrooms, plus a separate guest house for when their children came to visit.

Margo tried to concentrate on their questions, but she hadn't been able to get the Broders, and what they had said to her, out of her mind—that Andrew wouldn't be happy until he had Francine back, that Margo was just second best. With all of her problems, with all of her doubts and insecurities, which came and went, she had never thought of herself as second best and she wasn't about to start now.

When she got home from the canyon she left her muddy boots in the front hallway and went to take a hot bath. Soon she heard a thud, followed by Andrew's voice. "Goddamn it, Michelle . . . can't you ever put your things where they belong!"

"They're not *my* boots! Why do I always get blamed for everything?"

Margo wrapped herself in a towel and rushed out of the bathroom to see about the commotion. Andrew had tripped over her boots as he'd come into the house and had fallen.

"They're mine," Margo said. "I'm sorry. Are you all right?"

"Bruised my knee," Andrew said.

She helped him to his feet.

"Sorry, Michelle," Andrew said, "it's just that it hurt like hell and I was mad."

"Yeah, well . . . it could happen to anyone, I suppose."

He leaned on Margo and she helped him hobble down the hall to their bedroom. He pulled off his jeans and lay down on the bed.

Margo rubbed his knee. "Did your parents get off all right?"

"Not without giving me hell."

"For what?"

"Where do you want me to start?"

"At the beginning."

"Okay . . . first, I have no job security. How am I going to meet my obligations, which, I assume, means my financial obligations to Sara and you."

"Me?"

"Yes. They see that as the man's responsibility. And they can't understand that freelance writing is a job. They want to know why I don't go back to the *Herald*. At least I had a pension plan, medical insurance . . ."

"What else?"

"Then there was the part about us."

"What about us?"

"That we're not setting a very good example for Sara, or for your children."

"Not setting a good example . . ."

"We shouldn't be living together without being married."

"What'd you tell them?"

"I told them it's not their business, and besides, we've been too busy to think about marriage."

Margo laughed. "I once told my mother the same thing."

"What'd she say?"

"She said, *Darling . . . there's no such thing as too busy.*"

Andrew laughed with her.

She lay down beside him and he ran his hand over her face. "They're usually not so difficult. I think they were just feeling self-conscious and had to put in their two cents."

"They asked me if I thought you really loved me," Margo said, "or if you were just trying to prove something to B.B." Her mouth felt very dry. She licked her lips and swallowed.

He pulled away from her and sat up. "Jesus! I can't believe they said that. They still think I want her back?"

"Yes. They're convinced she's the reason you came here."

He shook his head and exhaled deeply.

"Is that true? Did you come out here to get back together with her?"

"Not consciously."

"Subconsciously?"

"I don't know. Maybe. I can't deny that I had this fantasy of getting back together . . . that enough time had passed to make it a possibility."

Margo untangled herself from him. She jumped off the bed and marched around the room, trying not to explode. "Did you make love with her . . . here, in Boulder?"

"No, but I would have that first night."

She sucked in her breath. "God, Andrew . . ."

"It was before I met you," he said.

"I know, but still . . ." She rested her hand on the old pottery lamp that sat on her dresser. She fought the urge to throw it at him. "Why didn't you tell me all of this before?"

"Tell you what? That I had some crazy notion of living happily ever after? What's so surprising about that?"

"Plenty."

"I would have told you before if I'd thought it was important . . . or if you had asked."

"Why should I have asked? I never thought about it until your parents put the bug in my head."

She walked across the room to the rolltop desk. She remembered her excitement on the day she'd found it in Caprice's shop. She had given it to Andrew on the night he'd moved in.

"But it's your desk," he said. "I can't take it."

"I want you to have it," she'd told him. "I love the idea of you working at it, using the cubbyholes to organize your notes."

"What about you?"

"I need more space anyway. I'll set up a door on sawhorses."

"You're sure?"

"Yes." She had painted the sawhorses blue.

Now she stood in front of the desk, fiddling with Andrew's collection of pens. "This is all a little hard to take," she said.

"Look, Margo . . . my fantasy of getting back together with Francine lasted for about ten minutes. And then I realized that nothing had changed, that nothing ever would, that we wouldn't have stayed together even if Bobby hadn't died."

Margo stacked his pens in a mug that had a picture of a dog on it. It was the only mug left from a set Michelle had given to her the last Christmas they had lived in New York.

"You were a fantasy in the beginning too," Andrew said.

"Me?" she asked, looking over at him.

"I'd been watching you for days. I knew you were Francine's friend, I knew I should stay away, but you were too appealing. So finally I worked up the courage to come over. I'd never done anything as ballsy as stripping off my clothes and sliding into your hot tub in my life."

"It was ballsy, all right."

For a moment after that neither of them spoke, but Margo was aware of the sound of their breathing. "Were you using me to make B.B. jealous?" she finally asked.

"No, but I liked the idea of her seeing that another woman, a smart woman like you, found me attractive."

"I don't feel very smart right now. I wish that you hadn't wanted her when you came to town. I wish I could be sure you had no ulterior motive when you met me, conscious or unconscious." She pulled down the top of his desk, then opened it again. "It would hurt too much to think that I've just been the pawn in some intricate game between you and B.B."

"How can you even think that?" he asked, his voice catching. "How can you doubt that I love you more now than I did in November . . . that I expect to keep on loving you more . . ." He stood up and hobbled across the room.

She held out her arms.

The graduates were called to receive their diplomas in alphabetical order. Margo was sure they would never reach the *S*'s, but finally, Stuart's name was called and Freddy jumped up with his Olympus OM2, complete with telephoto lens, to catch Stuart, smiling broadly, as if he had the world by the tail, not at all as if he believed he were a failure at eighteen.

After the last graduate received her diploma the chorus stood and sang. Puffin was in the first row, dressed primly, like the others, in a black skirt and white blouse, hands clasped in front of her waist. Margo turned around and smiled at Clare. Clare touched Margo's shoulder.

A few days ago Margo and Clare had been talking about raising kids, about the way you feel their pain as well as your own and Clare had said, "Puffin is still heartbroken about breaking up with Stuart."

"Has she told you why they broke up?" Margo asked.

"No . . . she won't say anything."

"Neither will Stuart."

"Do you think they were sleeping together?"

"I don't know."

"I gave Puffin a sex information book and told her if she had any questions she should come to me. But she never did."

Margo laughed. "I gave one to Stuart too."

"Puffin wants to go away for her senior year," Clare said, "so I'm taking her to look at Fountain Valley next week. She's having a hard time. I think it has to do with not knowing what's going to happen with Robin and me . . . not knowing whether we're going to stay together this time."

"Do you know?" Margo said.

Clare shook her head. "I wish I did. It's going a lot better since he took over B.B.'s business. He has a sense of purpose now. He doesn't mope around the house questioning the meaning of life."

Margo had noticed the change in Robin too. Since he had volunteered to take over B.B.'s business a month ago, he seemed more interested in life.

"I'm good with real estate," Robin had said one night when the four of them were having dinner in Denver. "And I'd like to do this for B.B., if you two have no objections."

"It's not our place to object," Andrew said. "And it's very decent of you to make the offer."

"I've written to B.B. and I've talked about it with Lewis," Robin said. "Lewis says I should go ahead. Of course, I won't be taking any commissions. Everything will be put away for B.B."

"It's a lovely idea," Margo said.

"Being semiretired I can pretty much do what I want," Robin said.

Clare and Margo smiled at each other across the table.

"Do you think it's possible to forgive and forget?" Margo asked after dinner, when they went to the Women's Room.

"Forget . . . never," Clare said. "Forgive . . . I hope so."

Margo had booked a table for ten at the Flagstaff Inn following graduation, more for the elegant setting and the fabulous view than the food, which was mediocre. She had requested a round table, but a long one had been set up, screwing up her seating plan. Freddy had already taken her aside that morning, insisting that the graduation lunch be on him. Well, why not? she thought. He was always quicker with his checkbook than with anything else.

When she had introduced him to Andrew, at the field, before graduation, Freddy had said, "So this is Andrew."

And Andrew had said, "So this is Freddy." Then both men had laughed self-consciously, but Margo had not.

Now, at lunch, the appraisals were over and everyone was behaving in a civilized way. There were no gaps in the conversation until Freddy, reminiscing about his student days at Penn, said, "Remember that weekend, Margo . . . you'd come down from Boston and it turned so cold I had to buy you a sweater? Do you still have that sweater . . . the one with the silver buttons?"

"No," Margo said, "but I had it for a long time."

Everyone was quiet for a moment. Then Freddy went back to his sole amandine and Margo, buttering a roll, thought, *This man was my husband. I lived with him for fourteen years. I made love with him one thousand four hundred and fifty-six times, more or less.*

Ready, Margo?

In a minute.

Now?

Yes, now . . . now . . . hurry.

Margo tried to imagine Freddy making love to Aliza, but she could not.

She reached for Andrew's hand under the table.

Aliza was telling everyone about the trip to Israel that she and Freddy were taking with Stuart and Michelle. "Three weeks . . ." she said. Her accent was halfway between Yiddish and British. "Everywhere from Haifa to Eilat."

"Andrew lived on a kibbutz for a while," Margo said.

"Really . . ." Aliza said. "I'm more of a city girl."

"When Abe and I went to Israel," Margo's mother said, "we visited a kibbutz."

"They were picking avocados," her father said.

Aliza turned to Michelle. "Next year, when you graduate, we'll go to Paris and Rome . . . yes?"

Michelle smiled halfheartedly.

Michelle had once told Margo that Aliza felt threatened by her, that Aliza was concerned that Margo would come back east and take Freddy away from her. *Don't worry, Aliza. He's all yours.*

*   *   *

The next morning Margo drove Andrew and Sara to the airport. When they got there Andrew went off to see about their seats and Margo and Sara stood with the carry-on luggage.

"I hope it goes okay with your Mom, Sara," Margo said.

"Me too."

"I know you've missed her very much."

Sara mashed her lips together and looked down.

"You know something, Sara . . . you've become an important part of my life. I've learned to like you very, very much in these past few months. And whatever happens in Florida, you'll always be welcome at our house." Margo had rehearsed this moment in her mind, but somehow her words sounded all wrong now.

"I had a nice birthday party," Sara said.

"I'm glad."

"Thanks for my new jeans and sweater."

"They look nice on you."

Sara looked down at her clothes. "Mom will probably say . . ."

"What?"

"Oh, never mind. It doesn't matter."

Margo hugged Sara, holding her close, thinking, *I should have hugged her more often. Why did I think she wouldn't let me?* There was so much to say, but it wasn't going to be said now. Maybe it would never be said.

"You'll remember to take care of Lucy?" Sara asked.

"Of course."

"And it's okay if she drinks out of your toilets."

"I thought she's not supposed to drink out of toilets."

"No . . . it's okay now."

Andrew came back waving their seat assignments. "Goodbye, Margarita," he said, kissing her. "I'll call you."

"Yes," Margo said.

"Come on, Daddy . . . they've already announced our flight."

"Oh, wait a minute . . ." Margo said, fishing a package out of her purse. She handed it to Andrew.

"What is it?" he asked.

"You'll have to wait until you're on the plane to find out."

*   *   *

"He's a lovely man, darling," Margo's mother said that night over dinner. "So, do I hear wedding bells in your future?"

"I don't know, Mother," Margo said.

"Why should they ruin it by getting married?" Michelle asked her grandmother.

"You think marriage would ruin it?" Margo's mother said.

"It might," Michelle said.

"Margo, darling . . . do you think marriage would ruin it?"

"No," Margo said. "I don't think marriage would ruin it."

"Then you wouldn't mind?" her mother said.

"Mind what?" Margo's father asked.

"Marrying him," her mother said.

Margo laughed. "No," she said, "I wouldn't mind."

"Mother, I'm shocked!" Michelle said. "I thought you believed that marriage was obsolete."

"No, Michelle . . . impossible, maybe . . . but not obsolete."

45

FRANCINE HAD GONE over this moment a million times in her mind. The bell would ring and she would walk quickly across the living room to the front door, open it, and there, looking exactly the same, except an inch or two taller, would be Sara.

Sara would say, *Hi, Mom . . .*

And Francine would say, *Hello, Sara . . .*

They would embrace naturally, as if they had seen each other yesterday, and then Francine would say, *Would you like a glass of juice?*

What kind have you got? Sara would ask.

Francine would show her into the kitchen, open the refrigerator and proudly display a jar of apple juice, a large carton of orange juice, and a six pack of V-8. Sara would laugh and choose the apple juice.

Then they would go for a walk on the beach.

Francine had moved into her own apartment ten days ago. She still lived at the hospital during the week, but weekends she was on her own. She was stronger physically too, exercising in the gym at the hospital and swimming laps in the pool. But not compulsively. If she skipped a day or two it didn't matter. The point, Dr. Arnold had explained, was to enjoy the exercise, not look at it as punishment. She had started to read again, novels with uplifting endings, and to listen to music. Sometimes, in the evenings, she would watch a movie on HBO, but nothing depressing.

She had become angry, rather than depressed, when she had found out two weeks ago that Lewis was footing the bill for her treatment. "It's my illness," she had told Dr. Arnold, "and I'll be damned if anyone else is going to pay for it."

"Fine," Dr. Arnold had said, "then pay yourself."

"That's exactly what I'm going to do."

For a while after that she'd felt ready to face the world, but her confident feelings hadn't lasted.

She still had not written to Sara. She had bought her a birthday card, but she had not mailed it. After almost four months a birthday card made no sense. She had discussed her fears about seeing Sara again with Dr. Arnold.

"Remember . . ." Dr. Arnold had said, "Sara will be uncomfortable too. She won't know what to expect. She may even be frightened. It's up to you to help her, Francine."

"But what will I say to her? How will I ever be able to explain all that's happened . . . and why?"

"You don't have to explain it all at once."

"What about next year? How do I tell her I'm not ready yet . . . that I can't take full responsibility for her? Suppose she thinks that means I don't want her?"

"Tell her the truth, Francine, in as simple a way as you can. Tell her that you're going to stay on here for a while longer. Maybe another six months. That you've made a great deal of progress, but you still need extensive therapy in order to understand what's happened to you."

"Suppose she hates it at Margo's . . . suppose she's miserable there?"

"Then we'll all have to get together and try to find a solution."

"Are you sure I'm ready for this?"

"I can't be sure, Francine, but if you want to see her, you should. Make the first visit short, no more than half an hour. And don't sit around looking at each other. Go for a walk on the beach."

"Yes, I know . . . a walk on the beach."

46

SARA SAT ON the plane watching her father open the package from Margo. It was wrapped in slick white paper with little red hearts all over it and tied with a red ribbon, as if Valentine's Day were in June, not February. When he'd finally opened it, Sara was disappointed. All that was inside was a big box of raisins. Not the most exciting gift in the world. But her father laughed.

The plane rose higher, the mountains disappeared below them, and still, her father kept laughing. Sara didn't see what was so funny until he showed her the front of the box. Where the picture of the raisin girl used to be Margo had cut a hole and had inserted a photo of herself wearing a dumb-looking red hat. Her father would not stop laughing. Everyone on the plane was looking at him. Sara was so embarrassed.

She had felt uncomfortable at the airport too, when Margo had gotten sentimental, telling Sara how much she had learned to like her. What did that mean, anyway—*learned to like her*—did it mean that Margo didn't used to like her at all, or that Margo hated her before but now she thought she wasn't so bad? Sara hadn't asked. And she hadn't said anything back to Margo either, even though Sara was sure Margo had expected her to say something like, *I like you too.* It wasn't that she disliked Margo. Margo was all right. So long as she didn't try to be her mother. If Margo ever pulled that Sara would tell her off. She would say, *You're not my mother, so don't try to act like one. You're not even my stepmother.*

ju're just some woman who sleeps with my father. She had
rehearsed those lines over and over, but so far she had not had to
use them.

That morning, while her father had been loading the car and
Margo had been upstairs in the kitchen, Sara had tiptoed down
the hall to Margo's bathroom and had put the envelope with the
Polaroid pictures back where she had found them, under Margo's
cosmetic tray. She could not go away for the summer leaving them
in her bottom dresser drawer and she couldn't take them with her
either. She had thought about cutting them up into little pieces,
the way Michelle had cut up Eric's postcard, but that seemed
wrong. After all, they weren't her pictures.

She wondered what this new summer camp would be like. It
was in Buck's County, Pennsylvania. Sara had never been to
Pennsylvania. You were supposed to do your own thing there.
Sara didn't know what her own thing was yet, but she liked the
idea of finding out. Maybe it would be painting. Margo had set
up the easel for her a couple of times, showing her how to use
watercolors and acrylic paints. She was not allowed to use the oil
paints though. They were kept in an old wooden box, which
Margo's parents had given her when she'd graduated from high
school.

Margo said she didn't have time to paint much anymore, but
she had shown Sara her sketch pad and Sara had been surprised to
find a charcoal portrait of herself. Margo had drawn her with very
big eyes, and no smile.

"When did you draw this?" Sara had asked.

Margo had checked the date on the picture. "March twenty-
fourth."

"I look sad."

"There's nothing wrong with looking sad sometimes."

"I guess."

Before camp Sara was going to spend ten days in Florida, visiting her grandparents. Grandma Goldy was learning to walk again
and Grandma and Grandpa Broder were going to take her to visit.
Also, her father would be with her for the first few days, so there
was really nothing to worry about. There was really nothing to

make her stomach jump all around or to make her grind her teeth at night. The dentist had asked, "Are you worried about something, Sara?"

"No, why should I be worried?"

"Because when a person grinds her teeth at night that usually means there's something on her mind. Something that's bothering her."

Well, there was nothing bothering Sara. Except, maybe, tomorrow. But she wasn't going to tell anyone about that because it would sound pretty stupid to say that she was worried about seeing her own mother.

Grandma and Grandpa Broder met them at the airport in Miami and they had time for a swim before dinner. The next morning her father drove her to Mom's apartment building in Boca Raton. It looked like all the others on the beach—a big white structure with balconies and a circular driveway lined with palm trees. She could not figure out why, if Mom was well enough to have her own apartment, she had not called or written. She hadn't even sent Sara a birthday card.

"There's nothing to worry about," her father said, parking the car. "She's probably more nervous than you are."

Sara nodded.

"I'll be waiting for you in the coffee shop."

"Why can't you come up with me?"

"Because Francine asked to see you by yourself and when I talked with Dr. Arnold she said that was a good idea." Daddy kissed her cheek. "Half an hour . . . okay?"

"Okay."

Sara walked through the lobby to the elevator, pressed *Six*, and said a little prayer as it carried her upstairs. *Please, God . . . let it be all right. Please don't let her ask me any questions about Daddy and Margo.* She got out of the elevator and walked slowly down the hallway, looking for *Six B*. When she came to it she took a deep breath and rang the bell.

Nothing happened. She waited a few minutes, then rang the bell again. Maybe her mother wasn't at home. Maybe her mother ad decided she didn't want to see Sara after all. Sara thought about leaving when the door opened.

Her mother was wearing a violet shirt, white jeans, and red canvas shoes. Her hair was cut short, with kind of curly bangs. She looked at Sara as if she had never seen her before.

"Hi, Mom . . ." Sara said.

She waited for her mother to say something, anything, but Mom backed away as if she were afraid. Maybe her mother didn't recognize her, Sara thought, so she said, "It's me, Mom . . . Sara."

Her mother just stood there against the wall and Sara didn't know what to do. Then, suddenly, her mother's face caved in. "Oh, Sara . . ." she cried, coming toward her. "Oh, Sara . . . I'm so sorry . . ." She took Sara in her arms and at the familiar scent, at the feel of her mother's arms around her again, Sara cried too.

Later, when Sara got back to her grandparents' apartment, she felt very tired. She went to the room she was sharing with her father to lie down. She needed time to think about all that her mother had told her, especially about Mom being married to Lewis, but not being sure that they would stay married.

"Does Lewis know about Bobby?" Sara had asked, as they'd walked along the beach together.

"Yes."

"You told him?"

"Yes, I did."

"Then it's not a secret anymore?"

"It was never supposed to be a secret. It's just that I . . ." But her mother didn't finish and they just kept on walking.

Her mother didn't ask her anything about Daddy and Margo, or about living at Margo's house, or even if Lucy was drinking out of Margo's toilets, which reminded Sara that she had brought a picture of Lucy for her mother to keep. She took it out of her pocket and handed it to her mother. Mom looked at it and smiled—a very shy smile, not at all like her regular smile, which showed all her teeth.

"Do you miss Lucy?" Sara asked.

"Yes," Mom said, "very much."

"We could probably send her to you . . . for the summer."

"That's very sweet, Sara, but I think Lucy should stay where she is."

When they got back to Mom's apartment Sara had a glass of apple juice and Mom said, "Sara . . . I don't know when I can come back to Boulder. I'm not completely well yet. I still have a lot to work out."

"When do you think you will come back?"

"Not for six months . . . maybe longer."

"But you're definitely coming back?"

"I don't know . . . nothing is definite for me right now."

What about me? Sara felt like shouting. *What's going to happen to me?* But she couldn't ask Mom. She would have to wait and ask her father.

"Can you ever forgive me, Sara, for the mess I've made of your life?" Mom asked.

"It's not so much of a mess," Sara said.

47

FRANCINE WAS NOT ready to see Andrew without the security of having Dr. Arnold nearby, so Andrew came to the hospital and they met in the garden, where Clare had visited a few months ago. But that had been before Francine could smile. She could smile now, although it wasn't easy, it wasn't natural. She had to concentrate and to spend time practicing in front of the mirror.

She stood stiffly as Andrew kissed her cheek. "Hello," she said, "sit down."

Andrew took the lounge chair, but he did not stretch out on it. He sat sideways and she sat on the straight-backed chair, facing him. "Well . . ." she said.

"Well . . ." he responded.

She looked away from him and watched two patients jogging on the path.

"The visit with Sara went all right?" he asked.

"Yes . . . why? Did she say something?"

"No . . . she didn't say anything."

"She seems so grown up."

"I know."

Andrew began to talk then, about Sara and school and summer camp, about the book he was writing on Florida's correctional system, an expression which made him laugh, and when he did she felt a pain in her chest, because she had always loved the sound of his laughter. He talked for ten minutes without a break.

"Well . . ." she said, "there's a lot to talk about, isn't there? A lot of water over the dam, as they say."

Andrew nodded.

"Water over the dam is a funny expression, isn't it?"

"Yes."

"I have a book of expressions like that . . . things to say when you don't know what to say . . ."

He nodded again.

She wished she had something to do with her hands. They were clammy and cold although the day was hot. She wished she had worn something with pockets. She wished she had some rubber bands. "Look, Andrew . . . there's just one question I need to ask you and that's this . . . is there still a chance for us?" She looked away as soon as she'd said it.

He took a long time answering and then said, "Not anymore, Francine."

She nodded. "I didn't think so, but I had to be sure because I'm planning the rest of my life." She did not know what she felt. She did not think it was disappointment or rejection. She did not think it was anger or fear either. Dr. Arnold would want to know. *What were you feeling?* she would ask.

"What about Lewis?" Andrew said.

"Lewis is waiting."

"He seems to care for you very much."

"I should hope so. He married me, you know."

They both laughed, but the sound of her own laughter was so surprising, she stopped abruptly.

Andrew took both her hands in his. "I'm sorry, Francine . . . I never meant to hurt you this way."

"Oh, I know that," she said. "And you can't take all the credit for my problems."

"I don't want to," he said.

After a few more minutes Andrew stood. "I've got to go now."

Francine stood too. "Well . . . it was nice seeing you again."

"It was nice seeing you too." He looked into her eyes, then he walked away.

"Andrew . . ." she called after him.

He turned.

"You did love me, didn't you?"

"Yes," he said. "Yes, I did love you."

She nodded. Now she knew what she felt. She felt tired. She felt incredibly tired. She did not want to plan the rest of her life. She did not want to plan anything. She wanted to lie down in the lounge chair, close her eyes, and go to sleep. But Dr. Arnold would be waiting, so Francine walked slowly toward her office.

48

MARGO WAS IN the hot tub. She had turned up the stereo so that she could hear the music as she soaked—Beethoven—perfect for her mood. She had said goodbye to her parents last night, and this morning, to Stuart and Michelle. Michelle had come to Margo's room at seven, carrying her cactus. "Will you take care of it for me, Mother?"

"Of course. I'll take care of all your plants."

"This one is special. And it only needs water once a week."

"Okay," Margo said, zipping up her dress. "And Michelle . . . I hope you have a wonderful trip."

"It's bound to be better than Camp Mindowaskin."

They both laughed.

Michelle placed the cactus on Margo's dresser. "I gave you a lot of shit this year, didn't I, Mother?"

"Enough."

"Of course, you deserved most of it."

"Maybe so."

"Well . . ." Michelle said, "aren't you going to kiss me goodbye?"

Margo was surprised. Michelle led her to believe she was no longer interested in parental affection. She walked across the room and took Michelle in her arms, kissing her cool, smooth cheek. "I love you," she said into Michelle's soft hair. "I love you very much. I hope you know that."

"I love you too," Michelle whispered. Then she broke away and said, "You know something, Mother . . . for a while I had my doubts, but you've turned out okay." She smiled, turned, and ran down the hall, calling, "Stuart, hurry up . . . it's almost time to go."

When they were gone Margo sat on her bed and cried. She did not feel sad. She felt emotional, the way she sometimes did at a tender play or listening to beautiful music or even watching the sun set. She felt a pouring out of motherly love, followed by an enormous sense of pride in herself and her children. She had made a lot of mistakes, but they had come through it together. They had come through it still loving each other and there was a lot to be said for that.

She dabbed at her eyes, blew her nose, then went to her bathroom to finish getting ready for work. She rummaged through her cosmetic drawer, searching for that new moisturizer she'd bought, and out of nowhere the envelope with the Polaroid pictures turned up. She had been over that drawer at least twenty times. Yet here they were. She thumbed through the pictures, satisfying herself that all five of them were intact. She laughed as she remembered the night she had posed for Andrew as Playmate of the Month. She remembered the lovemaking that had followed too and she felt a twinge. How could the pictures suddenly have reappeared? Unless . . . unless Michelle had taken them in the first place and returning them was her way of making peace. Yes, that must be it. There was no other explanation.

Years from now Michelle would probably tell her the truth. *Remember those ridiculous Polaroid pictures, Mother? I thought they were rather kinky at the time . . .*

Yes, Margo would say, *I remember.*

The phone rang then, startling Margo. She climbed out of the hot tub and ran into the house, naked and dripping, with Lucy at her heels. She answered, breathless, on the fourth ring.

"I have a person-to-person call for the Sun Maid Raisin Woman," the operator said.

"Yes," Margo said, laughing.

"Is this she?"

"Yes . . . yes, this is she."

"I have your party, sir."

Andrew came on the line then. "Hello, Raisin Woman. How's it going? Did everyone get off on schedule?"

"Yes. I'm the only one left. I was soaking."

"Wish I were there to keep you company."

"I've heard you pass out from the heat."

"Not every time. Only when I'm overly excited and have had too many brandies."

"Oh, so that's it."

"Uh huh."

"How's it going down there? Has Sara seen B.B. yet?"

"Yes, briefly. It went okay."

"And have you seen her?" she asked.

"Yes, late this afternoon."

And . . . she thought, but he didn't elaborate. She would have to ask. "Have you decided yet?"

"Decided what?" he said, as if he had no idea what she was talking about.

All right. She would spell it out for him so that there could be no misunderstanding. The truth was always easier to take than the imagination. "Decided what you're going to do?"

"It looks like Sara's going to live with us, at least for next year, maybe longer. Can you handle that?"

She didn't know whether to laugh or cry. "If you didn't come back, I was going to burn the rolltop desk."

"Didn't come back? What are you talking about?"

"Nothing . . . forget it." She wished she could reach through the phone and grab him.

"Can you handle having Sara?" he asked again.

"Yes, I can handle having Sara. I'm glad I'm going to have another chance with her."

"And can you handle this?" he asked. "I've been thinking that . . . well, you know how we've been too busy to talk about . . . look, I know the idea scares the shit out of you, but I made a list tonight of all the reasons . . . and they're all *our* reasons and they all make sense . . . so will you think about . . . no pressure, I promise . . ."

"How about the end of August?" Margo said.

"The end of August?"

"Yes, when all three kids are here, before Stuart leaves for college."

"You're serious?"

"You know I'm a serious person, Andrew. Besides, I love you."

"I love you too. And I miss you. I've been sleeping with the raisin box under my pillow."

"I've been sleeping with Lucy."

"She's better than a raisin box."

"But not as good as you."

"I'll be home in three days."

"I'll be ready."

She hung up the phone, went back outside, and lowered herself into the hot tub. For once, everything was turning out right, she thought. Not that she'd ever doubted, seriously doubted, that he would come back. After all, they loved each other. He wasn't going to just throw it all away. But having everything turn out right was a scary idea, even for an optimist. *Look,* she told herself, *you deserve it. You've paid your dues and so has he. Besides, this is real life. Just because it's all going your way tonight doesn't mean that tomorrow won't bring surprises. So count your blessings and be happy.* Isn't that what her mother had told her when she was a little girl? *It's okay to count your blessings, darling, so long as you remember to knock wood, after.*

"I'm knocking wood, Mother," Margo said, as she rapped her knuckles against the cedar tub.

Then, just to be sure, she did it again.